THE
WOOLSORTERS' PLAGUE

To Marianne Gearhart —
With admiration
and best wishes,

Clint Nagle

April 2012

To Marianne Gearhart –
With admiration,
and best wishes,
[signature]
April 2012

Nagle's second novel is another blockbuster. It is a high intensity novel of international intrigue with a race against the clock to stop another terrorist attack against the United States. The surprise ending will give you some sleepless nights.

James Zumwalt, bestselling author of Bare Feet, Iron Will

The Woolsorters' Plague is so authentic and compelling, you'll forget it's a novel. I ignored work and family and finished it in a day and a half. Chet Nagle has the authority of a man who lived the scenes he writes about. A tremendous book.

Tucker Carlson, Editor-in-Chief, The Daily Caller

Chet Nagle

THE
WOOLSORTERS' PLAGUE

Århus Publishing

Author's photograph on back cover by William Remington

ISBN (Perfect Bound): 0-9778108-7-9; 978-0-9778108-7-1
ISBN (Hardcover): 0-9778108-6-0; 978-0-9778108-6-4
ISBN (eBook): 0-9837075-0-2; 978-0-9837075-0-9

Library of Congress Control Number: 2011908788

Printed in the United States of America
First Århuſ Publiſhing Edition 2011

For Dorothy,
my constant partner.

PROLOGUE

Ufa, Bashkortostan
Russian Federation

Their silent prayers were ignored by the telephone. It paid no attention to the two men who sat at the splintery old table staring, willing it to ring. At times the men looked into each other's eyes, or glanced at the pistol next to the telephone, but their attention always returned to the stubborn black instrument.

They ran out of small talk ten minutes after they pulled up chairs in the cavernous office of the manager of Ufa Regional Airport, and they now sat in silence. The room was cold and damp and they were not comforted by the dull light of Russian winter poking through a grimy window in the western wall. Two naked bulbs dangled over them, their weak yellow gleam picking out faded colors in a flag in a stand behind the table—and the sheen of gun oil on the pistol.

Colonel Vladimir Iliyich Asadullin, commander of the 131st Regiment of the Russian Federation's Strategic Rocket Forces, sat in an ancient swivel chair. He squinted at the telephone again, tapping a fat forefinger on the pistol. Opposite him was a slender bearded man wearing a sable-collared cashmere topcoat and a splendid astrakhan fur hat.

The colonel looked away from the telephone and checked his wristwatch for the tenth time. Then he glared across the table, slowly raised the pistol, and fired directly at the face three feet away. The slender man did not flinch when the roar sent a bullet snarling past his ear and into a photograph of Prime Minister Putin on the far wall. A moment later, a lump of plaster fell into the echoing silence.

"Okay, skinny man!" Asadullin's jowls shook with pleasure. "You are goddamn tough. Like me. But you piss your pants, yah? Now stand up. Show Vladimir Iliyich!"

The slender man's face was impassive. He stood, took a folded silk square from his breast pocket, and removed his hat. He carefully dusted gunpowder residue from the tight curls of lamb's wool, donned the hat, and then dabbed at his shoulders. He refolded the handkerchief, replaced it, and opened the coat to display his trousers. They were quite dry.

"Okay, okay. Sit down!" The smile slid off Asadullin's broad cheeks. "But next time I kill you. *Da.* You die in that chair where you sit. I shoot that little scar on your face if you do not do all, *all* what you promise me you do." Perfumed with peppermint vodka, the words made brief vapor clouds in the still and frigid air.

"My dear friend, it will all happen just you were told. There will not be a scintilla of deviation." Unlike the colonel, who spoke a crude Bashkiri dialect, the bearded man spoke those consoling words in flawless Russian. Without a glance at the smoking weapon the Russian dropped on the table, he pulled the fur collar of his topcoat closer and smiled.

"In a few minutes, colonel, your son telephones from London and you will hear that your money has arrived, exactly as was promised. Then we can both go back to our warm homes. Ramadan begins tomorrow, and you begin your fast as a very wealthy man."

Asadullin belched and focused on the man before him. He was sure this was not some loyalty test. This was not an elaborate entrapment orchestrated by Moscow secret police, not some new trick. No, this was opportunity of the once-in-a-lifetime kind, and he would handle it perfectly. He had been tested many times in the years since his father had shot himself. The old man was First Secretary of the Central Committee of the Soviet Socialist Republic of Bashkiria—and he had to shoot himself! Why had he tried to help that madman Rutskoi? Crazy.

In 1993, Vladimir Iliyich was an athletic forty-seven-year old colonel. He had graduated from the elite Frunze Military Academy and was a rising star in the army, thanks to his father's influence. That was the year when Rutskoi seized the Moscow White House. That was the year his father had ordered one of his Bashkirian motorized infantry regiments to Moscow to support Rutskoi instead of the government. Yeltsin stopped that train dead in its tracks with one phone call.

Young Colonel Asadullin saved himself by volunteering for the war in Chechnya, and served bravely in that terrifying bloodbath. But despite his war record, he remained permanently under suspicion and permanently stationed in Ufa, his career a black hole in the universe of ambition. *Sins of the fathers and all that crap.*

Was he supposed to radiate gratitude from head to toe because he had not been put up against a wall and shot for his father's "treason" against Russia? And what was Mother Russia now, that mighty fortress he and his father had defended so gallantly? *A worn-out peasant that Putin's thugs are raping one more time, that's what!* But now, in the final years of service necessary to qualify for his paltry pension, in the scant months remaining to create a scheme to provide for his old age, this little bearded man magically appears.

The colonel belched again. No more cheap vodka for him after today. From now on he would drink only the best. Top shelf all the way. He would be no chip off the old block—a loyal stupid soldier, dead by his own hand. No. He would seize opportunity by the throat. The *right* opportunity, unlike his silly old man.

"Fifty millions dollars, not one kopek less!"

"Of course, colonel. That is precisely as we agreed."

The slender man languidly swept his gaze around the room. Beyond the broad north window snow showers veiled a cargo plane. It sported insignia of a Bulgarian charter company, and long vapor columns rose from heaters attached to its engines. Surrounded by military vehicles, the big Hercules squatted on a snow-banked parking apron.

"Colonel, I hope you will notify the airport manager to release my aircraft as soon as you receive your call from London. I really must leave before the weather worsens."

"Nothing! Nothing moves in this shit-hole airport without my permission! And if you—"

The phone suddenly decided to ring and interrupted the colonel's rising voice. He switched on the speaker, picked up the pistol, and looked meaningfully at the man opposite him.

"*Da?*" He smiled. "Ruslan, my son! How is shopping?"

"Good, father, good. The store has everything you ordered." The voice from the telephone's speaker was tinny but clear.

"Everything? All suits and shoes are there? Every one? All in my name? You have seen them all?"

"Yes, father, I have seen them, and they are all here in your name. Only you must give the store the correct receipt."

"Good. I understand. Now you wait in London. Your mother and me, we begin holidays with you in two days. I bring receipt and I pick up all clothes on first day I am there. Enjoy hotel. Goodbye, my son."

Asadullin placed the vintage soviet telephone on its cradle with exaggerated care, and then searched for the holster buried in folds of fat around his waist. He was trying to be nonchalant, but excitement was overpowering him. His eyes blinked rapidly and then squeezed shut in concentration while he fumbled with the heavy pistol.

"Okay, Arab oilman big shot. Whoever you are. Get on airplane and go to the devil. Now I call airport manager and move away my soldiers."

The colonel picked up his radio, spoke a few words, and the armored personnel carriers surrounding the Hercules slowly rumbled away. Then the colonel punched in another channel and contacted the airport manager. Within seconds the manager spoke to the airfield's tower and then to the plane's pilots. A minute later its four propellers began to rotate, one by one. Bracing his hands on the desk, the colonel heaved to his feet. His chin jutted forward when his visitor began to speak.

"My dear colonel. Our transaction is complete, and we are both satisfied. Before I board my aircraft, I would very much like to join you in that drink you offered."

A smile lifted Colonel Asadullin's broad Mongol cheeks again. Maybe this fancy fellow was not such a pompous ass after all, he thought. But before he could pick up the bottle the visitor delicately placed a hand over the greasy tumblers.

"Please. Allow me, colonel. In my country, a man happily serves a drink to a friend and a new partner. And today, you might even be called my *benefactor*."

The slender man over-filled the colonel's glass, pouring vodka over the thumb and forefinger of his gloved hand.

"Ah. My sincere apologies, dear colonel. I think the excitement has made my hand quite unsteady."

"Small waste of vodka. Never mind. Soon I buy my own vodka factory. To wealth and health!" The colonel downed his drink and, with a flourish, slammed the glass down on the desk.

His visitor did the same and said, "That is very true. It is impossible to enjoy wealth without health, colonel." He peered out the window again. "I must hurry now. The airport manager is on the apron, and I don't want to keep the poor man waiting in the snow."

Poor man waiting in the snow. The colonel buttoned his jacket. By the Devil's balls, for fifty million dollars I would roll naked in the snow on the main street of Ufa!

The two men left the double doors open as they walked from the office, side by side.

Minutes later the Hercules was climbing rapidly, turning south. It would eventually cross Kazakhstan and Uzbekistan before skirting the western shores of the Aral Sea. Then it would cross the Turkmenistan border near Ashkhabad and deliver its cargo to the holy city of Mashad, in the Khorasan province of the Islamic Republic of Iran.

In the small and luxurious passenger compartment, the bearded man accepted a glass of wine from the handsome cabin boy he had chosen for the long journey. He selected a slim Cuban panatela from the humidor, happy that his visit to the semi-autonomous Republic of Bashkortostan was ended.

It took his Muslim network in Russia three years to locate Colonel Vladimir Iliyich Asadullin. They had focused on finding an officer disillusioned with his government. Resentful. Perhaps in dire financial straits. Preferably a Muslim.

Sipping the wine, he thought he felt a warming glow from the five crates in the cargo compartment behind him. What a bargain. Fifty million dollars for all four, plus that little demolition device. A bargain even at twice the cost!

Clawing up through dense clouds, the plane finally burst into sunshine. Turning away from the glare, the bearded man absently fingered the small crescent scar under his right eye.

That fat Mongol idiot should be feeling the first effects of the Ricin by now, he mused. The thugs in VEVAK, the Islamic Republic's successor to the Shah's SAVAK assassins, had assured him their experiments proved a mere tenth of a milligram of Ricin would easily kill a two-hundred-pound man. He dropped twice that much in the colonel's vodka. And most delicious of all, if that letter of credit in London was not cashed within three days, or if the beneficiary died during that time, the funds revert to that very private and very personal account in Zurich. It was simply too delightful.

Then there was that son in London. What was his name? Ruslan. Oh, dear. Poor Ruslan. He would slip and fall to his death this very night from his Piccadilly hotel window. Accidents happen.

He swirled the last of the wine in his glass, and breathed its rich bouquet. If only the great Islamic Republic of Iran paid him better wages for his management skills—why, he would not be forced to take such drastic measures. Still, at this rate it would not be more than another year before he could buy that lovely Greek island near Lesbos.

The dark and bearded man laughed for the first time in days.

CHAPTER 1

The Pentagon
Arlington, Virginia

A stocky figure wearing a bright orange ski jacket and gray dress slacks skipped down the steps of the Pentagon's River Entrance. The taller man trotting alongside wore a black car coat that flapped open in the chilly breeze to reveal a belt holster. It was six o'clock in early December, and sunset had arrived over an hour before. The two men were in cold dark shadows when they paused at the waiting limousine.

"This is getting ridiculous, Jake. I told CID at least a dozen times I don't want a bodyguard and I don't need a bodyguard. I'm just meeting a pal for a drink after work."

"Secretary's orders, sir."

"I guess you don't read the newspapers. Secretary Blackman has been dead for three weeks."

"Yes, sir. But Secretary Horton hasn't changed the standing orders. And after last week's threats on your life, we don't figure he will."

"For Pete's sake. Maybe the new budget cuts will get you guys out of what's left of my hair." He turned toward the car and muttered. "And I'm not so damn old I can't take care of myself."

Grinning, the bodyguard closed the passenger door and climbed into the front seat. Next to him, the driver looked into the rear view mirror at the face that always made him think of a middle-aged cop.

"Where to, sir?"

"Let's go to that Irish pub in Pentagon Row. You know where it is?"

"Yes, sir, Mr. Adams."

Jeremiah Adams' Pentagon title was Special Assistant for External Affairs, a job that gave him unfettered access to the Secretary of Defense. Philip Blackman had been Director of the Central Intelligence Agency when he left Langley to run the Department of Defense, and he had brought Adams with him. For the next seven years Adams was his "go-to-guy" for informal inter-agency liaison and, most importantly, his chief coordinator of the covert war against Islamic terrorists. His career as a CIA clandestine field officer, an undercover spy, had given Adams a cynical and pragmatic mind-set. It also had given him a tough physique and a nose he described as "only slightly broken." Desk work had begun to push his belly over his belt, but long days and nights in the Pentagon had dulled neither his attitude nor the razor blades in his stare. At fifty-two, Adams had finally achieved the notoriety he wanted: terrorists feared him even more than they hated him.

The courtyard of the shops on Pentagon Row boasted an outdoor ice skating rink. It was a far cry from the glitzy rink at Rockefeller Plaza in New York, but it was popular with the locals, their kids, and the shops around it. Half-frozen skaters became good customers for pizza, hot chocolate, or a drink at the nearby Irish-style saloon. Its mullioned window facade, wooden floors, and dark booths were reasonable imitations of the real thing, and except for the 'no smoking' signs a Dubliner might enjoy it all.

Twenty shopping days before Christmas Eve, and the "Sine Irish Pub and Restaurant" was packed. The bodyguard took up a strategic position on a corner of the bar as Adams made his way to a booth that held a huge and tough-looking African-American with a closely shaved scalp. He wore the uniform of a navy captain that sported the golden aiguillette and badge of an aide to the Chairman of the Joint Chiefs of Staff. Unzipping his jacket, Adams sat opposite and aimed his chin at the aiguillette.

"Tell me, Bainbridge, will a bevy of young lovelies fall into my arms if I wrap some of those chicken guts around my shoulder?"

"Absolutely. And it works best on uniforms, formal wear, and classy outfits. Just like that elegant thing you're wearing tonight."

Adams looked down at his gaudy ski jacket and frowned. "Too cold for my blazer, and I couldn't find..." He noticed the glass waiting in front of him. "What's that?"

"Southern Comfort."

"You remembered, darling." Adams raised the tumbler and intoned, "Confusion to the enemy." He touched his glass to the captain's brandy snifter.

"And so say we all, " came the reply.

The ancient naval combat toast brought tight smiles to both men, and they sat silently, warmed by their old friendship.

"It's been weeks," Adams finally said. "So how're they hanging, dog robber?"

The captain took another sip of cognac. "Aides to admirals aren't called dog robbers in this man's navy. That's Army talk."

"I don't ask and I don't tell, sailor." Adams scanned the crowded room. "Crap. This place is just like the Pentagon and Langley. Nothing but spooks and white sidewall haircuts. What's your fascination with this *Sine* saloon, Walt?"

"The old Irish word is pronounced *Shee-nay*, Jay. It means nipple."

"That figures." He scanned the room again. "You want nipples, next time I pick the joint. We'll hit Good Guys in Georgetown."

The big captain laughed. "We'd both get our clearances lifted."

"Not to mention the pain sweet Jennifer Bainbridge would hand you. Or what the—aw, hell." Adams reached into his jacket and scowled at the vibrating Blackberry. He studied the screen for long moments and looked up.

"The Iranian bastards are hanging three protestors every day now." Adams pushed the phone back into his pocket. "And Hezbollah is on the move again. Sorry, amigo. I got to head back to the ranch."

"Have another drink. Jay."

"So we're not here for Gaelic lessons. What's up?"

"I need a favor." Bainbridge signaled to a passing waiter and pointed at their glasses.

"You're buying another drink? Must be a biggie."

"No, not a big favor. It's easy-peasy. All I want is for you to get my boss an appointment with your boss."

Adams looked away and mumbled, "I can't."

"All right, then. So would you please explain what's going on in your shop? The Chairman of the Joint Chiefs of Staff wants to talk to the Secretary of Defense and some flunky locks the door? What the hell is *that?*"

"You're talking about me or Beauchamps?"

"You don't run the Secretary's appointments diary, and you've never told me the Secretary is *simply too busy* to see my boss. I am talking about some idiot named Aubrey Beauchamps."

"I wish I could help, Walt."

Adams was still looking away when the drinks arrived. Pulling his snifter closer, Bainbridge pushed a glass toward Adams and waited. Silent, Adams stared into space.

"Okay, Jay. Maybe you can just tell me why the Secretary has a hard-on for my boss. We can't be frozen out much longer or the press will—"

Adams swiveled around and snapped, "Are you threatening me with your newspaper cronies, Bainbridge?"

"No way. I'd never go to the media on this. But their hounds sniff fresh meat and I can only sidestep them for so long. Help me out, buddy."

Adams picked up his glass, drained half, and said, "Beauchamps is a clown, Walt. He came off the Hill with Horton. God knows what he did for a living up there, but he was a senior guy on Horton's senate staff. He controls all access to the Secretary now. He doesn't tell me squat, and I can't get in to see Jelly Roll either. And that is the whole truth and nothing but the truth, so help me."

"Jelly Roll?"

"Jelly Roll Morton. I figure it fits the new Secretary."

"You mean Ferdinand Joseph LaMothe, the 1920s cathouse piano player?"

"Well, yeah."

The captain rolled his eyes and smacked his forehead.

"Some idiot is keeping Jay Adams from talking to his boss, a boss who just happens to be the Secretary of Defense. No one else can talk to the Secretary either. That is weird." He smacked his head again. "No, that is *dangerous*."

"Keep your voice down and don't act so crazy. Half the spooks in town are in here tonight."

"Fuck 'em." Bainbridge ran a hand over his gleaming ebony scalp. "If the Secretary is holed up in his office and no one can get to him, then who's at the wheel? Who's minding the store?" He closed his eyes." I don't believe this."

"Believe it. I can't even brief him on the raid status." Adams couldn't resist looking around to see if anyone had heard him. Reassured by the noise level in the pub, he whispered, "My team is almost on station now, and I'm not sure I can give them a green light."

"Jay. That op order was chopped all the way to the White House and back. Everything is in motion now. I even confirmed the position of the carrier strike group before I left my office tonight, just in case you asked. What could possibly be stopping you from giving the final okay?"

"I always got a nod from Blackman before pushing the button."

"Blackman is dead, and his replacement acts like he's crackers. So let him and his idiot gatekeeper learn all about it from CNN."

"I suppose you're right."

"Sure I am. Remember what Annapolis taught us. It's easier to seek forgiveness than it is to get permission."

The two men locked eyes, smiled, and raised their glasses again.

"You are a fountain of good advice, dog robber. I'll try to get your boss that appointment, but don't hold your breath." Adams zipped up his jacket, stood, and raised an eyebrow at the bar. The bodyguard started to the door. "I've got to take off, Walt. Thanks for the drinks. Next time is on me at Good Guys."

The captain grinned. "I'll be waiting for my invite to another Adams victory celebration—with nipples."

"From your mouth to God's ear."

CHAPTER 2

Naval Special Warfare Command Headquarters
Coronado Island, California

Lieutenant "AP" Cristani and Hector Hernandez, his platoon chief, pushed through the doors of a SPECWARCOM briefing room. The two men were products of the Navy's most grueling physical and mental training program, and they looked it. Cristani's blocky torso filled his fatigue shirt, the pale eyes and skin from his Corsican ancestors a sharp contrast to Hernandez' swarthy complexion and flat-muscled frame. But the pair moved with the same coiled and ready strength. They were SEALs.

Rear Admiral Robert Bancroft, Commander of SPECWARCOM, was waiting for them, his unlit cigar slowly migrating from one corner of his mouth to the other.

"Lieutenant Cristani and Master Chief Hernandez, reporting as ordered, Admiral."

Bancroft stood in front of a curtained wall map. "At ease, gents. Sit. Fresh coffee in the jug." He waited until they settled into chairs and then pushed words around his cold cigar with practiced ease.

"You got a peculiar warning order two days ago and you got some questions, right?" Bancroft picked up a coffee mug emblazoned with two gold stars, his name, and the motto, 'Sea Air Land—SEALs.' He answered his own question.

"Right. That warning order didn't say squat, except you depart today with nothing but fatigues and civvies. So you want to know why this procedure? Because that's all the gear you'll need. Mission equipment is on *Ocean Princess*, moored across the bay. That ship is your home for the rest of this year. You join her crew, cross the Pacific, and three weeks later you arrive at Bandar Abbas, here in southern Iran." The Admiral swept the curtain aside and poked a stubby index finger into the map.

"You go ashore, complete your mission, and return to the ship. She continues her voyage through the Suez Canal, you debark in Cyprus, have a few beers, and fly home commercially." His cigar drooped slightly. "I regret you and your troops will not be with family and sweethearts at Christmas. They'll all be invited to dinner at my quarters on Christmas Eve." He cleared his throat and turned back to the map.

"*National Geographic* has a research team on *Ocean Princess* that's cleared to visit Taib, a beach town one hundred clicks east of Bandar Abbas. They'll be looking for busted pots left by Chinese merchants who bivouacked there a thousand years ago. As it happens, the ship's crew is from CIA Special Activities Division. They'll give you detailed briefings on the mission while you're at sea, and assist with training and practice. My little talk today isn't necessary. It's just my way of saying how much I really care."

The two SEALs grinned.

"There are two Land Rovers as deck cargo for the *Geographic* expedition. They go ashore the morning you arrive, and you will use them for your mission. The vehicles are well-equipped. Perfect for a desert exfiltration should, ah, unforeseen problems arise during your time ashore. When you reach the target, there will be an extraction team from Oman standing by offshore. If you have to go to the beach instead of back to the ship, they will come close inshore for a pick you up. Escape across the desert is the last choice. Any questions?"

"*Ocean Princess*?" Hernandez raised his eyebrows. "A *macho* name, Admiral."

"I tried for the *Love Boat*, but she was booked." Bancroft did not return Hernandez' smile. "And for some reason, Iran Air didn't want to charter me a cargo plane."

"Hey, you want to make that trip on a sub, chief?" Cristani said. "Screw that. An *Ocean Princess* is just fine by me. We'll have Christmas cotillions and shuffleboard tournaments while we cruise under starry Pacific skies." He rolled his coffee cup between callused palms. "What about tactical gear, Admiral? Are we going to be in the water?"

Bancroft tapped a red circle on the map. "The target. A military research compound in the desert, sixteen clicks from the port. No swimming, unless you miss the boat today." He faced the two SEALs and added, "The peace-loving ayatollahs promised their citizens a New Year's gift for their big *Norooz* holiday in March. Our spooks found out what it is—they bought some Russian nukes to put on the *Shahab-4* missile they got from North Korea."

Cristani leaned back in his chair and whistled. "The Iranians are buying nukes from Russia and missiles from North Korea? That's nice."

"Yes, lots of key missile parts come from those crazies in Pyongyang. Anyway, Iran is mating the Russian warheads and *Shahabs* in Bandar Abbas right now. They'll be able to move at least one of them to a test-range in January. That's why the hurry-up mode. Another reason for our timing is that *Carl Vinson* transits the target area at exactly the time you arrive. You'll mark targets for her aircraft, and they deliver special New Year's greetings. Prior to that, you penetrate the facility, photo the warheads and missiles, and bring back some hard evidence." The Admiral's cigar became the ominous semaphore his men knew well. "But your core mission is to assist *Vinson* to destroy those buildings, and anyone in them."

The Admiral softly repeated his orders, "I say again, your mission is to destroy that place completely." He sipped lukewarm coffee and grimaced.

"You'll be equipped with Iraqi weapons and gear captured during the current war and Desert Storm. CIA fixed the junk so it works okay. Everything you carry, AK-47s, silencers, comm headsets, night vision gear, explosives—everything will appear to be Iraqi or old Soviet gear. Your boot soles have Iraqi markings, your buttons say Saddam was your daddy, and you'll drop Iraqi documents during the mission.

"We don't have floor plans, but CIA's worked up guesstimates about what's where. There are no underground facilities, so we don't need to call in a B-2 from Diego Garcia with bunker-busters."

Bancroft tapped a satellite photograph taped to the wall map. "Your opposition. This is a Pasdaran barracks near the target compound that houses a platoon of thirty-five. That makes it three-to-one odds. With prep and surprise working for you, the lucky guards will be having dinner with mommy in Tehran when you arrive."

He tried another sip of coffee and dropped his cold mug on the table. "You get area coverage via the ship's satellite antenna. An E-8 JSTARS bird will be close offshore on a training mission from Oman. She'll give you radar cover and jamming until you exit the target area. JSTARS will talk to you via *Ocean Princess*.

"Inland you pick up a Baluchi scout. English-speaker. He's a battle-hard soldier, and the spooks are very proud of him. Listen to what he says and take care of him. He knows the turf."

"Sir, will the Iranians believe—" The Admiral stopped Cristani with an upraised hand.

"Will they believe that some leftover Iraqi Republican Guards or crazy Sunni jihadists made a raid from a desert hideout? Even with what's going on in Iraq and Afghanistan these days, that's not very likely. But they'll be glad to put the blame on *anyone* instead of admitting the Great Satan did it." He smiled into the silence.

"Anything else? Okay, you clear San Diego harbor in an hour. Kiss your buddies goodbye, grab your sea bags, and double-time to the boat landing. Dismissed."

Chairs scraped, the SEALS stood to attention, and then they headed to the door. Watching them leave, the Admiral rumbled, "May God speed and protect you."

Bandar Abbas Harbor
Islamic Republic of Iran

The Hindu Kush, soaring "Roof of the World," falls westward from Afghanistan to sprawl across Baluchistan, its ice fields and frozen lakes glittering like scattered crystals. Mountains melt into desert hills and boulder-strewn valleys that roll in rocky waves across Iran and down to the Arabian Sea. Near that sea, close to the ancient port city of Bandar Abbas, a shadow moved in a shallow ravine inhabited by stunted tamarisk trees. The dark shape flowed into the silhouette of a tamarisk, paused, and became a shrub. Eleven other shrubs drifted across the sand to form a ragged circle.

The shadows were not desert vegetation. They were SEALs, direct descendants of the famed World War II "frogmen." Darkest of these shadow warriors are in DEVGRU, and their Gold Team—the premier assault team—was now standing on the soil of Iran. Three more commandos were on a ship docked in Bandar Abbas harbor, a freighter that made three weeks of port calls in the Philippines and India to off-load frozen seafood as a cover for its real mission—delivering the Gold Team to Bandar Abbas.

The commandos had walked off *Ocean Princess* forty minutes before their scheduled time to arrive at the target. Dodging through a gap cut in the chain link fence around the docks, they found the Land Rovers in the car park, tossed in their uniforms and equipment, and raced out of town on the Kerman road.

Ten miles later they were three hundred yards from their goal. They swapped their civvies for Iraqi uniforms, checked their weapons again, and found the Baluchi scout, Daud Bux Marri, waiting. Setting up a guard perimeter in the trees, they sent him out to reconnoiter. The hard men sheltering in the gully knew the tamarisk groves around them offered no protection, and the waning moon was not their friend.

Standing close to Hernandez, Cristani saw a phantom flitting through the trees along the northern bank of the *wadi*. Even though pickets signaled the scout's return, brilliant red dots from laser sights riveted on the Baluchi's lean figure. They stayed on him as he walked toward the lieutenant and master chief.

Cristani's night vision goggles showed the returning scout as an indistinct figure, a blurry green outline in the moonlight. *That is one creepy character*, he thought, *a raggedy-ass scarecrow. But he's quiet. And when we finally spotted his hide he just walked up and saluted. Picked me out as the boss, right off. Not bad.*

"Greetings, my commander," Daud Bux Marri murmured, moving closer to Cristani, "Let us now kill Persians."

His night vision headset pushed up on his forehead, Cristani looked at the laser dots dancing on Bux Marri and waved his arm. One by one, the glowing spots disappeared.

"Greetings, Daud. How is the target?"

"The fence is close, there." The scout pointed to the northern rim of the ravine. "Two men guard the south gate. Two at the east gate. One soldier stays in the big building and one light shines in the second floor. The bunker is dark. Soldiers in barracks watch the football on TV."

"Late arrivals? New activity?" Cristani could smell the scout's musty clothes and the tang of some unfamiliar spice.

"No, commander. Nothing." Bux Marri drew himself up and was still. He glanced at the high-energy chocolate bar Hernandez was unwrapping.

Cristani leaned toward his platoon chief and whispered, "Okay, Deacon, plan A is still on. Chunk's team secures the east gate, plants the laser, and takes up positions near the barracks. He recons the bunker. Our teams enter the south gate after Motown's crew secures it. He stays put while his troops plant charges in the big building and join the blocking team at the barracks. Your team follows my team through the front door and hits the main deck with Daud. I'll check the top deck and that light. Remind Chunk not to fiddle with his damn laser. It's *off* until he gets the word."

Hernandez nodded.

Cristani looked at the somber Baluchi guide. "Deacon, give Scarecrow here his AK, water, and a chocolate bar." He unsnapped the cover on his wristwatch. "Time to move out."

"Here you go, scout," whispered Hernandez. He handed the Baluchi a foil packet, canteen belt, and a silenced rifle. Then he turned away, genuflected, and bowed his head. As he knelt in the sand, the tall frame of Gunners Mate John Gorski, the platoon's heavy machine-gunner, loomed over him. Gorski shifted his demolition backpack of Czech SEMTEX explosives and eased close to the kneeling master chief.

"Say one for me, Deacon," Gorski whispered. Hernandez looked up and stood.

"I already did, Chunk. But God told me you better start sayin' your own." He looked beyond Gorski at another shadow kneeling in the sand.

"Why don't you ask Motown to say one for you?"

"Already did. But you know when he's praying. Won't listen to a fuckin' thing.

Machinists Mate Rafael "Motown" Hanna was born in the Oak Park suburbs of Detroit twenty-two years ago. Proud Americans, his family claimed an Iraqi heritage that began in 45 A.D. with the conversion of the Chaldeans by St. Thomas. Together with Egyptian Copts, Yemenis, and Palestinians from Jordan, Syria, and Lebanon, the Chaldeans were part of a large Middle Eastern neighborhood that sprawled across the Detroit suburbs.

Though the Hanna family was one of the few in the neighborhood to take to the streets in anger after the 9/11 attacks, Mrs. Hanna was still horrified when she learned her brilliant son gave up his Stamford scholarship to join the Navy. The last member of the Hanna clan to return to the Middle East had been her father, an Allison engineer who helped build a gas turbine factory for the Shah. Her son was the first Hanna to set foot in Iran for two generations, and he arrived not as a builder of gas turbines, but with other skills. He was a master of destruction.

Hernandez and Cristani rejoined their squads and were greeted by a sizzle in their right earphones, the command side of their headsets.

"This is Henhouse." The first UHF transmission from *Ocean Princess* was crisp and clear. "Iron Eye sees no traffic inside fourteen clicks. Two Hammerjacks inbound. ETA at IP is fifty-five minutes. Acknowledge."

Cristani checked his wristwatch, clicked his throat mike twice, and heard the reply, "Roger, Little Chicks. Henhouse out."

The SEAL Lieutenant visualized the "IPs," the Initial Points for bombing runs. Last night, while Bandar Abbas slept, he and Hernandez cut a hole in the port's fence and slipped into town. They set up two radar reflectors, each resembling a bare umbrella frame with too many spokes, at locations the CIA team selected. One was an outcropping of rocks northeast of town, and the other the roof of an abandoned warehouse. The low-flying carrier planes would be guided to the reflectors, and when they were close, they would see them as bright spots on their radar screens. Each was a precise start for a bombing run to the target compound miles away.

Cristani wondered if anyone had spotted the reflectors, or the hole in the fence. He pushed those thoughts out of his mind. It was too late to worry about any of that.

A hand signal from Cristani, and Hanna led his two SEALs forward to take up point position with the Baluchi scout. The four-man team jogged over the northern edge of the ravine with the main body of SEALs behind, their formation ghosting across featureless sand and gravel. Lights at the target were immediately visible on the horizon.

The first minutes went exactly as planned. The two guards at the main gate were startled by red dots glowing on their faces, and before they could blink they died as silent bullets slammed into their foreheads. Less than a hundred yards away, the east gate guards were watching a football game on a portable television set. One leaned forward to adjust the picture and gasped as a knife plunged into the hollow of his neck. The other guard fell next to him, groaning.

Crouching alongside the gatehouse with Hernandez and Hanna, Cristani breathed "Chunk" into his mike. A pair of clicks answered and the leader motioned his teams forward. Front doors of the building were unlocked, and the raiders poured silently into the entranceway and main stairwell with Hernandez and two SEALS spinning left, almost pushing Bux Marri into the corridor. Cristani and his men leapt up the stairway to the second floor.

Hernandez loped around a pillar in the center of the long hallway, and ran full tilt into a guard. The soldier's surprise twisted into a silent screams as he reeled under the shock of bullets driving him to the floor. Bux Marri fired too, adding to the surreal noise of muzzle gas, stuttering slaps of automatic actions, and the jingle of spent brass casings bouncing and rolling across the floor. A sound like metallic surf washed through the smoky air.

In the dim passageway a toilet door opened and an Iranian officer, one hand pulling at his trousers, raised a pistol. The first booming shot smashed into the Baluchi's ragged vest, the second hit Hernandez in the thigh. When the chief dropped to his knees, the Iranian leaned forward to aim a killing shot, but before he could fire again the wounded scout lurched across the SEAL, materialized a dagger, and with a deep grunt drove it home. The rest of the team ran up to a bloody heap of dead and wounded bodies.

On the floor above, Cristani and his squad heard the shots just before they burst through a door with leaking light around its edges. Inside, two men stood near a lab table crowded with racks of electronics. They wore white smocks over uniform tunics, and when the door slammed open they struggled to free their pistols from beneath the lab coats. They died before they could fire a shot. Three rapid clicks in the left earphone of Cristani's headset, followed by three more, told him that two of his men were down.

Motioning to his team to check the rest of the floor, he raced down the stairs to find Hernandez, Bux Marri, and two Iranians sprawled in pools of blood. Doc Dolan, platoon medic, already had a tourniquet on the chief's thigh and was pulling apart the scout's vest and shirt. The Baluchi looked stoically at the bright red blood frothing from the hole near the center of his chest.

Cristani pointed at the other man in the team. "Plant your charge and take Deacon's pack with you. Then join the blocking team at the barracks. Move it!" The SEAL ran down the passageway and disappeared around a corner.

"How is it, Doc?"

"Deacon's hit in the leg. Through and through. Clean. No damage to the femur, no major blood vessel damage. He'll be able to do a fast stagger with some help. The scout here..." his voice softened as he looked up at the lieutenant. "Sucking chest wound. No exit wound and way too much blood. Maybe an artery got nicked. Maybe even his spine."

"He can walk?" Cristani saw Dolan go poker-faced.

"Okay, I'll deal with it. Take my charge topside after you place yours down here. Move out, Doc." Cristani stooped over the fallen scout.

Dolan was standing with a satchel charge in each hand when another door opened, this time behind the crouching Cristani. A disheveled woman appeared, dressed only in an open uniform tunic and holding a small pistol before her like a chalice. Before either SEAL moved, bullets from the Baluchi's rifle ripped by them and spun her around. She staggered into a clumsy pirouette across the legs of the dead Iranian officer, waving her handgun. The scout shot her again.

"They are pigs, the Persians. Pigs." The Baluchi spoke to a wide-eyed Cristani, who had leap-frogged aside when the scout fired.

"I did not count these two, commander. The unclean woman must come here with day guards to sleep the night. I am sorry for this." The scout coughed wetly and added, "We fight swine."

Hernandez tightened the tourniquet on his leg and croaked, "The Scarecrow saved my dumb ass, boss."

Cristani looked at the downed chief and the blood-soaked scout. Then the hiss in his right earphone returned.

"This is Henhouse. Hammerjacks ETA now forty-seven minutes. Iron Eye sees no movement near you. Acknowledge." Cristani hit his mike twice.

The expected reply came, "Roger, Little Chicks. Henhouse out."

Cristani motioned Dolan to get moving with the satchel charges and glanced at his wristwatch. *All this carnage in eight minutes?* Abandoning radio discipline he pressed his throat mike.

"All hands. Voice report. Keep it short. Motown?"

Hanna was behind sandbags that ringed the gatehouse, watching the entrance road and the southern approaches. After dropping their explosives at the corners of the main building, his teammates were hidden in the shadow of the Pasdaran barracks.

"Charges placed. Blockers set. Out."

"Roger. Chunk?"

"Charges placed. Laser standby. Blockers at the barracks. You gotta see this shit, AP—this place is hot!" John Gorski, the big California body-builder, tended to be less than terse on the radio.

"On the way, Chunk."

Leaving Hernandez and the Baluchi propped against the corridor wall side by side, Cristani started toward the rear of the building. He grinned at them over his shoulder, his teeth gleaming in a broad smile that split his black face paint.

"You guys don't run off anywhere, okay? I'll be right back." He keyed his mike as he jogged. "Topside team, report." Cristani kicked through the rear doors and was almost to the bunker before his team checked in.

Second in command of Cristani's team, First Class Yeoman Toussaint had a Masters Degree in IT and was tasked with collecting computer data. He rasped, "Deck secure. Charges placed. Five hard drives. We're on the main deck, dragging Deacon. Raggedy Andy won't move."

"Roger. I'll get him. Hustle out." Cristani checked his watch again. *Almost back on timeline.* Not long before the Hammerjacks arrived.

Gorski was waiting at the east door of the rear building, a long and windowless bunker. He led Cristani inside, closed the sliding steel door, and said, "We're gonna lose night vision, boss, but check this place out!" With that, he switched on the lights.

The building was a huge weapons depot, with sleek shapes on racks that reached to the rafters, twenty-five feet above. Two cylinders rested on dollies in the center aisle, each fifty feet long and four feet in diameter. Wires like dissected ganglia dangled from their blunt ends. The *Shahab-4* missiles were waiting for their warheads. With a 1,200-mile range, the rockets could reach southeast Europe, India, and the entire Saudi Arabian peninsula. A missile strike against Israel or the vital bases in Oman would be easy.

"Bingo, Chunk."

Gorski nodded vigorously, unzipped his knee pocket, and produced a small Geiger counter. "I got hardware I could reach without climbing racks and busting everything open. Too much here to check out, but I got some good circuit boards. Now watch this!" The SEAL passed the Geiger counter over a conical green shape with several open access plates. The unit buzzed madly. "This fucker's a nuke!"

Cristani's mind recoiled as he looked at a nearby storage rack. It held another conical green shape with Cyrillic markings. He said, "They're the nukes for sure, and their hot guts will be spread all over this place in minutes." The Geiger counter continued its rasping buzz. "Put that thing away. I hope you didn't screw with this open one, Chunk, or you'll be glowing in the dark. You got pictures?"

Gorski nodded again, and said, "Got those tanks in the back, too."

Cristani looked at the row of tall stainless steel containers lining the rear wall. They were the biological agent storage tanks the spooks described, right down to the chugging refrigeration units. *Some nasty crap is going to get splattered around here real soon.*

Cristani's headset hissed again. "This is Henhouse. Iron Eye holds no movement inside fifteen clicks. Hammerjacks ETA at IP now thirty-eight minutes. Acknowledge." Clicking his mike twice, Cristani headed for the door.

"Turn on your laser and we haul ass!"

Gorski hit the wall switch. Fumbling in the dark, the two men shouldered the door open, pulling down their night vision goggles as it swung closed behind them. Gorski skidded to his knees in front of a small tripod, flipped a toggle switch and was rewarded with a green indicator light. The laser target designator was bouncing its beam off the steel door. Gorski ran toward the south gate while the lieutenant charged back through the rear door of the main building. He found the Baluchi scout alone, slumped against the wall.

"Okay, Scarecrow. Let's get you moving. Nobody gets left behind." Cristani knelt and put an arm around the fallen man's shoulders.

The scout gently pushed the cradling arm away. "I cannot rise. This is the place I die, my commander." The Baluchi looked at the AK-47 on his lap, its long sound suppressor resting on his tattered trousers.

"You leave me this rifle?"

"You have made it yours." Cristani slowly straightened. "I was proud to fight at your side, Daud Bux Marri. You honor your family. And you honor me and your comrades."

The Baluchi looked up, blood running down his chin. "One day, I will see you in paradise." He gagged and recovered his voice. "But do not join me this night. My beautiful *houris* must first prepare the feast for you." He pulled a dagger from his belt and raised it.

"For my son. I took it from a Yemeni dog I killed in Kandahar." His voice fading, he added, "Go with God, commander." When the SEAL leader nodded and took the dagger, Bux Marri's chin dropped to his chest and his eyes closed.

Then Cristani ran. He hurtled down the access road to the main gate, keying his mike and growling, "Move out, Motown! Blocking team, everybody—flank speed. I'm right behind you and I'll kickass stragglers." The hiss came again.

"This is Henhouse. Hammerjacks ETA now twenty-nine minutes. Clear target. Clear target. Acknowledge." Cristani keyed his mike twice and increased speed. Fifty yards ahead he saw the four men of the barracks blocking team scrambling through the gate. The others were disappearing into the darkness beyond. *Back on timeline!*

The SEALs tumbled into the *wadi* that hid their vehicles. Half-dragging Hernandez, they scattered papers, uniforms, and weapons as they scrambled through the tamarisks. One squad erased tire tracks while another drove the Land Rovers to the road, throwing more equipment from the windows as they climbed. The last thing to go were the boots, tossed out of the crowded vehicles as they wrestled themselves back into civilian clothes.

Sprinting down the road in the lead vehicle, Cristani received another message just as the Bandar Abbas dock lights appeared.

"This is Henhouse. Iron Eye holds you one click from base. Hammerjacks ETA in twenty minutes. Base is ready to roll, so move it, Little Chicks. Henhouse, out."

Cristani keyed the mike twice, crushed the headset against the Land Rover door, and sailed the pieces into the night. They crossed a culvert and swerved into a parking slot fifty yards from the hole in the fence. Beyond were the dock, the freighter, and safety.

High above the Straits of Hormuz, seventy miles south, an Air Force Boeing 707 rolled to a heading that would take it home to Oman's Masirah Island airbase. The powerful radar in "Iron Eye," the E-8 JSTARS airborne command post, saw the two Land Rovers stop and disgorge twelve commandos. It also tracked super-carrier USS Carl Vinson, as she and her escorts plowed through the waters of the Gulf of Oman, one hundred twenty miles southeast, nosing toward the Indian Ocean. But attention at the JSTARS main tactical console was focused on two blips crossing the Iranian shoreline at high speed. Encrypted commands were sent.

"Hammerjack Two, this is Iron Eye. Your IP nineteen clicks dead ahead. On course. Maintain launch speed. Hammerjack One, your IP now seventeen clicks. Come left to course 280. Maintain launch speed. You are cleared hot. I repeat. Hammerjacks are cleared for launch."

The Boeing F/A-18E Super Hornet strike fighters each carried a different version of 2000-pound "smart" bombs—Guided Bomb Units. The GBU-24 Paveway III on the centerline hard points of Hammerjack One would home on the laser target designator Gorski had activated near the weapons bunker. The Paveway riding on Hammerjack Two was guided by the GPS satellite system. It would navigate to the roof of the building the SEALs had packed with nine demolition charges.

Bandar Abbas boasts a great array of antiaircraft weapons. Besides hundreds of gun emplacements, the coast is studded with Russian SA-10 Grumble missile sites backed up by old Hawk installations and numberless short and mid-range missiles. Iran's greatest concentration of fighter aircraft, besides those near Tehran, was also based at Bandar Abbas. So even though the only active radar was at Bandar Abbas airport, and all military radars were silent, an EA-6B Prowler electronic warfare plane sent from the Vinson took no chances. Hugging the coast east of Bandar Abbas, its jamming signals blanketed the entire area. Even if a missile site operator accidentally activated his radar when the Super Hornets crossed the coast, he would be as puzzled by the failure of his equipment as was the radar operator at Bandar Abbas civil airport.

Hammerjack One crossed its IP. The pilot squeezed the trigger on his stick and pulled up sharply into a steady climb. Fighting the pull of five gravities, he rhythmically grunted as his G-suit pulsed and seized his legs and abdomen with a grip that forced blood back up to his head and prevented a blackout. He roared up, his aircraft riding a twisting column of flame.

The pilot fought G-forces turning his arms into lead until finally, the jolt came. His weapons system had released its winged bomb. The fighter was now at 3,000 feet, and it might have appeared as an eight-second blip on Bandar Abbas airport radar if it had not been smothered by the *Prowler's* jamming. Separating smoothly from the aircraft, the huge bomb continued its climb. The pilot rolled away and down, racing his plane back to the coast. A second later, Hammerjack Two performed the same maneuver, and it too dove back toward the shoreline.

Far above them, the two stub-winged bombs continued their arc into the night sky. Glittering patterns of frost diamonds grew on their chilled gray skins as they silently rose to 7000 feet, over a mile above the desert floor. The first bomb saw its target, illuminated by Gorski's target designator, and gracefully nosed down into a whistling glide, its laser-seeking eye fixed on that bright spot, far below.

As the second bomb climbed, its electronic brain converted GPS satellite signals into target coordinates. Then it too pitched over, adjusting its course for the bigger building, rolling gently as it dove. The giant bombs fell as if they were riding wires attached to their destinations.

On arrival, *Ocean Princess* had notified Bandar Abbas harbor control that her departure time was Thursday morning, and her captain had obtained all the required clearance documents and approvals. No one in the harbor master's control tower remarked on the ship that took in her mooring lines and eased away from its dock, setting course south, into the Gulf.

At that moment, the fused nose of the Paveway lance thrown by Hammerjack One ripped through the bunker door and detonated in the middle of sixty conventional missile warheads, three SEMTEX demolition charges, and explosive shells around the cores of two nuclear warheads. The bomb from Hammerjack Two nailed the nearby building's roof like a Ramset rivet, its detonation shockwave igniting demolition charges at the building's main supports. The pile-driver blows hit the compound like gigantic one-two punches.

Rivaling the aurora borealis, pulsing flashes lit up clouds over Bandar Abbas city, heralding the shuddering blasts that rolled in, echoing from the north. Windows rattled and cracked. The ground shook. A growling rumble brought the city's inhabitants running into the streets, fearing an earthquake. Barefoot people in bedclothes heard the rolling thunder and saw fountains of fire and skyrockets of debris sail up hundreds of feet as secondary explosions rocked the night. Fire engines, police cars, and military vehicles raced out of Bandar Abbas, their sirens screaming chaos.

The amazing light and sound show that woke the city was seen in the northern Makran hills and far out to sea. And it was seen by the pilots of the Air Force Boeing 707 far above, as it wheeled south toward Oman.

On the bridge of *Ocean Princess*, Cristani and Hanna also heard the rumbles and saw the multi-colored lights that blazed and sparked along the northern horizon. In the cool harbor air above them, a column of smoky heat rose from the ship's raked stack as her turbines wound up and she gathered speed.

"Some of the neighbors might be enjoying those holiday fireworks." Like the other SEALs, Cristani knew about Hanna's Middle Eastern ancestry.

"There is a God, boss. And we are His instruments of justice."

Cristani pulled two cigars from his breast pocket, and they solemnly shared a match. Savoring their traditional victory cigars, the SEAL lieutenant and his teammate went below to the sickbay.

Hernandez was fighting sedatives as Dolan and the ship's doctor worked on his torn leg. He looked up when Cristani came through the door and slurred, "Scarecrow... did he make it?"

"No go, Deacon." The weary lieutenant watched Hernandez fight sleep. "But we'll drink to him at McP's Pub in a couple of weeks."

"Yeah... a damn good man. We gave those turkeys something to remember... Happy New Year, AP. You too, Motown..." Hernandez sighed, and let his eyes close.

The SEAL team had indeed given many people things to remember and things to do, beginning with the stevedore who was always dozing on the dock near *Ocean Princess*. When the Americans returned—yes, he heard them talking—and ran up the gangway, his eyes glittered under the brim of his dirty cap as he counted their numbers. He saw one was limping. He saw they no longer carried the bags they had taken from the ship an hour before.

The sky over Bandar Abbas was still exploding when the stevedore left the pier and hurried into town. Tomorrow he would drink smuggled beer with his friends at the Homa Hotel. But tonight the concierge will send a fax to Tehran. The dark and secret man there would know what to make of this strange night.

CHAPTER 3

Golestan Palace
Tehran, Iran

Lean birches in the sheltered palace garden still wore some wilted summer leaves, and he enjoyed their anxious flutters as they struggled not to fall. He was early for the meeting, but then he was always early for meetings. He brushed a manicured finger over the crescent scar high on his cheekbone and stared through the tall windows. Dressed in a white turban and brown robe over an immaculate taupe tunic, a slender and bearded man was alone in a large room full of ornate Louis XV gilt furniture.

He had been in this room many times when the Shah was in power. In fact, he worked for the Pahlavi government until the start of the revolution led by Ayatollah Khomeini. Before those troubled days, this Tehran palace was used by the Shah's sister, and he met the princess here whenever she took an interest in officials who were spending her brother's money. She made sure she always got her share.

Now the palace served the masters of the Islamic Republic of Iran, and he worked for that government, too. But he was no longer just a clerk on General Toufanian's staff, buying American weapons and lining the general's pockets. Naturally, he lined his own pockets too, which proved to be prudent considering the time spent in exile during the revolution. Still, he was not forced to give much money to the victorious ayatollahs before they asked him to return and work for them. However they grumbled, he knew they needed his encyclopedic knowledge, his contacts, and his organizational skills. They needed him more than they coveted his money.

He turned his emerald ring in the sunlight, enjoying its green fire. The stone was one of a pair General Toufanian had made into cufflinks. But in the end, he mused, emeralds and bribes could not save the fool. *He should have fled to Paris, too. Now all that remains of him are two green jewels carved with a word from the Koran.* He turned the stone again and thought about its mate in that lovely modern ring waiting in his Paris flat.

He came to his feet as the doors swung wide and four figures sailed toward him, three in billowing robes, one in uniform. It was just as he had anticipated: Admiral Shamkani, Minister of Defense; Ali Yunesi, Minister of Intelligence; and Doctor Ebtekar, Minister of Environment. Then came the man whose face was in a golden frame high on the opposite wall—the Supreme Leader of the Islamic Republic, His Excellency Ayatollah Seyyed Ali Khamenei.

When the four were seated at the table he took the humblest seat, farthest from Khamenei. Tea, sweets, and pistachios were placed before the silent men. When the last tea-boy pulled the doors closed as he left, three of the men spoke at the same time.

"Everything—radioactive! And biological—"

"Attackers! Hundreds—"

"*Shahabs* destroyed! Delay is—"

In the midst of pandemonium, the slender man was motionless, watching. Then came a single whispered word that stilled the room. "Silence."

The room became a diorama of men frozen in mid-gesture.

Ayatollah Khamenei was seventy-one years old. Unlike his predecessor, brooding, tall, dark-browed Imam Khomeini, this man was short, round-faced, and wore horn-rimmed spectacles. His eyes bulged with anger as he slammed his bony fists on the table as if they held invisible truncheons. Bowls and glasses rattled.

"You are here because what happened at Bandar Abbas is the responsibility of each and every one of you. It must be explained to the Leadership Council, to the Supreme Defense Council, to the parliament—and to the people! You are here to work together, not to blame others! I am understood?"

All eyes focused on the furious little man. For he was the *Faqih*, the ultimate power in Iran and a man whose word overrides acts of parliament and any other cleric. He was head of the Leadership Council that oversees all affairs of the Islamic Republic. He was the *Marja Ala*, spiritual head of Shiite Muslims and keeper of the will of the Twelfth Imam, the *Mahdi*. He would be the first to bow before that messiah when he rises from the Jamkaran well in the holy city of Qum to lead the faithful to glory. But before that day, the *Faqih* must be obeyed.

Khamenei's gray beard trembled. Finally, when there was no reply to his outburst, he looked at each face around the table and then spoke in calm, tutorial tones.

"By the Holy Word, we think to be the first power in all the Middle East, and *this* happens? We burn in our own land. Tell me, who burns us?" No one replied. "Very well, then. Admiral, you answer first. Who destroyed our laboratories and our weapons?"

"It was the work of Baluchi commandos from Iraq, Eminence. We found weapons and clothes and documents. We even found the body of a Baluchi in the ruined laboratory building."

"So, we are humbled by barbarians. No doubt they came to visit us from the Kurdish oil fields in the mountains of Kirkuk. And how did they get to Bandar Abbas, admiral? Through an oil pipeline? And to where did they disappear?"

"We are searching the area, Eminence. We will find them and their spies. We..." The admiral's voice trailed off.

"I am relieved to hear you are so confident." The gray beard trembled again. "What an idiotic thing to say! Go immediately to Bandar Abbas! Stay in that poor city until you can tell us something that makes sense. And before you leave Tehran," his voice took on a hard edge, "before you leave *today*, Shamkani, be sure to give Doctor Ebtekar"—he shot a glance at the unhappy Minister of the Environment—a complete list of your weapons and deadly things that were strewn across our countryside by those mysterious Baluchis, so he can clean it all up. Go!" The Admiral rose and looked neither to the left or right as he strode toward the doors.

"What are you waiting for, Doctor Ebtekar? Go with him! Go, before all of Bandar Abbas dies from radiation and disease." The doctor silently followed the admiral out of the room.

"Now, Minister Ali Yunesi, what does our all-knowing intelligence service think about the disaster? What do your VEVAK informers and spies tell us?"

"It is true, Excellency, it looks like the work of Baluchis from Iraq. Or remnants of the old Republican Guards. But how did they get to Bandar Abbas? How did they escape? How could they carry enough explosives to—"

Ayatollah Khamenei's gnarled fist swept a bowl of almonds to the floor.

"You ask me questions? You ask *me*? I want answers, not questions. Go back to your torture rooms and your godless thugs. If you cannot bring me the bodies of those who raped Bandar Abbas, then bring me their names. I will find competent men to deal with them. Go, and pray the council does not send you to one of your own dungeons."

The Minister of Intelligence left the table and quickly crossed the room. When the door closed, Khamenei turned to the window and gazed at the dancing birch leaves. In the morning sunlight, his spectacles became opaque mirrors. He slowly stroked his beard, and it was a full minute before he looked at the slender man and spoke.

"Who?"

"The Americans."

"How?"

"They came from a merchant ship in the harbor, and left the same way."

"Why?"

"They must have learned of the nuclear warheads for the *Shahab* missiles."

Khamenei stood, raising his right hand as if he was about to give a sermon. The hand began to tremble violently. He looked at it for a moment, then quickly pressed it to his chest and closed his eyes. His sibilant words were blistered with rage.

"Satan." His eyes opened. "The Great Satan. How—how *dare* they! They invade Iraq. They invade Afghanistan. Then those infidel swine come here—here, to our own sacred land. Kill our people. Destroy our property. Do they think we are one of those peasant countries? One of those—those—"

"Banana republics."

"Yes. Banana republics!" Khamenei was silent for long seconds. Then he sat, clasped his hands, and smiled at the man sitting halfway down the long table.

"Speak to me, my son. Tell me you have more than knowledge. Tell me you have a plan to give us our revenge—revenge we must have to restore our honor and to teach the Americans and the world to respect us. Tell me."

"I have plans, my Supreme Leader, and I have begun to act. Give me your blessing and I will use new weapons to strike at the Americans. At their homeland itself!"

"New weapons?"

"Yes. It will be difficult and it will be expensive, but I can do it."

"Always expensive. And it will be dangerous too, no doubt." Khamenei shook his head, his face impassive. "You know the Americans are completely mad. Terrorists. They are capable of committing all crimes against Muslims. Anything."

"When I find men who can do the work, and when I find a military man of courage and skill, I believe I can strike at America as they struck at us."

"With commandos?"

"No, Eminence. We will use very powerful weapons made by Russia, even more deadly than their atomic bombs. We will use Palestinians that Hizballah will send to us, so if they are captured we can deny them. And when they are trained as I have planned, the Americans will not be able to prove we are the hidden hand. Completely mad or not, they never act without proof."

"True." Another long moment passed, then Khamenei added, "What will you destroy?"

"Americans."

"Many?"

"Tens of thousands. Perhaps hundreds of thousands."

Khamenei's eyes opened. "You still have Russian bombs?"

"Yes, Exalted Leader. We lost two of the bombs at Bandar Abbas, but the other three nuclear weapons are still safe in Tabriz. Even so, I must tell you that the chessboard is complex, and I am not yet sure of how we can best move. Only give me your blessing, and I will present a complete plan to you in one month. Six weeks at most. Then you may decide to use the weapons and fighters I will have made ready. Or not."

"Could an atomic bomb be taken to America and then be detonated from Tehran? Could I push a button and do it?" Khamenei's eyes glittered behind his spectacles.

The bearded man thought for a moment and answered, "Yes, Eminence, but not without great difficulty and risk of failure. I must respectfully advise against it."

"Never mind. It was a prideful desire born of anger. But as you ask, your work in this matter has my blessing. Prepare all things for my approval, and may God guide your hands." Khamenei moved to leave and the younger man stood respectfully.

"Stay here, my son. I will send them to clean the table and carpet and serve you the delicacies you enjoy. I know you are fond of this palace and this room. While you eat, think of how you will feed *me*. How you will feed my anger."

He turned abruptly and swept out of the room, leaving the door open behind him to allow the servants to enter. The slender man remained standing, settling his robes in pleasing folds, waiting as tea-boys swept up spilled almonds and set the table for his solitary meal. His thoughts uncoiled like waking serpents.

Who is that man who just humbled three powerful ministers? Not a demigod like those who came before him—the unloved Shah, and the turbaned usurper. No, not a demigod, but a mortal angry enough to dare to attack America.

And who am I? I am Morteza Dehesh, servant of ministers, and once the servant of demigods. I enjoy being a servant. I enjoy being feared, to roam the corridors of power, to make those arrogant westerners bleed. Or pay. Or both.

Smiling, he looked over the backs of the servants cleaning the carpet. He did like this room. It was a beautiful and proper place to peer into the fearsome kaleidoscope that was beginning to rotate in his mind. Terrible weapons... then he remembered the man who could steal them from the old Soviet storerooms!

He made his first decision. After lunch he would command his ablest and fastest courier to travel to the north. North, to contact a man in Russia who would bring him the weapons he needed.

CHAPTER 4

Pentagon power begins in the "A Ring." Surrounding a small inner courtyard, it is the smallest and innermost of a nest of five-sided corridors. Expanding through B, C, and D Rings, power gathers authority as it radiates out to the prestigious E Ring, with its windows on the Potomac and the Washington skyline. The office of the Secretary of Defense is on the E Ring, overlooking the River Entrance Terrace and flanked by offices of aides and chiefs of the military services. Plans do not always originate in that elegant office, but the military's deadliest plots are always approved there.

The winter sun was gone, and the room next to the Secretary's suite was growing dark. Outside its tall windows the dusk of a clear winter sky was turning to purple, and the only light in the room flickered from four mute television sets and a computer screen that displayed a satellite image of southern Iran. The screen's hard gleam etched the profile of Jeremiah Adams as he leaned across his desk, examining the digital imagery though drugstore reading glasses. He hummed the cheerful and tuneless melody he usually reserved for grilled steak.

"Decon trucks," he muttered, leaning closer to the monitor. "Looks like those troops are in biohazard gear, too. The whole area must be crawling with nasty microbes. It's a crying shame, for sure."

Pleased by the proof of a perfect job by Bancroft's SEALs and *Carl Vinson's* aircraft, he resolved that when he finally had a meeting with Secretary Horton the first thing he would ask the Secretary to do would be to send each unit a "Bravo Zulu," the traditional naval message of congratulations: *Well done!*

Adams wondered when he would have that meeting. In all of December, the new Secretary granted just one meeting to the Joint Chiefs, and only because they insisted on it in the name of national security. The Middle East and North Africa still smoldered after being ignited by a wave of popular uprisings that demanded regime changes, and American lives and interests needed military protection. But besides that solitary meeting, Secretary Horton had not allowed Adams or anyone else to formally brief him about forward planning.

The new Secretary's self-imposed isolation meant that only plans already approved would be implemented. All new operations were stalled until he could be briefed, could give his approval, and could coordinate action with his cabinet colleagues and the White House. Though his new boss had tossed a peculiar monkey-wrench into Pentagon routine, and despite the resulting delays and postponements, Adams doggedly soldiered on. The Christmas raid on Iran went well, other actions were being planned, and he remained hopeful that approvals would come. And come sooner rather than later.

Adams' chief worry was that the theocratic rulers of the Islamic Republic of Iran promised a world without the United States and Israel. They were working hard to make that dream a reality. The endless Afghan war complicated Adams' work, and America's festering problems with nation building in Iraq added still another dimension. Money and soldiers had postponed Tehran's plans to make Iraq a slavish satellite, so while the mullahs waited for the infidel invaders to leave, they redoubled their efforts to be the greatest power in Islam, a model for all the Shia, Sunni, Ibadi—all Muslims everywhere. To reach that goal they must intimidate their neighbors, so the mullahs intensified their program to acquire nuclear-tipped missiles. When they acted on that plan, so had Jeremiah Adams.

The SEAL raid on Bandar Abbas was part of a policy Adams helped create. Instead of just responding to terrorist strikes by Iran, Pentagon strategy became proactive, and covert forces went into action anywhere a threat was discovered. Multi-service, multi-agency, and sometimes multi-national, the aggressive policy had excellent results. Adams reveled in the complex work, but life on the job hit a speed bump when Secretary Blackman died on Thanksgiving Day.

The new Secretary of Defense, Frederick Horton, was a senior and highly visible Mississippi Senator elevated to the Cabinet by a White House concerned with the coming elections. Still, despite the usual backdrop of politics, it was known that he took his new job seriously and, despite a self-imposed seclusion, he worked long hours. His courtly style was complemented by bulldog jowls and a rotund frame under rumpled linen suits. Most days he looked quite like the portraits of his Civil War predecessors.

His chief of staff, dapper Aubrey Beauchamps III, was a stark contrast to Horton. Tall, slender, impeccably dressed and groomed, Beauchamps was the scion of a family that had contributed generously to Horton's senatorial campaigns, so when the new Secretary moved into the Pentagon, Beauchamps moved with him. Expanding the power of his new job, Beauchamps carefully controlled access to the new Secretary. He monitored Horton's complex stream of communications and paperwork with zeal, telling anyone who would listen that the task was a no-brainer for a Yale graduate. Above all, he wanted everyone's business with the Secretary to be his business too, and he insured that with surprise visits to offices of senior Pentagon officials.

So when fluorescent lights in the adjoining room stuttered and lit, Adams blinked at the lanky silhouette in his doorway and knew it could only belong to Beauchamps. He sprang erect, automatically hitting the computer screen's blanking key.

"What?"

The shadow lazily reached out, switched on the overheads, and drawled, "If anyone was still defending democracy late on a Saturday night, I'd bet it would be you, Gerry. I'd bet you were sitting here on Christmas Day, too."

Adams ground his teeth whenever he heard Aubrey Beauchamps' carefully oiled voice. It sounded exactly like a State Department officer who always referred to his opposite number in India as 'my little brown brother in Delhi.'

"You'd win both those bets, Beauchamps," Adams snapped. "And like I told you before, don't call me Gerry. Gerry Adams is an IRA dickhead."

"Oh. I am so sorry—*Jay*. I forgot your friends call you Jay. Please forgive me. Jay." The smile on Beauchamp's tanned face widened to an open-mouthed grin that showed his beautifully capped teeth. "Secretary Horton was planning to messenger this letter to you tomorrow, but I thought it would be nice to hand it to you tonight. Personally."

Beauchamps held out a sheet of heavy executive stationary embossed with the unmistakable seal of the Secretary of Defense. Adams ignored it and looked at the Hermes silk tie and the flat lapels of the suit standing in the middle of the room. He had another vague thought about replacing the tired blazer draped on the chair behind him. Then he shrugged.

"Thanks for going to the trouble, Aubrey. Just leave it on the desk and I'll get to it later tonight." Adams lit up the monitor and a National Security Agency emblem and a log-in box appeared. "Shut the lights off on your way out, please."

"You better read it, Gerry. Ah, sorry—*Jay*. Then you can forget about work and go home to celebrate. Enjoy Sunday on your boat." Beauchamps strolled to the desk, dropped the letter on the ink-stained blotter, and stepped back. Adams studied the paper for a long moment. Then he pulled the eyeglasses from his face, looked up, and sighed.

"What is this supposed to be?"

"Why, it's a draft resignation letter, of course. *Your* resignation letter."

"So you talked Jelly Roll into firing me. What for?"

"Oh, no, no." The smile became a sympathetic pucker. "You're not being *fired*. You are *retiring*. Your early retirement is part of a downsizing caused by budget reductions. Surely you must have seen that happen before." The wolfish smile reappeared and he nodded at the letter, adding, "After the resignation paragraph, did you see where you thank the Secretary for your Meritorious Service Medal?"

They locked eyes. Finally, Adams ended the growing tension with a chuckle and wagged a finger at the letter on his desk. "It was damn good of you to personally bring that around, Aubrey. I appreciate it."

"Really?" Beauchamps frowned. "I thought—"

"No, really," Adams interrupted. "I know how hard it is to tell a guy he's no longer needed. It's tough. Takes guts." He rose, walked to the front of his desk and sat on the edge, looking up at the taller man.

"Tell me, Aubrey, what's going to happen to my shop when I'm gone? Gonna be closed up? My position abolished?"

Beauchamps casually surveyed the office, and replied, "Oh no, Jay. The job is much too important to abolish. It will continue—after you vacate these spaces, naturally."

"What the hell? Are you engineering my resignation because you want this office? I don't need it. Take it. I'll move to the A Ring. I'll do my job in a broom closet on a folding chair."

"Ah, Jay. The job this office represents—well, the door is just where it should be. Facing the Secretary's inner office. Sorry. I'm afraid there will be no more limos or bodyguards, and you'll have to turn over the keys to the suite *and* the job. Along with that blonde secretary. What's her name? Suzy? I've got plans for that cute little ass." Beauchamps' smile flashed again. "Face it, Jay. There are those who can carry out your mission with style, and who can grow this office into its proper size and influence." He brushed imaginary lint from his lapel.

"I see. Style, size, and influence. I guess that's sadly lacking around here." Leaning forward, Adams again considered the clothes in front of him, taking in the wingtip shoes.

Damn. Where does he get them polished like that?

"And speaking of style, Aubrey, I thought you classy Ivy League guys always got a lady's name right. Her name is *Sophie*, not Suzy. Sophie Giltspur." Adams pushed away from the desk and stood very close to Beauchamps, smiling. "And next time you say her name, peckerwood, hold your mouth just right—or I'll kick your balls into your watch-pocket." Then Adams moved chest-to-chest with Beauchamps and stepped on one of his visitor's shoes, grinding his sole into the gleaming toe.

Beauchamps' eyelids fluttered, but he did not back away. "Get off my foot, Adams," he sputtered, "Don't make me show you why I was captain of the Yale boxing team." He raised a hand to push Adams' chest—and the rest happened instantly.

Adams jabbed his thumb into the back of the hand on his chest and smoothly peeled it away and down. The classic judo move brought Beauchamps to his knees, and when Adams twisted his arm, the lanky man was on his face with a knee in the small of his back. Adams leaned forward, close to the head on the carpet. He could smell floral aftershave lotion as he hissed into Beauchamps' ear.

"You ever put a hand on me again, tough guy, I'll rip it off and shove it up your ass. And if you so much as touch Sophie Giltspur's hair, I swear to God I'll find you, tear your head off, and ram my fist down your throat. Read me?"

"Uh. Agh."

"Read me, you dandified prick?" Adams increased pressure on the arm.

"Yes I read you!"

The two were silent for long seconds. Then Adams sprang to his feet. He watched Beauchamps rise just as quickly and assume a boxing stance.

"Go ahead, Yale champion, take your best shot. Go for it. Or get the fuck out of my office and hop back up on Jelly Roll's lap."

Eying Adams, Beauchamps slowly lowered his fists and backed toward the door.

"You're a lunatic, Adams. A violent lunatic. And the Secretary knows who started that 'Jelly Roll' business. He told me he'll do something to pay you back if you're not out of here very soon." He paused in the doorway, adjusting his tie and settling his jacket. "Actually, that letter on your desk takes care of that rather nicely, doesn't it? The Secretary expects you to make this office available in ninety days. So sign the resignation letter, leave it on my desk, and collect your medal. Then disappear, Gerry." He walked back to the door and turned, arching an eyebrow.

"About your secretary—" Beauchamps quickly stepped backwards into the room behind him as Adams lunged toward him.

"How many times I got to kick your butt tonight—you over-dressed cockroach? *Never* call me Gerry. Now don't let the screen door hit you in the ass on the way out, boxing team captain."

Adams slammed his door shut, snapped the lock, trudged to his chair and leaned back into the smooth leather. He sat absolutely still, thinking about the past ten minutes, then said softly, "The miserable little shit." He opened a lower desk drawer. It was deep, designed to hold file folders, but instead it held a half-gallon bottle of Southern Comfort and a Waterford crystal tumbler. Pouring an inch of the dark liquor, he leaned back again, grimacing. He felt as if he had been stabbed in the gut.

As always, the medicinal tang of the sweetened bourbon helped. It was his favorite sipping whiskey since midshipman days, when a proud uncle and aunt collected him from Annapolis for holidays. As soon as they passed the town limits they would hand him a fifth of "Comfort." Ducking his head in the back of the cavernous '58 Packard, he would take cautious sips from the bottle. Though they found it hard to approve of alcohol, they knew it was his way to relax at the end of school terms, and that he did not abuse it. The bourbon was also a target of his secretary's wrath. She would say, with a carbon steel rasp in her voice, "You drink entirely too much, Jeremiah Adams." Then she would get him two ice cubes from the small fridge under her desk.

Beautiful Sophie Giltspur. Those looks and lineage made her the most aristocratic secretary in the Pentagon. And she'd hit her stride on their first day together.

"If we are to work well as a team, you will understand that I am not your *secretary*, I am your *assistant*." She squared her slim shoulders when she made that pronouncement. It had set the style between them for the following seven years.

Seven fat years. That great figure, those great clothes—smartest and toughest gal in the five-sided doughnut. Held her own with the boys. Didn't tolerate much in the way of bad manners, though.

He remembered the army two-star who breezed into his office with no appointment, snarling, "Out of my way, girlie, or I'll go through you instead of around you." Sophie made it a point to meet the Army Chief of Staff at the next JCS social bash. She smiled her dazzling smile, complimented the trim physique his polo ponies gave him, and got herself invited to exercise those horses at his Fauquier County farm. The two-star wound up exercising troops in Alaska on his next tour, wondering what had happened to his third star.

Do not screw with Sophie Giltspur was the watchword of the executive staff. Not that Adams hadn't thought about it. After a long night's work during their first month together, he bought dinner at the Ritz Carlton in Pentagon City and then parked in her guest slot at River House. He looked earnestly into her blue eyes, stroked the glossy ash blonde hair, and tried on his best boyish smile. She reached over, squeezed his knee and stopped his hand from turning off the ignition.

"Please drive me to the front door and then go home, Jeremiah. We have another long day tomorrow." Her smile was dazzling. "And remember, you must ask daddy for permission to court me before you get midnight coffee privileges."

'Daddy,' Sir Basil Giltspur, died three months later and Adams never had a chance to meet him, much less get permission to grope his daughter. In the following years their friendship grew steadily warmer but never seemed to ignite.

Still, working with her he felt he had another arm, and she became the honest and trusted critic of his thinking. She was his co-pilot.

Sir Basil's death made Sophie a rich woman, and when Adams asked her why she did not quit her job, she answered, "I continue to work because it gives one dignity, Jeremiah, a character trait you should cultivate." He could not figure out what she meant half the time. Why, he already did the work of three men, dignified or not. But what would happen to her when he left? She could never work with Beauchamps, he knew that for sure. He also knew if she heard about his forced resignation letter from anyone else she would put him on her permanent shit list. No getting around it, he would have to call Sophie tonight.

Leaning forward he methodically stabbed the buttons on his ancient phone, hefting the substantial handset with satisfaction. 'Those new phones made in China by political prisoners don't weigh a damn thing,' he often said. 'They fall off your desk if you just look at 'em. Besides, those damn coiled cords always get tangled into knots.'

Sophie answered on the second ring, "This is Sophie Giltspur. Who is so impolite as to call during the dinner hour?" Adams felt like a telemarketer.

"I just got fired, Sophie."

"Oh, Jeremiah. I'd hoped the letter might not ever be delivered."

Sophie already knew about it! She beat the CIA with points to spare. Then she answered his unspoken question with, "The Secretary's secretary likes to be seen at the opera, and she was in my box Thursday night for *The Tsar's Bride*. She fell asleep right after she told me she'd typed the draft letter for Beauchamps."

"So why didn't you tell me yesterday? Or today?" Adams did not know why her words made him feel so wounded.

"I planned to intercept the Secretary's messenger and take you downtown to lunch at Café Mozart. So I could tell you myself. When there was no messenger, I thought the idiots had reconsidered." Her voice softened and she added, "I am sorry, really sorry, Jeremiah. What will you do about it?"

"I don't know. I scared Beauchamps out of my office after he delivered the letter. Maybe I ought to visit Jelly Roll and step on his shoes, too."

"Put all that out of your mind tonight, Jeremiah. Finish that Southern Comfort, instead."

He grimaced. Does she have a video bug in this office?

"Go to your beautiful home in Onancock and ask that newspaperwoman to massage your temples. Then come in late on Monday, and we'll talk about it. Do drive safely. Goodnight."

The line went dead, and Adams stared at the handset. Then he grinned and thought, if I could resist choking her blue in the first week, I'd kick down her door and propose. Bad idea. She'd probably shoot me before I was halfway across the threshold.

Dropping the phone, Adams picked up the crystal tumbler, spun his chair around and scanned the television sets on the credenza. He let his mind freewheel as he sipped the whiskey, waiting for national and international news.

CNN was doing their seven o'clock roundup. There were hints of trouble in places Adams knew well, places where American resources were spread thin. In silent scenes flickering on the muted sets, Adams saw Blackbeard and Henry Morgan, instead of Osama bin Laden and Imad Mughniyeh. It was the green flag of Islam these days, instead of the black Jolly Roger. And like eradicating murderous buccaneers, Adams knew that destroying these 21st century Islamic pirates would require international agreement to close down their safe havens. Fat chance, he thought. In the meantime, an aroused and angry United States would have to send pirate-hunters and rat-catchers to places like Bandar Abbas.

It was also clear to him that the terrorists had become smarter in the last few years. The dumb ones got killed or rounded up, and Darwin's "survival of the fittest" left the crafty ones alive. Evolution worked for all creatures, good and evil. He flicked on the sound and listened to a CNN commentator reporting in front of a burning mosque.

"An intense blaze has destroyed this mosque near Medina in the Kingdom of Saudi Arabia. Witnesses say a fire started in the mosque cellars that resulted in a series of large explosions. An unknown number of clerics, together with several Palestinian pilgrims on a religious tour, were killed in the blaze. A government spokesman said there will be a full investigation..." Adams muted the sound again.

Unlike the CNN commentator, Adams knew the names of the dead "pilgrims." They were senior members of the *Izzedine al Qassam*, a military wing of Hamas. He also knew what caused the huge arsenal in the mosque to explode. Bancroft's Coronado ninjas had struck again, with help from a revitalized spook network, local agents, and commandos from Britain's SAS. Stealth warriors do not leave footprints.

CNN switched to canned footage of a street corner in some Arabic town. Adams watched, sipped his sweet bourbon, and considered the vast amount of government disinformation fed to the citizens of most countries. Just as the mullahs knew who had blown up Bandar Abbas, the Saudi government knew who did the deed in Medina. They knew whose whip was on their backs, but they could not prove it. They could not even admit there had been an attack on the terrorists that they harbored.

Looking into his empty tumbler, Adams knew the war on the Islamist killers was soon going to be none of his business. He tried to imagine himself a bystander in the days and years to come. Doing what? The only love he ever had was his job, and that was being taken from him. What a cheerful prospect.

His bleak reverie was punctured by a click from the digital wall clock: the large numerals read 19:10. He switched off the televisions, dropped the tumbler into the drawer and hit the computer's off button. Then he pulled the metal ID card from the STE phone, flipped the card into the safe under the credenza, slammed the door shut, spun the dial, pulled on his blazer, and opened the door to the dark corridor. It was late. He would really have to roll to get to the party where he planned to see 'that newspaperwoman' again.

Adams patted his jacket and trouser pockets. Everything was in its place: Keys, eyeglasses, Blackberry and, as his had aunt instructed long ago, 'A gentleman's pocket essentials—a comb, a clean handkerchief, and a decent penknife.' He had it all, except the knife was a four inch razor-sharp blade in an 'assisted opening' handle. She could not have dreamt of his need for the .40 caliber Glock in a belt holster.

At a rapid pace through familiar halls, he soon reached the southern corridors of the E Ring, a route he always took in memory of the ONI friends he lost there on September 11, 2001. On that day, airborne suicide terrorists destroyed the super-secret Chief of Naval Operations Intelligence Plot, the aviation gasoline fireball incinerating 42 out of 50 people on watch in the heart of the Command Center. The gaping hole in the building was long gone, unlike the graveyard in his heart, and as he walked the corridor's new floor he felt his missing friends marching by his side. He had learned a long time ago how to blank out faces that bubbled up from his subconscious, but tonight he was reaching out for the memories. He silently told his friends about losing his job, and then promised he would continue the war against their murderers in any way he could.

The guard at the door to South Parking recognized him, but checked the ID card clipped to his lapel anyway.

"Have a good evening, Mr. Adams."

Adams returned the smile, wondering if the grandfatherly man could hit the ceiling with a bullet from his sidearm. On the other hand, he did not have much doubt about the rifle-toting Marine standing nearby.

Arlington night air in January was cold, and Adams trotted briskly to his parking slot a dozen yards from the door. His supergrade civil service rank came with a coveted parking space near the building, and on winter nights like this he was thankful that rank still had a few privileges.

The waxed silver skin of his Yukon Denali reflected constellations of parking lot lights, and a long thin pennant hung limply from a short mast on the top rack. Not that Adams needed help to find the huge SUV in any crowded parking lot. He just liked to think of the vehicle as his personal command with its own commissioning pennant. Rounding the rear hatch he heard an anxious whine through a side window. Ranger, his big Labrador, was glad to see him.

Sophie had given the dog to Adams two years ago, a bright-eyed and affectionate Christmas present. When he complained he did not know the first thing about raising a puppy, Sophie said Ranger would provide him with much-needed domestication. She looked after the dog when he traveled, but otherwise the Lab was always with him. If he could not take a dog into places like the Pentagon, he would leave him in the Yukon, crack the windows, and visit him every few hours for a walk and a treat. Adams would rise during long meetings, saying, "Excuse me, folks. Gotta walk the dog." Friends knew he meant it literally. Others thought he drank too much coffee.

Ranger leaped through the door, shook himself vigorously, and nosed around nearby cars. Adams watched him course back and forth, sniffing tires.

"Over here, boy! Nail this Mercedes. Belongs to that jerk on the Joint Staff." Adams encouraged Ranger to cock a leg on vehicles owned by Pentagon officials who were particularly useless or dense. It was a target-rich environment.

Adams climbed into the Yukon, started the Vortec V8, checked the gas level, set the trip calculator, then whistled for Ranger.

Sophie was right. To hell with all of it.

He opened the roof and looked at the clear winter sky. Diamonds on a black display tray, the stars were distant, cold, and indifferent to prayers and pain.

Suddenly the kind of ache that makes your eyes sting welled up in his throat and surprised him. He frowned to smother a groan. He was fired. It was over, finished, done. He looked up at the stars again.

No, it was not over. The job and the office were finished, all right, but something was coming. Something was reaching out to find him. He could feel it.

With a last look at the stars, he closed the roof.

CHAPTER 5

Damascus International Airport
Syrian Arab Republic

A sliver of the waning moon was rising in the eastern sky ahead of the aircraft that flashed over desert steppes toward Iraq, bound for the distant border of Iran.

Settling into his luxuriously upholstered seat, former Soviet General Anatoliy Kostevitch blew a long and satisfied sigh, loosened the belt over his hard paunch, and watched the lights of Damascus disappear beneath the accelerating jet.

This is the way to travel, he thought. Better than what any general on the fucking army payroll can get.

The undercarriage of the Gulfstream V whirred into the fuselage, cabin lights came on, and the flight attendant appeared with another chilled vodka. She was a Tatar. He had noticed the amazing gray eyes after a long appraisal of her curves and large breasts. Legs like a wild white mare. Yes, he day-dreamed, she was surely a more beautiful aide-de-camp than any of the dozens he'd had during his long career. Unfortunately, those Tatar broads have crazy brothers and uncles with knives, so there won't be any bouncy-bouncy tonight on the fold-down bed in the rear of the cabin. Just as well. There were things to review with his hard boys after he checked on progress to Iran. When he had polished off his vodka he would go forward and visit the cockpit. No hurry.

The twin-jet aircraft belonged to Lukoil, the giant Russian energy company. It had delivered the company's First Vice President, Sergei Popov, to Damascus for talks about developing a new Syrian oil field. The *LUK* logo was painted into a small red square on the tail fin, but the rest of the unadorned fifty-million-dollar aircraft spoke volumes for its owners. Rolls Royce twin turbofan engines could drive the plane at near supersonic speed for 7,000 nautical miles, enough to range back and forth between Damascus and Tehran seven times. With fuel to spare.

The Lukoil vice president owed his friend, General Kostevitch, a colossal favor for saving him from lethal disgrace fourteen years ago. Popov, a rising KGB officer back then, had been photographed being much too intimate with a young corporal in the army's Moscow steam baths. "Mistaken identity," Kostevitch had written on the military police report, and the corporal was transferred to a facility in Kazakhstan from which he never returned. Kostevitch still had the report and the pictures. He took them from his office along with hundreds of other files after that drunk, Yeltsin, fired him in 1994. They were useful stuff. Certainly more useful than the Lenin Prize that Gorbachev gave him for developing binary nerve gas. A sneer twisted the general's thin lips as he reminisced. Yeltsin used all of my hard-won prizes and citations for toilet paper, the lard ass, just because I sold some lousy second-rate chemicals to the Libyans. This time, he thought with mounting satisfaction, this time he'd *really* show them.

When a courier from an old Iranian contact arrived in Moscow, Kostevitch called in a few IOUs, got two crates loaded onto the Gulfstream, and made preparations to close a deal in Tehran during the Lukoil trip to Syria. When Popov and his delegation climbed off the aircraft in Damascus, Kostevitch and his two men would simply remain on board while the fuel tanks were topped off. Now, in the early hours of this fine Sunday morning, they continued to Tehran.

The trip details were widely discussed on unencrypted telephone lines, by email and by fax, and included mentions of three men in the vice president's entourage who were to deliver a Lukoil work proposal to Iran. No one, inside or outside Russia, thought the side trip to Tehran was the least unusual, though sanctions on Iran were getting tighter. Everyone knew that money spoke all languages and crossed all borders.

On the long leg from Moscow to Damascus neither passengers nor crew were introduced to Kostevitch or his two assistants and, when the vice president and his entourage deplaned, the general was left with a large red binder for the Iranian Petroleum Authority. The Lukoil vice president had ostentatiously given him the bogus proposal book before they left Moscow.

"Give my personal regards to the Minister," Popov told Kostevitch loudly. "I'll see you when you return." Simple cover stories were always the best cover stories.

Kostevitch knew the Lukoil vampires were a gang of reactionary opportunists, and that they were bleeding Mother Russia's veins for their oil profits. But this was New Russia, where you adapt or die, and his mother had raised no fools. He downed the last of his vodka and gave the glass to the Tartar goddess whose legs reached all the way to paradise. When she left, he closed his eyes for a moment and grunted to himself, *Soon it will be done, Anatoliy. Soon.*

Surging to his feet and striding to the cockpit with the vigor of a younger man, the old general shook his head when he looked inside. The aircraft instrument panel was just four large computer screens stretching across the space below the forward windscreens. On the LCD displays were colorful virtual engine instruments, navigation charts, radar, approach plans, and even a weather map. Look at that, he marveled. God knew what else that crazy smorgasbord of lights can do. The American *Star Wars* wizards were no joke.

"So, pilots, where are we now?" The general had never lost his command voice.

"We are just here, sir." The pilot almost added, 'Comrade General.' A former Soviet fighter pilot, he was one of the few who recognized Kostevitch when he climbed into the Gulfstream in Moscow. Leaning forward, he punched two buttons and pointed to the center screen where a small aircraft icon moved across a display of the terrain below.

"So, what about 'no fly zones?' Are we going to be shot down by some American cowboy?" The pilot thought Kostevitch's laugh sounded a bit hollow.

"Not likely, sir," he replied. "Things have changed in Iraq since the invasion. Those old zones are now irrelevant, and we have over-flight permission from Baghdad control. Anyway, you can be sure an American AWACS radar plane is tracking us, and they can see we're on the approved course. Look here, sir," he tapped more buttons. "These show borders of the old northern and southern zones forbidden to aircraft over-flights." Bright lines appeared across the terrain map marking the 33rd and 36th parallels.

"As a precaution, I intend to stay between those latitudes, stick closely to our flight plan, and make correct reports. We are perfectly safe, sir." The co-pilot touched his control column and the aircraft icon skirted the southern "No Fly Zone," turned slightly to the southeast, and moved directly toward the outline of Baghdad, 550 kilometers away.

"Good." The general looked at the bright moonlit desert below. "How much time before we land?"

"It's 690 kilometers from Baghdad to Tehran, so if the Iranians allow us a direct flight path after we cross their border, it is less than two hours before we land, sir. Perhaps less. I'll keep the track plot and ETA on the display screen over your seat until we land." The pilot's hint inviting the visitor out of the cockpit was not lost on Kostevitch.

"Good," the general repeated. "Good. Keep up the good work. And don't worry about Iranians. They give you whatever you want. Let me know if they don't."

He backed out of the cockpit and made his way to the two men in the rear, his hard boys. They had laboriously hauled two rope-handled wooden crates through the doors to the rear baggage compartment, and were now roping the boxes to the rearmost seats. Each man had an AK-47 rifle slung across his back—the AKS-74U paratrooper version, with a grenade launcher mounted below its barrel. Rising from their task, the men nodded to the general. The three bulky Russians stood silently, looking down at the boxes.

"Well, we land in a couple of hours, lads. There's still a little work for us to do when we arrive, so no more vodka for us until we celebrate on the way home. Any questions?" Kostevitch stared at the expressionless faces before him. The taller man spoke up.

"*Nyet*, Comrade General."

Kostevitch grunted an unintelligible reply, returned to his seat, and fell heavily onto the cushions. With a last longing look at the back of the flight attendant's skirt, he sank into the soft beige leather and closed his eyes. Thanks to that scar-faced *kozyol* in Tehran, he thought, in a few hours he would be a very rich and very successful businessman.

CHAPTER 6

The Hermitage
Onancock, Virginia

The Yukon Adams drove to the Chesapeake Bay Bridge was two years old, and he maintained it like an airplane. Its 320-horsepower engine could easily tow 8,400 pounds, and the big SUV had often eased his fishing boat down marina ramps. Then he bought *Pilgrim,* a forty-five foot cruiser moored at Wachapreague. He lived on that yacht for six months during restoration of the "Hermitage," a Flemish bond-brick house built in the 1700s. On Westerhouse Creek, near Onancock, it was minutes away from the marina on the Atlantic coast. As he neared the Bay Bridge, his mind wandered over days spent looking for a country home, and the joy of finding the perfect place.

Sophie Giltspur was the first person to visit the Hermitage. He remembered making her close her eyes on the turnoff, nudging her when they finally parked at the porch.

"Okay, open 'em up!"

Sophie spent a full minute appraising the peeling paint, the missing roof shingles, and the broken window panes backed with cardboard.

"Well, what do you think? Grand, isn't it!"

"I should not describe this unfortunate house as grand, Jeremiah."

"I know the big girl's been neglected, but with some restoration, paint, and a few new fittings, she'll be as good as new."

"One might say that about the Titanic."

"And, when I take you to Wachapreague for a gourmet lunch on *Pilgrim*, you'll see how close she is to this fine house. Docked right on the Atlantic. Perfect."

Sophie was unimpressed. "Exactly why did you buy this home? To judge by its size, I imagine it was expensive, even though it's quite a long drive from the city."

"Deduct interest on the mortgage from your income tax, figure the capital gains, and it's a lot cheaper than renting a small joint in the city, believe you me."

"So you bought this tatty colonial mansion because it's near a marina, and because it's a good tax deduction."

Adams looked at the house, then around at the patchy lawns, the tired shrubs, and the copse of trees along the creek that needed pruning.

"No, I bought this house because it's a long ways from *everything*. Sometimes I want to be with myself. I want to listen to music I like, to read books I like, to walk through those trees over there and watch Ranger swim in the creek. Sometimes I get out of bed in the middle of the night, sit in that rocker on the porch, drink a beer, and listen to the crickets. I'll fix it up, Sophie."

She watched Adams slip into daydreams, then gently touched his arm and said, "I know you will, Jeremiah, and it will be very beautiful."

Adams climbed onto the porch and examined a corner of the roof that looked like it was disintegrating.

"Woodpeckers." He shaded his eyes. "Didn't notice that last week. I guess the timber up there must be chock full of tasty bugs."

"Speaking of tasty things, when are we going to that gourmet lunch on your boat? I'm famished."

Sophie was unimpressed by her first look at the Hermitage, but she pitched in to help with the restoration. During those busy weeks that seemed so long ago, they sketched plans, assembled tools, bought materials, and hired local craftsmen. Adams and Sophie even set up a secure telephone and computer network so he could spend more time in Onancock. With first class communications on hand, he could stay in touch with the Pentagon as well as supervise the restoration. Sophie spent Sunday afternoons with him, bustling around the house and cooking lunch.

In three months, essential repair was done and Adams took over the fine work and detailing. He even found time for spring boating, and for learning about neighbors and nearby towns.

The city closest to Onancock was Wachapreague. It was not much to Adams' liking despite its marina and being "Flounder Capital of the World." He only went there to take *Pilgrim* out to sea, or for an occasional meal at "Captain Zed's," the harbor's private marina, restaurant, and bait shop. Historic Onancock, on the other hand, had a sleepy charm he found restful and therapeutic.

Happy in the best of two worlds, Adams made the long drive to the Pentagon without grumbling, sometimes skipping a day at the office in favor of "cyber-commuting." With Sophie to back him up, he did almost as much work done at computer consoles in the Hermitage and *Pilgrim* as he did at his office desk. During difficult foreign operations, he slept at the Fort Myer Bachelor Officers Quarters, where he kept a change of clothes. The previous Secretary of Defense never cared where his special assistant worked or slept, just as long as the wheels were turning. Those were good times.

Adams wrenched himself back into the painful present. *I didn't think Horton knew I was alive until tonight. Did he fire me because of my work routine? My clothes? Nuts.*

As they wheeled east on Route 50, Ranger came up from the rear to squeeze into a front seat and get his ears scratched. Adams loved the way he and the dog and the car fit together. Stroking the dog's glossy coat was great stress relief, and the vehicle was an aviator's joy to drive. The Yukon's custom performance package included a computer chip fuel monitor, a forced air injector, polished headers, and a panel of gauges. Growling through side exhaust ports, the souped-up engine devoured the miles, and after they crossed the bridge it was only a two-hour pull to eighteenth-century Onancock, a cocktail party, and a calm weekend on the boat.

Adams surrendered the last of his toll tickets at the western plaza and began a two-mile climb to the central span, two hundred feet above the bay. Watching shore lights fall away below him, he felt like he was flying a plane in a curving takeoff. He never tired of crossing the gigantic bridge, and he was certain he could feel his blood pressure drop when he topped the span. Up there, looking at the bay, Adams gave thanks again for the great oceans protecting the flanks of the United States. *No enemy navy can dream of crossing those waters and hope to survive.* Heading down for a landing on Maryland's Eastern Shore, another two miles away, he checked the trip computer again.

"Okay, my canine co-pilot. At this rate, it's just one hundred and ten minutes before we can pee on our own trees."

At precisely eleven o'clock, the Yukon passed Onancock's first gas station. Adams always filled up at Woody's because he stopped there for directions on his first visit to the town and found a sign in the unisex toilet: "If you don't like this restroom, find another!" The restroom had no toilet paper, no mirror, a dirty toilet seat of uncertain color, and a floor puddled with varicolored fluids. It reminded him of Saudi Arabia, and Ranger never tired of the smell.

He was pleased to be arriving before midnight and reckoned Carlotta Truitt, 'that newspaperwoman,' would still be at Tarik Kasim's party. He was Onancock's resident Lebanese rug merchant or, as Kasim liked to say, "Delmarva's foremost dealer in fine carpets."

Kasim made no bones about being enamored of Carly. In fact, when Adams first met her at the carpet seller's Thanksgiving gathering, Kasim referred to Carly as his 'date' during the dinner. But Adams read a different message in her body language and made sure to get her phone number.

Thinking about Kasim and Carly, Adams picked up speed on Market Street, Onancock's main drag. After a squealing right turn at East Street, he passed the modest monument to General Bagwell, the old Cokesbury Church, and saw that both sides of King Street were jammed solid with parked cars. The party was in full swing. Finding no space in the street, Adams gunned the Yukon over the curb and onto the lawn in front of the rambling frame house. He grinned at Ranger.

"Faithful dog, anyone tries to get in, you're cleared to hang teeth in their butt. Unless it's a curvy lady with long red hair. In that case, you invite her inside, lock the doors, and call me."

Adams swung down to the lawn, ran a comb across his temples, and took the porch steps two at a time. He opened the door and was enveloped by a sigh of warm air that carried perfume, music, the woody smell of fireplaces, and a tumbling mix of a dozen loud conversations. He tried to isolate Carly's voice in the babble.

"Aw, damn—you made it!" Kasim pulled a long face and then laughed as he pumped Adams' hand, adding, "You know, Jay, I'm not going to introduce you to any more of my women." He leaned close and whispered, "You should also know that Carly told me if you didn't come tonight she was going to marry me."

"What, and become a Muslim?" Adams was craning his neck to find Carly in the closely-packed crowd.

"Of course. She must convert to the true faith! How else does she meet my father and sweet mother in Beirut?"

Adams finally spotted a mane of red hair across the room and started to move away. He looked back at Kasim with a thoughtful frown.

"Listen, sport, why don't *you* convert instead? I'll be your godfather." He laughed at the expression on Kasim's face and added, "When you're a Christian, I bet you'll become a monk and join a monastery in the Italian Alps. You'll weave carpets and sell them to the locals. When your business is going good, Carly and I will visit on a skiing holiday and smuggle in some Chianti for you. How's that for a plan!"

Kasim's cool stare followed Adams until he was swallowed by the crowd.

CHAPTER 7

Mehrabad Airport
Tehran, Iran

Twenty minutes after the sun cleared the far crest of the Alborz Mountains, the white Gulfstream appeared, a gleaming white arrow over Mehrabad airport. General Kostevitch watched the wing dip to reveal the main runway and its shorter parallel mate. Then he watched the concrete strips slide right to line up with the nose of the descending aircraft. Touchdown was followed by instructions from the tower, and a battered "Follow Me" truck led the plane to an abandoned terminal building. Three black vans waited in the cold morning shadows.

The jet's stairway unfolded, reaching for the ground, and the engine behind the stairs spooled down. Its twin continued to run, powering the aircraft's lights, radios, and air conditioning system. The Russian pilots had little confidence in the quality of the airport's fuel, ground power units, or service personnel, and they had insured they had more than enough fuel onboard for the return flight to Syria—or to almost anywhere else in the Middle East. The aircraft continued to whine, poised to leap back into its element, as a phalanx of swarthy men in black suits advanced from the shadows. They were led by a slender bearded man in a fur-collared topcoat.

When the pilot started for the door with the plane's landing documents, Kostevitch waved him back to his cockpit seat.

"Sit, pilot. I deal with this myself. Do not worry. These people will forget about all their formalities today. You must only be ready to leave in fifteen minutes. Or on my orders."

Buttoning his jacket, the general lumbered down the stairway with one of his "lads" following him, cradling a rifle. Kostevitch paused on the tarmac, looking at the bearded man in the front rank of the silent gathering. Then the general and his aide advanced on the group like a pair of rhinos.

"So, it is really you, my interesting friend." It was the command voice again. "Let us do this quickly. *Da?*"

Two airport officials appeared, their hands fluttering like disturbed pigeons. One shouted over the engine noise and said, "You cannot leave this aircraft until landing documents are processed. You must shut down the engines!"

His companion began to yell about passports when the slender man, his eyes fixed on Kostevitch, flicked a finger at the officials and said, loud enough for everyone to hear over the noise, "Thank you for your help. Now leave us." The customs and immigration officers ducked their heads and scuttled toward the dark terminal.

"Let us walk together, Anatoliy Ivanovich." The slender man never failed to impress Russians with his language skills. "Do you remember my name? It is Morteza Dehesh."

He removed his glove and offered his hand. The general folded it into his bear paw with a half-smile, and they looked into each other's eyes. There was no warmth in either man's hand. Releasing their grip on each other, they walked away from the aircraft, the general signaling his aide to wait at the stairs. Like a pair of colleagues on a university campus they walked with hands clasped behind their backs, side by side, heads together. On the terminal walls above them, graffiti scrawled in blood-red paint proclaimed *Marg bar Amrika!* "Death to America!"

Kostevich studied the profile of the man walking beside him. "Of course I remember your name, Mr. Morteza. I also remember you are a very clever man, and sometimes also very dangerous. So let us do our business in the good old Russian way. Quick and clean."

"Will you come with us to the city, General? It is not far, and we would be delighted to show you some of Iran's famous hospitality. Shut down your aircraft and bring your friends. We have surprise gifts for you all." Dehesh's neat beard parted to show white and even teeth.

"I do not like surprises and my friends, as you can see, are not friendly. You and your people should be careful not to underestimate them. The aircraft cannot be shut down because that would make me and my comrades even more unfriendly." The general's voice was a low rumble, but quite clear in spite of the airport's background noise. "So, Mr. Morteza. You contact me. I am here. Now give me what you promise, I give you what you want, and we part. If that is not what we do, I leave immediately."

Kostevitch glanced over his shoulder. His aide was waiting at the foot of the stairs, looking impassively at the small knot of men in front of him. They were foolish to stand so close together. Josip, in the aircraft's doorway above, could easily get any that he might miss.

"Please, please. Let us not have any misunderstandings, my dear general." Dehesh turned back toward the aircraft. The general reversed course at his side, keeping the smaller man between himself and the aircraft doorway above them. "Everything you told my courier that you require is here, waiting to be examined."

"Show me. And just so we understand each other, I know you will go to great trouble to find me if what I bring is not as I promised. *Da?* Be sure I do the same for you." The general stopped alongside his aide.

With a slight shrug, Dehesh beckoned, and four men emerged from the gloom, each lugging a metal attaché case.

"I will begin. Here is what I brought for you."

Dehesh signaled for a case to be opened. Kostevitch bent over it and lifted one of the bright yellow bars. It was deceptively heavy. On its face was stamped, "Banque Credit Suisse–999–One Kilo." Almost two and a half pounds of pure gold.

Dehesh nodded at the case and smiled sardonically. "Do you wish to see them all, my dear general?"

Closing the metal case and nodding his approval, Kostevitch motioned to the man in the doorway above. "Bring down one of our boxes, Josip. After Ivan takes this case up, he will take your place at the door."

Seconds later, Josip came down the stairs, sliding a long wooden crate along the steps. It hit the tarmac with a dull thud.

"Open, if you like. Quite safe." It was the general's turn to smile.

Hesitating for a moment, Dehesh knelt to unfasten the wing nuts securing the lid. Inside, two large brushed stainless steel cylinders nestled in padded supports. Each was featureless except for complex fittings at one end that were covered with waterproof plastic shields.

Kostevitch looked down at the kneeling man. "All bombs are safe, I assure you. But do not play with them, please, unless you are expert. And even if you are expert, do not open them until I am high in the sky." The general laughed raucously. "Now give me your other cases, and I send down my last box."

Dehesh straightened, smiling. "Would you like my men to help load the attaché cases into your aircraft, general? No? Very well."

The heavy cases were hauled up the stairs by Ivan, one at a time. Watching him, Dehesh produced a leather cigar wallet from his topcoat, opened it, and held it toward Kostevitch. The general looked at it, frowning.

"I do not smoke those things."

"Pity. They're excellent imports from our friends in Cuba." Dehesh clipped one, struck a match, and drew on the slim cigar until it glowed brightly.

"You light a match next to my airplane? It could explode!"

"It would not dare," Dehesh answered dryly. "Not while it is in Iran."

The rope-handled crates rested on the tarmac, and the aluminum attaché cases had been stowed aboard the aircraft. The group of black suits looked at Dehesh expectantly. Above them, both armed men were alert in the aircraft's doorway.

"It seems our business is done, general, and I wish you a safe journey home." He extended a gloved hand. Kostevitch glared at it, motionless.

"Ah, I apologize for my rudeness." Dehesh laughed and removed his glove.

The Gulfstream's stairs retracted just sixteen minutes after they touched the tarmac of Mehrabad airport. Starting the second engine and calling the tower for takeoff instructions, the pilots rounded the corner of the abandoned terminal and taxied toward the runway. Even before the aircraft was on the centerline, the engines' whine turned into throaty roars and the aircraft accelerated rapidly into the brightening Sunday sky. Morning's shadows pointed west, toward Damascus, three hours away.

An hour after the Gulfstream departed, Dehesh and two men in uniform were seated at a library table beneath a delicate Venetian glass chandelier. Dehesh spoke softly into a telephone pressed to his ear while the two officers sat attentively on the edges of their chairs, eyes riveted on the man at the head of the table. They waited with folded hands, not touching the glasses or bottles at their places. Returning the phone to its cradle, Dehesh looked around the table.

"Please forgive my poor hospitality, gentlemen, but our Supreme Leader must be kept informed of our progress." He pressed a button on the leg of the brass-inlaid table. "Now we will have our tea and sweets. Do either of you care for anything else? No? Let us begin then, to enjoy this most excellent day." Dehesh made no effort to conceal his joy.

"We have all that is needed! Whatever else may happen, everything is in our hands at last." Looking from face to face, he paused at the stern man on his right.

"Return to Lebanon today, colonel, and be sure to be quite invisible. Meet with our friend who pays the Hizballah assassins. Tell him he must send us the two men he found in Israel. They must arrive in Tabriz this week, and you will personally arrange every detail of their transportation. They will not travel commercially, and they must not know where they go or the identity of their guides. I am confident you will not fail us in this matter, yes?"

"It shall be done, Excellency."

"Good. Give your colleagues in Lebanon the new encryption system. Tell them they will have a message from me tomorrow evening, and that they will use only the Internet and the steganography code to reply. They should tell me exactly when the men begin their journey to Tabriz. Remember, no telephone, no radio. Nothing but computers and the new code."

"It shall be done, Excellency." Once again, the reply was crisp and hard.

"Major Doctor!" Dehesh turned to the smaller man on his left. "Your task is to tell me today that the weapons we bought are exactly as promised. And tomorrow, you and your staff begin preparations to receive two students. They will arrive at your laboratories in Tabriz in a few days, and you must be ready to train them on these new weapons and the nuclear weapon you already have. You will carry out all training at the university and the camp nearby. The colonel will provide you with instructors for the military arts, but you must conduct the technical training yourself. You understand what to do?"

"Yes, Excellency." The doctor shifted slightly on his chair.

"Very good. Please consider yourself to be under my wing, Major Doctor. I will protect you, and I will give you all that you need to complete your important work." Dehesh regarded both men with a wolfish smile.

"Years ago, that insane President Bush named us part of an 'axis of evil.' He equated us to starving North Koreans and filthy Iraqis. His advisors promised to see *me*," he looked from face to face, "and *you*, destroyed the way they destroyed Saddam Hussein. But now, with the help of Allah, I will destroy *them* and that new fool in their White House! With your help, of course." He leered at his guests again.

"I realize it is still early in the day, but perhaps you'll join me in a toast to our success before you leave on your important missions?" Dehesh gestured, and the officers looked at the traditional ranks of bottles, carafes and tumblers at each place.

"There is an excellent Napoleon brandy there. Or orange juice, if you prefer it." The two officers looked up at Dehesh, waiting. He laughed.

"Soon we have our tea, but now it's brandy for this servant of Allah and Iran, and also for his loyal companions!" They each poured brandy into their glasses. Dehesh sniffed his goblet and then stood, glass held high.

"May the Great Satan burn in his own atomic fire!" The two officers also rose, and they all drank deeply.

What a silly thing is this toasting and talk of Allah, thought Dehesh, just the sort of nonsense military men expect. Nevertheless, the brandy fired a welcome inner glow, and he enjoyed the beginning of a bubbling exhilaration. Soon his hand would reach out, across six thousand miles—and seize the heart of America.

CHAPTER 8

Gaza beachfront

His own mother would not have recognized him. Imad Fayez Mughniyeh would have been very disappointed if she could, since his new face had cost him a small fortune and a great deal of pain. It was the latest in a series, and with color contact lenses, hair transplants and a new passport, it transformed him from a vicious Hizballah "freedom fighter" into an elegant Jordanian businessman.

At an oceanfront table of Gaza's famous *El-Amhal* restaurant, Mughniyeh savored a Cuban Monte Cristo cigar, an *après* lunch coffee, and an unusually warm January afternoon. Others on the terrace moved their chairs to face the sun, enjoying their desserts and the mild ocean breeze before returning to offices and shops. His chair was turned away from the ocean so he could scan the street. New face or not, he was cautious, besides, he was waiting for two important guests.

Wanted by the CIA, Mossad, and an army of bounty hunters, the Lebanese assassin managed to survive and prosper. His 1985 stint in Arafat's Force 17, a bodyguard unit with useful connections to Iran's Pasdaran, got him invited into Osama bin Laden's inner circle. He helped that religious zealot plan an audacious attack on New York and the Pentagon years ago. And then there were those three truck bombs in Lebanon.

Those bombs were the first of their kind, demonstrating his terrorist genius. Killing 241 Marines drove the Americans out of the Levant, the main purpose of the bombs. And though the French did not seem to notice their own 57 victims, the Israelis were quite another story. They would never forget or forgive their 60 dead, and Mughniyeh knew they would never stop chasing him, never tiring of the hunt. So even though he was called on for other tasks, quiet periods in the Bekka'a Valley were prudent for him these days. Iran took good care of their Hizballah terror army in Lebanon, and as head of "foreign operations," master terrorist Mughniyeh felt relatively safe there.

Yes, things here in Gaza were dangerous, but until he could retire into permanent obscurity he danced to the tune of his protectors. Although uncomfortable at times, it was not a bad life between missions, and killing Jews and their friends paid well. He pulled at his jacket to make sure he was not creasing the back of his Armani suit. In many respects his job was like any other stressful work, and whether in corporate boardrooms or Beirut alleys, the luxuries were delicious. The main thing he had to do was stay alive.

Mughniyeh had never met the stern-faced Colonel who appeared with the Hizballah overlord at breakfast in Beirut yesterday. But as instructed, he was in Gaza today. He was ordered to interview two men, and if they were satisfactory, dispatch them to the Jordanian border. He was then to send an email coded with the steganography disk he had been given. Whatever the devil that was. His Hizballah paymaster told him little else, except that time was of the essence.

He drew gently on his cigar and looked up at the restaurant sign, *El-Amhal.* "The Hope." Well, his hope was this job would be over quickly, and that he would be safe at home for dinner tonight.

Then he spotted them, sauntering toward the terrace. There was the Palestinian, Ghazi Abu Shakir, former university professor, towering over his runty sidekick. He watched the duo step up on the terrace and walk forward uncertainly. At six feet, Shakir was tall for a Palestinian, and had the gaunt look of an El Greco cardinal. His red hair and blue eyes spoke of a Crusader's visit to the Holy Land eight hundred years ago.

Mughniyeh followed them with hooded eyes. Once the beard was shaved off that tall one, he mused, he would have the exact western look that was needed. The other—what was his name? Ah yes, he is called Mahmoud Jabber or something equally atrocious. A killer from the Nur-Shams refugee camp, strong and motivated.

Ten months ago, Mughniyeh read of Jabber's parents refusing to leave their home in the West Bank, and then foolishly discharging an antique shotgun in the direction of an Israeli patrol. The house was bulldozed flat with them in it, and their screams would echo forever in Jabber's bruised mind. He was also a trifle stupid, and had proved it more than once. But even that drawback, Mughniyeh knew, could be useful—very useful, if handled by a good leader. Could the Palestinian Shakir be that leader? It is always hard to know such a thing before it is tested. One thing is certain: they were joined at the hip. Their friendship was forged by the violent deaths of their families and shared hard times in the refugee camp. Mughniyeh stood and waved at the two men.

"Saleh, Ahmed, over here!" He waited until they were a few steps from his table, and then added loudly, "Excellent! I see you bring your samples, my friends."

The one named Shakir narrowed his eyes against the Mediterranean sunlight and walked to Mughniyeh's table, trailed by his companion.

"You are from Jordan? The buyer for export dolls?"

"That's me." Mughniyeh extended his hand to each in turn. "Sit down, sit down. We have much to talk about before I return to Amman. You have had lunch?"

"We have eaten, thank you." Shakir dropped his voice. "You are completely crazy. Mossad or some Israeli aircraft will arrive in five minutes and kill us all."

Mughniyeh responded in an even lower tone. "If you learn how to hide in plain sight, my fiery-haired Palestinian, you will also learn that you will live longer." He smiled. "The Mossad is probably at the next table, eating a *halal* chicken. Relax. Have a cigar."

He offered Shakir a Monte Cristo and a silver cigar cutter. Jabber watched the exchange, his eyes sliding back and forth like black abacus beads. Mughniyeh turned to him, still smiling, and raised his voice.

"If I do not offer you a cigar, my muscular friend, it's because I know you certainly do not smoke. That's why you're so strong and healthy, yes?"

Jabber grunted.

Opposite them, Shakir clipped his cigar, dropped the cutter to the table, and then leaned toward the cedar wood match Mughniyeh held. His eyes never left the face of the man across the table. Mughniyeh returned the stare with professional interest. This Palestinian was a rare gem, truly. He shifted to English.

"Are your dolls as beautiful as those pictures you sent? Can you write advertisements for us in English? We get lots of English-speaking tourists, you know."

"Damn right. I know exactly what all your Western tourists deserve. Check out this sweet little dolly." Tapping ash from his cigar, Shakir passed Mughniyeh the box he carried under his arm.

Praise Allah, Mughniyeh thought as he opened the box, and praise be to Shaitan, too. What a marvelous American accent he had! Tucked into the box was a cheap bisque doll from the *souk*, slightly soiled by the well-oiled Browning pistol nestled in its dress. He closed the lid and returned the box.

"*Magnifique. Très jolie.*" Accents in Mughniyeh's leaden French were born in the mountains of the Levant.

"*Merci, monsieur. Vous êtes très gentil.*"

Shakir's reply was Paris-perfect. *Parfait.* Yes, Mughniyeh concluded with growing enthusiasm, this teacher speaks at least three languages fluently. He reverted to Arabic.

"Very well. Of course, you understand that sometimes we have also French clients for our products. So, to begin, I take four dozen. But you must ship tonight." His voice dropped. "It will be tonight. Do you understand?"

The red-haired man nodded.

Ghazi Abu Shakir was not like ordinary men, Mughniyeh thought. *He was like me.* Those intense blue eyes had not wavered for a moment. Steady they were, as if I had trained him myself. The smaller one, on the other hand, was jittery as a weasel in a cage. Turning to him, Mughniyeh gestured toward a glass and spoke in English.

"Have a cognac my strong friend, it will relax you."

"God forbid!" Jabber raised his hands in horror, gibbering in Arabic.

Mughniyeh smiled wryly and then said, "I am told you have English. Let us practice. How are you called in English?"

"My soldier name—Saleh Al Din Al Tubar."

Mughniyeh nearly choked on his cognac. Merciful God. This orphan calls himself "Saladin the Hatchet."

"What? You think I am clown for you?" A mosaic of purple blotches appeared on Jabber's face, and the tablecloth bunched under his clenched fists.

Mughniyeh rushed into the breach with whispered Arabic. He did not want to lose this idiot and, more importantly, his blue-eyed comrade.

"No, no, my friend. Your marvelous *nom de guerre* was surprising, that is all." Mughniyeh recovered his composure with visible effort and managed to smile.

"By the way, did you know there was an 'Al Tubar' in Iraq, years ago? No? He was a murderer who chopped up his victims with a hatchet. He was eventually hanged by Saddam. So you might reconsider your adopted name. It puts the great Saladin alongside an executed axe murderer."

Jabber crossed his arms and glared.

Mughniyeh decided ironic comments could only antagonize the dolt, and sucked on his cigar. After a few steadying mouthfuls he looked at Jabber through a cloud of aromatic smoke.

"So, Saladin, let us continue our English. What do you think of bisque manufacture? You are a bisque expert? What is your work in the doll factory?"

Jabber looked from Shakir to Mughniyeh and answered, "Yes. Factory. Good work. Good doll." Jabber lapsed into silence, his gaze darting about the terrace.

Mughniyeh concluded it was useless to test him further. This angry little man, he was certain, was entirely too nervous under the least pressure and had nothing resembling English language skills. Either drawback alone was a major liability for a covert mission in the West. And together? Together they might mean disaster. Still, dwelling on negative thoughts could ruin his own mission today. He was under orders to interview two men and send them on their way. Here they were. And his safe-house in the Bekka'a was waiting.

The master terrorist drew on his cigar again. These two were just as he had assessed them from their files. One was a hard and intelligent man who happened to be a multilingual academic. The other was a willing assassin who spoke poor Arabic and worse English. One pure gold, the other dross. But with those dead pale eyes and that superb education, Shakir was as perfect a team leader as anyone could hope to find, even if handicapped by a moronic partner he loved as a brother. The baleful Basilisk eyes told it all—the professor could be made into an implacable messenger of death.

"Your name, Ghazi—it means warrior," Mughniyeh remarked to Shakir. "But in honor of your education and languages, shall I call you 'Professor?'" Before the Palestinian could reply, he answered for him. "Yes, I think so. The sobriquet suits you perfectly."

Through it all, Shakir's unblinking stare had not changed. When his words came, they were stone hard. "Call me what you will."

Mughniyeh knew the challenging tone was not bravado. Not after he had read the detailed history of the man's life. Not after he had read the tortured history of the man's life. Still, he must try to plumb the depths of his agony and learn how much pain remained.

"I am told you studied at Columbia University in New York. Two years?"

"Yes." The calm and direct stare remained fixed on Mughniyeh's face.

"Then your father died. You came back here to run the family restaurant?"

"Yes."

"And you found time to study and teach languages at Bar-Zeit University?"

"Yes." Shakir drew on his cigar and added, "Why do you ask things you already know?"

"Was the restaurant business good, Professor?"

"Yes."

"You had a wife and a child?"

The Palestinian flinched, but his gaze steadied.

"Yes."

"They were killed?"

"Yes." Without looking away from Mughniyeh, Shakir ground his cigar into marble tabletop.

"How did they die?"

Shakir's eyes closed, and Mughniyeh could not see the crowded restaurant that appeared behind the eyelids. He knew all about it, of course, but he could not hear the beat of an Israeli helicopter, or the explosions of Hellfire missiles and the screams of lunchtime diners. Or smell the charred flesh. He waited, and then recoiled from what he saw when the blue eyes finally snapped open, brimming.

"Whoever you are," Shakir's voice was still steady, "if you speak of that again, I will kill you."

The silence held only a gull's cry and the scrape of Jabber's chair as he leaned closer to the table, looking daggers at the man from Beirut.

"I am sorry, "Mughniyeh said, "but you must understand it was necessary for me to ask such things." He cleared his throat and examined the ash on his cigar.

"This mission," asked the Palestinian in a steady whisper, "we are to be martyrs?"

Shakir's words were almost inaudible, just loud enough to reach across the table and include Jabber. Mughniyeh relaxed. He guessed the Professor wanted to be sure his companion was part of this dire conference. Good. He wanted this dangerous ascetic and his dim bulb partner to fully understand what was at stake.

"You were told weeks ago, Professor. No suicide. Such missions are given to religious robots. But what you will do is dangerous, extremely dangerous. And extremely secret. So if you will not face danger, leave now. Go back to your fly-blown Tulkarem camp and the Al Aqsa Martyrs' Brigade." Mughniyeh lifted his chin and shifted in his chair to contemplate the glittering Mediterranean.

"You do not tell us what we will do? Or where we will go?"

The Lebanese terrorist thought he could feel the heat of Shakir's focused gaze on the back of his head. He turned to meet the pale eyes again and said, "As Allah is my witness, I do not know." Mughniyeh shrugged and lifted his hands. After all, he really knew very little. *Go to your death, Palestinian. Or return to be a leader of dead men, like me.*

"But be sure, Professor, you will stab the hearts of Americans and Zionists. That is certain. So I tell you for the last time, if you must know details of the mission before you begin, go back to the camps. But if you are not old women looking for gossip in the *souk*, then ready yourselves. No tearful goodbyes to family and friends. Leave your life here. Leave it this very night. And if God wills it, you will be *living* heroes when you return."

Shakir broke off his stony examination of Mughniyeh to look at Jabber.

"You are with me, my hatchet?"

"I go with you to kill Americans and Jews, Ghazi."

Then Shakir turned back to lock eyes with the dandy in the expensive suit, the smooth linen shirt, and the woven silk French necktie.

"My friend Jabber and I have no families. Our family is *jihad* now. If you send us, we will go to kill the American and Zionist murderers."

"Good." Mughniyeh rose and extended his hand. When they were all standing close together, he leaned forward and whispered again.

"You need only the clothes on your back. A guide will find you at the Jericho Casino before midnight, and from there you go to your destiny. May the Prophet's blessings be on you both." He stepped back and raised his voice.

"Be at my hotel at six sharp tonight to sign the agreement. I thank you for coming, my friends, and I want you to know it has been a great pleasure for me to do business with you." He looked at the table. "Ah, yes. Don't forget your bisque doll. It's a fine example of the work you will be doing for my firm."

Silent, Shakir took the box, tucked it under his arm, and strolled off the terrace and down into the street, trailed by his small companion. Mughniyeh remained standing, watching them walk away and disappear. He was certain they would bravely attempt whatever task they were given, and Shakir's gifts might even overcome Jabber's shortcomings. The soulless Professor was truly a unique gift from heaven. If he survived his mission, whatever it is, he will certainly be invited to become part of his Bekka'a Valley army.

Mughniyeh settled back into his chair and examined the throng of afternoon shoppers in the seashore street. His practiced eye saw nothing unusual.

What will those two be ordered to do? And where will they do it? Welcome to the assassin's shadow world, my comrades. May Allah protect you. And me.

He waved his cigar at the waiter, and pointed at his empty coffee cup.

CHAPTER 9

The Hermitage
Onancock, Virginia

Aromatic cedar branches hissed and popped in the living room fireplace. Adams could hear the cheerful sound at the center island in the kitchen, where he was rattling a Martini cocktail shaker. He did not like gin, and if a guest asked for it he would say, "I don't have any. Gin makes your breath stink. Makes some people want to beat their grandmothers." But guests could always join him in his ritual sundowner—a very dry vodka Martini with a twist of lemon peel—or drive home sober.

Adams was expecting Carly to stop at the Hermitage for a drink before their Saturday night date. They were going to the town manager's annual bash for Onancock's residents—all five hundred voters—and he hoped Carly was well on her way from her Salisbury office. The sun set early in January.

Carrying the shaker and two glasses to the living room, Adams caught a glimpse of himself as he passed the Chippendale mirror in the connecting archway. A habit born of solitary days in the house, he muttered as he walked to the fireplace with Ranger at his heels.

"Damn hair's going and the spare tire's growing." He explored the chipped edge of a front tooth with his tongue. "So it must be my sexy smile that drives 'em crazy."

He placed one glass on the mantelpiece and poured the icy drink into the other. Breathing the fire's balsamic perfume, he took an experimental sip and then stepped back and dropped into his reading chair. Ranger made certain no food or games were on offer and then stretched out in his usual spot near the hearth.

Staring into the burning oracle that lives in every fireplace, Adams heard himself ask, "Okay. Unemployed middle-aged bureaucrat lives alone in mortgaged house in Onancock. Then what happens?"

No answer. Not that he needed a fireplace prophet to confirm he was really sidelined this time. Small consolation, he thought, but at least he gave that prick Beauchamps a kick in the slats. And he had escorted Carly to another party last week, so maybe there was a bright side to that resignation letter after all.

Sophie held the fort at the Pentagon and they talked often, usually via the encrypted cell phone always on his belt. And he had gloried in a whole week of handling tangible things. Tools, grout, brick glaze, and wood oil filled his hands and senses and the interludes between messages about soldiers, war machines, death and destruction. But no matter how busy he was, he could not shake the depressing thought that his job, and all the excitement that went with it, would soon be ended. Even long hikes with Ranger could not distract him.

He did have to admit it had been a fascinating life, even with a bad start. His parents were killed by a drunk driver when he was five. He could not recall much about them, but memories were very clear when he thought about the iron-ribbed Presbyterian uncle and aunt who took in the orphan and raised him in Rockbridge County. Twelve years on that hardscrabble farm had built character, and the uncle and aunt helped him grow as hard as a hickory stump. So when a letter from the Naval Academy sprung him from the Blue Ridge Mountains, he vowed never to return to that tough life. But his aunt and uncle were so proud of him he did go back, and as often as he could.

He made up stories to add humor and excitement to their idea of what life was like on an aircraft carrier and in the CIA. Their favorites usually involved Ted, his co-pilot and a character even Hollywood could not invent. Like that time at Breezy Point Officers Club. Adams' squadron was fresh off the North Atlantic, and all the pilots were gathered in the bar before going home. It was a tradition that drinks were ordered until the first sweetheart or wife telephoned, and that hapless officer paid for it all. No wife had called for ours when a captain's wife, the airbase Jezebel, made the mistake of leaning her décolletage over a nearby table and putting her posterior in Ted's face. The only thing heard in the silent wake of her scream was Ted's career sizzling over a slow fire. With a trembling finger pointing at the offender, she shouted into the silence: "He—he bit me on the ASS!" Ted's ass was saved by the laughter of a hundred aviators.

It was hard to find amusing tales about his CIA years, though. The best he could do was tell them about a night HALO jump from 20,000 feet and landing in the middle of a Pakistani village latrine. He left out the part about his sniper rifle and what happened to the Taliban assassin.

They both died while he was with the submariners off the Chinese coast, tapping Russian communications cables and fishing for their test missile warheads. His uncle's aorta ruptured—dead before he fell off his John Deere tractor. His aunt followed two months later. Bad heart, the doctor told him. But Adams knew it was a good heart, a heart broken by losing the man she loved so quietly and so deeply.

When he returned from the South China Sea, he made a visit to the Warm Springs churchyard to put flowers on their graves. Sole heir, he sold the house and land, put the money in high tech mutual funds, and was amazed how it grew each year. The wealth added to a guilty feeling that he should have been there to somehow protect them from death, and visiting the graveyard intensified it. After those first flowers he never returned.

Fifty-two years old, Jeremiah Adams had done it all. Naval aviator, Office of Naval Intelligence, a stretch with the CIA, field ops in strange and awful places. Planes and parachutes and submarines. Hurting people and breaking things. Finally a senior berth in the Pentagon and no more field work for the "old man." He did get to see the Pentagon big picture though, and sometimes he could even paint parts of it with his own colors.

Never had crayon scribbles on my walls. Dumb to shuck off every gal who wanted to be my one-and-only. Dumber to leave a widow with kids. Well, whatever the right thing might have been back then, I'm sure flying solo now.

Ranger sensed his somber mood and left the fireplace to shoulder Adams' leg and then sit heavily on his shoe.

"Yeah, I know you're always on my side, buddy." Adams leaned across his knees to scratch the dog's coat and was rewarded with a wet tongue. "Nice. But it's not exactly the kind of companionship I was thinking about."

The fire seemed to glow more brightly. Sunset.

"Damn, I'm getting to be a maudlin old fart." He leaned back and sipped his drink. "Maybe I'll teach you to talk, Ranger."

Headlights flashed across the far wall and Adams snapped out of his reverie. He jackknifed out of the deep leather chair and walked to the windows. Ranger ran to the door and whined.

"You're right, boy, it's her. And she likes you too."

He watched Carly Truitt unfold from her Porsche and stretch like a marmalade cat. Suddenly she looked up at the house. When Adams opened the door and started across the porch with Ranger, she froze them with a shout.

"Hey, you guys, stop right there! I don't need a butler and his dog. What I need is a drink. So you and that hound go back inside and get busy. When I lug in my stuff, there better be a hot fire and a cold drink waiting." She smiled the smile that lit up the party Wednesday night. Tall and lithe, with dark red hair and very green eyes, she moved and dressed like a woman confident of her beauty.

At the end of Wednesday's party they had snapped together like magnets. Ten minutes of fierce fumbling in the Yukon ended in gasps when Ranger poked them with a cold nose. After the hilarious zipping and buttoning, they agreed it would be a good idea to get to know each other before acting like hormone-soaked adolescents.

"We'll be grownups for a while," she said. "Besides, I must see how an old bachelor lives, so I can figure out what kind of germs I get by kissing him."

He drove home that night certain she was not like those faded flowers he peeled off the bar in the Fort Myer Officer's Club. Or like staffers on the diplomatic cocktail circuit, always anxious to see what was in his BOQ room. And now she was at the Hermitage!

"Aye, aye! No quarterdeck honors for Admiral Carly. Lieutenant Ranger, send the side boys below."

Adams pointed Ranger back through the porch door, and her voice followed them inside, "You men can tell me what a side boy is while I'm thawing out next to your fireplace."

That's when his cell phone buzzed. He put the shaker down, pulled the phone from his belt, and growled, "Adams. Speak."

"Jeremiah, you are not Captain Kirk on the starship Enterprise." It was Sophie, with her magical talent for timing. "I'm calling in hopes you'll be in the office on Monday. A few things do need attention." She paused. "And I believe we may be able to stop that resignation letter business, too. Mr. Beauchamps was by twice this week to see if you had signed it. It seems to me he is entirely too anxious." Adams could visualize Sophie's patrician profile as she spoke.

"Hey, what makes you think I want to stop anything, kiddo? If Horton wants to toss me out on my butt, there's not much I can do except complain about it like some big ninny. And I'm sure as hell not going to rot in some consolation job. So, if anything hot is going down, please encrypt the data and send it by email. Okay? Now I've got to go. Have a great weekend." He caught his breath and added, "Say, why not plan to come out here next week for a day on the boat?"

"That newspaperwoman is there, is she not? I shan't keep you, Jeremiah. The most urgent of the messages will be sent to you this evening. Please find time to read them between Martinis." She hung up. Looking at the drink in his hand, Adams wondered again how she did that remote vision thing.

Then the door slammed open and a clothes bag flew into the foyer, just missing the long case clock. Arms full of car coat, makeup kit and shoe bag, Carly nudged the door closed with a knee and turned toward the fireplace. Firelight burned copper glints into her full mane, her cheeks were pink from the cold, and her eyes were emeralds. Standing with a glass in each hand, Adams was transfixed. Ranger, on the other hand, bounded forward joyfully, aiming to give Carly's legs the serious sniff test.

"Whoa, whoa, whoa! Hold on, mister cold nose!" She tried to deflect the dog with her makeup kit.

"Ranger! Heel!" The dog jerked to a stop and trotted back to Adams.

Carly's eyes widened. "You certainly have the big guy well-trained. I'm impressed."

"We're all well-trained around here."

"Okay, sailor, bring that drink over and welcome me in to inspect your hovel." Carly dropped her coat and bags in the entranceway and stepped into the room. Adams came close enough to scent her perfume, and handed her a glass. He watched her out of the corner of his eye while she surveyed the room and then moved off toward the shelves of books.

"Looks like you are a reader. Lots of military stuff. Politics. Novels. Poetry, even." She sidestepped along one of the high bookcases fronting a wall of bare brick and oak beams, running her fingers across book spines.

"Organized by subject." She raised an eyebrow at him over her shoulder.

"Well," Adams said, "it's easier to find things that way."

"Marcus Aurelius, Elizabeth Barrett Browning, Frost, Shakespeare... and Robert Service, of course." She moved to an old painted country chest that had been converted into a music center and CD storage shelf.

"Down in the land of the midnight sun, where the men moil and muckle for gold, there is Jeremiah Adams of old." She bent to study the row of CDs. "And you are a music omnivore. Bach, Dire Straits, Enya, Sibelius... all in alphabetical order." Adams raptly watched her nose wrinkle when she smiled.

"Yes. I've been told I do it because I'm a Virgo."

Carly moved toward the huge fireplace the colonials who built the house used for cooking. She stopped in the center of the room, slowly pirouetting to look at each wall, the Federal period furniture, the paintings, and then the Persian carpets.

"I didn't expect this, Jeremiah Adams. Not at all."

"Um...what?" He blinked uncertainly and looked around the familiar room.

"A tough guy lives alone in a rural town. Likes parties. Likes a drink or two. Can discuss anything. No visible means of support. That man's home is not—it's not this. And a tough guy definitely does not have rickrack fencing along his driveway." Her voice trailed off. She ran her tongue along the edge of her glass and eyed Adams, waiting.

"Ah. Well. You should know I had the health department and exterminators in here yesterday. I try to get them to visit on a regular basis. They empty the rat traps, recycle beer cans and wine bottles, and dispose of anything Ranger kills and brings inside. And I realize that rickrack fences belong in Albemarle County, but I like them here anyway."

"So. Looking at all this, I see you as a mature and attractive gentleman, a little on the rough side. You live with your dog, set in your ways. Maybe retired. Or maybe a hit man for the Mafia. Who *are* you, Jeremiah Adams?"

"I'm the Special Assistant to the Secretary of Defense for External Affairs."

"And what do you do?

"I work for the government." Adams heard his words and winced. The standard bullshit answer. He decided to drop evasive language used by almost every government employee in a sensitive job.

"Okay, I told you Wednesday that I work in Washington. What I didn't tell you is that I work in the Pentagon and lead part of our secret war against terrorists. We go to distant places and stop them before they hurt us. When I was a little younger I was a rat-catcher myself. I went to countries you've read about, and probably some you haven't. I went there to find the bad guys—kill them. Now I try to help the people who took my place. I think about what the troops in the field need, and then I try to con our politicians into giving them what they need. I plan. I worry. I have bad dreams." He looked at her hopefully. "That's pretty much it."

"Sounds like you're a terrorist too."

"C'mon, Carly. I said they were *bad* guys. Murdering rats. We find out what they're planning to do and then we try to talk them out of it. If they don't listen to reason, we take preemptive action and fix the problem any way we can. But we always make sure they're bad guys."

"Always? I bet it's not that easy. And even with sugar on it, what you do still sounds like terrorism to me." She did not wait for a reply. "Why do you do it, Jay?"

Adams avoided her eyes. Looking into the darkening windows, he said, "It's what I do, Carly. I am what I am."

Carly grinned and said, "I yam what I yam? You mean mysterious Jeremiah Adams is really Popeye the Sailor Man?"

Adams continued doggedly, "Anyway, it looks like I'm out of it for good now. I think I've been retired." The last word soured his mouth as he said it.

Carly's playful grin softened into a warm smile. "Oh, that's good, Jay. Very, very good. I don't think I could be best friends with a terrorist. But anyhow," Carly overrode Adams as he started to object, "I want to hear all about it. Or as much about it as you can tell me." She moved close to Adams. Her hair brushed the edge of his mouth and, before he could touch her, she danced lightly aside.

"But right now I've got to change for that party. Show me where I can find a chair and a mirror, and I will astound you with what an expensive dress and eye shadow can do. You, Mister Cold Nose, can come along and chew on my underwear." She motioned to Ranger who wagged his tail and looked up at Adams.

"Go for it, boy. Drag some of that underwear back here—with her in it!"

When she returned to the fireplace twenty minutes later, Adams was in his party clothes, staring at the flames, drinking the last of his cocktail. Carly came up behind him and whispered in his ear, "Save a sip of that for me."

Adams spun around. "Yow! Never creep up on me like that! I almost..." He stepped back and slowly moved his gaze from the bronze lipstick that matched her neck scarf, to the low cut forest green silk dress, to the figured tights that disappeared into her stylish open-toed heels.

"Woman, you could make a monk reconsider his vows." He kissed her shoulder. "So let's bag going to town and have our own party. Right here."

"No can do, naughty monk. I've got to leave the festivities way before eleven so I can get a good night's sleep. Big staff meeting tomorrow, bright and early."

"Two cars?"

Carly took the glass from his hand and set it on the mantelpiece. "Sorry, Popeye, two cars. That's sad—I was really looking forward to all of us jamming into your front seats and Ranger drooling on this dress. Nothing helps a party like a little sexy gossip. But I've got to get back to Salisbury tonight."

Adams loaded her garment bag and other cases into the Porsche, then led the way to town in the Yukon, talking to Ranger in the passenger seat next to him.

"I love the way she smells too, boy, but she can't come back after the party and sit by the fire with us. It's going to be a great night anyway."

Adams did have a great night, even if it started with Carly's comment about him being some kind of terrorist. He promised himself he would explain his work to her more clearly, next time they were together.

The 'mature and attractive gentleman' part was okay, though. He hoped nothing would ever spoil that.

CHAPTER 10

Jericho Casino
Israel

A few years after Austrian International Holdings gave birth to the Jericho Casino, the sturdy infant was killed by the Israeli government. Jewish high-rollers from Jerusalem and Tel Aviv, who happily poured millions of dollars into the casino coffers, were stopped one day by a police cordon and turned back. Terrorism in Israel and the endless battle in the Gaza Strip made visiting the Palestinian casino too dangerous for Jewish gamblers. Besides, there was not enough tax money collected from the casino for the ruling party in Jerusalem to risk the serious political fallout if Jews were killed on the road to a roulette wheel. The trickle of tourist gamblers from abroad dried up too, and leaders of the Palestinian Authority were unable to revive casino profits they had been putting into their struggle. And into their Swiss bank accounts.

Politics and corruption on all sides meant the casino had to go. Austrian investors, leaders of the Palestinian Authority, and Israeli politicians all licked their wounds and let their cash cow starve to death.

Under a gibbous moon, Ghazi Abu Shakir sat in a dilapidated deck chair on the dead casino's portico and considered the sobriquet he had been awarded earlier that day. Even Jabber had begun calling him "Professor." What's in a name, he thought, it's just something to put on a tombstone. They can put anything they want—his head snapped up when a bush trembled in the weed-choked parking area below. Peering into the shadows, he saw a small figure crawling in the tall grass.

"Come up here, Jabber, you idiot. From whom do you hide?" Lolling in the chaise, the Professor felt his thoughts fall from the clouds veiling the moon and land in the stink and sounds of the Akabat refugee camp across the road.

"You can't be too careful," answered Jabber, his coarse whisper loud enough to still the night birds. Despite the cool air he gripped his Kalashnikov with sweaty palms, his eyes riveted on the entrance to the parking lot and the road beyond.

The Professor was about to speak again when he heard a leaf crunch in the darkness behind him. Before he could turn, a soft voice hissed in his ear.

"Your friend is a very foolish man. Tell him to leave his rifle and join us here. If not, you both die where you sit."

The Professor called out softly, "Mahmoud Jabber, my hero, my deadly hatchet. Our guide is here on the terrace, and his friends are somewhere near you in the bushes. So please leave your rifle on the ground when you come up. Otherwise we will immediately travel to glory."

Jabber jerked. There were dark shapes moving near him, and he eased back into denser bushes. Then he saw the Professor rise, a park statue silvered by moonlight with a shadowy figure standing close behind. It was not the Israeli Army or Shin Bet agents that surrounded them, because they would already be dead. He got to his feet, reluctantly dropped his rifle in the weeds, and climbed onto the portico.

From where the trio stood, it was five miles to the border with Jordan. Jabber returned Shakir's smile. He knew that very soon they would be on their way to make bloody history, rifle or no rifle.

An hour later, the Professor, Jabber and the guide eased through rank undergrowth along the bank of a muddy creek that marked the border with Jordan. The fabled Jordan River had been reduced to a trickle by the thirst of Israeli desert farms, and the turgid water stank of agricultural and domestic effluents. An occasional bit of unidentifiable garbage pimpled the greasy surface as it floated by. Wading across the sewage, the three men paused to scan the guard tower that rose up before them.

Seven hundred miles northeast of Israel's West Bank, it was less than an hour before the start of a new day in Iran. Major Doctor Saleh Suleiman, soldier, physician, and an expert in battlefield pathogens, tossed his lab coat on the office couch and dropped beside it. The Tabriz University building was deserted, except for a small team preparing a lab room. They worked to detailed orders and specifications delivered by a daily courier from Tehran, and if any of them wondered why they were preparing such a strange training setup, they said nothing. They quietly arranged video displays, equipment, and textbooks.

The Major Doctor's work was on a tight schedule. Yesterday, he received a coded email message from Morteza Dehesh himself, telling him two students were on their way to Tabriz and should arrive in less than three days. He would be ready. He would train them to use the things locked behind heavy vault doors only five meters from his office. How plain and featureless those cylinders are, he thought. Well, simple containers or not, those weapons were just as the Russian supplier promised. They could kill tens of thousands—hundreds of thousands. Even more would die if the weapons were delivered under exactly the right conditions. The nuclear 'suitcase' bomb next to them in the vault might possibly do the same, even though it was a low-yield weapon.

But the Major could not imagine how Dehesh might carry out his plan. How could such large and dangerous things be smuggled into America? How could detection be avoided at the border? Impossible. And Dehesh must know that if he used these weapons on America, they would identify the attackers, and then... then! For such a monstrous insult America promised, years ago, to obliterate the attackers' homeland with nuclear fire. Oh yes, and he was sure they would do it. They would utterly destroy Iran.

The Major leaned back into his couch, eyes on the ceiling, thinking. This idea to attack America is impossible to carry out, so it must be a twisted plot to test loyalty, to test internal security. Dehesh, with his expensive clothes, his jewelry, and his painful courtesies—there was something seriously wrong with that man, something frightening. It was a bad day, he reminisced, that day he called me to Tehran. Nevertheless, the man is terribly powerful, so there is no choice but to carry out the training, wait, and see what happens. He groaned aloud and decided he must go home and get some sleep or fall from fatigue.

Major Doctor Suleiman wearily pushed up from the couch. He reached out, switched off the lights, and walked to the parking lot inside the heavily guarded compound. Home, on a quiet tree-lined street in the Tabriz suburbs, was only half an hour away. Naila would be waiting for him, reading. She was always reading when he came home, whatever the hour. Then, sitting by his side with her head on his shoulder, she would watch him eat the supper she had prepared hours earlier. Finally, he would breathe a goodnight kiss into little Jamshid's curls and, at last, sink into six hours of sleep.

A solitary zephyr stirred the dust as the doctor walked across the parking area. At his car, he looked past the gate and into the tranquil road that led home. Dehesh would never risk such joy and serenity, he thought. He would not make some silly toast like, "Death to the Great Satan," and then attack the Americans. He gazed at the sky over ancient Tabriz. No, that is unthinkable.

The Hashemite Kingdom of Jordan

The Professor whispered to their nameless guide, "When we get through that hole in the wire fence, guards in the tower will see us. If they do not shoot us out of boredom, they will invite us to be the guests of their young king." Jabber softly snarled in agreement.

"Have faith, travelers. Was there not a way through the West Bank wall, the new 'Matzos Curtain' built by the Jews? A miracle, yes? There will be another miracle, and those *Bedouin* guards will be blind, *insh'allah*."

The guide brought the luminous dial of his watch close to his face. When the minute hand was precisely ten minutes after the hour, he lurched toward the border.

"Quickly," he said. "We are almost there—move!"

The Professor and Jabber stared at the Jordanian army watchtower that guarded the approaches to the Allenby Bridge to the south, and the King Hussein Bridge to the north. They saw silhouettes moving on the roof of the tall fortress, backlit by road lamps along Route 449 farther inland. At last they ran, scrambling to catch up with their guide who was passing under the tower with long, loping strides. Kicking through the sand, they felt their shoulder blades itch, waiting for the impact of bullets. Nothing happened.

The vehicle on the shoulder of the road in Jordan was a battered Chevy Blazer, engine rumbling. Covered with a vast assortment of dents and a layer of desert dust, it looked like hundreds of others except, perhaps, for new all-terrain tires and three spares bolted to the rear hatch.

Two men exited the Blazer and opened the rear doors. They waved to the guide, who had stopped to push the Professor and Jabber forward. The guide waved back, then wordlessly turned on his heel and slipped back through the makeshift hole in the border wire.

The Professor and Jabber settled on dust-covered rear seats, doors slammed, and the Blazer sped down the road to Amman. For such an unkempt car, the small SUV seemed to have a powerful engine that ran very smoothly.

"So, we go to Amman?" The Professor tried to find a comfortable position on the lumpy seat.

"No. We go around. Seventy-five kilometers past Irbid you cross into Syria, near Dar'a. In two hours you are there, without fail. Maybe less, *insh'allah*." The driver spoke Arabic with an accent the Professor could not quite place. Iraqi? In any event, it was at least a hundred and fifty kilometers across the desert to the Syrian border. They would have to drive quickly over the pot-holed roads to be there in only two hours.

"Then where do we go?" the Professor persisted.

"Not we. Only you two. When we get to the border you meet our friends. Then you are truly on your way." The driver paused, as if for effect, and added, "You cross to Syria and then you go to Kurdistan. *Insh'allah.*"

"And what do we do when we get there?" the Professor asked. But this last question went unanswered. The drivers, relieving each other at the wheel at thirty-minute intervals, remained silent for the next two hours.

Besides an occasional truck, there was nothing much to see in the night that streamed by the dirty windows. Sometimes there were distant lights or fires. Once, they made a brief stop at a trucker's canteen where the drivers bought them tea and sticky honey cakes. After that, they passed the Jordanian spur of the great Saudi oil pipeline that sprang from Dammam and snaked across a desert of ancient volcanic debris. Jabber dozed while the Professor wondered about the powerful effect the barren land of the Middle East had on the great powers, on Israel, Jordan, Iraq, Iran, and finally—on himself. The desert night, deep with stars, held no answers.

Crossing the Syrian border was uneventful. Leaving their passengers in an off-road gully near the fence, the drivers wheeled the Blazer away without a word, a wave, or a handshake. Minutes later another guide appeared to perform another border miracle, and they were in Syria. Bounced around the back of a pickup truck like sacks of cheap rice, they traveled a few kilometers into the dark countryside and stopped between treeless walls of a *wadi* near the border town of Dar'a.

Their poker-faced drivers motioned for them to disembark. Producing guns, they ordered their passengers to remove their clothes. Jabber's eyes rolled wildly. The Professor reminded the enraged man he would likely have demanded the same thing, if the situation were reversed. The drivers confiscated a knife Jabber had concealed in a sheath taped to his thigh, and the two travelers were allowed back into their clothes.

"I want that knife back," Jabber complained. The drivers said nothing as they leaned against the truck, fingering their weapons. It seemed like an hour in the chill desert air, but only twenty minutes passed before the helicopter appeared. Black and unmarked, its blades whistled above them as a side door slid back and they were motioned inside. The door closed and they lifted off.

The Professor examined the large cabin. He did not know what kind of helicopter it was, but it seemed to be some kind of VIP aircraft. The padded bench seat facing the rear was covered in a plush striped fabric, and the passenger seats were deep and comfortable. Maybe a general's aircraft? A company aircraft? The Professor studied the Syrian flag taped to the bulkhead behind the unblinking stare of the guard facing them. The small banner did not look very military or very permanent. All the side windows were painted out.

Shouting above the engine noise, he addressed the guard, "What is this? Avis rent-a-copter? Why can't we see outside? And why do you need that weapon? We are not your enemies. We are just pilgrims traveling through the holy land of Islam."

The guard neither smiled nor replied. Jabber examined the guard and his machine gun and stoically asked, "How far is it to Kurdistan, Professor?"

"I think it is at least seven hundred kilometers to Syria's northeast border with Iraq and Turkey. Kurdistan is part of the territory Kurds claim as their homeland, if that is where we are truly bound. Where we ultimately go and what we do there is still a mystery, my fierce comrade. This entire trip is a mystery. At any rate this is a speedy machine, so I think we could be near the border by dawn." The Professor slowly shook his head. "I feel we are prisoners, even in Syria."

"Yes. We are prisoners. We are prisoners because whoever is in command does not want us to know anything or anyone," agreed Jabber. "They worry about what we know and what we can tell if we are captured and tortured. But I will never be taken alive. Never." He looked up at his companion with a theatrical scowl.

The Professor nodded, closing his eyes. "We have only our first orders. Patience, Jabber, patience. All will be revealed."

The Professor and Jabber were dozing when the helicopter touched down on a deserted dirt road. Unceremoniously prodded from the aircraft while the blades were still rotating, they crouched and ran as the helicopter lifted off and disappeared.

"Professor, is this Kurdistan?" Jabber asked, his eyes darting anxiously.

"I don't think so, my orphan. But let us ask that limousine driver over there." The Professor pointed to a tanker truck parked alongside the road, headlights dimmed. They strolled to the driver, a short swarthy man wearing baggy pants and a wide sash. He was leaning against the front fender, watching them and taking enthusiastic bites from a huge sandwich.

"Good day to you," said the Professor. "Are we in Kurdistan?"

"Good day to you, and welcome to Dayr az Zawr. You are in Syria, but in one hour you will be in blessed Kurdistan, *insh'allah*." The driver's three-day growth of beard cracked to reveal a gleaming family of gold teeth.

"And how are you called, my friend?"

"Driver."

"Of course, of course. What else could you possibly be named? And to where do you take us, driver?"

"I take you to Mehabad." The golden family reappeared for a second. "In the homeland of the crazy fire-worshipers."

"And what roads do we take to get there?" asked the Professor.

"From here it is three hundred kilometers to Mosul. Then another three hundred kilometers from Mosul to Mehabad. There I leave you."

The driver offered the two travelers a flask of tepid tea and large *shawarma* sandwiches dripping with olive oil. He looked on paternally as the Professor and Jabber attacked the food.

"Good, eh? When you finish, take a piss and climb inside. We want to be far from here before the sun is up."

"Where are these cities he talks of, Professor?" Jabber's mouth was stuffed, and morsels of oily bread escaped to make patterns on his chin and shirt.

"Mosul is in Iraq, Jabber. And Mehabad is in Iran. Between those cities there are some interesting mountains. The Zagros." The Professor looked east, where the new day was beginning to etch a thin yellow line across the horizon.

"And how long will it take to reach Mehabad, driver?" the Professor asked.

"One, maybe two days."

"Will we be able to cross Iraq safely? It is a troubled country."

"Put your trust in Allah, and in your magic driver." The golden smile gleamed in the dark. "Get inside and we go."

The Professor and Jabber wiped greasy hands on their clothes and walked toward the cab of the truck. Closer, they saw flags on short front fender posts and a symbol painted on the doors. The design had horizontal stripes of red, white, and green, and a central sunburst.

"What flag is that?" asked Jabber.

"That, I believe, is the 'sunny flag' of Kurdistan. The Kurds have no country since they lost independence in 1848. Then all their leaders were shot in 1927. But they still have a flag, and of course they have tribes that will not agree on anything other than they want to have their own country."

"Ah. Then they are like the Palestinians, yes?" Jabber asked.

They had reached the cab, and he opened the passenger-side door. Before the Professor could reply there was a shout from behind them.

"No, not in front! Here. Through here." The driver was on top of the tanker body and was pointing into an open access hatch.

"We swim in oil?" Wide-eyed, Jabber backed away.

"Don't be crazy," the driver cackled. "The back of my tank has beds and blankets. Even electric light. Only the front of the tank is with oil. I take it to towns near Mosul and Arbil. Even in such a good Kurdish truck, how else do you think I take you across Iraq without a knife in the ribs? Now get in and we leave. Or else you run alongside and sing to me." He cackled again.

The Professor sighed, climbed the ladder to the top of the tank, and peered into the hatch. In a rear compartment of the tanker's cylindrical body he could see a dim bulb, two pallets, and a short-legged chair.

"This is really quite clever, Jabber. Come, we will discuss the gory details of Kurdish history while we relax in our cozy steel schoolroom. Our magical driver will do justice to his Savile Row suit and drive us swiftly and smoothly, just like James Bond. Climb up here, my friend, and let us go on to our glorious destiny."

The driver slammed the hatch over his passengers, mounted the high cab seat and, with a gear-grinding lurch, they were off to the east. It took two days of bouncing across mountain roads to reach Mehabad. Along the way the Professor and Jabber acquired a taste for Kurdish food, a smattering of obscene Kurdish phrases, and a collection of bruises delivered by the walls of their hideaway. Sleep was possible only when the rollicking ride paused for a few minutes to allow a delivery of oil. The driver did not seem to need sleep, so neither passenger got much rest during the entire trip. They were so sleep-deprived, that after the truck finally arrived at Mehabad they could never recall the last leg of their journey—in yet another helicopter.

They arrived in Tabriz during a dust storm, under a blood red sun.

CHAPTER 11

Two weeks after the Professor and Jabber arrived at Tabriz University, His Excellency Deputy Vice President for Executive Affairs Morteza Dehesh was in Tehran, eating supper at his library desk. He always enjoyed the simple meal of grilled minced lamb with polo rice, sumac spice, and warm flat bread: *Chelo kebab* and *lavash*. It was an honest Iranian meal that was the usual preamble to his long and solitary evenings. With a small house staff and four assistants, he spent most days in Tehran in a house at the end of a minor street. He only left his office for rare appearances at government gatherings where his absence would be noticed by gossips and spies—or for an occasional weekend at his flat in Paris.

Dehesh worked long hours without guidance or interference from the Vice President for Executive Affairs, who was nominally above him, or even from the more senior First Vice President. Summaries of his reports sometimes went to President Ahmadinejad, but it was to Ayatollah Khamenei, the Supreme Leader, that he always reported. Dehesh was Iran's *de facto* chief intelligence officer, and his power was as awesome as his public persona was humble.

He rolled a mouthful of vintage Margaux across his tongue. Unlike many of his countrymen who abused drugs, he had only two small vices: vintage French wines and Cuban cigars. Some whispered his vices also included his four handsome assistants and the household tea boys. Dehesh knew the rumors. *Women. In Paris you can smell their sex even through silks and perfume. They were a clinging, cloying, greedy nuisance. In Tehran they are hidden under the chador, thank God.*

Computer speakers behind him chimed, and he turned away from his supper to examine the screen on the credenza behind him. Probably another email from Doctor Suleiman. I will have to watch him carefully, Dehesh thought. The good doctor seems too nervous about his work.

As ordered, Suleiman became Dehesh's pen-pal from the hour the Palestinians arrived in Tabriz, and he sent long progress reports every day. The plan was unfolding smoothly. It was a good plan, even if Dehesh had no one to whom he could brag. The Russian weapons and the two Palestinian assassins were safe in the doctor's training camp, and there was little risk of being identified with the plot. Iran's involvement would be invisible, even if things somehow went wrong after the Palestinians landed in America. His plan provided deniability and the assassins were expendable. In fact, he intended to expend them as soon as their mission was completed. Then there was the second delightful gambit. He was sure that the elegance of it all was what gave him that erotic dream last night, and the night before.

Ayatollah Khamenei still raved about humiliation and losses from the American raid on Bandar Abbas, so he was easily convinced to play his part and grant the plenipotentiary powers Dehesh needed to act decisively. Act he had. Once final arrangements were in place, there would be little left to do but watch it all unfold.

So, what was this now, this latest bulletin on his computer? Dehesh refilled his wine glass and called up the message. As he expected, it was from Doctor Suleiman in Tabriz. He inhaled the wine's aroma and speculated on the contents of the coded email. Perhaps the Palestinians were getting bored or restless. Maybe they could not learn their complex tasks. Maybe they were out of control. He hoped not, because then his timetable would suffer. In that case, the Palestinians would suffer too.

The screen showed a set of colorful photographs. Two downloaded, then a third. It must indeed be a long message. He inserted a computer disk containing the steganography code VEVAK promised him America's NSA geniuses could not break. Then he clicked on the appropriate icons. Postcard pictures of Paris cleared and he leaned forward to read the revealed text. Columns of details and dates showed that training at Tabriz was on schedule. Smiling, Dehesh lifted the secure phone and asked to be connected to the commander of the naval base at Bandar Abbas. It was time to begin the next act of the opera.

Bandar Abbas Naval Base

At long last, the KILO class diesel submarine named *Yunes* had become the pride of the Iranian underwater fleet. Side number 903 was delivered by Russia's Novgorod shipyard in 1996 at a cost of three hundred million dollars, and for over four years the sub suffered one humiliating problem after another. Superstitious sailors whispered that a boat named 'Jonah' could never have good luck. They wondered why she had been named for a crazy prophet who saved the Assyrians in Nineveh—and after being eaten by a fish! But with the new batteries from India, her performance became superb. During the following twenty months Captain Jamshid Bakhtiar Reza stropped the crew to a razor's edge. He trained or replaced men until he was satisfied his sailors could operate the sub better than any Russian crew.

This afternoon, as black-hulled *Yunes* passed the breakwater after a long training patrol, Captain Reza was suddenly uneasy. The base commander's car was waiting on the pier. Admiral Ali Shamkhani seldom spoke to his unit commanders at social events, never mind leaving his office to greet returning ships or submarines. Reza felt the hairs on his neck ripple. Was it Minou? The children? What was so important that the admiral could not have sent him a radio message?

Tangy air of Bandar Abbas harbor swirled around his perch on the submarine's sail, high above the weather deck. Harbor odors sometimes reminded him of home-cooked meals and Minou's warm arms, but this day he felt none of that homecoming joy. He scanned the pier with stabilized binoculars, examining the familiar Mercedes while the glistening sub glided past the ferry docks toward its berth. His lean face was taut with worry.

After they tied up and were connected to power from the pier, the diesels were silent. Reza returned the salute from the guard at the gangway and stepped ashore to salute the admiral. Returning the salute, the admiral saw the unspoken concern on Reza's face.

"Your family is fine, Jamshid, everyone's fine. No need to worry But I'm sorry to tell you that your reunion with them is delayed until much later tonight." Admiral Shamkhani walked off the pier with Reza as the sub's mooring lines were doubled. "I'll take you to the airfield and tell you what details I know on the way. In a nutshell, you're going to Tehran to meet a very senior government official, and you must leave immediately. Our base aircraft will wait and bring you back tonight." The admiral squinted into the sunlight. "Here, this way."

The driver held the door for the two officers, hoping the grim-faced submarine captain would not leave his stink on the limousine's upholstery.

"May I first shower and change into a clean uniform, Admiral?" Reza knew he was a nauseating bouquet of diesel fuel, sweat, and recycled air, just like the rest of his crew.

"If a civilian will keep a submarine commander from his waiting family, then he will learn his first lesson about submarines at the same time." The admiral laughed and clapped a beefy hand on his captain's shoulder. "I've never told you this,

Jamshid, but you are the best sub skipper in the navy. As far as I am concerned, you smell delightful! It's the sweet scent of *Yunes* and her marvelous crew."

The Mercedes 600 stopped at the main gate of the base. Even with an admiral's flag streaming at the front fender it had to undergo a detailed inspection. After the mysterious disaster at a secret facility north of town, security around Bandar Abbas had become uncomfortably tight. Finally past the gate guards, the admiral raised the glass partition that sealed them off from the driver, and looked thoughtfully at the officer next to him.

"Listen to me, Jamshid. I don't know what waits for you in Tehran, except that the man you will meet is very powerful. Yesterday Admiral Mohraj ordered me to send you to Deputy Vice President Morteza Dehesh immediately upon your return. You should know that whatever title he may use, he is the head of our most serious intelligence activities. He reports directly to Ayatollah Khamenei himself. We were told that *Yunes* is now under his direct command for some mission that Admiral Mohraj and I know nothing about. And that's it. All of it."

Reza considered this startling news. If his superior officer and even the commander of the entire navy did not know what *Yunes* would be ordered to do, what terrible thing could it be? And to be under the direct command of a civilian?

"Admiral, with respect, what if this mission—or whatever it is—what if it's not, ah, what if it's not reasonable?"

Reza waited in vain for an answer. Shamkhani lowered the divider window and kept his eyes fixed on the road ahead. Nothing else was said during the rest of the journey. At the airport, the propellers of a Dornier 228 turboprop were already turning when the limousine pulled up to the stairs. A quick exchange of salutes and Captain Reza was airborne.

CHAPTER 12

Koucheh Bazorgeh
Tehran, Iran

It is six hundred-fifty miles from Bandar Abbas to Tehran, so it took over two hours for the Dornier to reach Mehrabad airport. Another black Mercedes was waiting, this one with darkly tinted windows.

Captain Reza did not visit Tehran often, and the bustling evening life of its twelve million inhabitants was overwhelming after tranquil Bandar Abbas. People crowded the parks and streets. Above them, construction cranes waded across the city like storks in a pond, their outlines reflected in the glass facades of new buildings. Long rows of streetlights illuminated wide boulevards brimming with cars and pedestrians.

The limo passed the old Hilton Hotel, now the Esteghlal Grand Hotel, and eased onto the crowded Chamran Expressway. A hundred yards further they turned into a dark and leafy *cul de sac*. It was *Koucheh Bahzorgeh*—Bazaar Alley.

The short street got its name from ladies of the night who took to selling their fleshy wares there during the reign of Shah Reza Pahlavi. He and they were long gone. Today, there were only two rusty fifty-five gallon oil drums waiting at the entrance to the narrow alley. Behind the drums a pair of guards sat on folding chairs wreathed in cigarette smoke, their automatic rifles across their knees. When the headlights of the familiar car flashed a recognition signal they sprang to their feet, slung their weapons, and rolled the barrels aside. Without slowing, the limo slid between the twin rows of sycamores that marched along the *jubes*, the curbside sewers that edge many streets in Tehran.

The door of the house at the end of the lane swung open without a knock, and Reza followed a servant into the dim interior.

"Captain Reza! How very kind of you to visit me on such short notice." Dehesh waved the naval officer into a comfortable chair in front of his desk. "Have you eaten? May I give you supper?" Dehesh's eyes were hidden in the shadows of the darkened library, but his disembodied hand floated above the polished desk in the cone of light cast by a tall gooseneck lamp. A single file folder rested before him, alongside a goblet of wine. "Or perhaps I can offer something else to help you celebrate this anniversary of our glorious revolution?"

"I'd forgotten today is a holiday. But no thank you, Excellency." Reza tried to see the eyes hidden in the shadows. "I did notice large crowds when we crossed the city, but I thought it was just a busy night in the capital."

"Ah, one should not forget to celebrate such things as a revolution." Dehesh's voice seemed to hover supernaturally in the gloom. "So if you change your mind about having refreshments, please tell me." His words rustled like fine silk.

Captain Reza watched the wine glass rise into the shadows and float back to the desktop. Pale hands then folded atop the file folder.

"May I come directly to the point, captain? I am aware that your beloved family waits for you." Silent, Reza watched the manicured fingertips raise the wineglass again and, after a pause, return it to the gleaming mahogany. "Can your submarine cross the Atlantic Ocean to America, put two passengers ashore and return? Undetected?"

Reza was struck dumb. When he was finally able to answer, his words were slow and cautious. "That depends on many factors, sir."

"Such as?"

"The first factors are the outcome of detailed preparations and a thorough review of my command's readiness. Then there are the proposed departure date, departure point, exact destination, weather, small boat skills of the passengers, and the return port." He paused and then added, "I assume you are speaking of a round trip, sir."

Dehesh suddenly leaned forward into the light. The intensity of his dark liquid eyes startled Reza. He thought they were kind at first, but as he looked into their depths he realized he was peering into deep wells of cruelty. He was grateful for Dehesh's next words.

"No martyrs are needed by me today, captain, whether they be on a submarine or elsewhere." The smile hardened. "But can it be done?"

Reza's mind ricocheted wildly. Unprepared for the question, he rapidly considered dozens of facts and variables. It was over five thousand miles from Gibraltar across the Atlantic to America and back. Stretching it very, very thin,

Yunes could stay at sea for forty-five consecutive days without refueling or provisioning. Maybe a bit longer. The American anti-submarine SOSUS system is no longer operational, but there were reconnaissance satellites to consider, as well as the awesome intercept capability of NSA. A ten-knot average speed of advance. Submerged all the way, snorkeling would be hard on the crew. But yes, it was possible. Barely possible. He answered the question simply.

"With some reservations, sir, it can be done." Dehesh's hand languidly waved him on and Reza closed his eyes, thinking aloud.

"I would be watched as I made for the Suez Canal. And then watched in the Mediterranean and watched all the way to the Straits of Gibraltar and beyond. The watchers are not insurmountable, though I think NATO will be concerned about such a voyage by an Iranian submarine, no matter what reason they are given.

"Then, in the eastern Atlantic, I submerge and disappear. I would need to know the overhead times of reconnaissance satellites from that point onward in case I had to surface. Fuel and food supplies limit the time I can loiter in American offshore waters. I could not spend more than a few hours there, at most. Weather is always a factor, though in this case it would primarily affect the landing. By the time I returned to the eastern Atlantic, NATO would be concerned about where I had been for so many days."

Reza paused for a moment and thought about the enormity of what he was saying. He thought the man in shadows behind the desk might say something, but silence still draped the room, so he spoke again.

"Of course, if I was forced to enter into combat, there might not be enough fuel for the entire return transit." The Captain paused and then added, "I would not like to risk losing crewmen taking those passengers ashore. But yes, it could be done. It could be done by *Yunes*, Excellency."

"You are reasonably certain of all that?"

Reza was certain. He was an avid student of submarine warfare and knew everything about the great history of German U-boats, from start to finish.

He answered, "The U-584 put saboteurs ashore in Florida, undetected. The U-202 did the same on Long Island. If ancient German diesel submarines could do that in 1942, then *Yunes* and I can do it now." He paused and added, "Satellites might see me if I am surfaced, but that would only be caused by a problem that would likely abort the mission anyway. The old SOSUS system would have easily been able to hear us when we snorkel, but the Americans have allowed the hydrophone arrays to fall into disrepair, and they are now used mainly for scientific research. They will not detect our diesels."

"Excellent! I have anticipated international concern about the reason for such a submarine voyage, so I made arrangements with the Russian shipyards to overhaul *Yunes* next month. That way, NATO and the rest of the world has an acceptable reason for one of our submarines to enter the Atlantic. A contract has been signed with a firm in Lisbon for diesel fuel and supplies. I have here tables of Atlantic overhead times of reconnaissance satellites for April and the first three weeks of May." He tapped the file on the desk.

"Our replenishment ship *Polyus* will meet your submarine in Lisbon and provide you with food and fuel after the trip from Bandar Abbas. On the return voyage, *Polyus* will be waiting in the Bay of Biscay, ready to sail west to meet you in case your fuel runs short. The passengers we speak of will be able to take themselves to land, once they are close inshore. And provoking combat is out of the question." Dehesh again leaned forward into the cone of light. "However, if an Iranian warship is fired upon, it is expected to return the compliment."

Dehesh looked steadily at Reza. "There is no doubt in my mind that your skills are equal to such a voyage, captain. But if your country calls on you to do it, is your patriotism strong enough to take your submarine across the Atlantic to the very doorstep of America?"

The two men stared at each other for a timeless moment. The ticking of the mantel clock seemed to stop.

Reza finally said, "Those passengers I would carry, Excellency. They are terrorists, are they not?"

"I prefer to call them my messengers. Why should that concern you?"

"I am a naval officer, Excellency, not a terrorist."

"Besides defending yourself, you will not be asked to commit any violent acts, legal or otherwise. And I do not believe a submarine that approaches American shores will be considered to be a terrorist by the Americans or anyone else. They move their submarines close to many countries all the time." The wine glass levitated into the shadows. When it returned to the desk, the rustling voice began again.

"We agree, then, such a voyage would be a great challenge. But what will you say if your country asks for an answer tonight? Yes or no?"

Captain Reza realized he was slowly nodding his head. Then he replied, "If I am asked... yes, I will do it."

Dehesh rose and extended his hand. Reza also stood and grasped the hand that materialized over the table. He was surprised to feel hard sinews move in the pale flesh.

"Your record indicates you are a very competent commander, Captain Reza, and now I know you're a true patriot as well. I'm impressed with your speed of reasoning, and that you did not speak of luck makes it all the more impressive."

Dehesh sat, leaning forward to remain in the lamplight. He added, "Anything you need, captain, besides a guarantee of good weather, I will supply to you immediately. Now, please sit and stay a while. Join me in a cup of my wine. We still have things to discuss on this historic night."

A wine glass appeared in the cone of light, and Dehesh slowly filled it with blood-red liquid. "By the way, you depart Bandar Abbas in the middle of next month, so we have just four weeks to become close friends."

Reza kept his face expressionless and sipped his wine. The aroma of the forbidden drink filled his mouth and nose and became a warm and pleasant sensation. Despite the effect of the wine, his mind held one clear thought.

From this moment on, my crew is in danger. I must not fail them.

CHAPTER 13

Tabriz University
Tabriz, Iran

Major Doctor Suleiman tried to find a comfortable position on the wooden folding chair. It was a practice session for his students. The Professor and Jabber wore wet suits and stood on the opposite edge of Tabriz University's large indoor swimming pool. Each had a folding-stock AKS-74 slung across his back and a sidearm strapped to his leg. Looking at the glistening rubber suits and the weapons, the doctor reflected that Jabber was hopeless in the classroom and labs, but showed a surprising ability to operate complex machinery and firearms. Then an instructor blew a whistle and thumbed a stopwatch.

Jabber pulled a lanyard attached to a long black bundle, and the two men rolled it over the tiled edge of the pool. It hit the water with a hissing splash, unfolding and inflating into a Zodiac "Futura Commando" with an Evinrude 50-horsepower outboard motor.

Floating at the end of its tether the boat took shape, and after rollup floorboards snapped into place, Jabber jumped into the rocking vessel with acrobatic agility. Disconnecting a heavy CO_2 inflation canister, he effortlessly tossed it up on the apron of the pool. In turn, the Professor swung two long stainless steel cylinders into the boat, along with two backpacks and a large aluminum suitcase. Jabber lashed the cylinders and packs to the boat and disconnected the safety lines as the Professor clambered down. Twisting toward the stern, Jabber adjusted the outboard's throttle, hit the starter button, and the Evinrude sputtered into a muffled growl. Hunched over, as if facing a stiff wind, they slowly motored around the pool.

"Outstanding!" The instructor's voice echoed in the pool enclosure. "Two minutes, ten seconds! Best time yet! Now, shut off the motor and get out. As soon as you deflate the boat, we do it again. This time you change places." The trainees groaned.

Even in his hard folding chair, Doctor Suleiman was happy. Technical training is half completed, he thought, and we are ahead of schedule for practicing this strange boat launching business. Dehesh had indeed sent capable instructors, just as he promised, though their background was not at all clear. Teachers at poolside today might be sailors—or not. After training sessions they kept to themselves, said little, and evaded questions.

Suleiman was also pleased that the theoretical laboratory lessons would be finished today, and they would then begin the last part of practical field work. Tomorrow the students go to a remote desert *wadi* for weapons training. He knew Dehesh was obsessive about secrecy, so the trainees were always blindfolded whenever they were outside the campus building.

The two men had already completed their classroom GPS lessons, and the instructors as well as the students marveled that the little handheld units could contain and display so much data. The units they used even had built-in base maps of American cities, rivers, lakes and coastlines. Suleiman shook his head, amazed Americans were still so free with such sensitive data. And it was all available for $311 each! Of course, the handsets only held maps of the United States—useless in Iran.

Climbing out of the boat, the weary students prepared for the next launch. Only the taciturn instructors at poolside knew the purpose of these inflatable boat drills, and the doctor had been unable to guess what it was. He only knew that whatever it might be, it called for many exhausting practice sessions. Surely the two trainees were not going to sail a rubber boat to America. Were they going to travel to American waters on a merchant ship and go ashore in a Zodiac? Whose merchant ship? The American Coast Guard will search the ship and learn of the plot. Then nuclear weapons would fly to Iran.

The doctor was deeply troubled by what was implied by the lab theory and field training Dehesh had demanded. He still did not believe Dehesh had permission to launch such an attack on America. *But what if he did?*

A mesmerizing sheen of rainbow colors gleamed on the pool's undulating surface. The outboard motor put an oil slick on the water that got thicker each day, and the doctor wondered if they could get rid of it before university students used the pool again, and started asking questions.

Sometimes he thought about the American military doctor who had invited him and Naila to become part of his family during a year of post-graduate work at Columbia University's College of Physicians and Surgeons. He remembered intimate dinners when they bored their wives with medical humor and problems. He remembered road trips to upstate New York for picnics and overnights at country inns. Visits to Cherry Valley. Fall foliage.

And then fate brought them together again at the London symposium on infectious diseases last summer. John, his American friend, had gone gray at the temples and had also been promoted to major. When he opened the beautiful briefcase the American officer gave him as a parting gift, Suleiman was disturbed to find a one-time pad codebook in it.

"Just in case," John had said. "Use it if you need it."

No. He would not think about that code book. All this bizarre training *must* be only an elaborate test of some kind. What else could it be?

It was close to midnight, and after-dinner lectures were over. The Professor and Jabber were finally in their beds. Lights were out, a guard dozed in the hall outside their windowless room, and the Professor's cigar glowed in the dark. Jabber watched the glow pulse with each puff.

"When do we leave this prison school, Professor? When do we go to America and kill those *shaitans*?" Jabber knew the target was the United States because that day they were briefed about parts of the eastern seacoast. They had begun to study maps of Washington, Norfolk, Baltimore and New York.

"When our good teachers think we are ready."

The Professor had found the microphone hidden in the overhead light fixture, and spoke as little as possible when they were in the dormitory room. That it was so easy to disable the overhead device told him there were others in the room not meant to be found. With that in mind, he never looked for them or voiced his suspicion that the training facility was in Iran. Still, he reflected, after that amazing ride in the oil tanker truck, they could be almost anywhere.

Portraits of unfamiliar swarthy men in western clothes were scattered here and there in the training complex, but the place still did not feel right. Well, all the secrecy was irrelevant because in a few weeks it would not matter one way or another. Their training was almost completed, and soon they would be given weapons that were truly awesome. If he was able to feel sympathy for Americans, or for anyone else, he would think that the weapons were—terrifying.

"Yes, but *when* do we get out of here, Professor? I do not mind the gun range, the boat practice, or even that obstacle course. But if I have to spend another day in that stinking lab with those cylinders and those cans I will kill that doctor

Mohammed. I will. And also instructor Mohammed at the pool." Jabber's voice was rising as he complained.

"Quiet, brave Saladin. Be patient. Two days ago our senior doctor Mohammed said we had three more weeks of training at the most. That means we start our journey on the twelfth of March. Not long to wait, comrade. Just remain your happy self and think of all the American Satans you will kill. Think of our slaughtered families. And then amuse yourself by wondering why everyone here is named Mohammed." The Professor looked at the light fixture and smiled into the darkness.

"Ah? That's right, they *are* all named Mohammed! Why do you think that is, Professor?"

"I have no idea. Now, let us sleep. Tomorrow brings more practice and training." He stubbed out his cigar.

CHAPTER 14

It was the dream again. He was in Gaza City, in the kitchen of the family restaurant, taking off his apron. It was lunchtime, and he would leave the cooking to his mother and spend a few minutes greeting new guests and gossiping with old friends. Somehow the Professor knew he was dreaming, but he stayed in the drama and played his part. It was the only way for him to see Salma and Yusef move again. To touch them.

"Don't be too long, Ghazi. We have many customers today and I will not be able to make all the dishes by myself." The face of the round woman in the plain black dress was creased by an infinite number of smile wrinkles and care lines.

"Only a few minutes, mother. And you have Adham to help you."

"Adham." The wrinkles regrouped into a scowl. "He cannot ladle *hummus* into a bowl without dropping it on the floor, never mind grind *kofta*. One day a guest will find Adham's finger in it." She waved a spoon at the hapless cousin.

Shakir heard himself laugh. It always happened the same way. "Only a few minutes, mother. You know our friends and neighbors are out there and I must be a good host. Give Adham a rubber knife."

Always happens the same way. First a kiss, and then he is outside among the tables, shaking hands with jolly Farid, the tobacconist. Then walking in the noonday sun. Then watching Salma spoon ice cream into Yusef's smile.

Happens the same way. A white Bronco pulls to the curb, the window rolls down, a hand beckons.

"Ghazi! Bring us *pita*, enough bread for the four of us. A nice *mezza*. You pick the dishes—but lots of your famous *kofta*."

He knew them. Three fighters from the Al Aqsa Martyrs Brigade and a greasy Fattah politician some said was a maker of bombs.

"Why don't you sit at a table? I'll give you one inside. Private."

"Better here. We wait for you and listen to Jews tell lies on the radio." The dark tinted window rose and covered the driver's smirk.

The same way. Salma waves and pulls Yusef back to her, stopping him from running through the sidewalk tables to his father. He waves back and ducks through the door into the cool interior, shouting to Adham to put together a *mezza*. For the Bronco. Quickly. His back to the door, he does not see the Apache helicopter descending into the street, hovering in the intersection fifty meters away.

THE SAME! The first Hellfire missile drills through the body armor of the Bronco and explodes inside the SUV. A blast of hot glass shrapnel from the vehicle's windows tears through tablecloths, dresses, jackets, and eyes.

He runs so slowly. He cannot get through the door to the sidewalk. Another rocket swirls right through the flaming windows of the Bronco and detonates in the middle of the sidewalk café. He writhes on the floor of the kitchen. Utensils and pots and food are smashed and steaming all around him. There is a profound silence. No screams. He is unhurt, and now he can run. He runs through the silence to the doorway, and then into the smoke outside.

Suddenly he can hear, and see, and smell. He hears the hissing roar of the burning vehicle mixing with screams of the wounded and dying. He sees flaming tables, chairs, and people. His first intake of breath sears his throat with the acrid smell of high explosives and burning flesh. He is running, running through the haze to the place where Salma and Yusef must be waiting.

Their table is overturned, the tablecloth on fire. Nothing else there except Farid, sitting in broken crockery, making a high keening sound like a nail dragged across slate. He has no legs.

And there they are, huddled in a corner of the cinder block wall next to the first row of tables. Salma's back is to him, arms wrapped protectively around Yusef. They cannot hear his shouting.

He is still running, running until he kneels in the glass and fire. He is reaching out, gently turning her toward him. Then he sees her face, black and glossy. The wounds on her cheeks weep a clear fatty fluid, like the split skin of a lamb roasted on a spit. He is afraid to touch the brown parchment stretched over her bulging eye sockets. Then he is reaching into her arms, pulling at Yusef. The boy's arms are slippery, and fall away from his grasp. He is looking at his hands and sees his fingers are papered with Yusef's skin. He sees the glistening pink muscles in the boy's forearms.

The dream does not awaken him. The colors simply merge and twist and darken. In the morning he will have the taste of blood on his tongue.

CHAPTER 15

Adams had been invited to two Onancock parties in as many weeks, and Carly was his date both times. She said she only went to parties to keep her journalistic eye on the county's social life, but he was happy to have her on his arm for any reason. He was certain she was the sexiest woman in Virginia—maybe in the world.

Between parties he got phone calls from Sophie, answered email and messages from military commands, and sometimes communicated with teams in offshore hot spots. The rest of the time was spent working on his house and boat, and this weekend he planned to show off *Pilgrim* to Carly if he could convince her to visit the yacht after the party. Retired life was turning out to be pleasantly busy.

Tonight's gathering was at Kasim's home again. The rug merchant threw a large party almost every month, inviting a wide range of Accomack County gentry. "Parties are good for business," he said. Like most of the others on the regular guest list, Adams came for the good food, drink, and gossip. This time he was determined to convince Sophie to join him and Carly, and had called her from *Pilgrim* during a break from polishing brass.

"You can't be busy every weekend, Sophie. C'mon, it'll do you good to take a break. Relax for a few hours, see some new faces. Folks around here will love you, and you'll enjoy the Lebanese food at the party. Absolutely delicious."

"I must be in the office tomorrow morning. We expect some important traffic from Pakistan."

"We always expect some important traffic from Pakistan. It'll keep for one day. Besides, I want you to meet Carly. You two will really hit it off."

"You are escorting Miss Truitt?"

"Sure am. Convinced her to take a break and abandon her newspaper desk early tonight. Just like I'm trying to convince you."

"The hosts have not invited me."

"No sweat—you'll be my date. Kasim will be overjoyed to meet a beautiful new customer for his carpets. And besides, it has been too long since we had some face time, don't you think?"

"Yes, Jeremiah. Too long."

"Great! So you'll come?"

"Yes, thank you. It's worth the long drive for an opportunity to discuss Mr. Beauchamps with you. What time should I arrive?"

"Beauchamps. For Pete's sake, Sophie, let's just forget that jackass and—"

"I shall be at the Hermitage by six," she interrupted. "Don't worry, I remember the way."

The line went silent, and Adams thumbed off his cell phone. Shaking his head, he picked up the Brasso and returned to polishing *Pilgrim's* bell. Beauchamps, he thought. At least that jerk won't be at the party. And after Sophie and Carly get to know each other, the three of us can be buddies. Pal around together.

Sophie had not yet appeared, and while they waited Adams and Carly were having pre-party sundowners in front of Hermitage's fireplace, listening to the New Age murmurs of *Enya*. The room was warm, and they were wrapped in a chrysalis of firelight, perfume and sound.

Carly stared into the embers, and he stared at Carly. She had kicked off her pumps and curled her legs beneath her, trailing an arm to scratch Ranger's head. The dog always posted himself next to the leather wing chair she had adopted as her own, the reading chair Adams used most nights to enjoy the faint traces of her perfume. Abruptly, she turned to him.

"Okay. Lipstick smeared? Spinach in the teeth? What?"

"Ah." Adams ran a hand over his jaw. She always seemed to know when he looked at her, and she always seemed annoyed.

"Okay. I just figured out who you really are. I mean, who you *were*. Wilding, the woman in *Mona Vann*. The painting in the Tate in London? Pre-Raphaelite model? Now that was a great school of painters, those Pre-Raphaelites." Adams felt idiotic. What a collection of dumbass things to say.

"I know about the Pre-Raphaelites, Jay." Carly cocked her head, the way she did when she studied something interesting. "You think I look like Alexa. The one they called the 'stunner.'" She giggled and sipped her drink. "After such outrageous flattery I'm sorry to say you don't resemble Dante Rossini in the least, even if Alexa was sweet on him. You're more of a William Hunt. Without the beard, thank God."

They regarded each other for a moment. Then Carly's soft whisper reached for him through the music.

"Jeremiah Adams, I like you. I like you very much. And I think I'm going to like you a lot more." He started to reply, but she put her finger to her lips, and breathed, "Just don't say anything."

She rose and approached his chair, barefoot. The nails on her long slender toes were painted a luminescent bronze that shone through her hose as she slid across the carpet. Then she was standing before him, stooping to bring her eyes close to his, and an ocean of dark red hair swirled across his face. He grasped her thigh and felt the wool dress slide smoothly against the silken surface beneath. As she bent and slowly brought her face closer, lights flashed through the front windows. *Sophie*. Turning away, Carly looked for her shoes.

Kasim's party was the usual crowded success. Sophie was an instant hit with the host and his Onancock neighbors, as Adams predicted, and the trio was quickly separated and moved around the room by introductions and conversation. Almost two hours passed before they drifted back together.

Standing between the women, Adams realized he had never seen Sophie in a revealing cocktail dress, and when his gaze traveled across her bare shoulders he found himself wondering what kept the front of the dress from falling off. And what she looked like without it.

"Admiring my necklace, Jeremiah?"

"Ah. Yes. It's very nice. Beautiful."

Carly peered down at Sophie. "That tri-color gold rope gives your diamond ear studs a lovely sparkle. It's very effective."

"Thank you, Miss Truitt. The necklace was a gift from my mother. Along with the rest of me." Sophie's chin was aimed just below Carly's neck.

Adams cleared his throat and said, "I'll get us fresh drinks, ladies." He backed away, got tangled up with Kasim homing in on Sophie, and paused long enough to watch Kasim produce his card and get a Pentagon card in return. Kasim studied it and asked for Sophie's home number, saying he was often in Washington and would just *love* to take her to lunch. Or dinner.

Wearing her "polite face," Sophie replied she seldom left her office during the day, including weekends, and rarely went out evenings. Kasim reddened and said he would call her office anyway, the next time he was in Washington. Moving off to the bar, Adams suppressed a strong urge to laugh.

Halfway to the bar, Adams saw that the party was rapidly winding down, so he returned and suggested they all go to Wachapreague for a nightcap on his boat. Sophie hesitated, then agreed to follow in her car.

When they reached the marina piers Ranger led the way to *Pilgrim*, his tail wagging at the prospect of a late night snack. Last on board, Adams pushed a series of circuit breakers and the long white boat sighed into life. They shed coats in the main lounge and Adams mixed drinks: two Martinis and "a very small vodka tonic." He dimmed lamps and toggled up music on hidden Bose speakers.

"...She's nobody's fool so I'm playing it cool...." Duke Ellington's *Satin Doll* was honey filling the cabin and flowing across the deck. Boats around them rocked to the slow Atlantic rhythm, and reflections of shore lights danced in reedy shallows along the inlet. For a moment, Adams, Carly and Sophie were lost in Ellington's magic. Then Sophie broke the spell.

"You've been on furlough for a month, Jeremiah. It is time you came back to your office to empty drawers and box up souvenirs. Either that, or you must stand up against the nonsense in the Secretary's office. I'll help you tape your cartons, or I'll help you feed the bureaucrats a large measure of common sense."

Carly was perched on the arm of a couch, Adams standing beside her. They were looking at the deep blue of the eastern horizon. Adams rocked on his heels in time to the music and finally answered.

"Sophie, these past weeks are the first long holiday I've had in more than two years. Maybe I should thank Beauchamps. Anyway, there's at least another month before my lease on the office is up, so there's no real rush. I'll get around to it. Maybe I'll start on it next week. Besides, you're handling communications as if I was sitting at my desk full time." He turned from the window to face the petite blonde. "You don't need me in the building, do you? Why can't we keep on the way we've been going?"

Sophie crossed the cabin, opened her purse, handed Adams a calling card and watched him read it. Under the seal of the Department of Defense was printed, "Ms. Sophie Giltspur, Executive Assistant, Office of the Secretary of Defense," and under that the suite number of the Secretary's office.

"Secretary Horton sent me those cards and asked me to be his assistant, Jeremiah. I told him I would take the position unless you returned to work next week. And I'd like another drink, please." Adams looked up from the card. Then he put it into his breast pocket, took her glass and walked to the bar.

"Horton and Beauchamps aren't teenagers, Sophie. They can run the shop."

"The Secretary is having trouble catching up with our on-going operations. He understands policy, but he is not very familiar with our capabilities. He needs help in planning."

"That's tough. All I want to do now is wind down current ops and make sure the good guys get home alive. New stuff belongs to new management." He handed Sophie her drink. "Look, Carly and I are planning to go out fishing tomorrow. We've got two cabins, and there's a bed for me here in the lounge, so we can all spend the night on *Pilgrim*. I'll take us out before dawn and when you guys wake up, we'll be in tuna country. I'll have us back for a late lunch, if you like. How about it? We can talk some more on the way out, or in, or both. Okay?"

Sophie glanced at Carly, who still studied the dark horizon.

"I think I'll go back to Washington now, Jeremiah. It's a long drive, so I shouldn't have this drink." She put her glass in the wet sink.

"Oh damn it, Sophie. Here." Adams snapped his key ring open and handed her a key. "Too late to drive to D.C. You'd fall asleep before you reached Salisbury. If you don't want to go boating, at least stay at the Hermitage tonight and then leave early in the morning. The alarm code is our office number plus two. Clean sheets and towels in both guestrooms. Please do it, Sophie. We can talk in the morning, over breakfast."

Sophie took the key. "Thank you for being so thoughtful. I'll put the sheets in your laundry bin before I go." She looked down at Ranger, who was sprawled on the carpet, looking from face to face.

"May I take him with me?"

"Sure. We'll be along in a few minutes."

She faced Carly and said, "It was a pleasure to meet you, Miss Truitt. I'll be on my way long before the breakfast hour, so I'll try not to awaken anyone when I leave. Goodnight." Gesturing at Ranger to follow, she was gone. They listened to her car drive away.

Adams slumped in a wide upholstered chair and downed the dregs of his Martini. What does Sophie hope that I'll do, he wondered. Does she think that I'd kiss Beauchamps' butt so I can work for a few more weeks? Suddenly, he was annoyed by the whole circus and pushed it out of his mind. He drifted on the music again.

Carly kicked off her shoes and crossed the cabin to Adams' chair. She sat in his lap, rested her head on his chest and said, "This is nice, Jay." She looked into his eyes and then traced the crease in his trousers from his knee to his belt. "Will we really be along in a few minutes?"

Lost in Carly's perfume, Adams felt himself surge against the thighs on his lap. He started to press his mouth to her breasts, but she gently pulled his head away. Turning to face him, she unbuttoned the silk blouse and arched her back.

Adams saw the delicate web of veins under her translucent skin. When his tongue touched the hard points of her nipples she ran her hand along his thigh.

Reaching under her, Adams picked her up and walked to the big bed in the forward cabin.

CHAPTER 16

Supper was unhurried in the empty Tabriz University dining hall, the plentiful food eaten in silence. Staff members at the table with the Professor and Jabber were pensive, avoiding their eyes. There had been no graduation ceremony before dinner, just a formal acknowledgement and a handshake from each of the 'Mohammed' instructors.

When the meal ended, the Professor and Jabber stepped into the entrance hall and were blindfolded, as they always were when taken outside the training buildings. Led to a Land Rover with blacked-out windows, they were locked inside. The two students were very valuable now. They had metamorphosed into weapons primed for an attack on America, the Great Satan itself.

It was a short drive to the helicopter pad inside the university perimeter. Helped from the Land Rover like blind men, the Professor and Jabber heard the familiar whistling beat of rotor blades and grunts and commands of people loading equipment. Airborne, they sensed they were rising very rapidly into the cooling night air. Then they felt the helicopter make swinging turns, orbiting, and then accelerating again. They could not know they paused for clearance from the air defense system around Tabriz, and had acquired a fighter escort that ceaselessly circled above them as they tracked southward.

Three hours passed. Jabber's complaints about his blindfold were answered only by the racketing blades above the dark cabin. Suddenly, a guard tugged off their blinkers. They were surprised to see the side windows of this helicopter had not been blacked out, and that they could make out lights of a town below. Then they were startled by flashing wingtip lights of a jet aircraft that materialized alongside. With a quick waggle of its wings the warplane disappeared, and the helicopter began a steep descent to a small airport.

On the ground, they were greeted by the usual armed guards and lack of answers to questions. But there were no blindfolds. They saw rope-handled wooden boxes containing the weapons they knew so well being trundled into a blue and white turboprop marked with insignia of the Iranian navy. Finally, through clouds of foggy breath, they watched the helicopter that had brought them lift off. A crewman in a naval uniform politely ushered them into the Dornier, and the Professor and Jabber buckled themselves into comfortable seats. Engines groaned and whined, their white-tipped props beginning to turn.

"You'll be glad to be out of this frozen cesspit, surely." The guard's Arabic was heavily accented.

"What cesspit?" Jabber peered suspiciously at the sailor.

"This dump. Bakhtaran. Now we go to a decent place. In summer it's hot as my Russian girlfriend's ass, but it's a great town anyway. Sailors' paradise." He grinned at their blank expressions.

"Bandar Abbas, you clowns! The jewel of the Gulf! We get there in three hours. All the hotels will be closed when we arrive, but if they billet you in our barracks I'll make sure you get a welcoming drink... not orange juice." He winked broadly. "There are other entertainments, too."

Jabber's scowl deepened, and the Professor nodded. Had it been Iran after all? During the weeks of training he often speculated they were in Pakistan or Afghanistan, but the "Mohammed" instructors could have come from anywhere. No matter. The Professor took the cup of juice offered by the sailor, drank deeply, and settled into his seat.

I am the hammer of vengeance, my dear wife and son. Soon I fall on your murderers.

Submarine Piers
Bandar Abbas Naval Base

When he spotted the truck heading toward his pier, Captain Reza stopped pacing on the cramped bridge atop the sail of *Yunes*. The camouflaged vehicle eased down the dock, stopped alongside, and four sailors jumped off the tailgate. Two figures emerged from the cab and joined them. Just as he had been told, there was a tall man and a smaller companion. Two wooden boxes and an aluminum case were offloaded from the truck, and then two bulky black shapes. The inflatable boats, he thought. Yes, there were the propeller shafts of outboard motors.

"Chief," Reza called down to the deck, "strike that cargo below immediately. See the passengers find their bunks in the forward torpedo room. Be sure the Master at Arms instructs them what to do and not to do, and that he relieves them of all weapons they have on their persons or in their bags. Escort them to my cabin after we are underway." He returned the Chief's salute. The officers and the non-commissioned officers on *Yunes* had been briefed on the lethality of their "passengers," but it did not hurt to remind them to be careful.

"Oh, another thing, Chief Ali." The Captain saw his Chief of the Boat look up again. "Once all hands are below, be sure our passengers are trained in water conservation and how to use the head. We don't want problems with fresh water—or toilet water—when we're running submerged. And there will be no pranks by the crew. Those men are not farm boy recruits."

Smiling this time, Chief Ali Shamkani saluted the bridge on the sail with a loud, "Aye, sir!"

The Captain returned the salute and turned to his Executive Officer, standing close beside him and observing the activity on the deck below.

"Let's line up the diesels and get underway immediately, Exec. I want to clear Qeshm Island before first light."

"Aye, aye, sir."

The executive officer's orders rang out on the intercom: "Now hear this. Set the engineering watch. Prepare to start engines."

Then came, "Set the special sea and anchor detail. Watch standers report to the bridge. All departments report readiness to get underway."

The exec noted the replies to his commands, turned to Reza and said, "Engineering and all departments report ready, captain."

"Very well, Esqual. I hear the lookouts coming up the ladder. Take us out."

The exec shouted to the crewmen waiting below, "Single up all lines. Stand by to cast off."

Captain Reza turned to look at the dark harbor mouth, and felt the last of the bridge watch move past him to their posts on the bridge. Moonset was two hours ago, and darkness enveloped the submarine like a black shroud. Soon he will move *Yunes* from her berth and slide her stubby bow into the Persian Gulf.

He knew the watchers will find them in the sunlight of the coming day. *Yunes* would be running on the surface when they would sight her, miles from the deep waters of the Gulf of Oman. Probably an Omani patrol boat would be first. But it will be quite another story when he no longer wished to be seen.

Koucheh Bahzorgeh

On the surface under diesel power, charging her batteries, Yunes was well into the Strait of Hormuz when Major Doctor Suleiman was ushered into Morteza Dehesh's library. Air conditioners labored behind heavy brocade curtains, and although it was noon on an unseasonably warm day, the library was shadowed and cold.

Sitting erect behind an ornately carved and gilt-encrusted desk, Dehesh waved the doctor into the seat opposite him and dismissed the hovering guard. Then he motioned for the doctor to choose from among the bottles and glasses on the low table next to his chair. Suleiman selected pomegranate juice and carefully poured it into a crystal goblet.

"So, we have finally begun. Is it not so, Major?" Suleiman saw Dehesh's eyes search his face, and thought that his smile seemed strangely fixed, almost comical.

"Yes, Excellency. The men, the weapons, and those rubber boats left Tabriz last night on a helicopter, just as your assistant instructed." Starting to wilt under Dehesh's penetrating stare and bared teeth, the doctor hoped he looked attentively calm as he tasted his sweet drink.

Dehesh's smile widened even more, and he leaned forward, his dark eyes glittering. "You understand how beautifully our plan has been crafted, do you not, Major Doctor?"

Suleiman uneasily lifted a shoulder, avoiding the eyes across the desk.

"Ah, but how could you? My dear doctor, I must apologize for all the secrecy. But now that our messengers are safely underway, you must be told how clever we've been. The wonderful details. After all, no one in Iran is more able than you to assess the carnage our attacks will cause—though the American media will be sure to tell us everything we'll ever want to know." Dehesh poured himself a glass of chilled white port.

"Simplicity is always best, don't you agree?" He ran his tongue around the edge of his cold goblet. "You know, of course, all the weapons originate in Russia, so they can't be traced to us. You also know the small nuclear weapon is enough to destroy the heart of a city, and the other weapons can kill tens of thousands. Perhaps millions. And you know the two Palestinian agents may think they were trained in Iran, but they cannot be sure. Unless you gave them reason to think otherwise?" Dehesh's eyebrows rose slightly. "I am advised one of those men is quite clever."

"Yes, he is well-educated, Excellency. But they were isolated at Tabriz University. Instructors did not mingle with them after classes. GPS training was carefully monitored, and I am sure they were not able to fix their position. They might even believe they were at a school in Afghanistan, or Turkey." The doctor did his best to sound convincing.

"Excellent. We can never leave too many false trails in the tasks we undertake. But in any event, it now matters little what your students believed in Tabriz." He paused for effect. "Because they are now at sea on one of our submarines!"

The uniformed doctor opposite Dehesh froze, his eyes blank and his face without expression.

Smiling, Dehesh lifted the fragile port glass and added, "We just received confirmation from Bandar Abbas that the historic voyage to America has begun. Soon the entire world will watch Americans suffer and die, and there will be nothing to connect it to us." He could not contain his triumph. "Perfect!"

Doctor Suleiman felt paralyzed when he heard the word "submarine," but he was still able to stutter, "Very clever. Indeed. Clever. Excellency." *My God! A submarine?*

"And in case you are not completely sure of our invisibility, doctor, you should also know the man who meets the Palestinians in America is one of my best officers. He will liquidate the men when their tasks are finished so they can never tell anyone how they brought such death to America." Dehesh cocked his head in an unspoken question and waited for Suleiman to speak.

"You've thought of everything, Excellency. I am sure it will be a great victory for our nation."

Behind his rapidly blinking eyes, Suleiman's mind was racing. *This madman has done it! He has launched the weapons against America. By all that is holy, he sent them on a submarine! Could the Americans stop it before it arrived? How soon could a message reach his doctor friend in the United States?* Suleiman was focused on a place far beyond Dehesh's cold eyes. He was calculating the earliest time he could return to his home in Tabriz, to the computer waiting there.

Dehesh leaned back in his chair. "I see by your expression you are stunned, major." He regarded Suleiman over his glass as he drank. "That is good. It tells me how surprised the Americans will be."

He raised a forefinger and pointed at the doctor, "While we wait for the great day of revenge to arrive, you and your family will visit Tehran as a reward for your diligent work. You will be my personal guests at the Esteghlal Grand Hotel for three weeks. All expenses paid. Your wife and son will enjoy the delights of the capital, and the research center at Damghan is at your disposal, should you need a laboratory.

"As we have done many times in the past, my people and I will work closely with you, doctor, every day. I want to help you advance all your special projects at Tabriz University and at Damghan. So, my personal driver will take you to the hotel now, and you can telephone Naila and Jamshid from your suite while you enjoy a celebratory lunch." Dehesh leaned back and beamed at his silent guest.

This monster knows the names of my wife and child! And I must visit him every day for three weeks. It will be impossible to find a private computer for an email to America without being observed.

"It's a privilege and an honor, Excellency," Suleiman said. "You are most generous to me and my family, and I look forward to working closely with you on my projects and research. Yes. A great privilege. And an honor."

A submarine! How long does it take for such a ship to sail halfway around the world? The first day he could get to Tabriz was three weeks away. Would there be enough time to stop a submarine?

Dehesh was talking, but his voice seemed to fade. It hummed and became a faint buzzing background for the single thought swirling in the doctor's mind.

Three weeks.

CHAPTER 17

Port Said,
Mediterranean Sea

Captain Jamshid Bakhtiar Reza was elated. *Yunes*, his magnificent submarine, had completed a night transit of the Suez Canal and was now on the surface, surging northwest into the calm waters of the Mediterranean. On the bridge, he looked into the darkness astern and saw the distant glow of Port Said, then he smiled at the huge Chief of the Boat.

"Chief Ali, the crew has performed to my highest expectations. I congratulate you and the officers. Thanks to you all, we've made a faultless voyage of over three thousand miles and, in a few days, we will see the Straits of Gibraltar and the Atlantic. Not one mechanical casualty. Not one operational error. Not even a sick crewman. Yes, we *can* do it, chief."

The big sailor thought about the tests yet to come in the Atlantic. Then he matched his captain's happy smile and said, "I'm proud to serve with you, sir. And so say all the men."

Reza had forged a passionate bond with his submarine. After participating in sea trials when *Yunes* was delivered, Reza returned to Russia twice for advanced training aboard Russian KILO submarines. He even suggested changes to standard operating procedures that, to his amazement, the Russians adopted. His personal library in Bandar Abbas contained more books on submarine warfare than all the other military libraries in the Middle East—combined. He packed himself with every scrap of submarine lore he could find.

The cool morning breeze freshened from the west, and Reza settled his cap firmly on his head. Besides superstitions shared by all submariners, Reza had only one visible idiosyncrasy. When *Yunes* was at sea he wore an officer's hat with a white cap cover, the unwritten prerogative of the old German U-boat commanders.

He adopted the white cap because his hero was Kapitanleutnant Reinhard Hardegen, commander of the famed U-123, the most daring and successful submarine commander in the German Ubootwaffe. Though life aboard those early submarines was primitive compared to *Yunes*, his crew still conserved fresh water and did not bathe or shave when at sea. So with his white cap, deep-set eyes, dark beard, and surrounded by the scruffy bridge lookouts, Reza could be Hardegen's twin.

Submarines in the 1940s were essentially submersible torpedo boats, so they performed better on the surface than underwater. *Yunes*, however, was a streamlined true submersible, and her maximum underwater speed was a brisk seventeen knots, almost twice her surface speed. Nevertheless, as long as his planned speed of advance was not threatened and the sea was calm, Reza ran on the surface a few hours every day and rotated the crew through fresh air bridge watches. He was using the long trip around the Arabian Peninsula and across the Mediterranean as a training cruise for the Atlantic crossing, slowly decreasing time on the surface each day. After departing Lisbon, they would be submerged for the entire Atlantic transit, charging batteries by running the diesels through the snorkel mast for long hours every day, day after day.

"Lieutenant Mostashar, you may take the conn." Reza's comment signaled his intention to leave the bridge and climb down to the control room. The young lieutenant moved forward on the bridge and saluted.

"You know the situation, lieutenant. Course 286, making ten knots on two engines. We are on planned course and speed, and at our planned position. There are two contacts, Alfa bearing 140 drifting right, and Bravo at 250 drifting left. Radar and ESM manned, with radar on continuous sweep. Four men on the bridge. You, me, and the two lookouts. No one is on the weather decks. Any questions?"

"No, captain."

"Very well. You have the deck. Don't hesitate to send for me."

Another exchange of salutes, and Reza eased through the bridge hatch and down the long ladder into the control room, pulling up the red-lens goggles dangling from his neck. He wanted to keep his night vision in case he had to return to the bridge before dawn.

The executive officer of *Yunes* was as short and wiry as his captain, and very taciturn. Navigator for the voyage, Lieutenant Commander Esqual Saduqi was bent over his plotting table when Reza dropped off the ladder, crossed the control room, looked over Saduqi's shoulder, and asked, "How's the fuel state, Esqual?"

Saduqi pulled a slim folder across the table and answered, "Engineering's latest colorful artistry, sir. Good rate of expenditure. Barring casualties we arrive Lisbon in good shape. Nomograph on top."

Reza opened the binder and studied the graphs. Glancing at Saduqi, he whispered, "You do understand making Lisbon from Bandar Abbas without refueling is a critical rehearsal for the long transit?" Besides the chief of the boat, Reza had told no one except his executive officer and engineering officer about the Atlantic crossing. "Precise fuel monitoring is essential, Esqual. And with these red-lens goggles, I can't see one of engineering's damn red lines."

Saduqi looked up from the plotting table with a rare smile. "Back to black, sir."

Reza chuckled, returned the binder to Saduqi, and hung his white cap in its usual place—a hook welded to the periscope housing.

"Fat Hassan should have breakfast underway in a few hours, exec. I trust you'll join me?" Again intent on the plotting table, Saduqi nodded. Long accustomed to the laconic nature of his second in command, Reza nodded in return and moved aft toward the galley and engine spaces.

The cook, Hassan Mostafar, was tall and lean, so military humor required the crew to nickname him, "Fat Hassan." He was always laughing at his own jokes, and his good humor was a pillar of morale on the submarine, not to mention his skill in the galley.

Before *Yunes* departed Bandar Abbas the spare torpedoes in the forward torpedo room were removed, leaving only those inside the six tubes. This made more room for food, water, and for the two passengers with their bulky equipment. Now, after three thousand miles, most of the fresh provisions were gone, though the fifty-five men on board were still far from exhausting the stores of frozen and dehydrated food.

The captain leaned into the galley and saw the Professor standing next to the cook, chopping potatoes and peppers with a large stainless steel knife.

"So, Fat Hassan, what delights are you preparing for breakfast? You and your unauthorized assistant."

"Captain!" Hassan's narrow face somehow found enough fat for deep dimples. "The Professor created an omelet that makes dehydrated eggs taste wonderful! He's a good chef, and he's very smart. He even knows some words in Farsi. Did you know he was a chef?" The cook laughed.

"No, Hassan, I did not know he was a chef." Reza cocked his head at the Professor and addressed him in Arabic.

"You were assigned to clean the galley because everyone on *Yunes* works while they are aboard, even passengers. You were not assigned to be a cook."

"I understand your reasoning, captain, though I'm not so sure my fellow passenger is overjoyed with cleaning up grease in the engine room." The Professor did not look up from his rapid slicing. "From each according to his ability, and to each according to his needs. A commendable philosophy, until one tries to apply it to the fields of economics and politics. Or to life in general."

"He was given a job commensurate with his lack of nautical skills, Professor, as were you." There was a meaningful pause. "And what else have you revealed to Hassan about yourself, besides your *nom de guerre* and your expertise with knives?"

Hassan spoke only a few words of Arabic, and he looked back and forth, sensing tension between the captain and the Professor.

"Only that I can cook, captain. If I hadn't explained I knew what to do with a pot and a chopping block, my friend Fat Hassan would never graduate me from scraping plates. And I would be eating green eggs for days."

The captain tried not to look relieved. No one in the crew knew the mission of the two passengers, or the nature of the deadly cargo they brought aboard *Yunes*. It had to stay that way until they were safely away from the American coast. The crew will learn about the nature of the attack on America from radio and television soon enough.

"Is your comrade still unhappy about the lack of daily prayers on this warship?"

Knife in midair, the Professor looked up from his chopping block. "I reminded my colleague that our *mursid* gave dispensation from daily prayer while we were at sea. The cleric explained that Allah can see into the hearts of the devout, where no man can see, and only He will judge our intentions, whatever our success in the *jihad*. The *mursid* told us we can concern ourselves with prayer when we reach land." The Professor resumed slicing peppers. "I also explained to my small associate that you would not turn the submarine toward Mecca five times a day."

"How do *you* feel about it, Professor?" Reza spoke softly.

Although he did not understand much of the conversation, the undercurrents in it disturbed Hassan, and he continued to watch the two men intently.

"I have a mission, and I must succeed. *That* is what's important, captain, and that is the only thing I feel."

Reza slowly nodded and then added a smile. He understood dedication and resolve, whether he saw it in a sailor or a civilian. Or in a terrorist.

"Chess after dinner, Professor? May I call you Professor?"

"Chess, if that is your pleasure, captain." The rhythmic chopping went on. "And as for Professor, I have answered to that name for many weeks."

The atmosphere in the galley brightened. Reza clapped the visibly relieved Hassan on his bony shoulder, and started toward the engine room.

"Aircraft! Aircraft! Patrol aircraft approaching! Captain to the bridge!" The loudspeakers carried Lieutenant Mostashar's voice throughout the submarine.

Anticipating a call to general quarters, two crewmen folded a board game and left the small recreation area, jumping aside to avoid the captain sprinting to the control room. Reza snatched his cap from the periscope housing and raced up the ladder to the bridge. Bracing himself next to the lookouts, he pushed the red goggles away from his face and scanned the sky.

Still a mile from *Yunes*, Italian Air Force Colonel Ugo de Poggi looked down at his prey. Commander of the 41st Stormo, 88th Gruppo based at Sigonella, he had ordered one of his Breguet *Atlantique* patrol planes to fly a training mission to Cyprus, and had joined the crew for what he called, "a personal refresher patrol." Actually, he wanted to fly the first NATO aircraft to meet the Iranian submarine reported to be transiting the Suez Canal. The message from Naples giving the submarine's position had arrived just in time for a pre-dawn interception off Port Said.

After an overnight stay in Larnaca, de Poggi drank a four o'clock morning espresso, kissed his sleeping Cypriot girlfriend, smoothed his uniform, and carefully placed his cap over salt-and-pepper hair. Then he drove an ancient Ferrari back to the airfield to check on the latest position of the KILO and to brief his crew for the patrol to Port Said.

Now there she was, a mile away, running on the surface.

"All right, TACCO, set up for a smoke-light and a buoy on your mark on top. She'll dive soon to get out of sight, and I don't want to lose her. Let's get some good sound data and earn our flight pay."

De Poggi approached the long wake of the submarine and pushed his turboprop aircraft into a graceful moaning descent. As he sped toward the submarine, he grinned when he heard the *Atlantique's* squealing radar altimeter. He was flying below 100 feet.

"In culo della balena!"

De Poggi's cheerful slogan was familiar to every crew in his command, and on this moonless night it looked as if he might really be flying into that whale's asshole.

"Standby! Mark on top in ten seconds!"

The TACCO was glued to his radar display, watching the range to the surface target close. Unlike the cockpit crew, he could not see the long phosphorescent wake of the submarine lengthen as its propeller churned through underwater clouds of Mediterranean photoplankton.

Lacking a distinct horizon, De Poggi set the radar altimeter to fifty feet and used the glowing scar in the sea behind *Yunes* to fine-tune his approach.

"Captain, what are they *doing*?" Chief Ali watched the aircraft descend, level out, and then race toward them along the glowing wake. The distance was closing very fast. "Look how low they are!"

The captain said nothing. When the aircraft thundered by, a few feet over their heads, he was the only man on the bridge who did not flinch and duck. Instead, he lifted his stabilized night vision binoculars and muttered, "Italian."

The crouching lookouts straightened in time to see two cylinders flash by and splash in front of the bow. One bobbed up burning, and began to trail a thin streamer of white smoke.

"Left full rudder! Lookouts, keep your eyes on that burning marker."

The submarine made a complete 360 degree turn and slowed near the drop point. Above, the patrol plane climbed away and was starting a wide circle. Reza glanced at the flashing wingtip lights, and then addressed the bridge watch.

"All stop. Lookouts, near that burning marker-buoy there is a metal cylinder with a light and an antenna on its top. Find it!"

Sure enough, bobbing ten yards ahead of the marker buoy was an aluminum cylinder sporting a meter-long antenna and a small electric light.

"Chief, maneuver alongside that smoke buoy. Have a lookout get down to the weather deck with a boat hook and snag the cylinder with the antenna. Make sure he is careful not to lose the hydrophones on the cable attached to its underside. Then he is to take it below. Quickly now."

In the aircraft above, Colonel de Poggi was gasping with laughter. He caught his breath and banked the aircraft sharply, beginning another descending turn.

"Skipper, the buoy was transmitting okay, and we got a few lines, but it went dead." The patrol plane TACCO was puzzled. "Set up for another drop?"

"Screw that." De Poggi was laughing again. "They'd probably steal our garbage if we dropped it close enough. Set up for a drop eight hundred meters northwest of their course. I'm making this pass just to get a look at that smart-ass *bastardo* with the white hat."

CHAPTER 18

Snuggling into bright blue rubber fenders, *Yunes* tied up alongside *Polyus*. The depot ship had docked two days earlier to await the submarine's arrival in Lisbon harbor. Captain Reza watched the sub's deck detail double up her mooring lines and secure the gangway between the two vessels. His crew could now rest, and his command would have a much needed cleaning and replenishment of fuel and supplies.

Reza had driven *Yunes* an astounding five thousand nautical miles from Bandar Abbas in just twenty-two days, and even with dive drills and relentless training he docked in Lisbon on schedule. Except for Jabber's constant grumbling, everyone on board the submarine had performed their tasks cheerfully and flawlessly, and for two days and nights their grateful captain would give them as much rest and relaxation as possible. He stood with his senior non-commissioned officer on the bridge, and they assessed what they could see of the port city.

"Secure the special sea and anchor detail."

"Aye aye, sir."

"When our comrades on *Polyus* finish admiring our beards, have the crew board her in groups of ten for showers, haircuts, and hot meals. They will take all laundry and bedding with them for replacement. Not washing. Replacement. When our first group is away, welcome the *Polyus* inspector and bring him to me in the wardroom."

Be sure to have Fat Hassan's shopping list. We'll review the lists for food, spares and repairs before I pay my compliments to the captain of *Polyus*."

Reza used his binoculars on the harbor front again, and continued his orders.

"All hands, except the passengers, have liberty ashore as planned. Passengers remain in the forward torpedo room until the visitors from *Polyus* leave. Advise the Master at Arms they will be confined to my quarters after that, and until repairs and replenishment are completed." Returning the chief's salute, he climbed down the ladder into the control room. His shower and shave could come later. The first thing he must do is prepare his command for its coming test.

Reza mentally reviewed the plan for the hundredth time. The day after tomorrow, *Yunes* will depart Lisbon and proceed north to the scheduled overhaul in Russian yards. She would make that appointment all right, but she would be twenty-eight days late. First, after veering west along middle Atlantic latitudes, she would travel three thousand nautical miles from Lisbon to the Virginia coast. *Yunes* would surface there and put her passengers ashore. Then, staying in the middle of busy and noisy North Atlantic shipping lanes, she would return to a point near Brest, where *Polyus* would be waiting. Besides the night of the landing, they would remain submerged—all the way to America and back.

Later, sitting in the cramped wardroom with his Executive Officer, Chief Engineer, Chief of the Boat, and the head maintenance officer from *Polyus*, Reza sipped his tea, basking in a profound sense of satisfaction his submarine and crew had given him during the past three weeks. After that heroic voyage, however, the submarine stank.

The fug that pervaded *Yunes* was a mixture of cooking smells, human smells, battery smells, motor smells and, above all, the smell of diesel fuel. Living with it, day after day, was one of the many things that Reza and the crew accepted and ignored. That did not mean they liked it.

The lieutenant commander from *Polyus* wrinkled his nose. Then belly laughs rocked his considerable girth and matching jowls.

"By Khamenei's beard! No, by *your* beard, captain, this tub stinks! What a smell." His friendly grin disappeared when none of the others in the wardroom smiled.

"That smell, lieutenant commander, is the first item on our list of requirements," said Reza. "You will send a cleaning crew here immediately. While your mechanics begin a meticulous check of our batteries, motors, and other equipment, I want you to make this vessel smell like your girlfriend's best perfume. You will replace mattresses and anything else that may have absorbed odors. Painting is not required, since it will not dry properly before we depart. Disinfectant spray and careful scrubbing will be satisfactory. Also, pull the torpedoes from the forward tubes and check each one carefully. Then return them to ready status in the tubes."

The third-most senior officer on *Polyus* stiffened perceptibly. "Any other special care you'd like us to give your rare fighting machine, captain?"

In the deepening silence, Reza leveled a long stare at the visiting officer. "You're aware of the priority status of this vessel and crew, are you not, lieutenant commander?" The roly-poly officer nodded.

"No head shakes. Speak up, lieutenant commander."

"I am aware, captain."

"Good. Stay aware. Here is a list of foodstuffs. Hassan, here, understands the exact nature of our requirements. He is ready to answer questions and supervise loading. If *Polyus* does not have the food we need, send a provisioning petty officer ashore with Hassan and buy it in the local markets. Also, our water storage tanks will be emptied, carefully cleaned, checked, and refilled. My engineering department's first petty officer will supervise that task." Reza paused to take another piece of paper from the tabletop.

"Here is a list of spares and consumables we will review at our first department head conference on *Polyus* this afternoon. Meantime, your maintenance crews will examine our batteries under the personal supervision of my Chief Engineer. The same goes for the motors and auxiliary pumps and compressors. And here's a list of all the other inspections and maintenance that will be done, from electrics to electronics, and from periscope to pisspot.

"We have less than two days to refit, so I want you here with me all during that time. You and I will work closely with both our crews until we cast off. Am I clear, lieutenant commander?"

"You are very clear, captain. May I make a suggestion, sir?" The rotund officer now spoke carefully.

"Of course."

"Why not have us follow you to the Russian shipyard, refueling and maintaining you on the way? We can easily match your best surface speed, and it would be good training for us all."

"Normally, that would be a fine idea. But as you must have been told, we are on an endurance voyage to simulate a war patrol far from Bandar Abbas. We will not be on the surface for long, if at all. And remember, the world will be watching this test of *Yunes* and of *Polyus*, her support ship. I know you and your crew will not let us down."

Looking into the intense gaze of the submarine commander, the chief maintenance officer of *Polyus* rubbed his jaw in silence. Then he hastily said, "Everything you ask will be done, captain, to the best of our ability."

Reza managed a thin smile. "I cannot ask more of you. So, if that is all for now, I'd like to see how my crew is preparing for their adventure in Portugal, and then wash my stink off. I'll remain aboard *Yunes* for the next two days except for a few walks on the pier. All of you, never hesitate to ask me anything, night or day. Questions? No? Then you're dismissed, with my thanks." They all rose, and Reza motioned to his senior chief.

"Chief Ali, I remind you that our two special crew members must be properly looked after until I can monitor them myself. See that they wear proper navy uniforms."

The chief saluted in reply, and Reza watched the group of men file out. His desire for a long hot shower was so intense it was almost sexual.

CHAPTER 19

While Captain Reza of *Yunes* was being piped aboard submarine depot ship *Polyus* on a sunny Lisbon afternoon, toiletry kit under his arm, five time zones to the west Jeremiah Adams and Carly Truitt were already showering.

Despite Adams' pleas, Carly had refused to move in with him, saying, "It's too far from my office Popeye, and besides, what would the neighbors think?" But they had spent the night before on the floor of the Hermitage's 'great room,' laughing under blankets in front of the huge brick fireplace.

"What the hell? Did you take my soap out of here, Carly?" Adams' growl filled the doorway of an upstairs bathroom. He saw Carly appear in the doorway of the opposite bathroom, steam swirling around her toweled head, her nude body a study in white and pale pink. *That's what Rossini was after when he painted Alexa Wilding!*

"Why sir, whatever do you mean? Here, have *my* soap!" Adams danced aside to avoid the bar she threw across the corridor.

It was first light on a clear Delmarva morning, and Carly's Porsche would soon be bolting up Route 13 to her office at the *Daily Times* of Salisbury. Founded in 1886, the *Times* was now owned by Gannett Publishing, like many other county newspapers bought up by the giant company. Carly was proud her name was still on the masthead as "President & Editor." When she sold the Truitt family interest to keep the paper alive, she fought to keep a small amount of stock and her title, saying, "Either this Truitt stays as big momma, or the paper dies a sad death." After she won a Pulitzer for a series on corruption in southern Maryland, Gannett was happy to have lost that battle.

Wrapped in a bulky Okinawa bathrobe with the obligatory tiger embroidered on the back, Adams was making his special brew of Jamaican Blue Mountain coffee when Carly joined him. In the new morning light, her dark umber suit and tan silk shirt were perfect complements to the kitchen's brick and wood decor. Watching her walk across the room, Adams pulled a basket of croissants out of the warming oven and marveled that every time he saw her was still the first time. *She belongs here with me.*

"No time for breakfast, cookie. Gotta get over to the shop and make sure last night's party makes Sunday's gossip column."

"Bullshit, Carly." Ranger barked his agreement. "There's no reason the boss of a well-trained outfit should be on deck twenty-four hours every day. The newspaper's not at war. Now sit down over there, drink coffee, eat a delicious yesterday's croissant, and give me a few more minutes to look at those long legs."

Carly draped her clothes bag over a chair. "Such a silver-tongued devil, Jay Adams. You and your hairy brown sidekick know just the right words to charm a girl." Her fingertips touched his cheek with a phantom caress, and then she sat at the place he set for her at the refectory table. Taking a bite of buttered croissant she returned Adams' stare. He was sprawled on the other side of the table, enjoying the way the morning light made a fiery halo of her hair.

Breaking into a grin, Carly absently reached into her purse and rummaged for a silver pill box. Shaking two tablets into her hand, she tossed them into her mouth and followed them with a sip of coffee.

"What's that stuff you're taking?"

"Dope." Carly was suddenly aware of the little box and dropped it into her purse. "It eases the pain of being away from you all day, sailor."

"C'mon. I've seen you pop those pills every morning."

"No you haven't. Anyway, they're vitamins and stuff for ladies. None of your business, nosey."

"Oh. Sorry." Adams flushed.

"You can be such a darling." She flashed the smile Adams treasured, and he brightened perceptibly. They sat that way until she drank the last of her coffee and suddenly rose. Standing behind her chair, she leaned forward and looked closely at Adams. "I like playing house with you, Jay."

He smiled broadly. "Me too."

"Do you love me, Jay?"

Adams' mouth worked silently. He got up, walked slowly around the table, and stopped just before he reached her. Carly was perfectly still, waiting.

"Damn, Carly, what a question. Of course I do."

"Tell me."

"What?"

Carly did not reply. Adams felt light-headed.

"You know I love you, Carly. With everything in me, I love you."

"I love you too, Jay. Never, ever doubt that."

They stood an arm's length apart, looking into each other's eyes. Then, picking up her clothes bag, she gently touched his chest and strode out of the room.

After the red Porsche disappeared Adams shifted his gaze to the creek, just visible though the woods beyond the driveway. Spring was early this year, and the trees wore the apple green of returning life. He thought about the coming day, about cleaning up fallen branches and pinecones, about the incredible mess Carly made of the guest bathroom. But most of all he just thought about her. Until the phone rang.

"I apologize for calling at such an early hour, Jeremiah," Sophie said. "And I do hope that newspaperwoman is off to her office or shopping or whatever she does to occupy her day."

Adams sighed. Carly's perfume still in the air and Sophie calls.

"No one here but field mice, a handsome Onancock redneck, and his ever-faithful dog. How're things at the five-sided doughnut? You're in pretty early for a Saturday morning."

"I'm always early on Saturdays, or have you forgotten what a real working week is all about? I'm calling now to find out if you intend to come to the Pentagon and tend to your pressing affairs. I'm also calling to ask if you've signed that letter Mr. Beauchamps gave you almost three months ago."

She sounded clipped, strange, and Adams wondered what was causing the peculiar tone in her voice. Then he said, "Sophie, a minute ago I wasn't planning to go back to the Pentagon in this lifetime. But if you say I have 'pressing affairs' that need my presence, I'll be in on Wednesday. Got a couple of things to do Monday and Tuesday. As for that resignation letter, the answer is no. I'm not even sure where the hell it is. Don't think it makes much of a difference, though, since the boss wants me to take a hike."

"You haven't sent the letter. That's good, Jeremiah, and it makes a great deal of difference. Though he's happily settled into your old office, Mr. Beauchamps mentions that letter rather often. When you come in next week, we'll sort out a few things."

"Roger. Like I said, I'll be in on Wednesday. By the way, how's life in the Secretary's office? Is the air sweeter over the River Terrace entrance?" Adams did not know why he was baiting his best friend. He felt slightly ridiculous.

"It's rewarding work. Sometimes tedious, but always rewarding. I'll see you in a few days, then. Please call as soon as it's convenient and let me know when you plan to arrive on Wednesday." She broke the connection.

Good grief, Adams thought, what the hell's eating her? Sophie would never let her new job go to her head. Whatever was bothering her, it didn't matter as much as a simple fact: she was right. Again. As always. It *was* time to get back and face whatever was lurking in the bushes.

CHAPTER 20

Eastern Atlantic Ocean
Latitude 38° 59' North—Longitude 10° 10' West

The sun was edging into the horizon. In a few minutes nightfall would paint a second black skin on *Yunes*. Even with a fresh breeze astern, spray from waves cresting the snub bow of the submarine reached as high as the bridge, and Captain Reza wiped his binocular lenses often. He looked up, high into the southern sky. It was still there.

The four-engine patrol plane had shadowed him since he cleared the Lisbon harbor breakwater. It was now two miles south, seemingly anchored to his sail by an invisible tether as it endlessly circled above. Pirouetting in the cloudless sky and illuminated by the setting sun, bright flashes reflected from its aluminum skin whenever it turned.

Reza saw the aircraft's colorful insignia when it made a low pass to take photos of *Yunes* an hour ago. A large "LA" painted on the tail and the squadron emblem identified her as an American navy patrol plane from squadron VP-5, the "Mad Foxes." His onboard library told him the squadron's home base was in Jacksonville, Florida, though this plane undoubtedly came from Rota, the Spanish base near Cadiz. They had won many awards for excellence, these Mad Foxes.

He could see that the aircraft's outboard engines were idle now, four-bladed propellers feathered. The pilot was conserving fuel, and must be planning to follow them for a long time. Reza smiled to himself in the gathering twilight. *Soon we will see just how excellent this Mad Fox might be. Very soon.*

Three thousand feet above, plane commander Keith William Patrick O'Connell leaned forward in his seat, focusing on the black shape two miles ahead, plowing north through the darkening ocean.

"Okay, TACCO, how're we doing?"

The Tactical Coordinator of the P3C-IV Orion had been monitoring the submarine's sounds since she sortied from Lisbon hours ago and had turned north to make a short trim dive. She was now back on the surface, her engine exhausts smoking profusely. O'Connell looked at the long smoke plume and listened to the wavering squeals flooding the sonobuoy hydrophones. He lowered his headset volume.

"It's a runaway steam calliope, TACCO. If that boat is even a half-assed example of the famous KILO, the best will be as easy to find as the worst."

"We don't have much trouble reading her," said the TACCO, "that's for sure. If you want more of her noise it's time to drop another buoy, but you ought to know I've recorded every squeak, rattle, and roll those diesels are making. She's one friggin' mess, Okie."

'Okie' O'Connell sucked on a cold corncob pipe as the distance to the submarine below closed. Nothing had happened for two hours. His mission was to monitor, not harass, and sonobuoys were expensive.

"Let's save the hardware," he answered. "It's a sinful waste and a pain in the ass to keep dropping them far enough away from the sub so they won't divert and pick 'em up." He had to smile as he thought of de Poggi's phone call a week ago about "that smart-ass buoy-stealing Iranian at Port Said."

"Hang in there, TACCO. Maybe they have a strong death wish, and they'll dive that black coffin again. Then we can drop a buoy and record the clang when they hit bottom."

It was 7:04 PM, and off the submarine's port beam the sun was touching the horizon. Atmospheric distortion had flattened the disk into a molten mass that looked like it would sizzle as it sank into the Atlantic. The patrol plane was almost overhead *Yunes.*

"Chief, go below and see those oily rags around the exhausts are thrown overboard. Lively, now!" Reza craned his neck to watch the plane pass overhead, and when he was sure its crew could not observe him visually, he keyed the mike for the internal speaker system.

"Engineering, secure noisemakers on the shaft. Stand by to dive!" Reza watched a crewman scramble through the after deck hatch after pitching smoldering rags over the side. He leaned into the mike again.

"Now, dive! Dive!" The lookouts scrambled down the hatch, followed by the executive officer and the captain, who pulled the hatch closed.

"Ooogah! Ooogah!" The klaxon sounded twice, and time-honored commands sang throughout *Yunes*. Reza had drilled his crew well. They could drive *Yunes* below the surface in twenty-five seconds, faster than the KILO's automatic dive system. Besides, he did not trust the Russian auto-dive technology and considered it to be a last resort, if that. What's more, he thought, for the maneuver he was about to execute, it would never do to execute a slow dive.

Sunset.

"Skipper! She's flooding ballast tanks! She's diving!" The TACCO lurched forward against the harness on his swivel chair, scanning sensor displays and pressing his earphones against his head. No doubt about it, the target was submerging.

O'Connell slammed his control yoke left and the Orion sluggishly rolled into a slow turn. "Copilot, start one and four. Hit it!"

Propellers on the outboard engines began to rotate as the 4600 shaft horsepower T-56 gas turbines awoke, their moans becoming screams. The Orion surged forward, deepening its diving turn with the added power.

"TACCO, set us up for an Alfa drop. Buoy, BT, smoke-light, the works. I'll come around to his course and we'll go for his sail, if I can see it. If there's no MAD contact, we'll drop on your best guess."

In just over two minutes the Orion was at five hundred feet, thundering toward the submarine's last known position.

"Mammy-huncher! The fucker's gone! Can't see a thing down there." Commander O'Connell peered at the dark sea below. "TACCO, speak to me! What's does FLIR say?"

In the new night's shadows, the submarine's wake and the swirl marking the spot where it submerged were invisible except, perhaps, to the Forward Looking Infrared equipment.

"Sea state is fracturing the IR return, skipper. I hold a possible surface scar along the target's last course. Standby. Standby to drop. Three, two, one, MARK!"

Two gleaming aluminum cylinders and a smoke-light arced out of the Orion as it howled over the spot the TACCO calculated to be nearest the submarine. O'Connell frowned when no signal arrived from the Magnetic Anomaly Detection equipment in the aircraft's long tail stinger. Steel in the hull of the submarine was too far away to detect. The Orion pulled into a wide circling turn to the left, and signals began to arrive from the sonobuoys.

"What've we got TACCO?"

There was a long silence as the plane charged around a circle O'Connell hoped contained the sub. The Tactical Coordinator anxiously scanned his console.

"*Nada*, skipper. Nothing from the DIFAR buoy." The TACCO was crestfallen. "The XBT shows a shallow layer at less than two hundred feet. He must've got under it before we hit datum. There's a real sharp layer at four hundred feet."

A thermistor on a wire stretching far below the SSQ-36 bathythermograph, the "BT" sonobuoy, had relayed a precise record of the temperatures of the sound reflecting layers below the sea surface. Temperature inversions were a submarine's best friend.

"Roger, TACCO. Believe the BT. Lower the DIFAR phones to four hundred feet and standby to set us up again. I want a MAD contact on that pisser."

There was another ominous silence as the patrol plane continued to circle around the flickering smoke-light that marked the datum point.

"TACCO?"

"Bad news, Okie. The CFS software is totally down. I can't move the phones. We can only drop manual-set buoys."

"Jesus wept."

The plane commander's mind raced across the options. Manually set an SSQ-62 DICASS buoy to ping at four hundred feet? What if he's below *that* layer? At a thousand feet? What if he stays *above* four hundred? Or two DIFAR buoys, one set at two hundred and one at a thousand? How about an SSQ-77 VLAD at five hundred? The plane commander forced order into his jumbling thoughts.

"Okay, TACCO. That Command Function Select failure screwed us big time. And I can't justify the expense of throwing away 62s and 77s. The CO would have my ass on a hotplate. Anyway, this fine day it's tracking we are, not harassing." O'Connell sighed and keyed the intercom again.

"We'll make three more orbits here, TACCO. If we don't get a MAD contact we'll lay a DIFAR barrier eight miles north, across his estimated course. Work up a four-buoy barrier, preset the buoy depth to alternate above and below the deep layer, and then stand by. He's got a date with a Russian yard, so he sure ain't going anywhere but north, and he can't loiter around here forever. Co-pilot, you have the conn."

O'Connell looked up from his instruments and out into the deepening darkness. He stared at the flickering smoke-light off the port wingtip and tried to visualize the submarine somewhere below.

"Say, TACCO? After we drop it, log that four-buoy barrier as essential training for CFS failure. The devil made me do it."

Three orbits later, the Orion banked sharply and moved its expanding search north of the invisible submarine.

Her racketing diesels were shut down when she dived, and silent electric motors were driving *Yunes* deep, accelerating her into the subsurface darkness. "Passing one hundred meters, sir. Steady on course 090. Speed twelve knots." Chief Ali glanced at his captain.

"Maintain twelve knots. Stay below cavitation speed. Level off at two hundred meters." Reza's eyes were closed, his head tilted back in concentration, hands pressed to each earphone of a sonar headset. In this contest, each minute was an eternity.

The hunter in the sky was still somewhere above, and Reza had twisted *Yunes* to the east, diving her toward the deep sound layer. He knew the big patrol plane would start by turning left, to the west, and by the time it arrived at the eastern edge of its circle the submarine *Yunes* would be below the layer, running silent and beyond the range of magnetic detectors. Understanding tactical doctrine of potential adversaries is essential, and Reza's intensive English studies repaid him handsomely this day.

"Level at two hundred meters, captain." Chief Ali checked the gauges showing the electric motors were drawing power from the submarine's massive banks of batteries. The seven-bladed screw silently churned the submarine eastward.

"Very well. Helm, now come right to course 275, decrease speed to ten knots. Keep silence about the boat. In a few hours we will be well clear of that aircraft and we can resume normal activities. Chief, my compliments to the dive watch for a job well done, and done in good time. Pass the word I will address all hands at 2200. It's time for the crew to know our mission. Commander Saduqi, you have the conn."

Five miles north, the Orion's TACCO glumly studied the displays arrayed in front of him and tried to visualize what the submarine was doing. It had disappeared without a trace. No screw cavitation, no machinery noise, no nothing. Even that shaft noise must have been some kind of decoy, or maybe they fixed whatever was broken. Anyway, he thought, we'll monitor the east-west sonobuoy barrier, and when he crosses it we'll get a good fix and work him over. Crafty sucker.

But *Yunes* never challenged the TACCO's carefully laid barrier of sonobuoys. Hidden under the thermocline's warm reflective layer and silently sliding west into the cold deeps, she lost herself in the crowded shipping lanes. The historic voyage across the Atlantic had begun at last.

Two and a half hours after diving, *Yunes* was twenty miles southwest of the Orion patrol plane and six hundred feet below the surface, advancing westward at a steady ten knots. It was time for Captain Reza to tell his crew they would be taking their small vessel across the Atlantic on a voyage to the shores of the United States.

"Chief, secure from silent running. It is now time to explain our mission to the crew. I will speak to all hands in ten minutes."

"Aye, captain." Chief Ali pressed the intercom transmit toggle.

"Now hear this. Secure from silent running and resume normal routine. The Captain will address the crew in ten minutes. All hands will cease non-essential activities at 2200 and stand by."

Reza remained in the control room, leaning against the console of the ANDOGA navigation computer, watching the automatic system that kept *Yunes* on course. He was comforted by the lengthening westward track, and he absently watched the plot for ten minutes as thoughts took shape in his mind. Then he stepped to the intercom.

"This is the Captain. Today we begin the mission for which we have trained every day for the past four weeks, and during the many months before we left Bandar Abbas. Our mission will take us across the Atlantic Ocean to the shores of America." He could see the wide eyes of the crewmen in the control room. He paused, waiting for his words to fully impact on the crew.

"Our mission is to deliver our two passengers and their equipment safely to America, undetected. We will then return across the Atlantic and meet *Polyus* to refuel at sea. Then we proceed to a shipyard in Russia. This challenging mission is made even more difficult because we must remain below the surface, except for the brief hours when we send our passengers ashore. The next days hold many dangers for *Yunes*.

"I have supreme confidence in each and every one of you, my shipmates. You are the best submarine crew in the Iranian Navy, or in any other navy. Now begins your greatest test, and each of you must perform your job perfectly. Each of you must be alert every moment." He paused again for emphasis.

"Remember always that this submarine is not in my hands alone. It is in the hands of every member of the crew, and our lives depend on each one of us. Whatever happens, let it be said we did our best, and that our best was truly magnificent. May the One God bless us all." Reza stepped back and Chief Ali took his place before the intercom microphone.

"All hands may now ask their officers questions about our mission. Officers will refer questions to the captain or exec, if need be. Orders that crewman and officers are absolutely forbidden to question or interfere with our passengers are still in effect. Now, return to regular routine." The hissing intercom clicked off.

After a stunned pause, every crewman not operating machinery or sensors crowded around their officers. The brains and blood of *Yunes*, her crew, seethed and bubbled with questions. But there was no fear. Unless Allah and the demons of the ocean deeps do not will it, they knew their captain would bring *Yunes* and her crew home safely.

The Professor looked up from his book. No need for him to ask about the mission.

Soon, my wife and son, soon your murderers will be your slaves in paradise.

CHAPTER 21

"Yup, real nice quarters. This classy joint really suits you." Adams looked over his shoulder at the outer office of the suite that housed the Secretary of Defense. "But the damn coffee always needs major help." After tasting it, he dumped the pot and refilled the coffee maker.

Sophie regarded Adams with her coolest and most level gaze. Dressed in a tailored dark blue knit suit, a simple diamond circle pin on her lapel, she was every inch the Executive Assistant to the Secretary of Defense.

"I'll ask Secretary Horton to put you on his personal staff as coffee steward, if you like. In the meantime, Jeremiah, drink tea. It's much healthier." She placed her bone china teacup on her uncluttered desk, took a small compact mirror from the center drawer, and began to repair her bright red lipstick.

"Why do you gals bother to do all that lipstick business? I mean, you just put it on and then smear it on a teacup. Then you break out a mirror and start it all over again."

"I'm sure you know it's rude to apply lip rouge in public, Jeremiah, but I'm doing it at my desk." She looked at Adams over the mirror and smiled. "Would you like to discuss the merits of waterproof lip gloss, perhaps? No?" She clicked the compact closed and stood. "Well then, did you have time to examine our old office? I made sure the door codes were not changed."

"Sure did. I skulked in before the new crew got to work." He glanced at the wall clock that showed half past seven. "Must be a bunch of slackers. Anyway, my desk was cleared out, pictures down, stuff out of the drawers, off the shelves, and everything boxed up in a nice heap in the reception area. Couldn't check file cabinets. Those combinations were changed. But I guess they couldn't deal with the big safe, so I rescued some files." He gestured to the box on her desk.

"They're my personal notes. I don't think they include any really classified stuff, so I'm taking them home. And my STE phone. I'll need it to stay up on the Intelink until NSA sends the men in black to confiscate it."

"A souvenir? Or are you thinking of actually doing some real work?" Sophie sipped her tea and raised her brows a fraction.

"Hey, kid, I was told that the Secretary of Defense—your new boss—has fired me. I'm canned, sacked, whacked, and out of work. Maybe even disliked. So last week I signed on as a visiting lecturer at the University of Maryland. I'll be telling the kids in Princess Ann about the real world and media distortions, and I'll need my notes to dazzle them with my great collection of dirty jokes. I'll use the crypto gear to stay up to speed on my current ops and help you to transfer them or shut them down. Or to brief SecDef."

"What makes you think the Secretary dislikes you, Jeremiah?"

"Okay. Give. What's going on?" Adams flipped the switch on the refilled coffee maker and sat on a desk edge.

"There are two kinds of people. Those who do the work and those who take the credit. Indira Gandhi said that one should try to be in the first group—there's less competition." Sophie waited for Adams to comment. Hearing none, she went on.

"The Secretary is still finding his footing on new ground, and like some other people I know, he is a proud man. He has asked for no help these past months, and is just now finishing his review of hundreds of files and years of programs. I am reorganizing files in the manner he prefers, and you may be interested to know that your resignation letter is *not* in the unfinished business stack. In fact, Mr. Beauchamps keeps it locked in his desk. I wonder why." It was not a question, and Adams remained silent, waiting.

"At this moment I think the Secretary knows very little about the nature and handling of your special projects, and absolutely nothing about your imminent resignation."

Adams loosened his tie and scratched the back of his neck. "For Pete's sake. If he just asks me, I'll save him lots of time. On lots of things."

"So say generals, admirals, and other senior civil servants. But Secretary Horton wants the facts without Pentagon snow jobs."

"What's all that got to do with firing me?"

"Heads may roll, but yours does not seem to be on the block." Sophie looked out the tall windows at the city skyline and then back at Adams.

"Don't you find it intriguing, Jeremiah, that Mr. Beauchamps asks me every morning to remind you to sign the letter he gave you? As you are fond of saying, he seems to be a loose cannon. So don't sign anything until I can tell you what's really happening. That is, of course, if you still want to serve."

Drawing a deep breath, Adams poured himself a fresh cup of coffee. "It's Horton's boat, and his cannons. As for serving in his new lash-up, I don't know. In our old office I was king and master of all I surveyed." He pulled a teacup over to the coffeepot.

"Okay, maybe I wasn't a king. But I was always the SecDef's loyal Jack of Diamonds. Now the set-up has changed, and your new boss seems hell bent on giving everyone in this building major heartburn. I've been doing lots of thinking out on the shore, and maybe it *is* time for me to step aside and let new minds tackle the problems. I don't think much of Beauchamps, but Jelly-Roll might see more in him than I do."

Adams carried a brimming porcelain cup to Sophie's desk and muttered, "Coffee just doesn't taste right in these flimsy things."

A uniformed woman Marine sergeant entered the office, glared at Adams, and sat at a desk near the door. She opened her purse and began applying a coat of lipstick so dark it matched her blue uniform. Adams watched for a moment, then shook his head.

"Okay, Sophie, you and that elegant BAM can start your day with a cup of Jeremiah Adams' industrial-strength boiler cleaner. I'll get me another ration at Starbucks when I clear Kent Narrows Bridge." He picked up his file box and the STE, bent close to Sophie, and added softly, "You know I won't sign anything from Beauchamps without checking with you."

Sophie pulled the teacup of coffee across her desk and smiled again. "Please remember to scratch Ranger's ears for me."

CHAPTER 22

Central Atlantic Ocean
Latitude 41° 01' North—Longitude 45° 18' West

Yunes swam beneath the Atlantic's surface like a steel microbe, a black bacillus making its way through the blood and toward the heart of its victim. Halfway across the ocean, and the submarine was still undetected. Never surfacing, it was never observed by the two thousand satellites orbiting above it, nor was it spotted by an aircraft, or by a ship, or by what remains of the Sound Surveillance System's long-range underwater listening arrays.

The SOSUS system had been extremely effective in finding Soviet submarines during the Cold War and for years afterwards. But when ultra-quiet nuclear submarines appeared, the budget masters in Washington thought the system was obsolete and did not fund improvements or maintenance. Since 1999, the few arrays not decommissioned are used mainly for scientific studies, monitoring sounds of sea-life and rumbles of undersea quakes. As a result, though the snorkeling diesels of *Yunes* sounded noisily along the ocean corridors every day, there was no SOSUS technician on watch to record her sounds, triangulate, and report her position to submarine hunters.

It was two hours before dawn in Bandar Abbas but on *Yunes*, cruising at periscope depth in mid-Atlantic, the crew was just finishing dinner. Captain Reza was in the control room, looking at the plots of two surface contacts being automatically tracked by the MVU-110EM torpedo fire control computer. It was another routine night.

"How goes it, Commander Saduqi?"

"We're on course and on time, captain, at periscope depth and standing by to snorkel." Saduqi gestured at the plotting table, and then joined Reza in bending over the wide area chart. *Yunes* was crossing the Atlantic Deep, and the ocean floor was an unimaginable three miles below. Reza turned his attention to the surface target plots.

"Esqual, what do we know about these two contacts?"

"Surface Contact One is a 290,000-ton crude carrier. She's a mile off to port. Her rigging and lights indicate she is probably *Eastern Star*, an old ship out of Houston. She is making twelve knots on a parallel course and slowly overtaking us. Surface Contact Two is to starboard and was acquired at long range, She's too far to work up a course and speed. Sonar just reported a loud shaft squeal. Should be easy to track."

"Very well. When do you plan to commence snorkeling?"

"Immediately, captain, with your permission. Sea state is calm and there is a low overcast and light rain. Watch-standers on *Eastern Star* won't be able to see our snorkel wake."

"Very well, you may commence snorkeling. Patch all internal communications to the squawk box."

The snorkeling watch was set in the control room, engine room and battery compartments, ready to start the diesel engines.

"Aye, captain." Saduqi nodded to the ever-present Chief Ali. "Up periscope. Stand by to raise snorkel masts and start the diesels."

The periscope hissed up and Saduqi draped himself over the handles. He slowly circled the periscope well, the beginning of endless observations that were made whenever the snorkel system broached the surface. It was essential to keep the snorkel head and exhaust masts well above water when charging batteries. They gulped down air and expelled exhaust fumes from the diesels turning the generator that charged the batteries. During this vulnerable time, the control room watch guarded against *Yunes* being noticed by a ship or an aircraft close enough to see the plume of spray, or the wake the masts carved in the sea surface.

Commander Saduqi completed his first survey of the horizon and saw only the masthead lights of *Eastern Star*, a mile to the south.

"Raise the masts and commence snorkeling."

Seconds later, the diesels began their clattering rumble.

Pleased with the smooth procedure executed by Saduqi and the snorkeling watch, Reza's thoughts turned to the regular after-dinner chess match with the

Professor. He was almost at his stateroom when he heard the words from the squawk box speakers.

"Conn, sonar. Surface Contact Two is closing rapidly. Now on constant bearing 081 degrees. Range 17,500 meters. Estimate course 260. Estimate speed twenty-six knots. Shaft squeal. Aural on both arrays. Very loud."

Reza's stomach contracted painfully. The starboard surface contact was rapidly approaching on a constant bearing. A collision course at twenty-six knots? What kind of ship could be approaching at twenty-six knots? He began to run.

Before anyone reacted in the control room, Reza bounded to the periscope and pushed Saduqi aside. Walking the scope around to 081 degrees, he shouted, "Chief, bring us up three meters. Quickly! Don't broach the sail!"

Nine nautical miles away *something* was approaching at high speed, and additional periscope height above the sea surface would extend the visual horizon to at least that distance. The Captain jammed his forehead into the rubber bumper above the optics, as if that might somehow increase his range of view. The dark night was made darker by the overcast, but a surface ship's running lights would be clearly seen at only nine miles. *Nothing!* It could only be a submarine. A nuclear submarine.

Realizing the sonar operator and watch officer could not yet understand that a threat was approaching, Reza stepped back from the periscope and rasped a series of staccato commands.

"I have the conn. Down scope. Secure from snorkeling. Secure diesels and shift to battery. Left full rudder."

On such a westerly heading, he thought, it's probably an American submarine returning from patrol, going home at a speed only a nuclear power plant could provide. Did they hear us? What if we're found and challenged? What if we're attacked? Reza pushed the thoughts out of his mind.

"Captain has the conn. Engine room signals diesels secured, captain. Main induction indicates closed. Scope and snorkel masts down. Rudder is left full." The chief's calm and measured replies came seconds after the captain's commands.

"Very well. Helm, come to course 180. Planesman, make your depth thirty meters. Engineering, give me turns for twelve knots. Maintain silence about the boat. Saduqi, refine the heading to intercept *Eastern Star*. Chief, check Lloyds. Get me the draft of that ship."

Commander Saduqi was first to reply, "Intercept course to *Eastern Star* at twelve knots is 183 degrees. Time to intercept four minutes forty-five seconds."

The chief's reply came ten seconds later. "*Eastern Star* draws eighteen meters fully laden, captain."

"Very well. Helm, come to course 183. That oil tanker goes to America, so she must be fully laden. Chief, make our depth sufficient for the sail to clear the keel of

Eastern Star by no more than four meters. When we approach the tanker, we will turn to starboard and match her course and speed. I intend to cruise directly beneath her bottom."

Before anyone could digest Reza's astounding orders, the intercom sounded again, "Conn, sonar. Target number two shaft squeal stopped. Aural contact lost."

Tension in the control room was heightened by Saduqi's soft tuneless whistling, as he worked the course change solution on his maneuvering board.

When Commander Saduqi gave the order that started *Yunes'* diesel engines, Captain Scott Mancini of fleet ballistic missile submarine *USS Maryland* was nine miles away. Sprinting home at twenty-six knots after a patrol north of the Faeroe Islands, *Maryland* suddenly acquired a singing shaft bearing, and her captain was not happy.

"Engineering, I hope you will be kind enough to advise your skipper of the situation back there." Mancini's sarcasm was not lost on his engineering officer.

"Captain, a main shaft bearing must've thrown some metal. We're checking it out, and I'll report as soon as possible. Recommend we reduce speed, sir."

"Okay, engineering. We'll ratchet down until the song dies. We weren't making a peep at twenty knots, so we should go quiet if we drop a few turns." Mancini looked around the control room for his coffee cup. "Make turns for twenty knots."

Going home to the Naval Submarine Base at Kings Bay, Georgia, Mancini was not very concerned about noise. The stealthy part of the last ninety days was getting his missile submarine on station unobserved and then remaining invisible. Relieved by a sister submarine, his objective now was to get the crew of the huge Trident sub back to their families and sweethearts, and *Maryland* had been doing an admirable job until two minutes ago.

"Conn, sonar. Possible snorkeling submarine bearing 261 degrees. Estimate range 17,000 meters. Estimate course 270. Faint lines. Bow array only. Target designated as Alpha Two."

Mancini was staggered. Then his command instincts kicked into high gear.

"Engineering, belay my last order. Slow to five knots. Helm, come right to course 350. Sonar, we're turning to put your arrays broadside, so put on your best ears. I'll be right there to take a look at your possible."

"Conn, Sonar. We've lost contact with Alpha Two. No further snorkeling lines. Alpha One is still classified as a large surface ship on the same bearing, range 18,500 meters, estimated speed twelve knots, course 270."

Seconds later, Mancini was peering over the head of the sonarman. They were both studying a screen displaying dozens of vertical lines that scrolled and wriggled in various widths. It was the "waterfall," a graphic display of sound that the sonar system pulled out of the ocean and analyzed.

"Okay, I see Alpha One. Now show me Alpha Two's snorkeling lines." Mancini watched the operator display a recording of recent sound traces.

"Look here, skipper, see that knee line? It was just seconds ago, and it's a classic signature of a snorkeling startup. Me, I never seen one of those out here in the jungle, but it's just like in the classroom. And the signature library shows it to be a lot like a Russian KILO class." The sonar operator twisted around in his chair and looked up at the bemused face of his commander.

"Well, I'm a raped ape. Hard to believe a Russian diesel boat would be out here in the middle of nowhere. That sure does look like start-lines, though. Well done, Hawkeye! I'm going to close as rapidly as possible without making too much noise. Then we'll take another look." Mancini paused and pointed to the sound traces of the tanker on the same bearing as the possible sub contact.

"Are you sure those lines couldn't have been caused by that big merchantman? By Alpha One?"

"Skipper, the shallow sound channel is so crappy tonight that at these ranges I wouldn't bet my ass on anything."

"Could Alpha Two be a Canadian Upholder, or maybe one of those Norwegian Ula boats?"

"If it's a submarine, skipper, I'd say it's a KILO."

"You've got the best ears in the squadron, so I'm assuming *something* is out there. Keep listening, and sing out if you hear a minnow fart." The captain shook his head at the waterfall then smiled at the sonarman and said, "Anyway, that was very professional work and I'm damn impressed."

Mancini left the sonar console and trotted to the main plotting table in the control room. He looked at the watch standers and shrugged his shoulders.

"Okay, troops, the grams are not exactly conclusive. If somebody snuck a diesel boat through all the ships out here without being spotted, it's a miracle. And what the hell it's supposed to be doing in the middle of the Atlantic is beyond me. But I do know it isn't one of ours because we don't have *any* kind of sub out here. Sonar thinks she could be a Russian. Anyway, we're going to take a brief detour and check it out. Helm, come left to course 260. Engineering, give me all the turns you've got below that shaft squeal. We're going hunting."

Five feet longer than the Washington Monument, displacing 19,000 tons, *Maryland* was twice as long as *Yunes* and five times its displacement. But despite its gigantic size, the ballistic missile submarine began to bull its way through the Atlantic, accelerating under the almost limitless power of its nuclear engine. At twenty-three knots, *Maryland* arrived two thousand meters from the last position of the "possible" submarine in less than twenty minutes. Slowing to five knots, her sonar screens were filled with engine sounds from the tanker ship three miles to the southwest.

"Sonar, you're not holding anything like a submarine, are you?" Mancini had refilled his coffee cup and was looking at the tanker's track on the main plotting board.

"No sir. No contacts besides Alpha One."

Mancini sipped his coffee. "Okay helm, come left to course 240. Let's make turns for twenty knots. Navigator, see that we pass two thousand meters astern of that tanker so we can take a peek at what might be off her port side. Sonar, when we're astern of Alpha One let me have one ping. No use annoying all the neighbors with anything more."

Eight minutes later *Maryland* was astern of *Eastern Star*, and her active sonar array boiled the water with a sonic shock wave that sledge-hammered into the tanker's hull and was heard on its bridge, eighty feet above the waterline.

Like a Remora fish attached to the belly of a whale shark, *Yunes* was cruising fifteen feet below the vast and barnacle-encrusted bottom of *Eastern Star*, pacing the tanker ship knot for knot, just ahead of its churning screw. When the lash of *Maryland's* sonar rang against the hull of *Yunes*, even her soft anechoic plating could not completely dampen a return echo. But that small echo merged with the much larger echo from the tanker's hull, and *Maryland's* sonar could not refine the simultaneous returns into two separate targets.

"Captain, sonar. Surface contact Alpha One bears 270 at 1900 meters. No other contacts."

"Okay, now come right to course 270. Slow to five knots." Mancini frowned at the silent control room as waiting for someone to explain the disappearance of Alpha Two.

"This is the skipper, Sonar. Could your line of bearing on Alpha Two be off? I mean, are you certain that Alpha Two was in front of that big tub? Or could that snorkeling have originated further out, somewhere on the line of bearing south of Alpha One?"

"Captain, I used both arrays on that fix, but at such a long range and with those weird skips in the shallow sound channel... yeah, it could have been further out." The sonarman did not sound happy.

"All right." Mancini looked down at the main plotting table. No explanations there, either. "Sonar, are there any other kinks in the thermocline besides the garbage in the shallow layer?"

"Yes, sir. There's a sharp inversion around a thousand feet."

"Very well. Helm, come left to 250. Maintain five knots. Navigator, put us on a course that goes right down that line of bearing to Alpha Two. Sonar, we'll try five minutes at five knots. You listen hard. Then we'll ping the hell out of the water ahead for five more minutes."

The long grey hull of *Maryland* slowly swung south.

Captain Reza was rigid, eyes closed. He forced his thoughts to squeeze out through the hull of *Yunes* and into the nuclear submarine lurking a few thousand meters away. What will her captain do? If he moves alongside the tanker and uses that gigantic sonar again, he would surely see him. But if *Yunes* tried to maneuver, if they tried to leave the shelter of the huge vessel above...

"Chief Ali," he whispered.

"Aye, sir," came the whispered reply.

Like the rest of the wide-eyed crewmen, the Chief of the Boat was motionless. *Maryland's* sonar ping had frozen them all in place when it crashed into *Yunes* and the tanker.

"Relieve the planesman, chief. On my command, you and I will take her down to a thousand feet. Closely monitor the temperature as we dive. We level off when we are below the deep layer."

"Aye, sir."

The chief did not have to remind his captain of what every member of the crew knew so well: test depth for Yunes was 985 feet.

An endless minute passed. Another. Then Reza's mind automatically began a checklist.

"Chief. How are the batteries?"

"Thirty-five percent, sir. If we stay at twelve knots we will only—"

"Chief," Reza interrupted, "I want a fast dive and I want a quiet dive. Do not let the screw cavitate. When we reach the layer you will reduce speed to five knots."

"Aye, sir."

"Chief. Use your phone, not the squawk box, and tell the forward torpedo room to make ready tubes one and two. Do not flood or open the doors. No noise."

"Aye, sir." The chief lifted a handset from a bulkhead cradle, spoke softly for twenty seconds, then carefully replaced it.

Three more never-ending minutes, and then they heard it. Sonar pings. A continuous series of sharp chimes had begun—to the south!

"DIVE! Dive now, chief!"

The deck tilted forward, steepened, and Yunes began its plunge.

"Right full rudder. Come to 350."

The whispered replies from the helmsman and the chief were tense.

"Rudder is right full."

"Passing through fifty meters."

Pause.

"Steady, 350 degrees."

"Passing one hundred meters."

Pause.

"One hundred and fifty meters."

Reza's gaze was fixed on the face of the depth gauge, its long needle dropping rapidly toward the bright red line at the 300 meter mark.

"Belay the meters, chief. Just tell me when the temperature changes."

"Temperature steady... falling slowly."

When the gauge showed 295 meters the chief hissed, "Temperature is steady!" Then the needle touched 300 meters.

"Temperature rising!"

"Now, chief! Level off! Five knots!"

Yunes passed through the warm layer and into colder water below. The chief wheeled the dive planes to full up position, his eyes riveted on the depth gauge.

"Steady, chief." Reza felt the deck begin to level as the gauge needle passed 305 meters, then 315, then 320, then slowly stopped at 323. There were deep iron groans as the steel muscles of *Yunes* fought the crushing weight of the Atlantic. They were 1,060 feet below the surface.

Silence returned.

"That's enough. Secure active sonar. All stop. Come right to 270." Captain Mancini took a deep breath as *Maryland* decelerated. "Hear anything, sonar?"

"No, sir, captain. We got no returns from active sonar and the only target I hold on aural is Alpha One, astern."

That tanker. Mancini's thoughts took form. What would I do in a diesel boat with a boomer on my tail? *Hide.* It must be that tanker!

"Give me turns for twenty knots. Navigator, take us right alongside that tanker. Make it 500 meters. Parallel her course. Sonar, when we come abeam of that big boy, use your gong. Two pings."

Maryland heeled into a sharp turn and effortlessly gathered speed. As she pulled alongside *Eastern Star* the sonar lashed out. Then again.

"Sonar, tell me something." Mancini was tapping his Naval Academy ring on his coffee cup.

"Nothing under that ship, captain. There was a faint echo in the far distance, but no definition. Could've been sea life, sir."

Sea life? Mancini gave his cup one last ringing tap and set it on the plotting table with a thin smile. If there's really a diesel boat hiding in the neighborhood, he mused, her skipper is damn good. To disappear that way is better than good. What did he do? Magically turn his boat into sea life? Mancini shrugged.

"Okay, troops, this exercise is over and it will be so noted in the log. Sonar, be sure to get those grams to squadron intelligence as soon as we get to Kings Bay. Now come right to course 265. Engineering, let's have turns for flank. And forget that squealing shaft. There's no cure like sea-cure, and we are now *secured!*

The two sonar pings were not followed by others. Then, when the shaft squeal resumed and faded into the distance, Reza stilled his growing premonition of disaster. Giving the conn to an awed Commander Saduqi, he left the control room.

Swimming in its salty haven below the temperature layer, *Yunes* continued toward her western goal, saved from detection by her ingenious captain.

Six days to landfall.

CHAPTER 23

Route 13
Salisbury, Maryland

"I like this place." Adams looked around *Flannery's*, an informal restaurant wedged into the intersection of Route 13 and Salisbury's business bypass. It was a warm day for April in Maryland, and he and Carly lunched at a sidewalk table.

"You know, Popeye, we've got lots of good restaurants in Salisbury. Some of them even have tablecloths." Carly's pale copper lipstick parted to show startling white teeth.

"Yeah, I've been in all of 'em. But ever since I found this joint on my first trip to Onancock, it's been hard to beat. They got a great selection of beers and damn good hamburgers. Okay, it doesn't have *Bizotto's* gourmet menu, but you never want to have lunch with me in Onancock anyway." Adams took a large bite of his rare hamburger while Carly picked at her salad.

"I would love to lunch with you in Onancock or anywhere else, but unlike some people, I go to an office every day. Besides, the way restaurants open and close on Market Street, *Bizotto's* might go out of business between appetizer and dessert." She glanced at her watch. "Speaking of business, I've got to scoot off to the *Times*."

Putting his beer bottle on the splintery table top, Adams looked at Carly with his version of a masterful Bogart smile. "Play hooky, Slim. It's Saturday. Let's take *Pilgrim* out for a few hours. Start the weekend. Go fishing. The Chinese say time spent fishing doesn't count against your life span. And you get to *add* time for nude sunbathing."

"Why do you always wear that blazer? And a turtleneck, too. It's a lovely day, darling, and you must be broiling in this sun."

Adams' brows drew together. "C'mon, you know why I've got a jacket on." *Why do women always change the subject?*

"Oh dear, I forgot you've got to hide that big pistol." Carly's smile slanted into a wicked grin, and she leaned closer, "But if you're a good boy and let me go back to work right now, I promise to take tomorrow off. We can lunch at *Bizotto's*, drink Martinis, run around Hermitage naked, then watch the sunset from *Pilgrim* while I polish your pistol."

Still grinning, she reached under the table for her satchel purse and then stood, tossing her jacket over a shoulder. Adams rose with her.

"Okay, okay. Just remember we get underway an hour before sunset. The seastate is forecast to be perfect. Like you."

Carly rarely kissed Adams hello, and never goodbye. Looking into his eyes, she stroked his arm, turned, and joined the pedestrians on the sidewalk. He watched her long strides until she disappeared into the throng.

Unlike some people, I go to an office every day. She did not say that to belittle him, Adams knew, but he somehow felt smaller and older. A guy is supposed to work, he mused, and work hard. If he's good at work he loves, then he has to find that work and do it, or fade away. Carly wants me to fade away—or change into a college professor. She's probably right. Rat's ass. Next thing she'll want me to do is smoke a pipe. Top it off, Sophie called and said Horton wants to meet me Monday. So my resignation gets set in concrete next week. My concrete booties. He had been thinking about what to do about that meeting for days. Stretching his back, Adams sat and motioned for the check. Still preoccupied, his mind would not leave the problem.

So after the Secretary cans me, I can teach a bit and maybe beg part-time work from some mercenary outfit. Do something useful. The past weeks' routine was getting tiresome: work on the house, work on the boat, too much booze. But what if he wasn't wanted by any outfit anywhere? He hadn't read a disturbing intel report in weeks, and he couldn't see any clouds on the horizon. Maybe the terrorists were on vacation. Maybe it *was* time to hang up the spurs.

Anyway, tomorrow night he had a boat date with the most beautiful and intelligent woman he'd ever met besides Sophie. Of course, Sophie didn't like boats much, but she was sure a damn sight more tidy than Carly. Neatness doesn't count in this game, though.

He signed the credit card slip and leaned back. He visualized being aboard *Pilgrim* with Carly, drifting six or seven miles off Wachapreague, full moon, calm sea. No crises, no chasing bad guys. It was going to be a perfect night.

He called the waiter back and ordered another beer.

CHAPTER 24

Western Atlantic Ocean
Latitude 37° 34' North—Longitude 75° 16' West

"Up periscope."

Electric tension filled the control room and vibrated throughout the submarine. *Yunes* was sixteen nautical miles east of Wachapreague Inlet Shoals.

Even before the periscope finished hissing up from its well, Reza's eyes were glued to the optics. He walked the usual orbit around the polished housing, scanning the surface. Then he spoke loudly, so all the crewmen in the control room could hear him.

"Nothing to see. Dense fog. Sea state is calm. Chief, advise our passengers they will be leaving us in two hours, and then get their equipment ready for off-loading through the forward hatch. Make sure both inflatable boats are ready to go up on deck. I want no errors or fumbling. After we surface, we will proceed on the diesels and charge batteries while we run in."

Commander Saduqi took over at the optics as Reza stepped back from the periscope to issue a command not heard since they headed west from Lisbon.

"Prepare to surface!"

Reza smiled at the nervous lookouts waiting in the control room. They wore red goggles, foul weather gear, and were anxiously fingering their binoculars.

"Your grandchildren and their children will speak of your bravery, men." Then he raised his voice, "Sonar, report depth and contacts!"

"No contacts, sir. Fathometer indicates twenty-five meters."

"Very well. Chief, take us up." Reza firmly settled his white peaked cap and stood at the foot of the ladder leading to the bridge atop the sail. The lookouts and watch officer crowded around him.

"Aye, aye, sir." Chief Ali pushed the klaxon three times, and then hit the intercom toggle.

"Surface! Surface! Surface! Prepare to start engines. Lookouts to the bridge."

Three blasts on the klaxon sounded for the first time in thirteen days. High-pressure air blew seawater out of the ballast tanks, and the gleaming black sail and decks of *Yunes* rose through the ocean's oily-calm surface. The submarine gushed foaming rivulets that cascaded back into the sea as Reza, Chief Ali, and the lookouts scrambled onto the slippery bridge. Fresh air falling through the open hatch brought smells of the Virginia marshlands a few miles to the west.

Days earlier, when they sliced across the Gulf Stream and bottomless Washington Canyon to reach the continental shelf, Reza watched the water depth gradually begin to shallow—from half a mile to mere meters. Periscope depth for *Yunes* was just shy of twenty meters, and it was finally necessary to come up. They would run on the surface over shallow water until they were at the drop-off point for the passengers, five miles east of Wachapreague Inlet shoals. Then the two passengers would use their inflatable boat to go to wherever they were going.

The fogbank lay thick on the slowly undulating sea surface, and though visibility was only a few meters in any direction, Reza welcomed the protection of its misty gray camouflage. Radar off, *Yunes* blindly groped forward in the night at seven knots, her growling diesels filling the banks of batteries with power. In two hours the deadly cargo would be delivered, and he could begin the return voyage.

Yunes was performing brilliantly, no problems and no machinery casualties, so Reza could not understand why a premonition of disaster dogged him. *Just nerves.* Understandable tension brought on by fatigue and the dangers of their long submerged transit. He concentrated on the thought that *Yunes* would soon be safe again, hidden under the surface, heading home.

Then, exactly five minutes before eleven o'clock, *Yunes* emerged from the fogbank into silvery light. The full moon was high in the eastern sky, a bright searchlight that silhouetted the figures waiting on the submarine's black deck. Aloft on the sail bridge, Reza scanned the shore lights scattered along the western horizon. Seeing the American mainland so close made him feel vulnerable and exposed, and he spoke softly into his lip microphone.

"Navigator, captain. Position."

The reply scratched in his headset, "Approximately five miles from Wachapreague Inlet, sir. Depth is now six fathoms. We're at the debarkation point."

"Very well. All stop. Chief, go below to the forward weather deck and help our friends over the side."

"Aye, Captain." The chief paused, "Ah, Captain. If the first inflatable works well, do we take the spare back below?"

Reza read the chief's mind and answered, "Absolutely. Our passengers told me you must have it as a small token of their appreciation for all the tender care you gave them on their first submarine voyage. If the first launch goes well, strike the other boat below." The Chief saluted, and slid down the ladder with unlikely grace.

Smiling at his disappearing back, Reza tried to ignore the uneasy feeling that dogged him. It must be proximity to that shore on the horizon, he thought, with its twinkling lights. The captain rubbed his thirteen day-old beard and wondered if the rumble of his diesels could be heard on the beach. *Yunes* was motionless, but her racketing engines were still on line, charging batteries and waiting to drive the submarine back into the fog bank astern.

Reza wondered how Kapitanleutnant Reinhard Hardegen felt seeing those lights in 1942 when he surfaced U-123 and began his astounding attack on shipping in these very waters. He surely stank of diesel fuel and body odor too.

Then there was a pop and hiss as the inflatable boat expanded on the deck below. Reza watched it splash into the sea, tethered close alongside. The deck crew and the two passengers worked with practiced ease to offload boxes and equipment. Then there were two shadows in the rubber boat, the tether was cast off, and with a muffled drone it was away. Reza followed the Zodiac until it disappeared, buzzing westward across the calm ocean. Beneath him, the deck crew manhandled the spare inflatable boat below. The chief would be pleased with his new toy, he thought.

Suddenly the starboard lookout hissed in his ear, "Ship! Ship! Dead ahead, Captain! There!" Reza's heart almost stopped.

Yes, there *was* a vessel! Coast guard? His night vision binoculars showed Reza what could be a private yacht a mile distant, dead in the water, with no running lights. From their small boat, the men in the Zodiac would not see it until they were almost upon it. But it was too late to do anything about that now.

"Engineering, this is the captain. Make turns for flank speed. Helm, left full rudder, come to course 090."

The deck crew below the sail looked up at him, startled when they felt *Yunes* lurch and begin to turn. They were not ordered to run for the open deck hatch, though, and no klaxon sounded a dive alert. It would take miles of cruising over shallow water before the submarine would dare to submerge, and the crewmen would have plenty of time to clear the decks and get below.

Reza looked at the nearing fog. Even though *Yunes* would soon be back in that comforting cloak, Reza knew the mist gave no protection against the radar of coast guard vessels. But at least he would be out of the bright moonlight.

"Navigator. How long before we reach deep water?"

In the control room below, Commander Saduqi bent over the navigation table with calipers.

"At this speed, fifty-seven minutes, captain."

Can't be helped, thought Reza, any more that I can stop that cabin cruiser from reporting us to their navy.

A minute later, when *Yunes* nosed into the edge of the fogbank, he thought he heard gunshots. No matter. His poisonous consignment had been discharged exactly as planned, and his submarine was still undiscovered. Nevertheless, as fog swirled around the bridge, a prickling of danger ran down his back again.

Twenty minutes before *Yunes* motored out of the fog and launched the Zodiac, Adams and Carly were sprawled on wide deck chaises on the fantail of *Pilgrim*, wearing down jackets against the night air and sipping Martinis. Ranger, full of a late dinner, snored gently in his favorite perch on the flying bridge above them. The white cabin cruiser drifted in a light offshore night breeze, four miles east of Wachapreague Inlet.

When the full moon rose from behind the fogbank that stretched before them, Adams switched off running lights and engines so they could enjoy a startling sight. Less than a mile away, a vertical wall of dense fog soared up three hundred feet, extending left and right as far as they could see. The fogbank was a milky barrier, a giant white mattress floating on the shimmering sea surface. It was a vast and surreal panorama.

"Popeye, you sure know how to arrange a boat ride for your girl." Carly's auburn hair was black in the moonlight, and she brushed the dark billows aside to look at Adams in the chair next to her. She could see his teeth gleam in the moonlight.

"Piece of cake, sweetheart."

"C'mere, tough guy, and tell me how much you love me."

Adams left his chair, crouched alongside Carly, and gently touched his glass to hers. They sipped a silent toast.

"You'll do, lady, you'll do just fine."

"It's not John Wayne I love, Jay. Tell me."

Adams stood, finished his drink and looked down at Carly. Once again, he saw her for the first time.

"I love you to the end of each day's most quiet need, by sun and candlelight."

Carly carefully put her glass on the deck, pushed her chair back, and stood very close to Adams. Then she breathed in his ear, "I love thee to the depth and breadth and height my soul can reach..."

Adams felt someone was watching them when they kissed. Impossible. But when he pulled her closer to his down vest, he looked over her shoulder at the moonlit fogbank. And froze.

"What the... " With an arm around Carly's waist, Adams pulled binoculars from the chart table and peered along the flickering avenue the moon traced across the ocean.

"Look at that, Carly. It's a submarine. It sailed out of that wall of fog like *The Flying Dutchman*." He laughed, handing the binoculars to Carly and pointing east.

"I see it," she said. "It looks like a big black square. Yes, it's moving, turning I think. I can hear its engine. Hear it?" Carly was leaning forward now, excited by the distant phantom. Adams heard an engine, too, but he knew the faint humming sound was not from a submarine.

"Keep an eye on that sub, Carly. I'm going topside to see what's heading our way." He sprinted up the ladder to the flying bridge, and when he looked east he saw a Zodiac bearing down on them.

"Looks like a landing party from the sub is going ashore. Our boys must be holding some kind of night exercise." Adams was joyful. "I might even know some of those guys!" The inflatable boat was nearing *Pilgrim*, closing rapidly.

"I see them," Carly shouted, still glued to the binoculars. "Looks like two men in that fast little boat."

"We better light up and get set to move, or those guys might run right into us. Then the Navy would probably sue me for repairs to the Zodiac." Adams chuckled, switched on *Pilgrim's* running lights, and started the twin diesels.

Ranger was awakened by the engine noise, and he barked enthusiastically. Adams did not see the winking light on the Zodiac, or hear the AK-47, but a silent fusillade tore into *Pilgrim's* superstructure, shattering the Plexiglas windscreen and punching holes into the fiberglass surround. Ranger howled when bullets whined, sparked and ricocheted off the instrument panel. Snapping at his hindquarters, he spun and fell from the bridge to the deck below, where he bounced off a chaise and rolled toward Carly.

"Sonofabitch!" Adams rammed the throttles forward and *Pilgrim's* bow rose, responding to the power of her flailing screws. He flipped a switch and the running lights went dark again as he spun the wheel. The big cruiser heeled sharply and turned away from the Zodiac, rapidly gaining speed.

"Jay, Ranger is bleeding." Carly knelt over the Labrador, pressing her hand against its flank. "Bring the first aid kit. Hurry!"

Adams plunged down the ladder, leaving *Pilgrim* to find her own way across the calm waters.

"Ranger! Those goddamn idiots shot Ranger!" He pulled a first aid kit out of the chart table and knelt next to Carly.

"The miserable bastards. By God, they'll wish they were never born. I'll see to that."

Pilgrim was speeding toward shore in a wide unpiloted arc. The black Zodiac disappeared into the darkness, increasing speed when it reached the mirror-flat water west of the Parramore Banks.

Hunched over his GPS unit, the Professor aimed the boat toward the mouth of Wachapreague Inlet, three and a half miles away.

"You're crazy, Jabber!" The Professor yelled against the wind as he turned the outboard engine throttle to its highest setting. "Why did you shoot at that harmless fishing boat? What if they radio the military?"

Jabber realized his mistake even as he pulled the trigger, but reflexes and fear had combined, and he fired the entire magazine before he could regain control of himself. He was also shouting to be heard above the slipstream and engine noise.

"I'm sorry Professor. I thought it was coast guards. Sorry. Maybe I miss." But he did not think so.

"We talk later. For now, look for the boat we must meet. It will be two miles ahead. And do not shoot that one, you idiotic assassin." The Professor suppressed his rage with difficulty. What else would this wild man do?

A mile away, Ranger had stopped bleeding, but Adams worried that internal hemorrhages might kill his friend before he could get him to a vet on shore. Working by moonlight, he and Carly put compresses on the wounds in the Lab's abdomen and wrapped him in a blanket. Then Carly sat back against the afterdeck railing, cradling Ranger's head and listening to the big dog whine with each ragged breath. Adams stood and looked down at the two figures.

"We've gotta get him to a vet. Keep him warm, sweetheart, okay?"

Carly nodded, eyes brimming with tears, and doubled the blanket over the wounded dog. With a glance over his shoulder, Adams climbed up to *Pilgrim's* bullet-riddled bridge. At full throttle, the cruiser would reach Wachapreague marina in minutes. Then the Yukon would get Ranger to the Onancock vet's home office before midnight.

In spite of the shooting and screaming, the two men piloted their Zodiac to the appointed meeting at sea, a mile from the shoals. A large private fishing boat flashed the correct response to their challenge, and they took the thrown line to be towed to a shallow gut leading to Wachapreague harbor. Once in sheltered waters, they transferred their cargo to the larger craft, sank the Zodiac, and cruised into the municipal marina. The small harbormaster's office would not open until six o'clock, and the watch-stander at the nearby Parramore Beach Coast Guard Station was dozing in front of his portable television set. In the early morning hours, no one saw three men leave a yacht, carry bulky objects to a black SUV, and drive off.

Only an hour since the two terrorists left *Yunes*, and already they were drinking tea in the home of the sleeper agent who had been waiting for them. It was midnight, and the Professor and Jabber were safely hidden in the bosom of the Great Satan himself.

Everything was going almost as planned.

CHAPTER 25

"That smells good."

Carly padded soundlessly into the kitchen, picked up a waiting cup of coffee and wrapped an arm around Adams, who was looking morosely at the day's first light. They both had an aura of soap and shampoo.

The vet had been more than cranky when they woke her at midnight, but when she saw Ranger in his bloody blanket she was suddenly alert, and pressed Adams and Carly into service as her surgical assistants. The wounded dog was very lucky. A single bullet missed his vital organs and blood vessels, the vet assured them, and after a couple of weeks of care in the hospital, Ranger would be his boisterous self again. Adams and Carly did not leave the clinic until the anesthetic wore off and Ranger licked at their hands. An hour later, bone weary, they were back at the Hermitage for showers and breakfast.

"It's going to be a long day for me and a very bad day for those crazy bastards who shot my dog. And my boat." Adams rubbed his hand across the shoulders of the barefoot woman at his side. "You were great, babe. On the boat and in the vet's office." He kissed her forehead. "Maybe you want to head upstairs and grab a nap? I'll call you after I find out a few things."

"You want to get rid of me, sailor? And here I was, just getting to know you."

"No way. If I could, I'd have you around my neck on a golden chain."

"My, my. The man I love is a cornball." A shadow crossed Adams' face. "But a manly-man cornball! I promise I won't tell anyone about your sweet and tender side. Well, probably only our daughters."

Adams' brow furrowed again. "Daughters?"

"Okay, sons and daughters."

"Get a grip, Carly—"

She leaned back into his encircling arm and grinned up at him. "Don't worry, darling, I'll get pregnant *after* the wedding. You like big weddings?"

"Ah. Sure. Sure, I like big weddings."

"*Our* big wedding?"

"Whatever you say, sweetheart." Adams pulled her closer, burying his face in her hair. "I never thought I'd like thinking about a big wedding. I mean *our* big wedding."

"That's lovely, Jay. You practice thinking like that. Meantime, let's do whatever you plan to do about what happened last night." Entwined, they walked out of the kitchen.

Adams had built a fire against the morning's chill air, and cedar logs sizzling in the fireplace were pushing cold shadows out of the great room.

"Warm your bones in that chair over there, beautiful woman. I've got a call to make and then I'll join you."

Adams gently pushed Carly toward the fireplace and settled into a high-backed chair in front of the long bank of computer and communications equipment. After punching a speed-dialer, he swiveled around and waited, watching Carly hug her knees and stare into the growing blaze. A sleep-burred voice answered his call.

"This is Admiral Tarsis. Whatever is getting me out of the bag at this hour better be unbelievably important. Unless you outrank me. By at least one star." The Commander of Submarine Forces Atlantic was still an hour away from his wake-up calisthenics.

Adams swiveled the chair away from Carly and his face hardened. "It's *damned* important, George. I want to know the names of the stupid bastards you put ashore last night."

"Sweet Jesus. Is this Jeremiah Adams? I thought you retired a month ago."

Adams grimaced. "Admiral, I am *not* retired. What I am is pissed-off. I want to know the names of those idiots your boat put ashore at Wachapreague last night. I also want to know where they are right now, or where they'll be later today. I intend to pay them a personal visit."

There was a long silence, and Adams frowned. "Are you awake, George?"

"Exactly what happened, Adams?" The crisp tone was reassuring.

"About an hour before midnight one of your boats sailed out of the fog five miles east of Wachapreague and dropped off some maniacs in a Zodiac. I was drifting in the vicinity watching the show, and then those—those *people* shot up my boat and my dog. I want their ass on a platter, George, and I want it now. I intend to do some very serious carving."

"You're sure you saw a submarine? Ah, forget that." Tarsis paused. "I guess you know what a boat looks like in fog." There was another pause. "You say Ranger got shot? He okay?"

"George. George, are you *listening* to me? What the hell's the matter with you? I want to know who those people are. I am going to visit serious shit upon them." Adams took a long breath. "Ranger's going to be okay, George. Which may be just enough to save the lives of those assholes, but don't bet on it."

"That's good, Jay. Fine." Tarsis sounded distracted. "I'm very sorry about Ranger. And about your boat, of course. Tell me, Jay, where're you now? At that old house you bought in Onancock? What's that name... the Hermitage?"

"Yes, I'm in Onancock, damn it, and—" Tarsis interrupted.

"That's fine, Jay, fine. I've got all the numbers for you out there. You'll be hearing from me in a few hours, max." The line went dead. Adams looked at the silent handset for a moment and then slowly returned it to its cradle. Carly was watching him through lowered lashes, and when he swiveled back to her chair she silently raised an eyebrow.

"Tarsis was very strange."

"How do you mean strange?" She watched Adams stand and walk to the fireplace, which was finally flooding the room with warmth.

"I think he doesn't know a damn thing about that sub or the people in the Zodiac. And Admiral George Tarsis is aware of the exact location and status of each and every one of his boats. So...."

"So?"

"So, that submarine was not one of ours. And whoever sent it and the landing party did not do it with US Navy permission." As Adams stared into the flames, Carly noticed his jaw muscles flexing rhythmically. Breaking out of his deepening reverie, Adams spun away from the fireplace and moved toward the stairs.

"What's cookin' sailor?"

"They've carried the war to our homeland again. It's time to dress, eat a high-protein breakfast, and make a lot more calls. Things will start happening before the sun is high or I'll start making them happen. So I'll need a pot of fresh coffee, trousers, and a kiss."

Carly unfolded out of her chair in front of the fireplace, and stretched her arms high. "Are you sure about all that, skipper? Maybe this is some sort of test or— or what do you call it? A war game?" Her voice did not hold much conviction.

"Tarsis doesn't play games with submarines. And those were real bullets."

"Okay, then." Carly managed to produce a small grin. "So it's coffee, trousers, and a kiss. Have I got that in the right order?"

"No, you don't."

Adams pulled Carly to his chest, breathed the perfume in her hair, and kissed her. He leaned back, lifted her chin, and looked into her eyes.

"Kissing you is first, babe. Always."

Carly stepped out of his embrace and flashed a brief smile.

"Get moving, sailor. I make coffee, you make trousers, and when I get dressed we both make some phone calls."

Adams grinned at her and turned to take the stairs two at a time. But the après kiss warmth did not convince him there would be much joy in the coming day.

CHAPTER 26

The large gray frame house was sleeping, blinds lowered and windows closed. Inside, in a second floor bedroom lit by a dim table lamp, two men were sitting close to a third man in bed. The two that were seated drank dark and pungent coffee.

"Jabber, hear me. Hear me, my brother! How do you feel? Speak to me." The Professor leaned close to the sweat-streaked face on the pillow.

"I feel like death, Professor. I cannot breathe. My body is so weak I cannot stand." Jabber's voice was reedy, and his eyes wandered around the room until they found the Professor's face. "I am dying?"

The Professor was relieved to hear Jabber's voice. "Don't try to be even more crazy than you are already. You have the flu or some respiratory illness. Something infected you in that sewer pipe of a submarine. Don't worry. Now listen carefully." The Professor leaned forward and raised his voice when he saw Jabber look away, gasping in pain and breathing hard.

"Listen to me, you idiot. I must go with our friend here to see the target, and to be sure of what we must do. I will also make ready the first weapon. I do not wish to do that near this house or this village. Listen to me!" The Professor reached out to gently turn Jabber's pale face toward him.

"You will stay here. You have water and orange juice on this table. Take these tablets, one every four hours. They are American flu pills, and they will help you feel better. There's food in the kitchen if you are hungry. Be sure to stay away from the windows if you go downstairs. Jabber! Are you listening?"

"I hear you, Professor." Jabber was suddenly alert, fixing his feverish eyes on the face above him.

"If anything happens and I do not return, you will carry on without me, just as we were trained. Your instructions for all the weapons are written in your book. See, I put it on this table. Yes?"

Jabber nodded feebly.

"I will leave the other weapons in the garage. If we're not back tomorrow, one of our friends in America will come here to guide you. Whatever happens, the only calls you answer are from this telephone." The Professor switched on a cell phone, and put it on the night table near the bed. Then he sighed in resignation.

"We have hidden your guns in a very safe place, Jabber, so don't bother to search for them. You won't need them. Do not leave this house until we return tomorrow. By then you will be better and you can help complete our mission. Do not answer the door if anyone comes. Do absolutely nothing, Jabber. Nothing. Most important, kill nothing. Don't kill a fly. Do you hear me, Jabber?"

"I hear you, Professor. I will pray for you today. And for me." Jabber's voice rasped wetly.

"Good. You pray. I must leave now, before the dawn comes. Do not worry, you will feel stronger tomorrow." The Professor leaned forward again and saw that Jabber had fallen into a troubled sleep. Taking a last look at the man tossing in the bed, the two men rose, stepped into the hall, and quietly closed the door behind them.

As they went down the stairs, the Professor murmured to his companion, "I do not understand how Jabber became so sick so suddenly. He was in good health when we left the submarine, and now he is sick. Very sick."

"Don't worry so much. These things happen. What could it be but a chest cold or the flu? You heard him coughing last night. He'll be with you when you strike your first blow, and he will join you in your glory."

"Yes, I heard him coughing." The Professor shrugged off his concern as they crossed the dark kitchen on their way to the garage. "Last night I saw the machine in the back of your vehicle. It is exactly what is needed?" The Professor glanced at his companion as the two men entered the shadowy garage.

"Correct, and the other one is the same. It's mounted in the Suburban over there. They're both exactly as ordered."

"Pray they are so."

The Professor checked the machine in the back of the black vehicle, comparing it to a twin mounted in a similar SUV parked alongside. Satisfied, he closed both rear hatches and crouched next to the two cylinders lying on the garage floor. Selecting one, he checked the fittings on it, then heaved the stainless steel canister onto the rear seats of the Suburban. It settled heavily, cushioned by its foam rubber rings.

The Professor closed the side door and said, "We will test the machine in the back of this vehicle when we are away from your lovely American home and curious neighbors. Let us now go, my secret friend." He glanced at the aluminum case in the corner and the remaining cylinder beside it, and made a mental note to hide them when they returned. In the meantime, they would appear harmless to any casual observer.

The electric garage door elevated silently, and the Suburban backed into the dawn. The Professor could just make out a dim light on the second floor of the house, and then the driver turned and wheeled them down King Street. Soon they would be on Route 13, heading to Washington, heading to the beginning of their destiny. Jabber should be with them, he thought, but some microbe from that filthy submarine had wounded him as surely as an enemy's bullet.

The Professor watched America roll by, and thought about Jabber's sickness again. It was not a good beginning.

CHAPTER 27

"Why do you always say I'm early to work, Jeremiah? The Secretary arrives promptly at seven-thirty every morning, and I always have the traffic and mail organized and waiting for him. Just as I did for you, if you can remember." Sophie was answering Adams' call to her Pentagon phone, and sounding all business.

"There's something important in the air," she continued. "The Secretary called my home an hour ago, and asked me to forward all calls from Admiral Tarsis to him until he's at his desk. He also said I might be hearing from you and if I did not, I was to call you this morning as soon as he arrived." Sophie paused until the silence became accusatory.

"I'm sorry, Sophie. I guess I forgot how fast bad news travels." Adams tried for an apologetic tone in his voice. "Look, the reason I didn't bother you or your boss at home this morning is that I don't think he knows much about submarines." He caught himself, "I assume you're referring to the incident last night?"

"The word 'incident' is a bit sterile, don't you think?" Frowning, Sophie stirred her tea vigorously. "According to the confirmation traffic on my desk, SUBLANT called CINCUSLANTCOM, who called the CNO, who then called the Secretary. They're all very concerned about this 'incident,' as you call it." Then her voice softened. "How's Ranger? Admiral Tarsis said he'd been wounded."

"Ranger's going to be fine. I'll be stopping by to see him today while you and your boss manage the nation's defense. Anyway, I'd like to be kept in your loop, since I'm going to harass Tarsis and some other folks today."

"It seems you *are* in the loop. The Secretary asked me to request you to stay at home so he can speak to you on a secure landline. That should be in few minutes, so if you must go out, please be sure to have your secure cell phone with you. Ah... just a moment, please." Sophie had covered the mouthpiece of her phone with her hand, and Adams could hear muffled voices.

"Secretary Horton has just arrived. Please stay by your phone until he calls you." The connection clicked and went silent.

Dropping the phone into its cradle, Adams turned his chair to watch Carly come into the room. Dressed in jeans, a woolen shirt and hiking boots, she winked at Jay as she added a log to the fire. Then came a distinctive warble, and Adams spun his high-backed chair around, slid a metal ID card into the STE unit, and lifted the handset.

"Mr. Adams?" The Secretary's digitized and encrypted voice boomed down the wire.

"Yes, Mr. Secretary. Good morning."

"In view of events last night, we have little hope it will be a good morning." Horton cleared his throat. "I regret I have not had the opportunity to meet you face to face before this unfortunate day. However, your reputation tells me you do not stand on ceremony. So, since Miss Giltspur assures me this is a secure line, I will come right to the point." Adams liked the Secretary's style.

"Admiral Tarsis tells me you saw a submarine put people ashore on the coast of Virginia last night. Both he and the CNO say the submarine was not one of ours, and that they do not know the nationality of the intruders. The submarine has disappeared, and so have the people who landed. Do you agree with that so far, Mr. Adams? And are you absolutely sure you saw a submarine disgorge a landing party?"

"Yes, sir. I was close enough to them to get my boat and my dog shot up by the bastards. Excuse the language, please." There was no inflection in Adams' voice.

"No apologies are needed, Mr. Adams. I want the bastards to whom you refer taken down immediately. Since you are the senior member of the defense establishment on the scene, I am asking you to take control of this incident until I direct otherwise, and begin the hunt for those people who landed on our shores. What sort of assets will you need to initiate your search?"

"With respect, sir, may I remind you I am no longer a senior member of the defense establishment? Or if I am, it's only until you accept my resignation letter."

Adams spoke those words through clenched teeth, and Horton inhaled deeply before he replied. "Yes, Mr. Adams, there is indeed the matter of your pending resignation. Miss Giltspur, you are still on the line?"

"Yes, Mr. Secretary."

"When we conclude this telephone conference, please ask Mr. Beauchamps to place himself on administrative leave until further notice. He's not to enter the Pentagon while on such leave, and you will inform security his building pass is revoked until I have time to personally deal with him. Is that clear? Yes? Good." Adams could hear springs complain as the Secretary rocked in his brass-studded swivel chair.

"I believe there has been a serious misunderstanding, Mr. Adams, and I would like to clear it up right now. May I ask if it was your intention to resign your position?"

Adams felt his chest relax. He wanted to jump out of his chair and run around the room, laughing. Then he saw Carly watching him, her lips curved in a faint smile. He realized what he really wanted to do was put the phone down and hug her. To explain he was not going to be a college professor. To tell her how happy he was. But he turned away and looked into the distance.

"No, Mr. Secretary. I did not intend to resign my position. I was led to believe that you—"

Horton interrupted, and said, "You were improperly led to believe things by an individual no longer relevant to you or my department, Mr. Adams, and I will be obliged if you will disregard anything he may have said or done. You will further oblige me by continuing to act in your position as my Special Assistant. In that capacity you will now assist in dealing with those men who secretly landed on our shores. Are we agreed?"

"Yes, sir. As to your first question, I'll need a little time to think the situation through in detail. For starters, though, I believe a multi-agency dragnet at this time would be a waste of energy and probably counterproductive."

"And why is that?"

"First, we don't know anything about who we're looking for, what they look like, where they are, where they're heading, or what they might be planning to do. Second, there'd be a chaotic turf fight between Northern Command, Homeland Security, the FBI, and state and local police forces. And that would create a feeding frenzy in the media. Then the public gets panicky."

"Very well. Nevertheless, it's not a good idea to sit on this. The media and our fellow citizens will not long forgive such silence, especially should...well, should bad news develop."

"Sir, if we had photos of the men who came ashore we could get them out to every law enforcement agency in the country. Grill informants. Pull out all the stops.

But what do we tell our cops right now? That there are some guys who illegally landed here and who might be planning to injure us? Those kinds of people come across our borders all the time these days. So, until we're smarter, a single helicopter with some troops to search the coast near Wachapreague might be the best first step."

The Secretary replied immediately, "What sort of helicopter and troops? What kind of equipment will they need? And exactly how long do you think other government agencies will remain ignorant of our actions?"

Adams was beginning to think this new Secretary might turn out to be one hell of a surprise for his critics.

"The 24th Marine Expeditionary Unit at Camp Lejeune just returned from Somalia. If the MEU commander can be persuaded to part with one of his new Knight Hawk helicopters and a sharp pilot, they'll be useful for things besides a coastline search. And as for other agencies, I recommend we sit on this for at least a couple of days. It'll take at least that long before they can catch up, anyway."

"Very well. I'll try to be persuasive with our Marine Corps with regard to their helicopter. What else?"

Adams' mind reached out to envision scenes yet to happen, and though he did not feel it happening, his body tensed and his eyes narrowed as his mind rapidly established parameters for the search. *Landing area... safe-house? Block roads up the peninsula... proximity to Washington? Vehicles... Communications... Did spooks see anomalies? Assets? Make something happen... shake the grate?*

Adams had metamorphosed into a practiced hunter. Carly shifted in her seat as she listened to him speak, her cheerful demeanor evaporating.

"Sir. Please ask Admiral Tarsis to look for that submarine. Then, besides the helo, I'd like a team of Force Recon Marines from the MEU, including a couple of swimmers and a communications expert. They should bring swim gear, an inflatable boat, tactical comm equipment, and small arms. I'll coordinate their activities from my home."

"Admiral Tarsis and I have already agreed an immediate search for that submarine is essential, Mr. Adams. So, besides the helicopter and Marines, is there anything else you need right now?"

"No sir. I'll let you know what's happening and what else might be useful as soon as things develop."

"Very well, a helicopter and a Marine unit will be at your disposal today. You will have a visitor from Admiral Tarsis, and one from the Office of Naval Intelligence. In the meantime, please keep your secure cell phone with you should you leave your home. Miss Giltspur and I will need to contact you from time to time. And of course, no one is to know about the landing besides those who are already aware of it, or who are sent to assist you. You agree we should keep this very close for the moment?" Adams glanced at Carly and wondered why she looked so unhappy.

"Of course, Mr. Secretary. No one except those who are already aware of it." At least he had a loophole that would allow him to keep Carly briefed, and he reckoned he would need it. He did not want to think about trying to tell her she did not have a 'need to know' about the landing.

"By the way, Mr. Adams, I have a question somewhat off the subject at hand," the Secretary continued. "Precisely who is 'Jelly Roll' Horton?"

Adams almost swallowed his tongue. "Ah. Um. Jelly Roll Morton, sir. *Morton.* He died in 1941. He was a jazz musician. Piano player."

"I see. Was he a good musician, Mr. Adams?"

"If you like jazz, sir, he was one of the greats."

"As it happens, Adams, I do like jazz music. I also believe Jelly Roll played in whorehouses, was a gambler, a pool shark, and a stage comedian. Isn't that correct?" Secretary Horton cleared his throat into the silence. "And I do hope Ranger, your well-known companion, makes a quick and complete recovery. I will call you later today."

With that, Adams realized Horton had gently dropped his phone back onto its base. What he could not know was that the Secretary then heaved himself out of his comfortable chair to head for Sophie's desk in the outer office. He had orders to issue before going to the White House.

Sitting in her adopted chair in the Hermitage, Carly drew her brows together and asked, "What was that all about?"

"A musician." Adams shook his head slightly. "This new Secretary is going to jack some people up *big time.*"

"No, not that. I mean about not resigning your job as an official terrorist."

"Sweet Jesus, not all that again. I'm not a terrorist, Carly. I'm looking for some dangerous people—people who are *real* terrorists. That's it."

Carly fixed Jay with a cool stare. "Okay, Popeye, here's the deal. You know I love you, and you know how I feel about your job. You're tough, but you're not a youngster anymore. So I'll worry, and I'll stand next to you while you find the men who hurt Ranger. No questions, no reservations. And when all this is over, we'll talk some more about big weddings. And about what we do. Or don't do. Deal?"

Adams was stunned into momentary silence. Whatever else happened, he was *not* going to lose this woman. While anxious thoughts roiled in his head, he noticed that Carly had a faint dimple in her chin when she frowned. Funny he never noticed that before.

He walked to her chair and put his face very close to hers, whispering, "Okay, it's a deal, sweetheart."

Too old for the job? Bullshit.

CHAPTER 28

Temperanceville, Virginia

At the Professor's insistence, the Suburban stopped on a side road fifteen miles north of Onancock. Dawn was ten minutes old, and the very rural town of Temperanceville was still asleep when the Professor stepped down from the vehicle.

"Wait patiently, my friend," the Professor said, "and keep the engine running in case we must depart quickly." He dried moist palms on the firm roughness of the new Levi jeans he had been given by the driver. They fit well, and the Professor's mind drifted to his college days in New York, a lifetime ago. *Two lives ago, the lost lives of my wife and my son.*

The driver grunted and handed the Professor a battery-powered remote control. "This will start that machine in the back."

The Professor buried his nostalgia, opened the rear hatch, and noticed the green road sign nearby. He turned to the man behind the wheel and said, "The sign says this place is named Jerusalem Road. You have a fine sense of history, my generous host. I hope Arab historians will smile when they write of this moment."

The driver shrugged and replied, "Let's finish this before some stupid farmer comes by and offers to help us."

The Professor looked down at the remote control. It was just like the units he and his "Mohammed" instructors had used during training classes. He depressed a button on the hand-held controller and heard the machine in the rear of the SUV cough before producing a businesslike buzz. Waiting a few seconds to insure it ran smoothly, the Professor depressed another button and the machine was silent. Pocketing the control and opening the side door, he reached under the seats and found a respirator facemask.

"This is not truly necessary, but it is good to be careful about all such things." The Professor's voice was muffled by the mask.

He bent, picked up a pinch of dust from the road's shoulder, and tossed it into the air. It drifted away from the vehicle and into the nearby field. Grasping steel loops welded to the cylinder's body, the Professor hauled the gleaming tube off the rear seat and cradled it in his arms. He walked to the open back doors of the vehicle, sat the cylinder on the tarmac, looked up and down the road, and then twisted a T-bar handle. He was rewarded with a brief sigh, and he then unscrewed the top of the cylinder as if it were the cap on a long and shiny jar of mayonnaise. Tossing the valve-top into the van, he looked into the interior of the stainless steel tube.

Just as in the training sessions, there they were—three plastic bags like big sausages, each filled with a tan flour-like powder. But these were not dummy training bags. One by one, he carefully transferred each sealed bag into the hopper atop the machine in the rear of the van and then locked down the rubber-edged hatch with its four wing nuts and bolts. Finished, he sealed the edge of the hatch with tape from the roll in his pocket, slammed the back doors and returned to the front of the van.

"That's it? That's all?" The driver looked back at the machine in the rear with undisguised suspicion.

"What did you expect, dear colleague? Armageddon on Jerusalem Road? I only vented the protective gas. Nitrogen. The machine will be ready for use as soon as the bags in it are opened."

The Professor pulled off his mask, climbed back up into his seat, and closed his eyes in satisfaction as the vehicle accelerated. They were almost ready to make their special visit to the Pentagon.

CHAPTER 29

A venerable but highly polished SH-3 Sea King helicopter settled into the south lawn of Adams' home on Westerhouse Creek. Leaves and small branches scurried in the tornado of its downwash.

Carly and Adams stood on the porch of the Hermitage, watching the helicopter's rotor blades slowly whistle to a stop. Two uniformed figures emerged and trudged toward the house, one carrying an overnight bag.

"You gents certainly know how to tear up a country boy's rhododendrons."

Adams knew both officers: Lieutenant Commander Skip Harding, the humorless aide to Admiral Tarsis, and Commander Fred Horst, an old friend from Office of Naval Intelligence days.

Horst looked at the tattered bushes, clapped a hand to his mouth in horror, and said, "Oh, dear! Write up a bill for Tarsis, Jay. Skip here is anxious to give the Admiral more bad news. Right, Skip?"

Firmly buttoned into his uniform, Harding was not laughing. He said, "I am sorry about your plants, Mr. Adams. Admiral Tarsis sends his personal greetings. He wants you to know he advised CINCLANT about the... " His eyes swiveled to the tall redhead casually leaning against the porch railing, watching the three men with cheerful interest.

"Oh, I'm sorry," Adams said, glancing at Carly. "Sweetheart, this freckled gent is Lieutenant Commander Skip Harding. He may look like a high school intern for some senator, but he's really an aide to Admiral George Tarsis. The man next to him is Commander Baron Sigfried zu Horst und Koberg. An old ONI buddy."

A distant birdcall was heard in the ensuing silence. Harding and Carly first gaped at Adams and then turned, as if they were synchronized by hidden wires, to stare at the slowly reddening Commander.

"For crissake, Jay," said Horst.

"Okay, everybody," Adams chuckled. "Fred gave up the title when he turned twenty-one at Annapolis and had to relinquish his dual citizenship. He's just Fred Horst now. I only mention it to give him a hard time for the damage to my lovely rhododendrons and to let you know that nobility is on the job. By the way, Skip, don't make jokes about Fred's Bavarian lineage. He is likely to inflict pain on you.

"And now, gentlemen, this is Miss Carlotta Truitt." Adams made a short bow in Carly's direction. "She publishes The Daily Times, Delmarva's finest newspaper."

It was the turn of the naval officers to gape at Carly. Horst recovered his smile first and said, "I heard you were retired, Jay. Are you a newspaper reporter now?"

"Damn it, Fred. I am not retired. And I'm not a reporter either. Carly was on Pilgrim when we got shot up last night, and she stuck around to give me a hand with Ranger at the vet's office."

Carly broke the strained silence that followed. "Why don't you invite these men inside, Jay, and offer them some coffee? I think the pot's still fresh." She moved back, opened the screen door, and stood facing the trio. No one moved.

Adams heaved a mock groan. "All right, all right. Let's get this over with. SecDef said the landing was to be closely held except for 'those who are already aware of it.' He also appointed me as senior officer present afloat, and as SOPA I have decided that Carly qualifies, especially since she was shot at last night. She's on board this exercise and stays in the loop until I say otherwise, okay?"

Adams waved the two officers toward the door, and Horst dutifully climbed the stairs. He paused at the door and looked back at Harding. The unsmiling Admiral's aide stood rooted to the walkway.

"Mr. Adams, sir. Admiral Tarsis informs you that neither the submarine," Harding glanced sadly at Carly, "nor the people it put ashore, belong to COMSUBLANT or anyone else in the defense establishment. He wants you to know he spoke to CINCLANT, who advised the CNO, who then advised Secretary Horton. There is now the highest possible 'need to know' restriction on any information about the incident." After another unhappy glance at Carly, he went on. "Commander Horst has been assigned to assist you in any way possible, and Admiral Tarsis instructed me to tell you he is also ready to help. He's checking every source of data available to him, and he's diverting an attack boat to the mid-Atlantic area. He believes that submarine landed terrorists last night. Or saboteurs."

"Tell George I'm grateful," Adams answered. "Tell him I'll keep him advised in return, including my bills for Horst's rations and quarters. And all those rhododendrons. Now come inside before you have some kind of seizure." Adams watched Harding blush again and heard Horst chuckle behind him.

"No thank you, Mr. Adams. I was ordered to deliver the message and Commander Horst, then return immediately with your reply. After I return the helo to CINCLANT, I will be your liaison with Admiral Tarsis. And the Admiral wanted me to be sure to tell you he has every confidence you will do a decent job here, even though you are old and retired. His exact words, sir."

Adams looked at the helicopter and realized its turbines were still running, the pilot waiting in the cockpit.

"Tell your Admiral as soon as my dog recovers he's going to bite the Admiral's ass. My exact words."

Harding looked horrified.

"Okay, Skip, off you go. Don't forget my message to George." Adams turned toward the door as the helicopter's blades began to turn. "And try not to screw up what's left of my lawn."

Leaning on the kitchen's center island a minute later, Horst was holding out a coffee cup to Carly and laughing. "Tarsis will shape him up, Jay. Or Skip will die trying."

They sat around the long refectory table dividing the kitchen's eating area. Horst continued talking as he spooned sugar into his cup.

"Okay, Jay, CINCLANT says you're not retired. I believe that. But I also believe you'll be more than retired if a newspaper article appears about the landing." He looked at Carly and added, "You agree, right?" Then Horst shifted his gaze to Adams. "So how's about we get her sworn in as a deputy federal marshal?"

"Why, so she can carry a badge and gun for protection? Or because she'd be a fed, with the usual penalties for revealing family secrets?"

"Jay, you know that pretty soon there'll be enough guns and badges around here to take care of any and all shooting problems. The bad guys are probably long gone from the neighborhood, anyway. What I'm saying is that while she's in the loop she'll meet all sorts of dumbass people, and it would be good if she had a title besides publisher."

Carly's palm smacked the table.

"May I say something? First, I don't like being discussed as if I'm not standing here. I'm not a dressmaker's dummy. My name is Carly, or Miss Truitt. Use one or the other, Commander Horst." She bit the end off each word. "And I understand what's at stake. I am not going to panic the public. I am not going to make trouble for Jay. So let's agree that I stay in the loop, whatever the hell that means, and I print nothing for now. As soon as the wraps are off, I will ask for and I will get permission to publish an exclusive." Carly looked from face to face, "Okay?"

Adams held up a hand, defensively. "Whoa! No one can stop you from printing an article about the landing right now. You were there. Your deal sounds fine to me, but Fred still has a point. We're going to give some people heart attacks every time you're introduced as a newspaperwoman."

Carly glared at the two men, but remained silent.

Adams turned to Horst. "I take her sweet smile to mean it's a go. Can you handle the swearing-in routine this morning, Fred?"

"You bet, boss. And this is good coffee, Carly. Thanks." The naval officer pulled a cell phone from his belt and started to punch in a number. He paused and looked up, sensing Carly's stare. "What? Change your mind?"

"Baron zu Horst und Koberg?"

"Standing before you in the Bavarian flesh."

"You do look the part. If I hear of a small country being plundered by a former naval officer with a blond crew cut, blond eyebrows and a blond mustache, I'll know who to call for an interview."

"You bet. My family motto is, 'Small countries sacked. Off-season rates apply.'" Horst finished dialing. Waiting for the connection, he looked around the kitchen.

"Splendid galley, Cap'n Bligh. When I get back from inspecting holes in your rowboat, I hope lunch will do your elegant décor justice."

CHAPTER 30

The Representative Condominiums
Arlington, Virginia

The two men were on a balcony that overlooked the Pentagon. The Washington skyline shone on the opposite bank of the Potomac.

"This building we are in, what is it called?" The Professor was looking at the nearby Pentagon through binoculars the driver had supplied.

"The Representative."

"It is not on the map."

"Of course it's not on the map. Why would it be on a tourist map? And don't spend all day on the balcony with those binoculars. Someone could be watching and see you."

"We are on the south side of the Pentagon. You did not tell us the exact position of this building. It is not an effective location for the weapon we will use."

"South side, north side, what's the difference?"

The driver set his pistol and cell phone on the antique desk near the balcony, being careful not to scratch its polished surface. "This apartment is only a place to rest before you and your helper carry out your mission." He smiled at the ornate furniture and silk carpets. "It's a lovely place, isn't it? When he feels better, your comrade can join you here. You'll have your own room with its own toilet."

The Professor frowned. His comrade, his brother, was sick and perhaps even more volatile than usual. Concern edged his words.

"We planned to use this apartment balcony for our attack."

"What! My condo? Never. The police would find out and tear it apart. I was told we should use the Suburban for the attack, not the balcony. That way we can get away from the Pentagon afterwards, and get to a safe-house."

The Professor slid the balcony doors closed, drew the drapes, and slowly turned. As he locked eyes with the driver, he removed his Glock pistol from its belt holster, letting his arm hang at his side.

"You will do all that I decide is necessary in order to succeed. Is that not how you were instructed, my friend?" He was annoyed by the sheen of perspiration that appeared on his companion's face. This man is a coward as well as a sybarite, the Professor thought. I will have to watch him carefully, and perhaps Jabber will have to deal with him when we leave Washington. Cowards are dangerous.

"Of course, of course. If the apartment is in the wrong place, we'll just find a better place." The driver's head bobbed up and down. "Where would such a place be?"

"I am thinking about that." The Professor placed his handgun on the table next to the other weapon. "So let us refresh ourselves and then drive your huge vehicle around the streets here. Yes?"

Twenty minutes later, they were back on the road.

"The Gaza waterfront was once as happy and beautiful as this street. But never again," the Professor observed. The Suburban was cruising north, back toward Army Navy Drive, and the Professor saw Monday shoppers thronging the entrance to the Pentagon City mall.

The driver grunted, "Gaza was never so clean."

Suddenly angry, the Professor forced his face and eyes to go blank. This man beside me cares only for his possessions, he thought, and I wish Jabber were with me instead, sick or not. Then, worried about how long Jabber might be ill, and what that meant to their plans, he found himself leaning forward, concentrating. They were cresting the rise just south of the Pentagon, and he saw entrances to the parking lots surrounding the massive building.

"Very good," he said, "Now drive back down your clean street, and get us closer to that building."

"It's not possible. See those police? See those military vehicles? See those machine guns? They are all around the Pentagon. You need a pass to do anything but drive into the visitor parking lot. I can only go around the north side and come back down the parkway between the river and the building. If you like."

"Do it."

It was the driver's turn to be angry. This imperious shit has some nerve, he silently raged, ordering me around after shooting at some fishing boat and fucking up the landing. We'll be lucky if the government doesn't start a big investigation. At least there were no news reports about the shooting at Wachapreague. His thoughts grew darker. It will be a real pleasure to kill this dog after his mission is over. Him and that little sick prick in my house. But first they must finish their mission. After they are successful others will come, and between taking care of these idiots and waiting for the next batch, life will be sweet. Sweet, as long as Dehesh is satisfied.

Driving along the Pentagon's north parking lot, he turned right and then swung south on a tree-lined road that joined the George Washington Parkway.

"Watch," the driver said, "The Pentagon will be on the right in a minute. Just through those trees."

"What is that over there? Boats?" The Professor looked down at the city map of Washington. "Ah, I see it here. It is the Columbia Island Marina. Turn in, turn in!"

They parked the SUV at the far end of the marina's parking area and walked along the docks. The Pentagon loomed close on the western horizon, just beyond the lagoon surrounding the marina's slips. It was warming into a perfect spring day, and birds called and fluttered in the giant pin oaks shading the water's edge.

"Who owns these boats? Admirals and generals in the Pentagon?"

"Maybe a few," answered the driver. "But most are owned by the local people." He looked through a locked gate at the cabin cruisers and snickered, "And their boats aren't half as good as mine."

"How do the owners get through these locked gates? Are there guards?"

"Of course there are guards—marina guards. And policemen. But the owners have keys to the gates so they can get to their boats." *You stupid peasant.*

The Professor looked across the pier to the marina's sloping boat ramp and then at the Pentagon. Just across the narrow lagoon, the building looked immense.

"Your boat. Could you drive your boat here?"

"My God. It would take forever. We'd have to go south to Cape Charles, then north up the Chesapeake Bay, then up the Potomac River. I could do it in a couple of days, but how would I explain why I took my boat on such a journey? And we'd have to anchor out in the river, since we don't have a slip at this marina. There are police boats that patrol the Potomac."

"That is unfortunate. It would be an excellent way to bring all our weapons into the city. Never mind, there are other ways to move them. Let us return to the vehicle."

The Professor slowly walked along the tree-lined waterfront, occasionally looking across at the massive gray building beyond the boat docks.

Even a casual observer could see that approaches to the Pentagon were walled and defended by police. Only fools would try to attack it on foot or in a vehicle. All those policemen and their guns served only to deter idiots and impress the foolish. The elegant attack the Professor and Jabber practiced so long ago was now made impossible because of the location of the apartment. The road west of the building was almost suitable, but there are still guards, and the nearby high ground is covered by official buildings in a fenced compound. But no knot was ever tied that could not be untied.

"Let us drive along the river. I would like to see Reagan National Airport, and the other marina near it. On the map it is called Dangerfield Island Marina. Then we can cross the river and tour Washington." The Professor turned in his seat to examine the driver's profile.

"I hope you do not mind driving me about, my dear friend, but it is necessary we find exactly the right place to use our weapons. We must select the correct weapon for the correct task in the correct place. After today I will do the driving, if you are getting tired of it."

"No, of course I don't mind. I'm not tired. We must do what we must do."

It was going to be a very long day, thought the driver. Probably no decent food or drink either.

CHAPTER 31

Turbulence again scattered leaves and branches in all directions across the Hermitage lawns. Looking through the porch window, Adams could not stop the corners of his mouth from sagging as he watched the helicopter lift off. An hour earlier, it had delivered a burly federal marshal who administered Carly's oath as a deputy and collected her fingerprints.

"We'll get a heliport license," he said. "That way, we lay concrete over all the damn grass and get a tax write-off."

Behind him, Horst joined Carly at the kitchen table and admired the lunch: A platter of hamburgers grilled on the indoor Jennaire, toasted whole-wheat buns, bleu cheese dressing on the salad, crisp shoestring French fries, and a bottle of vintage Burgundy. Horst beamed.

"The catering in this heliport canteen looks great, deputy marshal Truitt. Just like home."

Carly motioned the men to sit down and said, "You will be happy to know that from now on we're specializing in health food at Hermitage Heliport. Lots of tofu and bean sprouts. This lunch was just to clear out the fridge before the grand opening."

They busied themselves assembling hamburgers and dishing out plates of salad and fries.

When everyone had a glass of wine, Adams raised his goblet in the old toast: "Confusion to the enemy." They all drank and then Horst spoke around a mouthful of hamburger.

"Whoever the enemy might be, they shot up your *Pilgrim* real good."

"What'd you find?"

"Holes. I dug out a few bullets and I'll have the lab look at them. My guess is that they're AK-47 rounds, and even if we figure out who made them, that won't tell us who fired them." He dipped a fry into ketchup. "Nice boat."

"Go through the drill anyway, Fred. We're going to cover every base in every damn ballpark. You check the bullets. Tarsis looks for the sub. And if Horton moves fast, we'll have a chopper full of Marines here today. I figure they can do a close search of the coast today or tomorrow morning, latest."

"What do you think you're gonna find?" Horst sniffed his wineglass and then peered at the wine bottle label. "And if this is regular mess deck fare, I hope we can finish the search in time for an early supper."

"That landing party had to be in a hurry to get to a safe-house, wherever it is," said Adams. "Especially after they ran into *Pilgrim*. They probably scuttled their boat instead of taking time to deflate it and hide it. That would take too much time, and I don't think they plan to leave the way they arrived, anyway."

"Where do you think they went?"

"That's the key question, pal, and there are lots of others. Like why use a submarine to land people when they could just walk across the Canadian or Mexican border? Whose submarine? And what kind of mission justifies the use of a submarine?"

Carly said, "Maybe they brought things with them that are too big or too complicated to walk across the border." Both men raised eyebrows and looked at her.

Horst cocked his head and said, "You know, Jay, Humphrey Bogart would say that marshal Truitt is not just a pretty face."

"You noticed. Well, I don't mean to detract from her deductive powers, but I've been thinking along those lines, too. Besides Washington, there are plenty of high value targets along the East Coast that justify landing a team and heavy equipment by submarine. And another thing. Countries with subs capable of crossing the Atlantic also have arsenals of very nasty weapons." A pall fell over the table as they thought of horrific possibilities.

"Any country that detonates a nuclear weapon on our soil would be flattened into a glowing parking lot. Who'd be so crazy..." Horst's voice trailed off and then he mumbled the list of nations operating long-range submarines. "Russia, China, France, the UK. It just doesn't make sense."

"You give that some thought," said Adams. "Meantime, our first priority is to locate the landing party and whatever they brought ashore. Or find the folks who met them in Wachapreague. We do that, we'll be on our way to knowing everything else."

"And how do we do that?"

"We think, we look, and we get lucky. Something will point us to where they are, or pretty soon we'll feel the ground shake and then we'll know exactly where the bastards *were*." Adams looked grim.

Carly spoke up again. "Maybe we notify State Police and the Sheriff's Office. Those guys know every nook and cranny in Accomack County, and they have helicopters and hundreds of cars. I can also get reporters from my paper and the *Eastern Shore Post* sniffing around. We can tell them we're looking for illegal immigrants suspected of some sort of serious crime."

"Nah, bringing in local law and newspapers would only be slightly better than calling in the FBI or Homeland Security. Either way we'd have chaos, only DHS and the feds would create it on a grand scale. We simply don't know anything about who we're looking for."

"If they're carrying radioactive material, maybe they'll get picked up at one of the nuke choke points." Horst dipped more French fries in ketchup. "Been reactivated, you know. They tell me they have better gear now."

"Those neutron sensors suck, Fred. But like I said, pray we get lucky." Adams was refilling his glass when the secure phone made its distinctive sound and he went to the comms table. It was the Pentagon. Sophie.

"I'm glad that newspaperwoman is now a federal officer, Jeremiah. I suppose that makes her one of the family?"

"For cryin' out loud, Sophie. You want a belly laugh from me, or is something useful happening at the seat of empire?"

"I apologize." Sophie did not sound the least contrite. "I called to advise you that Secretary Horton called from the White House after briefing the president. The Secretary will order the Marines and the helicopter from the MEU to fly to you as soon as he returns to his desk, which should be in ten minutes. He intends to review the situation with you this evening. The president was advised by the Secret Service to move the vice president and part of the government out of Washington to a secure location."

"Oh boy, here we go. Okay, thanks, Sophie. I'll be standing by." Adams replaced the receiver and returned to the luncheon table.

"Okay, the bad news is that we now have the attention of the maximum leader himself. The good news is that the Marines will be here today."

Carly rose from the table, stretched, yawned and said, "While you two greet more helicopters, I think I'll make a quick trip to the vet's office and check on Ranger."

"Those troops won't be here for hours. I'll go with you." Adams returned Carly's smile.

Horst shook his head and said, "Ducky. While you two are snuggled up in that Porsche, I'll just hang out here, do the dishes, vacuum the carpets, and answer the phone. Just remember, I don't do windows." He reached across the table. "These French fries are cold—but good."

CHAPTER 32

The driver of the black Suburban grimaced when he rounded the circle on the Virginia side of the Arlington Memorial Bridge. The setting sun was in his eyes, and he was forced to slow as they bumped along the cobblestone road leading to the Arlington military cemetery.

"What's to see here?" he asked. "It's just a lousy cemetery, and it's getting dark."

"Our passing by does not disturb the dead, my loyal friend. It is the living we intend to disturb, and we must examine all possibilities. But you're right, it will be dark soon. We should leave this road before we reach those gate guards, and go south." The Professor looked at the map on his lap. "We pass the Pentagon again on our way back to your apartment. Drive as slow as possible without attracting attention."

"Okay, I will." The driver's glum face darkened. "But we had no lunch, except water and tuna salad sandwiches from a sidewalk vendor. Now we go to my condo where there is only cheese and stale crackers. Must we live like mice?"

"No, we will have food."

"Excellent! Where shall we eat supper? I know a good Lebanese restaurant on Twenty-Third Street," the driver offered.

"McDonald's. We will get the famous Big Mac and eat in your apartment. Our rest must begin early tonight. We rise before dawn to return to your other home and learn if Jabber's sickness delays us." The Professor put a forefinger on the map and traced the outline of the Pentagon, then the Federal Triangle in downtown Washington.

It must be very difficult to get close to the Capitol Building or the White House in a vehicle, he thought. That is a problem. Still, all the important buildings are clustered in the center of Washington, near the Capitol, and the hill there is high enough. East of the city, the hill is not good for anything but the nuclear weapon. And even if we detonate it on the hill, it is too small to destroy the entire city. The mission must change. A better plan is hidden somewhere on this map.

They were rolling south on Jefferson Davis Highway, passing the east side of the Pentagon. The Professor looked at the building and examined the police vehicles parked under the trees at each intersection.

"Tell me, my patient driver, did you see the van and military vehicles near the big bridge we crossed this morning? Is that van over there the same thing?" The Professor indicated a long trailer parked next to an armored personnel carrier. A soldier behind a pintle-mounted machine gun watched the passing traffic.

"That van you saw on the Bay Bridge is probably what they call a nuclear weapons choke point," replied the driver. "Inside are sensors that see a nuclear bomb. When a bomb is detected, Delta Force soldiers will take it. But I don't know about the van we passed. Maybe it is for construction workers." The driver glanced at the Professor's profile. "Didn't they tell you about choke points?"

The Professor ignored the question. "You think such a system works well?"

"Who knows? Until this day no one's tried to bring a nuclear bomb to America. But anyway, I think the sensors aren't very good."

"How do you know about nuclear sensors?"

"Newspapers." They drove on in silence.

The Professor's mind turned inward. Choke points. They are astounding, the Americans. But their technology cannot save them.

I will kill Washington.

CHAPTER 33

"Damn, even health food attracts helicopters."

Adams heard the approaching aircraft just as he, Carly, and Horst were sitting down to a supper of soup, salad, and a freshly baked organic cherry pie.

The waning light burnished the dark skin of the Nighthawk, the MH60S helicopter assigned to the Marine Corps MEU at Camp Lejeune, North Carolina. Adams walked out on the porch as the rotor blades wound down. A Marine captain in a camouflaged field uniform trotted up to the steps.

"You are Mr. Jeremiah Adams, sir?"

Adams nodded.

"May I please see some ID, sir?"

Poker-faced, Adams produced his ID holder and offered it to the Marine, who matched the photo to Jay's face and then returned it.

"My men and I are at your disposal, Mr. Adams. Colonel Kelly would like to inform you that he's loaned you fifty percent of his airborne penetration capability. He says that if you bend his tin he will come up here and bend you. He also said his feelings were hurt when he was not invited to your retirement party. Sir." The captain saluted smartly as Adams' eyes narrowed.

"You tell Walt he'll be spraying his rosebushes a long time before I retire, damn it. You may also tell him, captain—captain what?" Adams leaned forward and looked at the nametag. "Alexander. First name? Christian. Okay, Captain Christian Alexander, let's relax and let my blood pressure settle down. Who are your troops?"

The captain produced a folded sheet of paper that Adams opened and held up to the dim porch light.

"Stand easy, captain. No inspection scheduled for today. Let's see, Sergeant Ari Lowenstein, Lance Corporal Anthony Loiacano, and Private Stanley Gryzbicki. Pilot is Lieutenant Peter X. Duggan. Reads just like Notre Dame's fighting Irish backfield."

The Marine looked puzzled.

Adams began to explain and thought better of it. "Never mind. Tell your people I'll figure out how to bunk you all in my guest wing. Rooms aren't fully furnished yet, so it'll be a little cozy, but they're warm."

"No thank you, sir. We'll bivouac in that field if I can trouble you for some potable water."

"That's not a *field*, captain, it's my *lawn*. Or what's left of it. The water hose is under this porch. Good well water." Adams looked at the helicopter, its engines still running, and asked, "Captain, I wonder if you'd mind making a couple of passes over the beach at Wachapreague? See if there's anything in the way of sunken boats, or maybe people and vehicles skulking along the shoreline?"

"No good, sir. We made a pass on our way up. The low sun angle makes it too dark to see much detail on the deck. The FLIR's no help either, and night vision gear is only useful when it's real dark and we're in real close. I suggest we fly over the beach at first light tomorrow."

"Okay. How're you fixed for gas? And how about chow tonight?"

"The helo got a drink from a KC-130 a few clicks past Norfolk. She's got full tanks." The Marine cracked his first smile. "And we're looking forward to our delicious MREs. Thanks just the same, sir."

"All right, Captain. But even tough guys like real food, so campfires are okay if you want 'em. You can borrow one of my vehicles and go to town for some carryout or supermarket chow if you don't want to eat MREs. Just don't roast my neighbor's horse."

"Very kind, sir. We'll police the area in the morning."

"Fine. Send Sergeant Lowenstein over here and I'll show him the bathrooms in the rear. I don't want a latrine dug in my lawn, and morning showers for five Marines won't run my hot water tanks dry. My compliments to you and your troops, captain. See you at oh dark hundred tomorrow morning." Alexander thanked him, saluted again, and turned on his heel to march back to the helicopter.

Adams watched him go. They'll sleep on the ground tonight, he thought, and be bright-eyed and bushy-tailed before dawn. God bless the Marine Corps.

CHAPTER 34

It was less than two hours into the eight-to-twelve watch and the Marine detachment at the Hermitage was bedded down near their helicopter, a lone sentry pacing the chilly grounds. Miles to the west, in the Representative condo, the Professor and his driver were sitting at a glass-topped table in a gilt and silk dining room.

"Filthy stuff. How can anyone eat such crap." The driver pushed his half-eaten hamburger away in disgust.

"The fried potatoes are quite delicious. You should eat some. We'll be on our way before dawn, and there may be no place to find breakfast for hours. Perhaps not until we reach the big bridge." The Professor was not very hungry either, but he forced himself to chew.

"I'll survive without that garbage. We have coffee."

"As you like, my good and faithful friend. Before we call Jabber, let us review the documents you have for me. I'll be driving tomorrow, and I should know what my drivers' license looks like."

"Here." The driver took a manila envelope from the credenza behind his chair and emptied the contents on the table. "This is your Virginia driver's license. Plus two credit cards and an American passport."

"They are all counterfeit?"

"They're all real. But they won't stand up to close investigation. Neither will you, of course, so I suppose they'll do." The driver laughed.

"How did you obtain them?"

"The driver's license was the most difficult. I had to show them documents that said you lived in Virginia. That was a small inconvenience. I got official receipts when I paid utility bills for an empty house in Norfolk I rented in your name. That's the name you see on the license. But then it took some time to find a colleague who looks enough like you so his photo on the license at least resembles you. More difficult, but it was done. Americans don't check such things carefully. Even the police.

"The rest was easy. The driver's license, the birth certificate, the Social Security number, and then the State Department mailed the passport to the house in Norfolk. Credit card companies beg you to take their cards. They even pay you to take them! And so here you are, an American citizen, with credit." He laughed again.

One by one, the Professor examined each document. "An American passport. That is more than I had when I was a student in New York. And who is this Jason Bodman I am supposed to be? He is a fiction?"

"He's dead. I looked up recent obituaries and deaths of people in Wilmington who were your age when they died. Then, before they could be notified of the death, I asked the Delaware registry for a certified birth certificate. I had to do some research to find someone who did not have surviving family, and I found Jason Bodman. Then I got his Social Security number and moved his ghost to Virginia before the state realized he was dead and updated their computers." The driver leaned back in his chair.

"Unfortunately, a serious check by police will show Mr. Bodman is no longer able to drive a car. You could think about asking for Social Security benefits, though." The driver smirked. "They'd probably even send you a check." More laughter.

"Very good indeed, my friend. When our mission is completed these will be useful papers when Jabber and I drive to Canada." He looked up. "You have more of these papers for Jabber?"

"Of course I do," he replied. "And when will you strike?"

"I must find perfect locations for the weapons, and the wind and weather must favor us. After what we saw today, I think we make our first attack soon. Perhaps in the next days. It will be more difficult without Jabber, but if he's not well, then you can help me."

"But I'm not supposed to be involved in the attack! I mean, not *personally*."

"You are already involved, dear friend, and since this apartment is not suitable, you may even be essential. So. Let us call Jabber. If he feels better, perhaps you can just watch it happen on your big television."

The Professor punched in the number for the cell phone they left with Jabber. It rang six times and switched to voice mail. He broke the connection and dialed again.

"*Nam.*" Jabber's voice was faint. Then he coughed an amendment to his greeting and murmured, "Hallo."

"Saladin. It is I. How do you feel?"

"I feel like death, Professor. I am coughing my blood now. Where are you?"

"I am coming back to you soon, my hero. I will see you early in the morning. Keep warm, drink water, take the pills, and have this phone by your side. Remember, it's not '*nam,*' it's 'hello.' Okay?"

"Okay. I forget." The sounds of wheezing and gagging coughs came through the phone. "I see you in the morning. *Insh'allah.*"

"No *insh'allah*, comrade. I will see you tomorrow and we will help you to get well. Now sleep." The Professor broke the connection. "He is very sick. We will leave here after two hours and return to your house. Then we must find a doctor for Jabber as soon as possible. So, where do I rest?"

"A doctor? How do we explain Jabber? If you must have a doctor then we move him out of my house and into a motel. You can call a doctor from there."

The Professor looked up from the cell phone and glared at the driver, his words coming as a rasping whisper. "You and I, we will do everything that is needed. Everything. Remember that. And now, show me where I rest."

The driver led the Professor to a room that, like the rest of the condominium, was furnished with a discordant but expensive collection of pictures, furniture, fabrics, and figurines.

"I suggest you leave me and sleep immediately, my dear colleague. We rise at dawn, and tomorrow will be a busy day." The Professor pulled back the coverlet on the king size bed and stood looking down at the black satin sheets. "I hope you also have such an interesting bed in your room."

An hour before midnight the Professor woke, drenched in perspiration, a sheet wound around him like a slippery black shroud. The plan, the egg of a fiery bird, had hatched in his mind. He had difficulty finding sleep again, and rolled about in feverish and restless discomfort. No matter. He knew what must be done with the first weapon.

CHAPTER 35

"Hey, deputy Truitt, would you slice up the apple pie? Then put some plates on the counter and I'll pass 'em out in the morning." Adams was leaning back in his tall ergonometric chair, working at his bank of computer monitors. Commander Horst sat in a smaller swivel chair at his side.

"What apple pie?" Carly asked.

"The non-health food *Mrs. Smith's* apple pie in the freezer that you're going to pop in the oven. It won't take long to bake. While you're at it, fill the coffeemaker and set the timer for oh five hundred. I'll take the pie out when it's ready, if you know how much time to set on the oven timer."

Carly was motionless in the doorway to the kitchen, and said dryly, "I am supposed to make you an apple pie for breakfast."

"Pie and coffee are for the Marines out there. They'll need some tasty carbs after those MREs. Around dawn I'll whip us up some scrambled eggs, bacon, and rye toast with homemade blackberry jam. And if you're real nice, a spare piece of pie can be yours, scullery wench."

"You just saved yourself a fat lip, sailor," Carly said over her shoulder. "And while you're worrying about those Marines, you should know that the towels and soap in the bathrooms back there are still stacked. I'd say no one was in there tonight, but the shower floors are wet."

Horst winked at Adams and said, "Guess they brought their own soap and towels along with their own helicopter."

Finding the frozen pie, Carly rattled a baking tray into the oven, set the temperature and timer and filled the coffeemaker. Then she climbed the stairs to the bedrooms saying, "Don't stay up late, my little darlings. Big day tomorrow." Her door closed.

"Yes, auntie," Adams muttered, staring at a monitor. He was about to speak when the phone rang. A screen in the console said it was Sophie, calling on the encrypted line. He lifted the handset and punched the flashing button labeled "Secure." The small screen then read "Full Duplex." There was a slight delay and he heard Sophie's voice, her precise diction unchanged by the encryption.

"Jeremiah."

"Good evening, Sophie. You E-Ring folks are sure working late tonight. Polishing the silver?"

"I'm as tired as you, and I am in no mood for poor attempts at humor. The Secretary wishes a word with you. Please stand by." The phone clicked on hold for a moment, then the voice of Secretary Horton boomed into Jay's ear.

"What is the situation, Mr. Adams?"

"The Marines and their helo are on my lawn, Mr. Secretary, and Commander Horst is in my home. All hands are ready for an early start tomorrow."

"I imagine you plan to search the oceanfront and surroundings for evidence of the landing. What do you expect to find?"

"I'm not sure, sir. Perhaps nothing. But we'll look hard for the boat they used when they came ashore. After running into *Pilgrim* they must've been spooked, and maybe they hid their boat where we can see it from the air. Anyway, we don't have much to go on right now. My guess is they were met by sleeper agents who took them ashore. Hell, they could even be in another state by now." Adams' fist clenched when he said the words, "sleeper agents."

"It does not sound promising, I agree. Perhaps we should alert Northern Command, the FBI and the other law enforcement agencies. It may be time to establish a dragnet."

"Sir, we still don't have any data on which to base a dragnet, so I can't change my recommendation. Northern Command was established with an eye to the 9-11 attack, and they're not up to speed for this kind of threat. Neither are the federal agencies and local authorities. On top of it all they have conflicting charters, so I still think there'll be a mass of confusion, turf fights, and public concern—maybe panic. Let's work it ourselves for two days, and then we'll review the situation."

"By then, the people who landed may have attacked us."

"True."

"Damn it all to hell..." Secretary Horton's voice fell, then returned firmly. "I count us lucky you were in their path when they came ashore. But even though only three admirals, ONI, the president, and I know exactly what happened, it's only a matter of time until it leaks out. To the press, perhaps." There was a long pause, "And what *about* the press, Mr. Adams?"

"If you're referring to deputy marshal Carlotta Truitt, she's agreed not to print anything until we give her the green light. She was on *Pilgrim* when the boat was attacked, and there's nothing to stop her from publishing what she's already seen. Anyway, I think she falls in the category of 'those who already knew of the incident,' don't you agree, sir?" *Damn, Sophie must have told Horton about Carly.*

"Deputy marshal Truitt. Hah! Now that is clever. Well, if her word has sufficient weight with you, we can let it go for the moment."

"Her word has all the weight in the world with me, Mr. Secretary, whether she's a marshal or not." Adams collected his thoughts. "By the way, sir, if we use military force, deadly force, on the soil of the United States, we need a presidential directive or we'll be breaking the law. And I'll need a directive just to get the kind of people and gear and cooperation we need out here."

"Mr. Adams, you are aware that I am an attorney, I trust? How do you think you got the Marines and the armed helicopter from Camp Lejeune? A copy of that presidential directive is in this office, and Miss Giltspur will attest to its existence and terms upon proper request at any time, day or night. Have anyone who balks at providing you with what you need call her directly. Anything else?"

Horton is the right man to sit in the hot seat after all. "Yes, sir. If we get lucky after we search the beach area, I'll need a pack of mean hunting dogs to follow the trail. Sophie should stand by for a call from Admiral Bancroft."

"Fine, Mr. Adams, do as you see fit."

"Oh, and one other thing, sir. Please ask DCIA if he has recent intelligence or rumors about a landing or a terrorist attack. One that involves a submarine." Adams knew Horton and the Director of the Central Intelligence Agency were good friends, and reckoned the DCIA would honor an informal request from the Secretary without demanding to be involved. At least, not immediately.

"Very well, Adams, I'll call him first thing tomorrow morning. If I called him at this hour he would be alarmed. You should also know Admiral Tarsis called me to say one of his submarines made contact with a foreign submarine in mid-Atlantic a few days ago. Hmm. Perhaps that's sufficient reason for a call to the CIA. In any event, please keep me informed." The Secretary's voice was wearing thin. "I think we should all get some rest now, Mr. Adams, and pray for God's protection. Good night." The line went dead.

Horst had been listening to the conversation on another handset, and when Adams put the phone down he said, "Why not use the SEALs from Little Creek? Lots closer."

"There's no big rush, Fred. But if we do go into action, Bancroft has a team I've used before. They can walk on water." He rubbed his jaw. "What the heck was that comment he made about one of our boats making contact with a foreign sub?"

"Beats me. I'll check what's on the gossip net." Horst swiveled back to the computer monitor in front of him. "There's probably not much info available, considering how tight-assed submariners are about giving it out. But it's worth a look-see." Horst peeked around the edge of the large flat screen display.

"You know, Jay, I expected good computer gear and maybe a STU-III phone, but you've got a digital STE, a window on Intelink, and encrypted mobile phones. Who gave you the board seat at NSA?"

"The work I did—the work I *do* for SecDef depends on broad access to intelligence. I guess NSA got tired of sending couriers to my office, so they sent me the STE and gave me Intelink access to save on gas. It's real expensive to drive back and forth these days, you know."

"Sure it is. And of course they know you've moved the STU-III *and* the STE *and* your STE ID insert out here to Onancock, and that you regularly access the jazz on Intelink from your living room?"

"Naturally. How else?"

"Okay, pal. It's pretty handy right now, but when this is over I suggest you seriously consider hauling Uncle Sam's hardware back to your Pentagon office." Horst turned back to the monitor as it presented a summary of the global submarine order of battle.

"Meantime, why don't you bag it for a few hours? I'll see you at reveille."

Squinting at his own monitor, Adams punched a speed-dialer on the secure line. "Thanks, but I gotta call Bancroft before I turn in. We don't have any new info on that landing party, but it can't hurt to be prepared. It's only, let's see..." he scanned the digital clocks above the console. "It's only 9 PM out there. He's probably still in his office." The telephone in California rang once.

"Admiral Bancroft here. Caller ID says this is Jeremiah Adams, defender of the faith in Accomack County. I surmise your retirement is boring, and so you make crank calls at midnight on an encrypted phone they forgot to confiscate from you."

"For Pete's sake!" *The bum word is everywhere, dammit.* "No retirement, Bob. I'm very much in business as we speak, and I need the loan of Cristani and three of his best. I need them in Onancock. Now. Yesterday would be better."

"My troops do not vacation on the East Coast, Adams. And if it is an official visit you want, I'm afraid you must show me first your penny."

"I got a presidential directive. Call Sophie Giltspur in SecDef's office. If she's not there when you call, no sweat. Her Pentagon phone will forward to her secure phone at home, and she'll confirm it. Don't worry about waking her up." *Revenge, Sophie, for ratting out Carly.*

"Okay. I'll start the troops on their way and confirm with Sophie later. Unlike you, she deserves a night's sleep. I figure you're probably sober, Adams, even if you are retired, and that you are fully aware of what I will do to you if that presidential directive does not specifically cover things like domestic deployment of my troops. Would you care to enlighten me with some details?"

"Damn it, Bancroft. I said I am not *retired.* And just for that, I definitely would *not* care to enlighten you. Tell Cristani and his lads to just bring their shooting irons. No swimming anticipated. And by the way, you'll learn from Sophie you have authority to commandeer space on any aircraft you like, military or civil."

"In that case, they will be at your doorstep before noon tomorrow, local time. Goodbye, Jay." The connection broke with a sharp click. Adams sighed, replaced the handset, and used his heels to pull his chair alongside Horst's position.

"Okay, Fred. Why don't you use one of the rear guestrooms when you're done. You go through the dogtrot off the rear deck of the kitchen. Carly says the towels and soap are still lined up, so use whatever suits you, and I'll wake you with some coffee."

"I think I'll rack out on that couch there, if it's all the same to you. I'll be closer to my computer in case there's an answer to my pleas for enlightenment. You notice it is also closer to the fridge, the beer, and the pretzels. And I hope you've got a decent porno channel on that big flat screen."

Adams patted Horst's head and said, "Don't ever change, buddy. You're a breath of spring in a staid and PC world controlled by pencil-necked idiots with no sense of humor. There's a blanket and pillow in the window seat. *Buenos noches, amigo.*"

It was an hour later when a creaky floorboard woke Horst. The only light in the great room came from screensavers on the monitors, but the glow was enough to illuminate a willowy shadow gliding across the hallway balcony between the two bedrooms above.

Horst pulled the blanket up under his chin. *Good old corridor creeping. Considering Carly's brains and beauty, it sure looks like Jay's luck with the ladies has finally turned. In a big way.*

CHAPTER 36

The dawn promised a bluebird sky. The Marines were finishing their MRE breakfasts and policing the area around the Nighthawk helicopter. In the kitchen, Adams and Carly were making breakfast, brewing coffee, slicing apple pie, and watching Fox News. Eggs and bacon were sizzling in a skillet when Horst's voice sailed in from the living room couch.

"You two look like a Norman Rockwell painting this morning. A marvelous picture of domestic bliss." Carly and Adams looked at each other across the kitchen's center island and traded smiles.

"Yes indeedy." Horst leered wickedly as he folded his blanket. "There's nothing quite like a night of undisturbed rest to perk a body up. Isn't that right, shipmates?"

"Okay wise guy, you want eats, get to work. Set the table, pronto." Carly was putting plates of pie on a tray. She wore an apron sporting a legend that said, "If Momma Ain't Happy, Ain't NOBODY Happy."

"I'm going to haul apple pie and coffee out to those Marines, and when I get back I expect bright and shiny faces, two eggs over easy, and very crisp bacon. The grits should be just about ready, too." Arms laden, she headed toward the door, a heavy auburn braid swinging behind her.

The search along the Wachapreague coastline would begin as soon as the sun cleared the treetops. Lance Corporal Loiacano had brought his manpack radio into the house an hour earlier, and it sat on the computer table, alongside crypto gear and secure phones. The corporal would act as a comms center for the air search and the supporting ground activity. Adams had the twin to the radio in the back of his Yukon, and Captain Alexander and Horst carried encryption-capable walkie-talkies.

Adams' plan was simple: The helo would search the coast, beginning a mile outside the inlet, then into Wachapreague harbor, and then over the watery guts that crisscrossed and drained the marshes like twisted varicose veins. It would carry Sergeant Lowenstein and Private Gryzbicki to act as lookouts and swimmers, if need be. Captain Alexander and Adams would be in contact with the helicopter from the marina parking lot with their walkie-talkies. Horst and Carly would remain at the Hermitage headquarters.

Breakfast was almost finished when Horst asked, "Okay, Jay. Who pulls what rabbit out of what bung-hole today?"

"Look, Fred, you know as well as I do that chances of finding anything out there are slim. But we're going to search the hell out of the coast anyway." Adams looked bleakly at the faces turned to him. "Even if it looks hopeless now, our activity is good for Washington's morale. Not to mention my own. So let's go to work and hope the people we're looking for screwed up somehow. It's a good day to ask heaven's Giftie for a break."

Adams carried dishes to the sink, his face reflecting his concentration. Why a sub? If they brought heavy or bulky stuff ashore, what was it? Nukes? Who met them? There's *something* I'm just not seeing. He could feel his subconscious nagging him, and he hoped his instincts would crystallize and identify the worry before disaster struck.

Outside the warm kitchen, the helicopter began to whine, the long folded rotor blades slowly stretching out like dragonfly wings, ready for flight. A silver Yukon drove past it, and its driver exchanged waves with the pilot.

The MH60S Nighthawk is a blend of Army's Black Hawk and the Navy's Seahawk helicopters. An example of this new class was hovering a few hundred yards east of Wachapreague Marina, and it looked particularly lethal. Festooned with sensors, it also had a searchlight, a rescue hoist, and an external heavy lift hook that could take a 9,000-pound load.

One hardpoint on the vibrating machine sported a six-barreled "minigun" that could belch 4,000 bullets per minute. Another mount held a *Hellfire* missile. The Sunday morning boatmen loitering on the dock near Captain Zed's bait shop were fascinated by the intimidating warbird, even though they had no idea what it was doing over their fishing grounds.

"Big Tooth, this is War Rocket. Do you copy? Over."

"Roger, War Rocket. Copy you five by five. Over." Captain Alexander was shading his eyes from morning sun that haloed the black helicopter. The encrypted transmissions had a tinny sound in his headset.

"Big Tooth, we've spotted something here that looks like a sunken boat. Tide's down and it's a few feet under the surface. Request permission to put a swimmer in the water. Over." The Marine captain raised an eyebrow at Adams who gave him an enthusiastic thumbs-up.

"Roger, War Rocket, permission granted. Get that sunken object hooked up and then haul it and the swimmer to the parking lot west of the marina. We'll be waiting. Out."

Adams studied the helicopter through his binoculars and watched it slowly descend into a hover just above the glittering surface. A figure jumped from the open door and splashed into the gut. In minutes, the Nighthawk was slowly rising, a taut cable below it attached to a dripping black shape. The diver mounted the formless shape, his SCUBA tank bright orange in the morning sunlight, and rode up with it on the rescue winch cable. Adams let his binoculars hang from the neck strap, and watched the helicopter and its prize approach shore. He saw that the glistening black mass had an outboard motor attached to it.

Our first break. Keep 'em coming Lord. And please tell me what the hell has me so worried.

CHAPTER 37

At the Hermitage, twelve miles west of the marina, Carly and Horst stood behind Lance Corporal Loiacano, who was seated at Adams' communications desk. They were all sipping coffee and listening to the chatter on the secure tactical net that was spilling from desk speakers.

They heard Adams say the helicopter had brought ashore a Zodiac "Futura Commando" inflatable boat, with its long-shaft outboard still attached. The rubber flotation hulls had slashes and punctures along their upper sides. It had to be the boat used for the landing.

"I'll be jiggered, Carly, they actually found it!" Horst punched the air in triumph. "Now all we need is a calling card in that boat to tell us who picked them up and where they went."

"Fred, who are those men who came ashore in that boat? I mean, where do you think they come from?" Carly gazed at the commander over the close-cropped head of the Marine on the chair between them.

"That's the sixty-four thousand casualty question, deputy. A good guess is that they're the usual suspects. Islamic terrorists. They're not letting bygones be bygones after what we did to them in Afghanistan and Iraq, you know. As far as the nationality of the gents who landed here—heck, they could've come from lots of places. We'd have a better handle on 'em if we knew who owned the sub that gave them the ride."

"I understand that. But I was thinking more about who could have met them."

"The sleeper agents?"

"Yes. Sleeper agents. Would those agents be Islamic terrorists? Would they be Arabs?"

"Look at it this way. The terrorists could've originated in Indonesia, Pakistan, Sudan, Somalia, or other hives of perdition, but odds are they're Arabs. If so, I doubt anyone other than a fellow Arab would be trusted to meet them. What are you getting at?"

"We have Arabs right here in Onancock. Well, one Arab anyway. What if he was one of the sleeper agents?"

Horst started to laugh, but the look on Carly's face checked him. Instead he said, "You know we can't go around rousting every Arab in the country, Carly. Who've you got in mind?"

"Tarik's the local rug merchant. He says he's from Lebanon, and he makes no secret of being a Muslim. And I know he's got a big fishing boat at the Wachapreague marina. Let's take a drive over to his house. It's just a few minutes away, and if he's not the sleeper agent I guarantee he'll be overjoyed when I show up. He's got the hots for me." Carly flashed her widest smile and started for the door. "Let's go. I'll drive."

"Carly, we're supposed to sit tight here." Horst watched her walking briskly to the door. "Hey! Wait! This is a real crazy idea, you know? Let's tell Jay where we're going, and then we'll cruise by this Arab's house to see if he's home. I guess that'd be okay."

"Don't you dare call Jay. He's busy with that boat they found, and my hunch is... well, it's probably just a hunch." Speaking over her shoulder, she continued toward the door.

"Okay, okay." Horst moved quickly to catch up. He looked back at the silent Marine facing the radios.

"Hold the fort, Loiacano. I'll stay up on the net and we'll be back in a few minutes. Want anything from town? We deliver." He waved his walkie-talkie.

"No thanks, sir."

The lance corporal swiveled around in his chair to watch them go. From the moment Carly showed up at dawn in her tight jeans, carrying apple pie and coffee, laughing and joking with the troops, she became the sweetheart of everyone in the Marine detachment. Loiacono called after the naval officer, "Would you like to take my sidearm with you, sir?"

"Got my own, thanks." Horst fought an urge to unholster his Glock and check it. "We won't need firepower anyway. See you later, corporal." This was not standard operating procedure, and it did not feel good.

CHAPTER 38

Wachapreague Marina

The Zodiac was laid out in the weedy field near the marina like a beached sea monster. Gas turbines cooling and ticking, the Nighthawk crouched nearby while the Marines examined the deflated rubber boat, carefully going over every fitting and compartment.

Adams stood up from examining the boat's interior. "Nothing useful in any of the compartments, but it's got to be the boat they used." His radio chirped, and he pulled it from his belt. It was Sophie.

"Jeremiah, the Secretary wants to speak to you." She paused, "And I am sorry I mentioned Carly being a newspaperwoman to him yesterday. I hope it didn't cause you or her any trouble." She seemed genuinely sorry, but before he could reply the line clicked, and Secretary Horton's voice overpowered the tinny earpiece of the walkie-talkie.

"How goes your search, Mr. Adams?" Horton was somber.

"It must be ESP, Mr. Secretary. I was just about to call and tell you we think we found the boat that was used in the landing. Doesn't seem to be anything in it to give us a lead, but we'll send it to ONI for a detailed examination. Not marvelous progress, sir, but it's a start. The Marines here performed with their usual excellence, and I hope you'll make a note of it."

"Splendid. It certainly seems your reputation is well-deserved, Adams." Despite his kind words, Horton's tone remained subdued as he added, "And I will also remember to mention the detachment to their Commandant." Horton cleared his throat, hesitated, and said, "I have some news for you too. A few minutes ago, CIA Director Black answered my request for information about rumors of submarines and terrorist attacks." There was a long silence, and while the radio sizzled a nameless anxiety came over Adams as Horton continued to speak in his usual measured cadence.

"Some weeks ago, the CIA received an unconfirmed report of an attack planned on the American mainland. Two terrorists were allegedly recruited in Gaza, trained in Iran, and transported to our shores by an Iranian submarine. Something called a KILO."

Adams exploded. "Damn! Why didn't they put the word out? Why—" Horton interrupted the outburst.

"Please, let me finish." Adams could hear blood pounding in his ears as Horton calmly continued. "According to an Iranian medical doctor, the terrorists were trained at a biological and nuclear school in Tabriz. They have a nuclear device with them, and a large amount of weapons-grade anthrax. The unconfirmed report indicates the bomb has a yield of about one or two kilotons. The anthrax spores are a particularly lethal type developed in the Soviet Union called Strain 836, and are transported in two large steel canisters. They can be modified into aerosol bombs when mated with the proper equipment. Each canister contains over fifty-five pounds of the spores." Horton paused, and Adams could hear him shuffle some papers.

"In addition, the terrorists are also reported to be carrying six small canisters charged with an antibiotic-resistant form of pneumonic plague. The targets of all this weaponry are supposed to be the Pentagon and major cities on the eastern seaboard—" It was Adams' turn to interrupt.

"Supposed? Mr. Secretary, they're *here*! Right *here*! Those scumbags, their nuke and their germs landed right where I'm standing! Why didn't the CIA warn us?"

"It seems the report the CIA received was from an Army doctor. He forwarded an email from an Iranian military doctor he tried to recruit at a medical conference last year. In the absence of corroboration or reports of submarines and the like, the CIA thought the email could be a message designed to provoke us into a national panic. They decided to check it carefully before alarming the intelligence community.

"Although he asked about my concern, I did not tell Director Black about the submarine you saw. In any event, he regretted the delay in promulgating the report, and said that—" Adams again interrupted the Secretary. His mind flashed to the Hermitage, and all he could visualize was Carly's face, framed by her auburn hair.

"Please stand by, Mr. Secretary," Adams said into the radio. He pushed a button on his cell phone and brought it close to his face. "Loiacano, this is Adams." His crushing grip on both handsets turned his knuckles white.

"Yes sir, Mr. Adams." The encryption circuits whined.

"Get Commander Horst on the line for me, okay?"

"The commander and the lady left base and went to town, sir. They took off a few minutes ago." Adams' mind cleared so suddenly he was light-headed. He *knew* where they had gone.

"Corporal, please think carefully. Did they say where they were going?"

"I'm not sure, sir, but the lady said someone named Tarik might be one of the guys we're looking for, and they went to check out his house."

Kasim. That sonofabitch. It was the name seething in Adams' subconscious all night. *Kasim! If he was the sleeper, then—*

"Mr. Adams, what is going on, please?" The flat tone of the Secretary's voice indicated his patience had worn very thin. Adams did not care.

"Mr. Secretary, I have an emergency and I will call you back as soon as possible." Adams abruptly toggled off the radio and clipped it to his belt. He concentrated on the cell phone.

"Exactly when did they leave the house?"

"About five minutes ago, sir."

"Okay. Now get me the commander on the tactical net or on his cell phone. I'll stay silent to keep the net clear. When you get him, tell him to hold his position, wherever it is, until I return. Under no circumstances are they to enter Kasim's house. Understood? When you contact the commander you call me any way you can. Got it?"

"Yes sir."

Gripping the cell phone like a relay-runner's baton, Adams bolted into a pounding run, savagely rummaging in his pocket for the keys to the Yukon. His hand was shaking as he jammed the key into the lock. Captain Alexander sprinted up alongside and almost saluted when he saw Adams' fierce expression.

"If you're in a hurry to get back to base, sir, the helo's ready to go."

"By the time you wind up your bird and get airborne, I'll be there. Get all hands and that Zodiac back to my house. Then stay on the tactical net and stand by at base." The last words trailed out the window as the SUV accelerated, bounced across the curb and swerved into the street, its rear tires firing crushed oyster shells across the road like buckshot.

Alexander jogged to the helicopter, shouting as he ran. "Okay, troops, saddle up! Pull that piece of black crap aboard and let's haul ass to base. Move it, Duggan!" The Marines scrambled inside and prepared to get airborne as the Yukon roared west out of Wachapreague toward Onancock.

Adams could not bear to wait for a message. He keyed the walkie-talkie.

"Base, this is Adams. Speak to me, Loiacano. Over." The circuit made mosquito sounds and then buzzed. "Frequency in use." Loiacano must be trying to reach Horst.

Adams tossed the handset onto the seat next to him and wheeled the Yukon past the Wachapreague volunteer fire department, accelerating on the straight road out of town toward Route 13. The Yukon careened past the farm fields west of town, its slipstream whipping the tall crepe myrtle trees lining the road. Pushing on the steering wheel, urging the big vehicle on, Adams remembered the Army anthrax training sessions last year.

Anthrax is older than recorded history, he was taught. A zoonosis, disease that can travel from animals to humans, it was the sixth plague that Moses sent Pharaoh and the "burning wind" in the *Iliad* that killed horses and dogs and soldiers. It was the "Black Bane" of the Middle Ages, a disease of sheep and wool merchants that was called the "Woolsorter's Complaint." But even in those septic days, few people got the disease and fewer died. Two centuries later, the Soviets turned anthrax into a weapon—Adams clenched his jaw—and now their damn Woolsorter plague is *here*. Over a hundred pounds of the stuff! A few years ago, just a couple of grams of crude anthrax in a handful of letters killed five people and put thirty thousand on antibiotics. What would a *hundred pounds* do?

If the scum that came ashore Sunday night have equipment to disseminate the spores, the old anthrax-by-mail episode will be a stroll in the park compared to what's coming. Plus pneumonic plague. Plus a nuke. The Yukon narrowly missed a farm tractor and avoided the ditch by inches.

Adams' face was a mask of worry. Trying to remember the treatment for pneumonic plague, he skidded onto Route 13, cut off a truck, and roared north toward the Onancock intersection. Bringing his cell phone to eye level he keyed Horst's number, and softly breathed a prayer.

I'll do anything, God, but please—please keep Carly safe.

CHAPTER 39

Jabber was sick. Very sick. He tried to rise for prayers when the first light of morning came through the bedroom window, but he could only roll out of bed and fall to the floor. He lay there for two hours, coughing and moaning. The fever seemed to come and go, but the nausea, the racking cough, and the agony throbbing in his chest and abdomen were endless. He drifted in a universe of pain. Then his eyes snapped open and his mind cleared. He knelt on the *sajjafiamda*, the prayer mat Kasim had provided, facing east. Groaning, he began to pray, eyes raised to heaven.

"*Allahu Akabar...*" Allah is great. Allah is just. Allah is merciful. Allah is... Jabber began the *Shahada*, the profession of faith intoned by hundreds of millions of Muslims when dawn swept around the globe to light the eastern sky over each believer.

At the end of the driveway below Jabber's sickroom, one of the garage doors at 175 Kings Road was open. A black Suburban SUV was parked in the closed bay.

"It looks like he's out, Carly, so let's shove off. I don't think we ought to be breaking and entering." Horst shifted uneasily in his seat. They were in the Porsche, engine idling, parked on the driveway in front of the open garage door. He studied her determined profile and tried again.

"Okay. If it's got to be breaking and entering, let's call Jay and get him over here with a couple of those Marines." He picked up his walkie-talkie.

"I hereby dub you Onancock's Marine for a day, Fred, and you just leave that radio in the car. I told you when we left the Hermitage that we were not going to bother Jay." She saw the naval officer's face set into a stubborn frown and quickly added, "Look Fred, this isn't just feminine intuition. About two months ago I was at a party here. It was so jammed I had to use the upstairs bathroom—the one in the main bedroom." She paused, her mind's eye looking back to that day.

"So what did you find in the bathroom?"

"Not the bathroom. The bedroom. A closet door was open, and I looked in." Carly reddened. "You know, to see what his wardrobe looked like."

"That's when you saw his camouflaged tutu. Pretty scary."

"There were no clothes in the closet. Just lots of radios and other electronic stuff. See that big antenna on the roof?"

"So? I saw that SSB antenna when we drove up. The guy's a ham radio operator. That's not a crime."

"That's what he said when I asked him about the radios. He also said the guns I saw were for protecting his carpet inventory from burglars." Carly killed the engine and swung her legs out of the sports car. "Anyway, we're not breaking and entering—the door's wide open. And what's the use of being a deputy marshal if I can't investigate a possible crime scene?"

She was not waiting for Horst to argue, and walked off. He sprang out of the car and entered the garage alongside Carly, who was heading for the connecting door to the kitchen.

"That's his other Suburban." Carly jerked a thumb over her shoulder. "See that magnetic sign pad on the side? 'Kasim's Karpets.' Should say 'rugs and drugs'." She opened the door to the kitchen, walked in, and paused. There was a faint voice in some far room, groaning rhythmically.

Horst touched Carly's shoulder, and whispered, "Hey, Carly, that's a Muslim at prayers. Let's take a hike."

"That's not Tarik's voice," Carly answered. She soundlessly climbed the stairs, Horst following.

When Carly pushed the bedroom door open, Jabber turned from the eastern wall and saw two figures through bleary eyes. Strangers. And one of them was wearing a black uniform. The enemy!

Delirious, Jabber's mind reeled. A good Muslim, he was unarmed at prayers and besides, the Professor had hidden his guns. The only thing left to him was the death spray—the same spray can he used on that thieving sailor the day before they left the submarine. The sailor did not fall then, but instructor Mohammed taught him that death came from the spray in the can. *My pack on the floor. Here it is—and my knife!*

Carly was framed in the doorway, eyes widening. Jabber's face was a horrible sight. The pneumonic plague had progressed to septicemia, and the flesh of Jabber's nose and extremities was necrotic, the dead tissue making him look like a clown in macabre black makeup. His shirt was stained with dried vomit, and bloody mucous dribbled from the corners of his mouth. Then it all happened in seconds.

Horst's cell phone rang and Carly's joined it, the noises galvanizing Jabber to his feet. Swaying, he lowered his head and lurched toward his enemies, the canister and knife in front of him like the horns of a charging bull. A misty cloud of spray reached Carly as Horst's arm came up, the dull black handgun appearing almost magically in front of her. The pistol roared twice.

In the small bedroom, the blasts were deafening. Two .45 caliber bullets smashed into Jabber's chest, hammering him back down into a twisted heap on the prayer rug. Her face dampened by the aerosol from the canister, Carly moved into the room with small hesitant steps, then knelt at the terrorist's side. Next to her knees, Jabber's hand opened and the can, wrapped in a bright blue *Arrid* label, slowly rolled under the bed.

"Get away from that little asshole, Carly." Horst's gun was still pointed unwaveringly at Jabber. "Get back!"

Carly looked at the eyes staring up at her and whispered, "He's dying, Fred."

Blood pulsing from the gaping wounds in his chest, Jabber was smiling as his shattered heart fluttered and spasmed. *Paradise! The first of the beautiful virgins, just as it is promised!*

The cell phones stopped ringing.

When Jabber finally went limp, Horst holstered his gun, pulled Carly to her feet, and offered her his handkerchief.

"Here Carly, wipe that deodorant off your face."

Taking the handkerchief as if in a trance, she turned away from the dead terrorist and absently dabbed at her face.

"It doesn't smell like deodorant, Fred. It's sort of musty." Her dreamy voice trailed her as she walked to the door, dropping the handkerchief.

As Horst bent to pick up the linen square he turned away from Jabber's face, its nose and ears black, necrotic. Then he followed Carly to the door.

"Hey, that guy attacked us with a knife. I *had* to shoot him. He was a sick and crazy bad guy." Carly did not respond. "We're not going to lose any sleep over this, okay?" He went on encouragingly, "Crazy guy or no crazy guy, we're both in one piece, and that's what matters. Right?"

Horst watched Carly drift out of the bedroom, and then spotted a small spiral-bound notebook on a table near the door. It was open to a page covered with neat Arabic script, and an Exxon roadmap of Washington lay next to it. He picked them up and followed in her wake, reading.

"Hang on a sec. Whoa! Look at this." Carly still did not answer. She continued her mechanical march down the stairs, reached the ground floor, and walked on. Still reading, Horst skipped down the stairs behind her, hurrying to catch up.

"Hey Carly, listen! I think this book is a plan to attack Washington. It's all in Arabic. Looks like... they've got a nuke! The book says they're going to attack the Pentagon with some kind of anthrax aerosol... and there's even supposed to be a sprayer machine and a nuke stashed in the garage. Right here!"

Horst looked up from the map and saw Carly crossing the kitchen like a zombie. He grabbed her elbow as they were passing the stainless steel double sink.

"Okay, deputy. We're stopping at the oasis." Holding Carly with one hand, he wet a dishtowel and held it up to her. When she did not take it, he briskly rubbed the cold cloth across her face, holding on to her as she started to squirm.

"What the hell are you *doing*!" Carly was sputtering mad, writhing and trying to twist her arm out of Horst's grip. He stepped back and watched color slowly return to her face.

"That's better." He anxiously scanned her face, trying to look into her eyes. "Uh, it was all pretty horrible, I know... but that guy was nuts. Came at us with a knife. I had to stop him, okay? We'll talk it out later, kid. You and me. Okay?"

"I've never seen anyone shot in my whole life," Carly retorted. She wiped her eyes with a tissue, then searched her shoulder bag for her lipstick. "I don't want to be an official terrorist like you and Jay. So you just un-marshal me, Fred. You un-marshal me as soon as we get out of here."

"You bet. We'll do whatever you want." Horst's relief at Carly's revival was clearly visible in his broad smile. "Anyway, looks like you were right about the guy who lives here. That Tarik guy?"

"I don't know who that poor man was. It wasn't Tarik." Her lips began to tremble. Horst took her elbow again, and was gently guiding her toward the front door when his cell phone beeped. He glanced at the caller ID numbers.

"It's the *jefe* himself. He's not going to be happy about us leaving home base or about... but wait until he sees these papers." He punched the green button.

"Admiral Nimitz speaking."

"Don't screw around, Horst! You left base without checking in with me. Exactly where are you?"

"We're at the home of some guy named Tarik, I think. We were attacked by a crazy sick guy with a knife and a can of *Arrid*." He glanced at Carly and dropped his voice. "That was a very, very sick Arab, dude, but he's out of pain now and on his way to paradise. We're okay. And the good news is we've got documents that show—"

Shouting, Adams cut him off. "What kind of can? What happened?"

Horst glanced at Carly, who was busily repairing her makeup. "I told you, the guy sprayed us with a can of deodorant. What's your problem, Jay? Like I said—" He was cut off again.

"Horst, I'm going to kick the crap out of you! Report!" Adams was screaming into his cell phone as he piloted the rocketing SUV up the access road from Route 13 to Onancock.

Horst looked at his phone, frowned, and slowly brought it back to his ear. He spoke in a serious monotone.

"Roger, Jay. We entered a gray house on Kings Road through an open garage door. Carly says the owner's name is Tarik. A car in the garage has a sign on it that says, 'Kasim's Karpets.' We went upstairs. There was a sick Arab praying in a bedroom. He came at us with a knife and a can of *Arrid*. Sprayed Carly. That was a weird thing to do, but he never got close with the knife. I downed him. He's dead. Carly says he's not Tarik. We're in the kitchen now, and she's putting on makeup. We didn't make a search, but there doesn't appear to be anyone else in the house. That's it, besides a map and papers we found that say the terrorists have a nuke and other weapons in the garage here."

"Oh, shit, shit, shit. Now listen up, Fred. You and Carly go out to the front porch. Sit in the rockers there, and don't do anything or go anywhere. Period. I'm seconds away and I'll explain everything when I get there. Got that? Sit tight!"

"It's not good, is it, Jay." Unease crept into Horst's voice.

"No, it is not good, buddy. Not good at all. Now just do what I told you, and I'll be right there. We'll deal with it." Adams cut the connection as the silver Yukon barreled into the heart of Onancock.

A can of *Arrid*. A can of... The words were a river of hollow echoes. He hit the cell phone's first speed dialing option, and then "encrypt." A short pause, and then he heard, "This is Sophie, Jeremiah."

"Sophie. Please write this down. Call the Marine Corps biowar incident response team at Indian Head. Tell them I want a full decon team and all their hardware in a helo and over to Onancock. Immediately. Tell them this is no drill, and they should come prepared to treat and evacuate two people and decontaminate a house. Suspected agents are anthrax and pneumonic plague.

"Their helo will be able to land in the street in front of 175 Kings Road. You've been there—Tarik Kasim's house. Explain what it looks like so they can find it from the air. I'll have emergency road flares lit in the street and on the lawns. Then call the Virginia Highway Patrol station south of Onancock. On Route 13. Ask them to send a couple of cruisers with at least four troopers. While they're rolling, they should ask the local cops to cooperate with me until they get here. Then call the nuke choke point at the Bay Bridge and have them send me a team to collect a suitcase bomb. I'm not sure it's in the house, but it could be. I'll be on scene in a minute, and I'll clear the street. Got all that?"

Sophie responded immediately. "I have it. While I make the calls I suggest you brief the Secretary about this."

"Put him on, Sophie. But please cut back in as soon as you know the Marines have lifted off."

"I will do so. Also, the SEALs you requested from Admiral Bancroft landed in Norfolk and are en route to your home by helicopter. They should be there within the hour. And Jeremiah..." Sophie paused. "I know you'll be careful."

The line clicked, and Adams told Horton that their worst nightmare was a reality. Seconds later, the hot tires of the Yukon squealed, jumped the curb, and settled into Kasim's lawn. Engine off, the big SUV rocked to a stop. Adams opened his door, eyes riveted on two figures sitting in the porch rockers, when his cell phone and walkie-talkie simultaneously signaled callers. Once again, he had a phone to one ear and a radio to the other. The radio crackled first.

"This is Captain Alexander, Mr. Adams. My team and the helo are at base and standing by, over."

"Okay, captain. I need you and two of your troops to come to me in town." Adams looked around Kings Road. The streets were deserted, and only three cars were parked on the road. If the owners were not home, the vehicles will have to be pushed out of the way to make room for the helicopters.

"Off-load the Zodiac, captain, then circle the town and fly west, over the main road through central Onancock. Before you reach the harbor, you'll see two short parallel roads near a small statue and a chapel. They intersect Kings Road. You'll see my vehicle on the north side of the road, on the lawn of a large gray house. You and two of your troops disembark. If there isn't room to land near the house, come down on the sling. Rifles and side arms. Any problem finding me, use the radio and I'll guide you in. Over."

"We've got rappelling lines, so we'll be on the deck there no matter what it looks like. On our way. Alexander, out."

Adams clipped the radio to his belt as he walked toward the house, speaking into the cell phone. "Adams here."

"Jeremiah, where are you! If you're near Kasim's house, do *not* go inside! Stop where you are, *immediately*." Sophie was agitated. Adams stopped ten yards from the porch; Carly and Horst were getting out of the rockers, moving toward the stairs to the lawn.

"I'm in front of the house, Sophie. Carly and Commander Horst are on the porch, coming down now."

"Jeremiah, please listen! Do not approach them and do not let them off that porch. The response team from Indian Head is airborne, and they called to say that no one should leave or enter the house under any circumstances until they arrive. Your report of pneumonic plague has them extremely worried. I gave them your cell number."

Adams was silent, considering the unsettling implications. Then he raised his free hand and shouted at the couple coming down the porch steps.

"Carly, Fred! Stay on the porch. Help is on the way. In a few minutes this place is going to get real crowded. Meantime, we've got to maintain some sort of..." he searched for a word, and then choked out, "quarantine."

"Quarantine." Horst's voice acquired a slight quaver.

Carly was continuing down the steps when Horst pulled her back toward the rockers. He whispered to her, his lean face bloodless.

"Carly? These guys, Carly—that guy upstairs—I think they might have biological weapons. We could be contaminated, and we've got to be checked out. Cleaned up. Until then, we've got to stay away from other people." Horst looked into Carly's horrified face. "Don't worry, deputy. We'll be fine. Let's just sit here and watch Jay work." He spoke to Adams a few yards away, motionless, phone still to his ear.

"Okay, Jay. We're going to sit here for a while, rock a little, enjoy the morning air. What are *you* going to do to earn your paycheck today, buddy?" The mocking words electrified Adams.

"Sophie, tell the response team to call me when they're five minutes out. I'm going to roust the local cops and get them to cordon off the street."

Rotor blades of Captain Alexander's Nighthawk flogged the air above him as the helicopter went into a hover over the road. Adams had to yell into the cell phone. "The cavalry has arrived, Sophie. When the state troopers get here we'll clear everyone out of houses on the street and get them to drive their cars away. There'll be plenty of space for the biowar team. Tell the Secretary this place is almost under control. I'll give him a full report soon."

Adams snapped the phone shut and heard sirens of police cruisers curving into Kings Road. They braked to a sudden stop when the drivers saw armed Marines sliding down ropes hanging from a hovering black helicopter.

CHAPTER 40

Kasim and the Professor were worried. They could not get Jabber to answer his phone all morning. Then, after an endless delay caused by an accident on the Bay Bridge, they arrived in Onancock to find a crowd blocking Kings Road and spilling into Market Street. Town police and sheriff's deputies were everywhere.

"My God! What's happened? Let's get out of here!" Wide-eyed, Kasim made a three point turn U-turn and started back toward Route 13. The Professor looked back, craning his neck to try to see over the crowd.

"Park here," he said calmly. "We will go back and find out what has happened. Perhaps it is just some accident."

"Are you mad? The—the police are everywhere! And soldiers! We—we must get away from here—escape before they see us!" Kasim was stuttering hysterically, eyes darting around the street.

"Try not to be a greater coward than you are a fool. There is much confusion here, and we will not be noticed if we do not draw attention to ourselves. Stop this car. Or I will stop it for you." The Professor's voice was colder than the pistol he jammed into the driver's ribs. Kasim stiffened and the car slowed, easing to the curb in front of the old Onancock movie theater. As the Professor moved toward the crowd, Kasim locked the Suburban's doors and muttered, "I will kill him. First chance. I will kill him, mission or no mission."

They walked toward Kings Road. Moving into the thickest part of the crowd, they cautiously squeezed closer to the police cruiser blocking the street. The sight that greeted them was stunning.

Two huge helicopters squatted in the middle of the road. Local police, state police, sheriff's deputies and armed soldiers were everywhere, setting up barricades. Kasim's house had become the center of an armed camp.

Bright yellow screens were standing across the front lawns, blocking the view of activity there, and figures dressed in helmeted orange spacesuits moved purposefully in and out of the front door of the house. Besides an occasional murmur in the crowd and the muffled whine of generators, the scene had the eerie quiet of a mortuary.

A bareheaded man dressed in a navy blue windbreaker emerged from the screens and paused in the morning sunlight. He wore a respirator and latex gloves, and was studying a spiral notebook inside a sealed transparent bag. Then he pushed the booklet into the hands of a space-suited figure next to him, along with the mask and gloves, and pulled a cell phone from his belt.

"That man is in charge here. Do you know who he is?" The Professor whispered into Kasim's ear.

"Oh no!" he groaned. "It's Jay Adams."

"Jay Adams?" Watching the man pace up and down, speaking into his phone, the Professor was almost mesmerized. Somehow, he knew that this man was very important to him.

"He's a kind of intelligence officer in the Pentagon. A big shot. And he knows me. He knows me very well." Kasim strained to keep his squeaking voice from rising into a scream. "If he sees me we're dead men!"

A bullhorn bellowed, "Sorry folks, you're going to have to move completely off this street now. Please move back. Move back. Residents of this street please check with one of the uniformed police officers. Everyone else, let's move it back." With that, two State troopers and a Marine advanced on the crowd packed around Kasim and the Professor.

Beyond lines of police and soldiers, the black helicopter's turbines groaned and its rotor blades began to turn. Looking around furtively, Kasim ducked his head as he and the Professor moved with the crowd and walked away from Kings Road.

Behind them, Adams continued speaking into his phone.

CHAPTER 41

Adams was in a waking nightmare. Sunday morning overflowed with dreadful purpose that turned Kings Road into an armed camp of security vehicles, helicopters, Marines, police, and a Marine decon team. A powerful force had gathered, and it was searching for the microscopic beasts that infected Jabber and had turned the gray house into a death trap.

Adams leaned against the Yukon, watching the decon team go about its methodical work. Every thought was painful. On the porch he saw Carly, ashen faced and trembling. Horst was sitting beside her, reading the terror plan in the notebook he'd found. Adams' love and his best friend were exposed to plague because of his bumbling. Somehow he would make it up to them. *I have to.* But when the CH-53 "Sea Stallion" delivered the biowar incident response team, all he could do was watch helplessly while the Marines erected privacy screens, took Carly and Horst off the porch, bagged their clothes, and led them into disinfectant showers. Even before they were dry, they were given massive injections of streptomycin, jammed into yellow coveralls, and put aboard the Nighthawk for the trip to Fort Detrick.

The detachment doctor would not let Adams hug Carly before they left. God, he thought, she looked so terrified. Her beautiful hair plastered around her face in damp strings, she sagged against Horst's arm, weak with fear. He could only shout encouragement and wave at them when they lifted off. Then they were gone.

Adams was overcome by dread. He had seen the body of the terrorist and what the plague did to him. Could that happen to Carly? To Horst? His fear changed into white hot rage. *Kasim. I'll make that bastard scream. And the other one...*

"What's the word, sir?" Captain Alexander's quiet question startled Adams from his bloodthirsty fugue.

"Ah. Alexander. I suggest you, Lowenstein, and Gryzbicki report to that doctor over there. He's in charge of this exercise, whether you outrank him or not. Get your shots, pills, gear, and orders from him. I'll be making myself useful too, as soon as I check in with the head shed." He returned Alexander's salute with a nod, and the Marine trudged off toward the house, followed by his two men.

Adams listened to his phone connect and synchronize with the Pentagon encryption circuits while he watched the Marines from the Lejeune MEU get their shots and respirators. Their assigned search areas would probably be away from the bedroom on the second floor, the hot zone reserved for the heavily protected experts from Indian Head.

"Sophie, here. What can I do to help you, Jeremiah?" Adams felt like kissing the phone. *She was a warm breeze on a cold day.*

"Thanks, Sophie. Please tell the Secretary that work is underway to decontaminate the house, the surrounding area is secured, and that I'll remain on the scene until things settle down." Before Adams could hear Sophie's reply his radio squawked. Yet again, he had a handset to each ear.

"Adams, over."

"This is base. The SEALs have arrived and request permission to join you and the other troops, sir. They say they brought their MOPP 4 suits, and they're safe to get into the hot area. Over."

"Negative, base. Tell them to sit tight. There are enough troops, cops, and confusion here for an all day parade down Market Street. I'll..." for a moment Adams's voice faltered. "I'll—you tell them to relax until further word from me. Adams out." He keyed the radio off.

"I gather Lieutenant Cristani has arrived." Sophie's voice was still firm and calm. Adams could visualize her eyes, cool blue under honey blonde hair.

"Yes, they're at the Hermitage." With the phone to his ear, Adams looked around the cluttered lawns of Kasim's house. "You know, Sophie, looking at everything that's going on here I'm damned if I can think of what to do with those SEALs. Or with myself, either."

"I will give your update to the Secretary." Sophie answered evenly. "I suspect there is not much you can do to help the decontamination teams at Kasim's house. So go back to the Hermitage, Jeremiah. Have one of those Southern Comfort drinks and sit on your porch. Your mind will clear and you will make a plan to find the terrorists. And do not blame yourself for what happened to Miss Truitt and the naval officer." The line went dead before he could reply. *Damn. That woman is a comfort.*

Carly and Fred. The thought of them isolated at USAMRIID lanced his mind with anxiety. But Sophie was right, as usual. Take a deep breath and get back to work. Push it.

While Adams was trying to order his thoughts, a Navy doctor walked up and politely told him he was of absolutely no use to the biowar team, and his SUV was in their way. The doctor suggested that Adams return to wherever he came from and stay in touch on the tactical radio net.

Adams started to remind the grim-faced captain of exactly who was in command of the crisis, but instead he smiled at the doctor, requisitioned five courses of streptomycin for the SEALs and Loiacano, and backed the Yukon off the crowded lawn. He cautiously drove through the silent crowd standing around the Bagwell monument, avoided looking into their eyes, and headed back to the Hermitage.

He was wheeling past the town's waterfront docks and the "Historic Hopkins & Bros. Store," when his radio buzzed again. The doctor reported that while his Tyvek-suited Marines were laboring up and down stairs to the hot-zone bedroom, Alexander's men searched the garage and found a cache of small arms, a long steel canister, five *Arrid* aerosol cans, an agricultural spraying machine, and a large aluminum suitcase. It had all been removed from the garage and disinfected, he added.

Adams told the doctor not to open the suitcase, and that a team would arrive soon to take it away. He thanked him for his prompt report, and then called the Pentagon to give Horton the first good news of the day.

CHAPTER 42

"Mr. Secretary, it looks like there were two of them, plus the sleeper agent that brought them ashore. Commander Horst killed one of the landing party in the sleeper's house. As for the book he found, I read most of it myself. Horst made the same translation." Even though alone in the car, Adams lowered his voice

"They were planning to detonate that nuke somewhere in Washington. They also plan to hit the Pentagon with anthrax from an agricultural fogging machine, as soon as wind and weather are favorable." He listened a moment.

"No sir. The notebook doesn't show timing of the attacks, but confirms the terrorists landed with a one kiloton suitcase nuke, two large cylinders of anthrax, and six aerosol canisters of pneumonic plague. It was the sleeper who bought those fogging machines. The bastard's a local. We found what I think is the nuke in the sleeper's garage, along with one big cylinder, five aerosol cans and one of the two foggers. Figuring the can near the dead terrorist is one of the plague weapons, we can account for everything except a cylinder of anthrax and a fogger. I assume the missing terrorist and the sleeper have the anthrax and fogger machine with them. That means they're armed, on the loose, and the Pentagon is their target. You'll have to consider shutting down the building, sir. Maybe start to evacuate Washington, too. If word leaks out about anthrax in the capitol area, roads out of town will be pandemonium."

Adams listened, then said, "I know a one-kiloton weapon sounds small, sir, but it's damned serious. Imagine the effect of a *thousand tons* of TNT detonated anywhere on Capitol Hill. Pack that nuke with cobalt or plutonium dust and our capital city would be out of business for years while we clean it up. Maybe forever. We're real lucky we found it."

He listened again, and replied, "Shutting down the Pentagon is a decision way above my pay grade, sir. But if you're going to hang tough, permit me a few suggestions. If they hit the building with anthrax from that fogger, they'll probably do it at night, or in the hours before dawn to avoid exposing the spores to sunlight and UV. They'd hope for a temperature inversion to keep the aerosol fog close to the ground, and a breeze for maximum dispersion."

"They'd have to put the fogger in a building window or a moving vehicle, upwind of the Pentagon. If they use a moving vehicle, the long cloud line of spores would infiltrate the entire building, infect everyone in it, and then settle in to wait for the folks in the morning shift. Plus it would get inside every house, car, nook and cranny in its path. No way to hide from it. A good westerly breeze would easily take it across the river into Washington and on into Maryland. Besides humans, those spores will get sucked into the lungs of every dog, cat, rat and bird for miles downwind—anything that breathes will die. It's a poor man's nuke. A city-killer."

Another pause to listen, then Adams said, "Starting right now I'd beef up patrols all around the Pentagon, especially upwind. Stop all vehicles that can carry anything bulky, like an agricultural sprayer. Inspect buildings on the upwind side, too."

Adams' eyes stung when he heard the Secretary's next question, and he answered in a tortured whisper. "I'll keep you informed sir, and I thank you for your concern. Miss Truitt and Commander Horst are on their way to USAMRIID right now. I'm sure they'll be all right. And I'll keep you advised of developments here." He broke the connection.

He was three miles from the Hermitage, still thinking about Carly. Raising his cell phone again, he thumbed the buttons.

"Doctor Holloway? This is Jay Adams. I hope you remember me, doc."

"Yes, Mr. Adams, I remember you. How are things down in the big city?"

"Not so good, doc. I can't give you details since your phone isn't secure, but we've had an incident—release of a pathogen. A response team is on the scene and is treating everyone who could've been exposed. One of the, ah, perpetrators is dead. Of gunshot wounds. The decon team doctor says he was in the terminal stages of pneumonic plague, and it would have killed him anyway, today or tomorrow. I can get his body transported to your facility if you want to do an autopsy."

"This release you talk about. Accident or intentional?"

"Intentional."

"I suppose that shouldn't surprise us, these days."

"No sir, it shouldn't."

"Well, I don't want to slice up the son of a bitch that did it. Not if he's dead, anyway. Take appropriate precautions and turn the body over to the local medical examiner. Be sure to warn him that pneumonic plague in a victim's corpse is infectious for almost a year. So, besides all that Adams, what assistance can we give you on the scene?"

"Thanks, but we don't need more help out here. Reason I am calling, doc, is that two of our people have been exposed, and they're en route to your facility in a helicopter. One is Commander Fred Horst, and the other is a federal deputy marshal, Miss Carlotta Truitt. They've had decon showers and streptomycin. The doctor here thinks they'll be okay if they finish the course of treatment. But I have reason to believe..." Adams' voice faltered for a moment. "I believe the strain of *Yersinia Pestis* used on them is weaponized, and may be highly resistant to antibiotics."

"I understand, Adams. We've already been advised that they are on their way up here. Do you know if they got a big snootful?"

"Marshal Truitt may have been exposed to a concentrated aerosol at close range. I'm not sure about the commander."

"Sounds like it's two for the slammer. We are assembling a team now to meet that chopper, and we'll do everything we can for them."

"I know you will, doc. If you don't mind, I'll check with you from time to time to see how they're coming along. Uh, doc... I guess you know this whole thing has a pretty high classification."

"You guess right, Adams." Holloway hung up.

Clipping the phone to his belt, Adams recalled the sight of Marines duct-taping the side doors, vents, and windows of Kasim's house, while others were carrying dozens of electric frying pans through the front door. Before the sun sets on Onancock, the house at 175 Kings Road will be sprayed with a hypochlorite solution and flooded with a decontaminating gas that will rise from formaldehyde crystals cooking in the pans. After three days there will be nothing alive in that house—no microbe, mouse or bug. He conjured up an image of Kasim and the terrorist tied to chairs inside the house when the gas started to rise.

Five miles from Onancock the Professor called a halt to their flight, and Kasim parked the Suburban in the rear of an abandoned gas station on Route 13. The Professor leaned back in his seat, eyes closed, deep in thought. Then he pulled an area map from the glove compartment and leaned toward the driver.

"Is there some other way we can go back to your Washington apartment, besides driving across the big bridge?" The Professor pointed to the Chesapeake Bay Bridge on the map.

"No. We could take side roads that parallel Route 13 and Route 50, but they all lead to the Bay Bridge. The other route stinks. See, here," Kasim jabbed at the map. "If we don't use Route 50 but continue north, we could avoid the bridge by driving all the way to Baltimore and then turning south on Route 95. We'd be lucky to get to Washington by dinner time."

"Stop thinking of your stomach, my brave friend, and think about that man we saw. That Jay Adams. Think about what must have happened to Jabber. Think about losing the nuclear weapon. Then think about losing all our weapons but the one we have with us now." The Professor glared at Kasim and then ran his finger down the peninsula and across the Hampton Roads bridge tunnel. Kasim looked at the map and then at the Professor.

"So, my clever driver. Can we go south?"

"Yes, we could drive south from here. In Norfolk we have the choice of going north on one or the other side of the James River. A very long drive." Kasim's voice trailed off, and he blinked his eyes rapidly. "My house... my business... "

"Your life's work is not with the carpet business, and houses are not important. Your true business is to help me complete our mission." The Professor's voice became harsh. "Soon, very soon, they will look for us everywhere. But perhaps they will not believe we will go south. Do it!"

By now, Kasim knew it was not a good idea to disagree with his passenger, and he turned the Suburban south toward the Hampton Roads bridge tunnel. The Professor leaned back in his seat, and was seized with a sudden coughing fit. He felt feverish again.

I am sick as Jabber was sick, he thought. Little time remains. That Jay Adams—surely he has read Jabber's book. So now I have only my dream plan to kill Washington. I must do it soon. Very soon.

CHAPTER 43

U.S. Army Medical Research Institute of Infectious Diseases
Fort Detrick, Maryland

The USAMRIID building at Fort Detrick is a cream-colored brick pile of typical government design, unremarkable except for a forest of vents sprouting from its roof. The dozens of crook-shaped pipes are attached to HEPA filters—High Efficiency Particulate Air filter systems—that crowd the building's top floor with pumps and ducting. Below the filter floor are the labs. They're under a constant negative air pressure that prevents their prisoners, microbes and viruses, from escaping. No air can get out of those rooms except through the HEPA filters above. Incredibly virulent viruses like Ebola and Marburg, rare hemorrhagic fevers, and dozens of other pathogens are being studied, probed, and classified in some of the labs. In others, countermeasures and vaccines are being developed for a host of biowar agents. USAMRIID is a very dangerous place. Yet its military and civilian employees do their work in a routine manner, they eat lunch in the cafeteria, get candy bars from the vending machines, and make telephone calls to their wives, husbands and sweethearts. They are just employees in an unusual government facility. They are very careful employees.

Horst and Carly looked down at the helicopter pad as the Nighthawk began to slow and lose altitude. Under the descending aircraft, an Aeromedical Isolation Team—

an "AIT" of two doctors and six nurses—was clustered around wheelchairs and a small ambulance.

Pushing wheelchairs and carrying stretchers, the team rushed the helicopter before its blades stopped turning. It was the opening scene from the old television series, "MASH." But this was no comedy.

The leader of the team wore a face respirator, and reached the open door first. He looked up at the two passengers who hesitated in the doorway. "I am Doctor Holloway, boss of this AIT and lots of other things here at Fort Detrick. Now jump down here, folks, and don't give me any arguments. Get in those wheelchairs or I'll have my gorillas strap you into stretchers." Holloway's voice was muffled by his respirator. "That vehicle will take you to the main building. I'll be waiting there." He turned to face the team clustered around the helicopter door and raised his voice so Carly and Horst could hear him too.

"Okay, troops, you know these people were exposed to pneumonic plague, and you know what to do. There's also a remote possibility of anthrax. They were treated at the exposure site by a biological hazard response team so they're not in aircraft isolator units. You see they're wearing facemasks. That's for our protection as well as theirs. Risk for everyone is low at this point, which is why I'm only wearing a respirator, but you will practice every precaution as you escort them to the slammer." He turned back to look at the two figures in the helicopter door, still speaking loudly.

"All this will be excellent practice for us, and I am sure the marshal and the commander will understand. Now get on down here." He turned back to the team.

"Remove their overalls and any personal effects. Bag everything for immediate test and decon. Check the helicopter, and start the crew on a course of oral Streptomycin if they haven't been already treated by the biohazard response team. Then they can take off. After you peel these two move them inside quickly, or they'll freeze their butts. We don't want 'em catching a cold before they get to the slammer. See you all there." He walked briskly to his car and drove off.

The isolation team was moving as the doctor talked. In minutes, Carly and Horst were in green hospital pajamas, sitting in wheelchairs, and ready to be hoisted into the waiting ambulance. Above her respirator, Carly's eyes were wide and darted from face to face as the team worked. Horst reached over and grasped her hand while they were being wheeled toward the waiting ambulance.

"Hey, Carly, no sweat. You heard him. These guys are using us for a practice drill. We'll be at a farewell banquet of their best hospital mush before you know it. Nothing to worry about, deputy. Okay?"

Carly nodded her head, not trusting herself to talk. The doors closed and the van moved off.

Carly and Horst were met at the building entrance by Doctor Holloway. The two wheelchairs, surrounded by the medical team, were pushed past the silent security guards, and down a highly polished corridor. They passed doors labeled "Anthrax" and "Tularemia" accompanied by squeaks from crepe-soled shoes and the mournful clunk of a warped wheel on Carly's chair. The caravan stopped before a stainless steel door that looked like the entrance to a meat chiller, complete with gauges and a small window. They had reached their destination.

USAMRIID's "High-Containment Patient Care Facility" is the only biosafety Level 4 facility of its kind in the United States. Fully equipped to handle patients with contagious diseases that have no cure, the facility is officially referred to as a maximum biological containment isolation suite. The staff calls it "the slammer."

A two-room suite, each section of the slammer has its own bathroom and toilet, and each is configured like a small intensive care room. It's all there: cardiac monitors, ventilators, oxygen, X-Ray equipment, blood gas monitors, and all the other instruments found in a superb health care facility, right down to a miniature operating theater. The slammer is a compact hospital—except its rooms are under negative air pressure like the labs around it, and every breath exhaled inside it leaves only through HEPA filters. The entrance is a double door airlock that leads to a decon shower, and everyone entering or leaving goes through the shower on the way in and the way out. Besides doctors and patients, nothing alive gets out— especially not microscopic things.

Holloway motioned for Carly and Horst to enter the open doorway, saying, "This isolation suite is designed for your protection and for ours. If you test negative, I promise you will be our guests for a very short time. The doctors in there are in positive pressure suits, and air coming into their helmets from those flexible hoses is so noisy they can barely hear themselves think." They could see two figures in space suits waiting inside.

"When we close these outer doors, you go past the changing room, skip the shower, and put on a radio headset the doctors will give you. That way you can hear each other. You can take off those respirator masks once you're inside. Then do what they tell you. I'll monitor the lab tests myself, and I guarantee quick results. Okay? Move it."

"I hope this is the best suite you've got," Horst said. "We don't mind not getting the penthouse, but we flew out here for first class treatment." No one laughed. Carly had a grip on Horst's hand that threatened to crack bones, and he could feel her trembling.

"Oh God, Fred. I'm never coming out of there."

"C'mon, kid, don't be silly. Even Microsoft Gates can't afford to spend a night in a swanky joint like this one. Listen, when they finish their tests I'll take you out for a champagne dinner in Washington. On me. Meantime, ladies first." Horst disengaged from Carly's grip with difficulty. She slowly entered the open doorway, and he followed.

The steel door slammed shut.

CHAPTER 44

"I wish our first face time could've been under better circumstances, Lieutenant Cristani. But I'm glad to see you and your men."

"Me too, Mr. Adams."

"Okay, you know about this stuff? Prophylaxis for anthrax exposure?"

Adams handed out syringes, streptomycin, alcohol swabs, and instruction leaflets to the four SEALs on the Hermitage porch.

"Yes sir. This stuff is standard Navy issue."

"Good. Let's go inside."

"Looks like you had a tough start to a bad day," Cristani offered, once they were all assembled in the great room.

"The lance corporal here told us about a commander and a lady fed who got hit with some kind of biological weapon brought ashore by terrorists." Loiacano avoided Adams' dark glance. "I'm sorry we weren't here to give those guys a special SEAL celebration when they got to the beach."

Adams suddenly felt very tired, and he fell into Carly's favorite chair, looking up at the four SEALs. They made the room look smaller.

"Say, Cristani, I've always meant to ask you about your name. What's the "AP" stand for?"

Before Cristani could reply, Chief Hernandez broke in and said, "AP stands for 'armor piercing,' sir. *My* initials are HE. They stand for—"

"I know, high explosive. You're the high explosive deacon." Adams managed to grin at the tough men in his living room. "Okay, grab chairs and spread out while I bring you up to speed. There's a coffee pot in the kitchen—and I'd be grateful for a cup myself."

In twenty minutes the SEALs learned about the events at sea and in Kasim's house: the submarine and the midnight landing; the arrival of the biowar response team; and the fortunate capture of most of the terrorists' weapons and a copy of their plan of attack. The SEALs already knew they were operating under an unusual presidential directive that empowered them to use deadly force on American soil.

There were a few questions when Adams was done, and then a long silence—finally Master Chief Hernandez spoke again. "We know about anthrax, sir. But what about this pneumonic plague weapon? I thought plague was something you caught from rats and fleas."

"That's right. The Latin name for plague is *Yersinia Pestis*. It's a zoonosis like anthrax, except the animal hosts are rats instead of sheep, and transmission to humans is by fleabites. The "Black Death" killed thirty million people in the fourteenth century. But during the Cold War some charming Soviet scientists weaponized plague in its *pneumonic* form. It's not like anthrax. Pneumonic plague is highly contagious. The victim coughs and sneezes and sprays the disease onto the next guy. Symptoms are not nice. Fever, bloody cough, vomiting, diarrhea, maybe septicemia. Unless it's treated *before* symptoms appear, the fatality rate is damn near one hundred percent. If you make those bugs resistant to antibiotics—you've got a major horror show."

The SEALs digested the lecture, and Adams' imagination gave him one depressing image after another of Carly and Horst at Fort Detrick. It was Tristani's turn to break the heavy silence.

"This 'weaponizing.' Does that mean the bugs are put in some kind of a weapon? I mean instead of being mailed, like those anthrax letters a few years back?" The SEAL lieutenant brought Adams back into the here-and-now.

"Not exactly. It means the microbes themselves are made into weapons. Anthrax spores are milled down to a tiny size that allows them to get past the defenses in your nasal passages, and then lodge deep in the lungs. They're made static-proof, so they don't cling together in lumps. Made resistant to sunlight. And like the pneumonic plague weapon, the bacteria are made resistant to antibiotics. Those anthrax letters were bad, but nothing compared to the stuff those terrorists brought ashore. A handful of weaponized anthrax dust contains millions of spores, and the two bad guys on the loose have almost sixty pounds of it, ready to go. Sprayer and all."

"Okay, Mr. A., I think we've got the picture," Cristani said. "We need to find those illegal aliens and secure their nasty germ weapons right now. Give us our orders and turn us loose."

"I wish I could." Adams stared into the cold dregs of his coffee. "Outside of a guess they're somewhere between here and Washington, we don't have any kind of fix on where the assholes are, where their hideout is, or when they intend to use that fogger on the Pentagon."

"Okay, even if they took off for Baltimore and Philly, there are four of us and you, Mr. Adams," Cristani said. "Let's work out a plan and get on their tails."

Adams looked from face to face, stopping at the SEAL Lieutenant.

"All right, Cristani. What we need to do now is get organized and accelerate. First thing, you troops take your gear to the guest rooms in the rear of the house. Any stuff back there belongs to Captain Alexander's team, and they'll be going back to Camp Lejeune today.

"Loiacano, call for a transport helo to collect you and your team and haul you all to Lejeune. The Nighthawk and pilot Duggan will be staying, once he gets back from Fort Detrick. We'll be needing that chopper for a while." The Lance Corporal turned to his radios, and Adams looked at the waiting SEALs.

"After you stow your gear, you men recon the house and make yourselves at home. Nothing is off limits except my bedroom. Cristani, you get the upstairs front guest room. RHIP still works in my outfit. Settle in and meet me back down here. We've got a pile of planning and actions to execute."

"Transport will be here in a couple of hours, Mr. Adams," interjected Loiacano. "I also called the captain and told him to return to base. Then I asked the state troopers to bring them in. Is that all right, sir?"

"Good headwork, Loiacano. When the SEALs stow their gear they'll relieve you on comms and you can get ready to head out with your team when they get here. Minus those radios, of course."

"Motown," Second Class Machinist's Mate Hanna, usually handled the SEAL squad's communications, and his face fell. "You mean I'm not going out with my team, Mr. A? I got to stay in here?"

The lance corporal broke in again. "I know the comms routine and this crypto gear, sir. Maybe I should stay so he can be with his outfit."

Adams looked at each man in turn and shook his head. "For Pete's sake. Didn't anyone ever tell you guys about volunteering? Okay. If SEALs can figure out how to cohabit with the Marines in those four rooms back there, you can *all* stay. Loiacano, cancel the transport helo. Then call Ms. Giltspur and get three HUMVEEs sent up from Little Creek. Two should have M60's on the roof, and will stay with us. The other one takes the drivers back.

"Then call Buddy's Barbecue on Route 13. Get large barbeque lunch plates delivered for us all. Pronto. Tell them the tip will cover the speeding ticket. They know this place, by the way, so don't shoot the deliveryman when he comes up the walk.

"Cristani, looks like you and Alexander will bunk in the main guest room. A Marine captain and a Navy lieutenant—roommates. Too bad it's got twin beds." Everyone laughed.

"The lieutenant and the captain will work out watch details. First comms watch starts at 1200." Command hardened Adams' voice, and the men around him heard it. They traded approving glances with each other.

Thirty minutes later, Adams swallowed a bite of Buddy's barbeque and watched Cristani fork in a large mouthful from the heap on his plate. When the officer looked up from his plate, Adams spoke.

"All right. The remaining terrorist is out there with Tarik Kasim. They're armed, they have a pile of anthrax, a delivery system, and they intend to attack the Pentagon. We don't know exactly where they are or when they intend to act. And that's all we know. Let's talk."

"You know about their plans because you read that notebook from the house, right?" Cristani splashed more sauce on his barbeque.

"Yes. It was an action outline left for the terrorist Horst killed. Sort of a backup plan in case something happened to the other joker or to the fogger. It also mentioned six cans of pneumonic plague and a nuke, but we got all those."

"So by now, the two guys out there figure we're all over their base house, right?" Cristani and Adams locked eyes, their thoughts beginning to synchronize.

"They might even have been back here a couple of hours ago. Sounds crazy, but I think I felt them near me." Adams' brows drew together. "But even if I'm a lousy psychic and they weren't back in town today, they probably called their sick buddy in the house. When he didn't answer they'd be alerted, for sure." He rose, took two writing pads from his desk, and tossed one to Cristani.

"Let's start the lists while we finish this barbeque. Might be the last good chow we get for a while."

At noon, when "Deacon" Hernandez relieved Loiacano on the radios, the two men at the refectory table were still scribbling. The other SEALs were finishing lunch and talking quietly. Adams glanced across the table.

"What've you got, Cristani?"

The SEAL team leader looked at his pad and pursed his lips. "We got to cover every option we can think of. First, they might be on the road right now. We need to lock down the highways. Second, they probably tried to communicate with their dead pal, and maybe with each other. We need numbers for their cell phones and wide area coverage for traces. Third, they may have been joined by other bad guys.

Fourth, they probably have a second base or safe-house close to the target. Nearby the Pentagon or maybe in Washington. We need... we need some good ideas on that." Cristani chewed his pencil. "Finally, they know we got their plan to attack the Pentagon from that notebook. They have to figure we're ready for that attack, so that means we've got to think of other target options they might have. And still cover the Pentagon." Cristani looked up. "For sure I've forgotten something."

"Not much. If you want to quit your west coast job, a slot's waiting for you in my shop. The main thing you didn't note," he rasped, "is that if they give me the least justification, I intend to kill that scumbag Kasim and his terrorist friend. Personally."

The room was still after Adams spoke. Then he added tonelessly, "Of course, you gents might get them first. Other than that, we track pretty close. One thing you don't know is we recovered a cell phone from the bedroom where the terrorist died. He must have dropped it in the crapper or something, so we couldn't get the call logs. NSA is working on it. But we still know a few useful things. Things like Kasim has another Suburban, a twin to the one in his garage. We know their primary target for the anthrax is the Pentagon, though we've got to consider that Washington is an alternative option. And I know Kasim has a boat." He consulted his notes.

"I also remembered his nearest showroom is in a shopping center on Route 13. That could be important if he kept records there. Kasim spent a lot of time in Washington. If he has an apartment or a house in D.C. there might be something about it in his office files, not to mention info about other cell phones. And I bet we can squeeze some good poop out of his employees when they show up tomorrow morning."

In SEAL tradition, all members of a team participate in planning an operation. Hanna's voice floated across the room from his seat next to Chunk Gorski.

"Why not break into the asshole's office now? Uh, excuse the language, Mr. A."

Adams and Cristani looked at each other blankly. Adams spoke first. "No apologies, Motown. We've got to stop thinking like nice civilians and more like warriors. And we need to think fast now, or we'll never nail the assholes."

He pointed his pencil at John Gorski, the squad's machine-gunner and said, "You've been pretty quiet since you got here, Chunk. Anything to add?"

"Great barbeque, sir." The laughter was loud and genuine.

"Another good point. Okay, now we got to work for our lunch. Deacon?"

"Sir?"

"Did Loiacano leave all the freqs and call signs on the desk? Yes? Good. Call the state troopers at Kasim's house. Tell them we need a cruiser here right away with at least a sergeant or a lieutenant in it. Don't mention breaking and entering the carpet store until I can talk to him. Got that? Hit it!" Adams spun his chair and faced the men in the room.

"Motown, you and the highway cop will kick down the door of Kasim's carpet shop and vacuum the place for papers, bills, insurance documents. Get anything that can tell us about his vehicles, phones, and especially about his houses or apartments. Also get the name, address and phone number of all the employees—we just might call on them later today. I know your folks taught you Arabic, so if you run into any of Kasim's people in his store today, impress upon them that we need their cooperation. Impress them firmly.

"AP, use my vehicle and take Chunk, a radio and a rifle to Wachapreague marina and check out Kasim's boat. The harbormaster will point it out. Search the boat and set up an ambush in case he shows up with his terrorist friend. I'll give you directions to the marina. Short drive. If there's shooting, Chunk, leave enough air in them so we can ask a few questions. If that turns out to be inconvenient, don't worry about it. We'll relieve you as soon as I get a local cop to take over. I'll stay here and set up the road nets. Loiacano, grab a rifle. You've got sentry duty until Alexander gets back, right?

"Okay troops." Adams smacked the tabletop. "If there are no questions, everyone saddle up and move out. AP, better take a look at this map before you lose my Yukon in the sticks." Everyone in the room was suddenly in motion.

When the front door closed, leaving him and Hernandez alone, Adams stood quite still for a moment, looking out at the sunny day. Things were starting to move. He turned back to the comms desk.

"Deacon, get Sophie Giltspur on the secure blower. Identify yourself and tell her she needs to talk to VDOT and the Virginia and Maryland State Police. We need complete eyeball coverage of highways north of here, across the Bay Bridge, and into Washington. She should also tell them we want coverage by remote TV monitors, police cars, helos—the works. The story is that we're looking for a late model black Suburban, with two escaped military convicts in it, armed and dangerous. Vehicle may have a sign saying 'Kasim's Karpets.' License numbers follow, but all black Suburbans are fair game. Got that? Okay."

He closed his eyes in concentration and then added, "Tell her I need phased array vans for cell phone fixes, and that NSA will call her for authorization for the domestic intercepts. Also tell her I'm going to hassle NRO for satellite coverage. Do it."

Adams pulled the phone from his belt and punched the buttons, speaking as soon as encryption circuits cleared and he had a reply.

"Jeremiah Adams here. Get me Admiral Tarsis, please."

"This is Tarsis, Adams."

"Admiral, we're shifting into high gear to nail that landing party before they get near their targets, but I haven't forgotten how they got here. Are you guys reaching out for that foreign sub? Figured out where it came from yet?"

Adams heard a deep sigh, and then the admiral said, "You know Adams, you really give an old sailor the red-ass. We've humped every conceivable asset to locate that sub. I contacted the Coast Guard and what's left of SOSUS. I had an informal chat with friends at NRO to see what image archives from Atlantic surveillance might show. And as the Brits are wont to say, 'We got fuck-all, mate.' That boat just appeared and disappeared. I sent an attack boat out to hunt for them the morning you called, and I told all my boats along the probable exit course to be alert for diesel boat activity. I probably pissed-off half my skippers with that order. Sounds like I don't think they're vigilant." Tarsis sighed again.

"Anyway, you should know that *Maryland* returned from her patrol and reported possible contact with a diesel boat six days before that landing at Wachapreague. Her grams show what looks like a Russian KILO class, snorkeling. *Maryland* couldn't confirm, thought it was spurious data, and broke off the search. If it was the sub bringing in the landing party, and if she made ten knots submerged, the location and timing would be just about right."

Adams began to sputter. "Russian sub? What the fuck is a Russian submarine doing off our east coast?"

"Take it easy, Jay. I said Russian KILO *class*, understand? The Russkis sold that boat to lots of people."

"Okay, George, whose boat is it? The goddamn Chinese? And how does a diesel boat make it across the Atlantic undetected?" Adams was controlling himself with difficulty.

"We don't know whose boat it is. Yet. The gram that *Maryland* recorded is short, and doesn't look like anything in our library. My people think it might match an Iranian boat that recently transited the Med on her way to an overhaul in a Russian shipyard. But they're not sure. As for funding to detect foreign submarines crossing the Atlantic, call your local congressman."

Adams ignored the sarcasm and growled, "Iranian? Are those crazies back in our face? George, find me that boat. Please? I'll deliver a message to them in the Atlantic, the Med or wherever the hell they are. I'll—" Tarsis cut him off.

"Calm down, Adams. I said my people are not sure. I'm casting my nets, and when I'm absolutely certain I know who is screwing around in my front yard I won't need your help to deliver them a message. You read me, mister?" There was barbed wire in the Admiral's voice.

"Ah. Sorry, George. I'm wound up pretty tight right now." Adams took a long breath and exhaled noisily. "I'd appreciate you keeping me informed of progress."

"Sure, Jay. I'll keep you informed. My troops have you second on the list of who needs to know." The admiral's tone softened, and he added, "How are Commander Horst and that young lady doing? Do the docs say they're okay?" Adams did not bother to ask how the Admiral knew about Fred and Carly being exposed to pneumonic plague.

"I don't know, George. USAMRIID will make it right, if anyone can. Thanks for asking."

"I like Horst. Tough as woodpecker lips. He'd look like an old-time Teutonic knight, too, if he wasn't such a skinny bugger. I only hope he wises up one day and comes to realize being your buddy can be slightly dangerous. As for that deputy marshal, I hear your lady's a natural beauty who deserves a submariner instead of a broken-down naval aviator. Bring her around to our quarters when she is out of the slammer. My wife says she wants to impart some words of wisdom to an accomplished woman who's wasting time on a retired Pentagon bureaucrat."

The line went dead as Adams' throat constricted. One smart Admiral. And a good friend. He was looking at his phone, thinking about calling USAMRIID when Hernandez piped up from the comms desk. "It's Motown on the radio, sir. Says they got lucky at that rug store."

CHAPTER 45

The Professor shifted in his seat and twisted around to look back at the Newport News tunnel exit behind them.

"Another huge tunnel," he mused out loud. "It's truly amazing how many tunnels and bridges the Americans build. Just like New York."

"No, it's not just like New York. This place is full of soldiers and sailors who get drunk and live in cheap houses before they get sent somewhere else. The people born here are farmers and small business people—or parasites feeding on the military bases. Not like New York at all. New York is beautiful. Beautiful people. Good restaurants." Kasim was concentrating on weaving through midday traffic. "That's where we should go now, New York. They're searching for us here, and Jay Adams knows me."

The Professor ignored the suggestion about New York. If he still had the pneumonic plague canisters he might consider spraying one into the New York Lincoln Center air conditioning system during a big concert. Washington's Kennedy Center, too. That would give cultured America an excellent taste of hell. But the spray cans were lost, so there was no point in making plans about music halls.

He thought about Jay Adams, and then about the military installations he saw during their drive through Norfolk. He checked the base perimeters shown on the road map. Many good targets. Maybe there was a base of helicopters and missiles the Americans were sending to Israel. But he did not know enough about surrounding terrain to plan a good attack. He had only one weapon now, and it was best to follow his death dream for Washington. He looked up at an overpass bridge.

"Stop driving so fast, dear friend, or we will attract attention. Stay with the traffic flow and follow that big vehicle." They went under the overpass. He looked back and asked, "Tell me about those cameras on the intersections. I saw them on the bridges and in the tunnels, too."

"They are traffic television cameras. VDOT monitors traffic in Virginia for rush hours and accidents. That sort of thing." Kasim slowed and pulled in behind another black Suburban.

"They monitor *all* the roads in Virginia?" The Professor could not smother the impulse to look around furtively. "Could they see us? Find us with those cameras?"

Kasim sneered. "I told you, they're traffic monitors. They don't look for illegal aliens or Palestinian freedom fighters."

The Professor considered that, and then he said, "If those cameras can see the road, they can see us. Especially this big automobile." He examined the map again, tracing roads with his finger.

"At this speed, we're only three hours away from your apartment. Perhaps we will be safe for three more hours. Perhaps. Drive very carefully, and no faster than the traffic."

He coughed. The pain in his chest was worse, and he was feverish again. I will be getting very weak soon, he thought.

Tonight must be the night.

CHAPTER 46

After Cristani returned from the marina, he and Adams were continuously on the phone and radio, monitoring the road surveillance network they had created. They now had three contact points: one for the VDOT camera system, one for state police cruisers stationed at main intersections along roads to the Bay Bridge and Washington, and a third for police helicopters patrolling Route 13 and Route 50 all the way to the Washington Beltway. From time to time they also checked on progress of the inbound HUMVEES and the decontamination team at Kasim's house.

In Onancock, Delta Force commandos confirmed the aluminum suitcase found in Kasim's garage was a small nuclear device, and took it to Andrews Air Force base. It would be examined by a California lab to determine its country of origin. It's not from Iran, Adams thought, they're still building big nukes. Anyway, it's off the playing field. But the anthrax... if they hit us with that stuff just right, it would hurt us a lot worse than a one-kiloton nuke. We've got to bag the terrorists before they can use that fogger on the Pentagon, or a big city like New York.

Three innocent black Suburbans had already been spotted and intercepted, their frightened drivers sent on their way. Mobile security units from DIA and ONI were near the Pentagon and setting up road patrols along every approach to the building. Helicopter crews glued to stabilized binoculars buzzed streets and bridges, looking into cars and scrutinizing pedestrians. Adams could not imagine how the terrorists made the big SUV disappear so effectively. He worried that if they did not find it soon, the surveillance net would be noticed and the secrecy lid would inevitably come off. Then all hell would boil over when the turf fights began. The Washington area would overflow with units of a dozen federal, state and city agencies, each with their own plan, each hyping the media. The public would go nuts. He was about to call Horton again when a police cruiser pulled up and Motown, a trooper lieutenant, and a small man carrying a file box got out and headed for the house. Adams met the parade on the porch.

Hanna smiled grimly and prodded the man toward Adams with a pistol. "Like I said, Mr. A, we got lucky. Hameed here really wants to cooperate. Right, Hameed? *Nam?*"

"I am only bookkeeper, sir." The short man was perspiring freely. "These men broke the office door sir, and came with guns. I am working on my records, sir. They make me come here. I am sorry, very sorry, sir. My wife and daughter are missing me, sir."

"Take it easy, Hameed." Adams smiled at the sight of Hanna and the policeman looming over the diminutive man. "No one's going to harm you." He turned to the laconic police lieutenant as Cristani joined them and motioned for Hanna to holster his gun.

"My compliments to the Virginia State Police, lieutenant. What's the bottom line?"

"This guy was in the rug shop when we, ah, found the front door open, Mr. Adams. He helped us locate those files, and has been completely cooperative. Says he doesn't know anything about a house or apartment in DC, or about any equipment that's not in the rug store. He says the owner keeps a lot of files in his house. Seems to think we're investigating their last tax return." The big trooper could not contain a rumbling chuckle. "That SEAL kinda terrified him, so we just grabbed all the shop files and records that looked useful. Uh, I mean he volunteered to bring them along."

"Okay, lieutenant. Great work. Hameed is going to be our guest until we search his boss's house. He might be needed to explain whatever paperwork we might find there. After that he's free to go home to his wife and daughter. Please lock him in your car until we can toss Kasim's house before they fumigate it. If we don't find anything he needs to explain, you can deliver him to his home, if you don't mind. His neighbors will be very impressed." Adams took the file box as the state trooper led the bookkeeper out to the cruiser.

"AP, Motown, sort through this stuff, please. We don't care about purchases or deliveries as much as we need cell phone numbers and a line on Kasim's hideaway."

He dumped the contents of the box on the refectory table in front of Cristani and looked over at Hernandez.

"Deacon, if the cops have finally showed up at the marina, ask them to bring Chunk back here. Then get me the latest fixes on the HUMVEEs position, Duggan's chopper, and Alexander. Ask Giltspur to get authorization for a bivouac area near the Pentagon for you SEALs and the Marines. We also need a spot on the Pentagon executive helo pad for the Nighthawk. Then I want our complete team to assemble here so we can move base to the Pentagon as soon as possible. We're going to get closer to the target." Across the room, Cristani dropped his head on the pile of receipts and moaned in mock distress.

"You mean I don't get to spend the night with that Marine? Darn. Maybe I can go south with him to Camp Lejeune after we round up the bad guys."

"That's truly sad, AP. As a consolation I'll make sure you guys get to sleep in the same tent tonight." Adams froze. Lejeune. *South!* He spun and faced the comms desk.

"Deacon, before you make those calls, contact VDOT and the cops, pronto. I want the road net expanded to cover Route 13 *south* from here to Norfolk, and then north from there to D.C. along Routes 64 and 95. Routes 5 and 10, too, if they have the manpower to check rural roads. Those terrorists aren't stupid. I'll bet they figured on roadblocks and took the long way around. Damn, maybe I *am* getting old."

Adams rubbed his hands together anxiously, and continued to speak at the busy chief's back. "Next, check with NRO for satellite coverage of those southern routes. I know they've got problems repositioning their birds, but I need their input *now*. Any static, you report them to Giltspur." Adams waited while Hernandez scribbled notes.

"Make sure NSA is setting up that cell phone net, and is moving their intercept vans to DC. If they have problems with domestic surveillance laws, be sure to give them Giltspur's number. I want immediate coverage on those phones as soon as we get their ID. Also have them check phone records for listed and unlisted landlines in the Arlington and Alexandria areas billed to Tarik Kasim, or a firm named Kasim's Karpets. That's carpets spelled with a K. Then tell Alexander to hold his position, and that we will join him at Kasim's house. We'll need him to help look for files in there before they finish sealing up the joint."

Adams walked to the door, checking battery levels on his radio and phone. He jerked to a stop when Cristani casually said, "Here are license and registration records for two Suburbans, and receipts for six cell phones. Four assigned to the store, and two for Tarik Kasim on Kings Road." Before Adams could give an order, Hernandez cut in.

"Hey, Motown, pass me those numbers from the lieutenant, okay? NSA says their cell phone net will be up and running for us in minutes, Mr. A. The cops and VDOT will start looking at those southern routes, too. I already asked NSA to send their intercept vehicles to Arlington and Alexandria and to move around the Pentagon area, so as soon as I relay those phone numbers, they'll find 'em. If they're turned on, that is."

A few minutes later Hernandez swiveled his chair to face Adams again. "We're in luck. NRO has a satellite in the right place, but no joy yet. They got gaps in coverage, but they're going to fix it best they can. No listed or unlisted phones in the Arlington or Alexandria area for a Tarik Kasim, or Kasim anything. I'll check on those new numbers right away." He returned to the blinking lights on his console.

Adams looked around the room at the close-cropped heads bent to their tasks and said, "Hot damn. I love it when a plan comes together like this." He permitted himself a half-smile and added, "I'm heading to Kasim's house with the bookkeeper. Now all we need is a little more data and a lot more luck."

Buoyed by the surge in possibilities, Adams was finally able to push dark thoughts about Carly and Horst to the edge of his mind.

The fist is closing, Kasim. Soon you will feel the pain.

CHAPTER 47

It had been a stressful day of long distance driving. Kasim and the Professor were tired. They had almost been snared by a roadblock on Route 95, but were saved by a WTOP traffic report explaining the cause of the backup. They immediately abandoned the interstate for Route 1 at the Fort Belvoir exit. Driving past Mount Vernon, they fearfully cruised up the George Washington Parkway and into Alexandria. Fifteen minutes later, they were parked in the garage of the Representative condo building.

During the entire trip the Professor had shielded his face from each VDOT camera that dotted the highway. He was right to think they were looking for him. CCTV had spotted the Suburban twice, once on Route 95 and once on Route 1. But roadblocks were set up too late, and dispatched cars and helicopters missed the fugitives before they were able to lose themselves in rush hour traffic.

"I feel they are close to us, my capable driver. It is now time to act quickly, before they find us." The Professor had the huge television in Kasim's entertainment center tuned to the weather channel. "A bomb does not depend on wind to destroy Americans, as does our brown powder. But at last Allah smiles on us. Tonight, the weather is perfect for the fogging machine, and it will kill many more than that small atomic bomb they captured. We will attack before they are ready."

"Tonight? You're crazy! Didn't you see those police cars and unmarked cars? They must have a description of the Suburban by now—it's a miracle they didn't see us before we got into the garage. We must wait a few days until things calm down."

"You think that man, your Jay Adams, will calm down in a few days? I think not." The Professor coughed and winced. His aching bowels told him he must use the toilet. He stood carefully, "We have perfect conditions for an attack tonight. And we will do it." The Professor left the room.

Kasim switched the television to the Playboy Channel and thought about the impossible situation. This sick madman will do what he threatens, no matter what the danger, and then guards around the Pentagon will kill both of us. If we even walk on the streets, police or unmarked cars will find us. What to do? Perhaps I could abandon him, or betray him to the police somehow. Or I could take the money from the company's account at PNC Bank and go to Canada. From there I could tell Tehran the crazy terrorist made some kind of mistake and was captured. That's it. Kasim's mind was racing, out of control.

The Professor returned and sat before the television set. He watched for a moment, sighed, and switched it back to the weather channel. The prediction brought a faint smile to his wan face. A light breeze from the west would begin at midnight and a temperature inversion would put a warm layer over the city, trapping cooler air below. An air quality warning would probably be in effect by noon. But there could be no warning from the weather channel about another kind of smog. The smog waiting in the Suburban parked in the garage below. The death smog.

The Professor fixed his pale dead eyes on Kasim, who was drumming his fingers on his knees and perspiring.

"We will stay together this night, my comrade. If you wish to pray now, I will pray with you. But if you try to call the police or destroy our mission, I will kill you. After we have done what we must do, then take your big car and run away. I will not stop you." He continued to stare balefully at the sleeper agent.

"I will be at your side all night." Kasim's voice wavered. "I would never betray you! Put such thoughts out of your mind. We rest, send out for food, and then you tell me what we must do—how I can help." His mind was racing again. Now I am well and truly dead, he thought. This insane killer can read my secret thoughts!

"Good. It will be as you say, my faithful comrade. At midnight we go to the garage and prepare the weapon in the vehicle. Then we shall leave here and strike a blow the Americans and the world will never forget."

The weather channel repeated maps predicting the midnight arrival of a cool night breeze. Though his chest pain was growing, the Professor's mind was clear.

Death drifts on wind from the west. Before sunrise it will find them. It will kill them. All of them. I must be strong for a few more hours, and it is done. Then I die like Jabber, and join my family. After I kill this seller of rugs.

Pain in his gut was wrenching.

The plague. Foolish Jabber. He killed himself and me. Perhaps he even killed that submarine.

CHAPTER 48

Adams and Captain Alexander's team searched Kasim's house for files and records. He urged them on because he feared there were only hours before the terrorists struck, and because he was desperate to get out of the steam bath inside his Tyvek biohazard suit. The frozen gel in the cooling vest gave only minor relief, and his breath in the suit's humid helmet was fogging the visor. He was close to passing out when they found a long file drawer in a closet, took the folders, and plodded outside.

Next to Alexander on the porch, Adams listened to his battery-powered blower labor to filter cool air into his suit. Panting in the jungle heat inside his helmet, he watched the Marine Captain slap the last file closed.

"Nothing in that file but a bunch of restaurant and gas station receipts. These other files are mostly about rug customers. One file has a bunch of pictures of the same guy posing with different gals. A couple of 'em are real swamp donkeys. I guess the guy in the pictures must be Tarik Kasim." The HEPA respirator muffled Alexander's voice. "There's even one with you in it, Mr. Adams."

"Let me see that file. Sonofabitch. If he has a picture of Carly in there I'll do things to him that—" Adams was interrupted by the Marine, who was balancing the small pile of files on the porch rocker seat.

"Nope. No picture of Miss Truitt in there. But when we grab his ass, let's do some fun things to him anyway."

Adams started to stagger off the porch and gasped, "Just leave those files there for the decon squad." Then he turned and stared at the rocker. "Where are those receipts from? I mean, what restaurants and gas stations?"

Alexander picked up a file, leafed through it and said, "Near as I can see, some of the receipts are for lunch at Chevy's, a few from Ruby Tuesday in Pentagon City and a pile from some Lebanese restaurant. Places like that. Gas receipts are mostly from an Exxon station on 23rd Street in Arlington. Couple of others here and there." He looked up at Adams.

"The gas station and those beaneries are near Pentagon City mall, a pistol-shot away from the Pentagon. I bet Kasim's got a place real close to there. Okay, leave all that crap, captain, and let's get out of these torture suits." Adams and the Marine slogged to the decon showers and dry clothes. Thirty minutes later, they stepped out of the Yukon and rejoined Adams' Onancock army.

"Okay troops, let's review the bidding." Adams was surrounded by the SEALs and Marines on the lawn in front of the Hermitage. The Nighthawk was back from Fort Detrick and dozed in the afternoon sun. Two camouflaged HUMVEEs, armed with M60 machine guns, waited next to his Yukon.

"We still don't know much, troops, but we have to assume the terrorists made it to the Pentagon area. According to the notebook, that's their prime target. Based on VDOT camera sightings and satellite shots at 1400 and 1530, we think they took the Suburban and the anthrax fogger north and disappeared into Alexandria or Arlington.

"We got no confirmed visuals. Their cell phones are off, so no joy there either. One thing is pretty certain, though, and that is they're not in Onancock or Wachapreague. I say we move this outfit up to the Pentagon area. Anybody have a better idea? Okay, we move out in twenty minutes.

"Cristani and Alexander, you're in the helo with me. That'll give us time to review options and do some thinking. Those familiar with them will drive those two HUMVEEs. Deacon, you get to drive my Yukon. Dent her and I'll slug you, even if I have to sneak up on you when you're asleep.

"Portable comm gear gets distributed between the vehicles and the helo so we can stay in touch. I'll take my laptop and the Intelink interface with me. Duggan, we're cleared to set down on the executive pad at the Pentagon, so get over to your beast and wind up the engines. Everyone else, try to stay closed up on the roads and rendezvous at the Pentagon helo pad."

Adams called the phone in the USAMRIID slammer again. Holloway had given him the number after he threatened to fly up to Fort Detrick. Still no answer.

CHAPTER 49

Lieutenant Duggan and the Pentagon helo pad crew chief were running checks on the Nighthawk's systems before the sunlight faded. Waiting for the HUMVEEs to arrive, Adams, Alexander and Cristani were sitting on the grass, watching the two men check the ammunition belt on the wicked-looking minigun. Adams' cell phone's chirping broke the dusky silence.

"Adams."

"Secretary Horton wants to know what's happening, Jeremiah. We have calls from government offices, two newspapers and a television station. They are wondering who authorized the activities at VDOT and on the highways. The president is concerned we have not alerted all the security agencies and the public, and the White House has called us twice. Not to mention the dozen calls we received from the citizens of Onancock who are wondering about helicopters and Marines. The president is considering activating the Continuity Of Government plan and sending the vice president and a good part of the government out of Washington."

Adams gathered his thoughts.

"Okay, Sophie. Sounds like you and the Secretary are making like little Dutch kids with your fingers stuck in a leaky dike. So here's a quick rundown. We believe the terrorists are armed with sixty pounds of weaponized anthrax and an agricultural fogging machine, and that they left Onancock to go to a hideout. It's probably somewhere near the Pentagon. The fogger is likely to still be mounted in Kasim's vehicle, which we've identified but haven't found. We didn't intercept it because I stupidly failed to block the southern roads. Right now I'm positioned right outside your back door, waiting for the SEALs and Marines to catch up.

"Our hope now is that the terrorists activate their cell phones. They don't have the latest models so NSA can't get a fix on them if they're turned off, even with *Trigger Fish* and *Swamp Box*. But the second they turn them on we'll get triangulation from the roving vans. So besides prayers, that's about it. Tell Horton I think the president should initiate the COG plan and get out of Dodge with his pals. Unless, of course, we find those bad guys real soon."

"You were *not* stupid about road blocks, Jeremiah. And no one doubts you are taking every step to resolve the crisis. I will pass your report to the Secretary, and I'm sure he'll wish to talk to you tonight." She hesitated. "And I'm sure you are worried about Miss Truitt, on top of it all. I'm very sorry she was exposed to those germs and is so ill."

"She's so ill? What do you mean *so ill*?" Adams was shouting. "What have you heard about Carly?"

"I really don't know much more than you've already told me. But perhaps you should call USAMRIID and check on things yourself." Before he could reply, she broke the connection.

Adams was furiously stabbing the buttons on the phone when it warbled. The caller ID showed it was an USAMRIID line.

"This is Adams!"

"Whoa! My tender young eardrums." It was Commander Horst.

"What's happening out there! How's Carly? How are you?"

"Looks like I'm fine. They're going to release me in a few minutes, after another set of PCR tests comes back from the lab. I've got a bucket full of needles and I've gotta jab myself regularly, but I should be with you before dinner. You're parked at the Pentagon helo pad, right?"

"Yes. We are at the helo pad. What about Carly, Fred?" Adams was having trouble controlling his voice.

"I was told she'll have to hang around here for a while, Jay. I don't know much else, other than she was exposed to a heavy dose of... the pathogen."

"Fred, you're in the same room with her, and you 'don't know much else?' Pardon my phrasing, but *bullshit!* Tell me what's happening right now, or I swear I'll pound your ass right back into intensive care."

"Wow! Hold on there, buddy. Fact is they moved me out of the slammer pretty early on. Seems my blood work and initial PCR tests showed no measurable level of infection. They wanted me to clear out so they could treat Carly without me being in the way."

"Horst, damn it, I am really going to—" The call waiting tone beeped. "You hang on, you hear?" Adams switched to the other incoming call.

"Adams!"

"This is Doctor Holloway, Adams. I just stepped out of a session with Miss Truitt in the isolation unit and I've got to get back in right away, so I'll make this brief. I promised to keep you advised, and I'm doing so now. Miss Truitt is a very sick young lady. She was massively challenged by the pathogen. A hell of a lot of bugs. Her condition is not responding to streptomycin, and we're changing the protocol right now. I don't have much else to report, but I'll call you later tonight."

"Doc, what's going on? I've got Commander Horst on the other line and he's fine, he says. Why isn't Carly okay, too? Can I talk to her? I can be up there by chopper in a few minutes."

"Horst is in fine physical condition. He was barely exposed, if at all. He's never had TB, and his lungs and immune system are in great shape. Then there are the matters of luck, genetics, and microbiology. I have the phones in the isolation unit shut off now, but I promise to turn them on before tomorrow morning. As for coming up here, I don't think that even you could shoot your way past our gate guards. Forget it. Now I'd like to gossip with you Adams, but I have to get back to my patient. There will be more news later, I promise you." The line went dead, and Adams switched back to Horst.

"Fred."

"Hey, buck up, amigo. She was sitting up and smiling when I left the rack in my half of the isolation room. She was glad to see the last of me. Look, Jay, I'll go back to the slammer before I leave and bring you a personal report on what's happening, okay?"

"Please, Fred. I'll owe you a big one. I can't get through by phone—Holloway's cut them off and won't let me visit."

"Give it a rest, Jay. There's a team of doctors in there, and they probably don't want to be bothered answering the phone. I'll see you soon. Real soon."

Adams looked at the silent phone and slowly returned it to his belt. A shuddering wave of helplessness washed over him.

Forty minutes later, the sun sank into a scarlet horizon. Blood red. Adams looked west and intoned, "Red sky at night, sailor's delight. Sure." He dropped next to Alexander and Cristani on the Pentagon's lawn, and they watched the sky change colors. As the light faded, they heard a distant siren approaching on the parkway. It was Horst, announcing his arrival a full minute before he arrived. Guards on the perimeter had been forewarned by the Secretary's office, and they waved the Crown Victoria through without the usual tedious checks. Siren dying, the car squealed across the access road, pulled up near the Nighthawk, and Horst jumped out. He marched up to the three men sitting on the grass, watching the last of the sunset and drinking coffee. Under his arm was a plastic box that looked like a small attaché case with a red cross on its side.

"Well, if it isn't Curly, Larry, and Moe." Horst's grin faded when he took in the bleak look on Adams' face. "C'mon, Jay. I saw her through the slammer window exactly one hour and fifteen minutes ago, sleeping soundly. Her phone's unplugged so she can rest. There's a medic in there, around the clock, and I asked one of the crew about her. He told me she was stable. And that is the God-honest truth."

"Thanks, pal. Like I said, I owe you one for looking in on her. Now you're back you can listen to TacNet reports from your fellow spooks as they wander around looking for those two pricks, while we heroes sit here snapping our snakes. And meantime Carly suffers in the slammer." Adams looked up, his face a study in gloom. "What's in your case, tough guy?"

"Syringes full of streptomycin. Couple of shots a day for ten days, so I'm carrying this box around wherever I go. And you should stop listening to the tactical net like some kind of ambulance-chaser. When they find them, the comm system will light up like Disneyland. Now rise up, amigo, and look at the wheels I used to break all land speed records just to be at your side. Take a look, shipmate. You'll love it."

Adams forced a wan smile, got up, and walked to the dark blue Ford sedan with Cristani and Alexander. Horst opened both front doors and reached in to pop the hood. Inside and out, the car was astounding.

"Ta DAH! My Spookmobile!" Horst was bubbling with enthusiasm. "She's a regular Crown Victoria Police Interceptor with fat tires. I had them put in heavy-duty gas shocks and tighten up the sway bars, for openers." He smiled paternally at the gleaming engine.

"Then they dropped in a Merlin II "509" with 540 cubes, polished aluminum Merlin rectangular port heads, and a supercharger. She's got 640 horses up front, goosed by that Holley 4-barrel carb and a blower." Horst gushed on, to the delight of Alexander and Cristani.

Adams sidled around to the open door and said, "What kind of boxes you put in it for the pilot?"

Horst joined him and began to identify the equipment surrounding the driver's seat. It looked like an aircraft cockpit.

"That's a GPS map overlay system, and over there are the usual phones, radios, CB, and police scanners. The keyboard is for the frequency-hopping datalink, and the other flat screen display is plugged into a custom laptop I can unplug and take out. I switch to the antenna suite if I need rock and roll. Otherwise..." he reached in to the steering wheel. "I make my own music!" He pressed the horn button and a siren erupted in an ear-shattering wail.

"So what d'you think about my go-cart? Pretty neat, huh?" Horst stepped back and admired the dark blue car.

"It's faster and better-equipped than the Yukon," Adams admitted. "So I'm shifting my flag to this vehicle as soon as I can plug in my PC card and bring up the Intelink. We might need real speed tonight or tomorrow, and this supersonic gas guzzler could come in handy."

"Gas guzzler? Hey, with her 13:1 compression ratio and some glow plugs I could burn peanut oil if... wait a minute. You're gonna let *me* drive it, right?" Horst followed Adams anxiously.

"Sure. You're the skipper and I'm the battle group admiral on board. We'll play sailors at sea."

Adams returned to the Yukon to pull the Intelink security card out of his laptop when his cell phone rang. Caller ID showed it was USAMRIID, Carly's phone number in the slammer. *Carly! Okay!* But it was not Carly.

"Adams? This is Holloway. We're with your Miss Truitt right now, and I'm calling as I promised. She is very sick, Adams. That fulminating plague bug resists every antibiotic we can muster, and she's starting to have serious trouble tonight." Holloway's voice was garbled by the radio headset he had pressed to the telephone mouthpiece. It was the only way he could telephone from his positive pressure suit.

"I guess you know she had a serious case of childhood TB, and her lungs and heart are in bad shape. Her immune system can't cope with this pathogen from hell, and we're getting very low on ways to help her. At least it is not the plague hybrid we've heard about with diphtheria toxin genes spliced into it. But if you still want to get up here, Adams, you might think about doing it now."

"I'll leave right away, doc." He choked the words out. "Please help her."

Adams was standing next to the Yukon's open door, and he could smell a faint trace of Carly's perfume on the passenger's seat. His eyes brimmed when Holloway hung up.

TB? Heart and lungs? Oh no. Those pills she was always taking...

Horst had walked to the driver's side of the Yukon to give Adams some privacy when he took the call. He reached inside when the SUV's radio squawked.

"Adams' base. Horst here."

"Lieutenant Hillman, ONI area coordinator, Commander Horst. We've blanketed all roads on the west side of the Pentagon sir, and set up a rolling grid that will intercept any suspicious vehicle before it gets near the building. Random DIA, Army, and Air Force patrols are covering the general locale as well. Nothing else to report, sir. Over."

"Roger. Base out."

Horst knew that what made the west side so special was the breeze that would come from the west that night. But hell, he thought, what if they've picked another target. Like the White House.

Before Adams could clip the phone to his belt it rang again. Ranger's vet said the Lab was ready to go home to convalesce, and his only problem was he missed Adams and 'that lovely young lady.'

Screw everything. Horst can deal with the scene here. I'm taking the chopper to Fort Detrick.

CHAPTER 50

Western Atlantic Ocean
Latitude 39° 45' North—Longitude 66° 00' West

Forty hours had passed since *Yunes* delivered its deadly cargo to the shores of America. Slipping eastward under the surface of the Atlantic at a steady ten knots, she re-crossed the continental shelf and passed over the Hudson Canyon deep. With two miles of water under her keel, she was well north of the Kelvin Seamount, on course to her rendezvous with *Polyus* in the Bay of Biscay. Captain Reza was in his cabin, grimacing at the bottle of cough medicine. When something tasted this foul, he thought, it should be a lot more effective. There were two quick taps on the compartment door.

"Captain? Captain, may we have a word with you?" It was Lieutenant Hossein, the ship's doctor.

"Come."

Doctor Hossein and Chief Ali squeezed into the cabin, crowding close to Reza at his fold-down desk. They were wearing facemasks, the N95 disposable respirators he had ordered when he was told about the nature of the cargo he would carry. The pain in his chest intensified when he saw the masks.

"Speak, Doctor."

"Captain, *Yunes* is dying. I thought it was flu when I saw so many men report to sick call yesterday, but it is not flu. I am now positive it is..." the doctor lowered his voice to a whisper. "It must be pneumonic plague. The chief and I don't seem to be infected, and there are two other healthy crewmen. When I realized what was happening I started us on a protocol of doxcycline hydroclorate and issued respirators to the four of us. The drug is not very effective once symptoms appear."

The doctor placed a respirator on Reza's desk along with a vial of blue and white capsules, and added, "You must wear the mask, captain. The plague bacteria are surely circulating throughout our air conditioning system. Take two of those capsules, to start."

"Why are you and the other two not infected?" Reza looked at the mask and vial of capsules. For the past day he watched his crew become sicker by the hour, and his hope that it was a flu bug was now gone.

"I do not know, captain. Perhaps we have not yet breathed enough of the germs, or perhaps our immune systems have protected us. There are always a few survivors of even the deadliest disease, it seems. But the five of us are the only crewmembers that are not yet sick or showing symptoms. Many of the men are very close to death, and the others are coughing their germs into the air. Start your treatment now, captain, and I will check all the compartments again. But I am sure there is not much I can do for the rest of the crew, sir."

Captain Reza hacked into his handkerchief. The two men recoiled, but could only move back inches in the small cabin.

"Like my crew, doctor, it appears it is too late for me to take pills and wear a mask. How long do you estimate before... before everyone dies?"

The chief's eyes above his respirator brimmed with tears as he answered. "There are only a few able to stand watch, my captain. I do not think the crew can operate *Yunes* for even one more day, and not a single officer can leave his bunk. Most men look like they have only hours of life left in them." His heavy brows drew together. "Captain, take the pills anyway. They still might work. Right, doctor?"

The doctor stared at Reza. Then he said, "*Takdeer*, captain."

"It is indeed my destiny, doctor." Reza stood. "Thank you for the thought, Chief Ali, but the doctor knows I am not suffering from the flu. A moment, please."

Reza took a tall dark bottle and three crystal goblets from a recess in the cupboard over his desk, and returned to his chair.

"I was given this very fine wine by a minister in Tehran. It was to be enjoyed when we saw the shores of Europe after our return transit. Perhaps you will join me now? It seems *Yunes* is on her way toward a different shore." The captain pulled at the corkscrew taped to the bottle. The two standing men were silent and motionless.

"Ah. You can't remove your respirator masks. Of course. And I suppose the glasses are contaminated too, like everything else on my beautiful *Yunes*." Reza began to cut the foil away from the bottle's cork.

"Tell me, gentlemen, what can four of you possibly hope to do?"

The chief glanced at the doctor, who still stared at the calm captain, and said, "The inflatable rubber boat, sir. The other Zodiac those shit-brained swine brought with them. Pardon me, sir. We could launch it and make for Canada. It's a long journey for a small craft, but I could rig a storm sail and use the motor sparingly. There is easily room for the five of us..." the chief's voice trailed off.

"A daring plan, chief, but there will be only four crewmen in your new command." Tossing the cork into a corner, Reza placed the bottle on his desk and sighed.

"Very well. Prepare yourselves to shove off in the Zodiac. When you are ready, you two meet me in the control room and send the other two to the engine spaces so we can bring *Yunes* to the surface. I will conn the boat while you go over the side." The Captain smiled at the doctor and the chief.

"Off with you now. You need to find foul weather gear, disinfect it, and prepare the provisions for your long journey. I too, must dress appropriately for this important day." He returned the salutes of the two men, and looked away as they left the cabin.

The five men still able to operate the submarine's complex controls brought *Yunes* to the surface. The automatic surfacing and diving systems were located in the control room, so three officers there and two crewmen in the engine room were enough.

When they were on the surface and running on diesel power, the doctor, the chief and the two other crewmen joined the captain in the control room. The only other man in the compartment was Abdul, the radioman, who looked out from his cubicle with fever-blind eyes.

Reza broke the awkward silence and said, "Very well. You assembled provisions at the forward torpedo room hatch, along with the Zodiac. Take it all topside, chief. I am sure you know how to inflate that boat. Launch it to starboard. There is calmer water there. Use your lifelines and take care while you move your supplies aboard the boat and lash them down. I go to the bridge now. When you have started your motor, give me a signal and I will go below to change course to starboard. That will give you more lee water. When you see the bow moving, cut the line and steer away." Smiling now, the captain looked from face to face, each masked with a respirator.

"Soon clean ocean air and sunlight will wash over you and your rubber lifeboat, and you won't need those things." He smiled again at the masked faces and went on, "Here, chief. Take my GPS unit and this chart. You were always a poor navigator."

Chief Ali looked down at the chart and GPS unit. Suddenly he stiffened to attention. His voice exploded through his respirator.

"Attention on deck! Form ranks for salute! Now—salute!" The four men held their salute until Reza returned it.

"I am proud to have served with you men, and with your shipmates. You are a credit to this boat and to the navy, and you leave *Yunes* with honor. Now go. Continue your part in her journey into history. Dismissed!"

As the men began to move toward the forward hatch, Reza paused on the ladder to the bridge.

"And chief. After you get the boat and supplies on deck, leave the forward hatch open. We'll get some fresh air in here, too." The chief raised his hand and started to reply, then stopped.

"Aye, sir."

Reza mounted the ladder to the bridge and the others continued forward, heading for the Zodiac waiting in the forward torpedo room.

In his blue dress uniform resplendent with medals, wearing his white cap, Reza stood stoically on the bridge, watching the four men below launch the rubber boat. When they were all aboard, and the outboard motor started, the chief turned to the bridge and raised his hand in a long salute. Reza returned the salute and went below, leaving the conning tower hatch open.

Crisp ocean air flowed down the hatchway and followed him into the control room. Taking the helm, he changed course slightly to the south and walked to the periscope.

There they go. My brave crew, off on another heroic voyage.

Returning to his stateroom, Reza left the periscope extended. It was the eye of a beautiful sea creature, he thought, that was dying. It looked down at the arrow of the Zodiac's wake, pointing hopefully into the sunset.

Sitting at his desk he filled the wine glass, drank, and examined the magnum bottle Dehesh had given him. It was a Margaux, 1998 vintage. The wine's magnificent bouquet was only slightly marred by his fever. *To Yunes and all who sailed in her! To her historic voyage!* He rose, drained the glass, picked up the bottle and walked back to the control room. Two men were sprawled in the passageway, one of them was Commander Saduqi. Reza paused for a moment to see if they were breathing, then stepped over them.

Radioman Abdul had fallen, sitting on the deck near his communications console. He was moaning and nodding his head, as if he was giving approval to some speech only he could hear. A cascade of vomit ran down his tunic.

Reza sat in Abdul's chair, refilled the wineglass, and listened to the familiar drone of shipboard noise as her diesels powered *Yunes* aimlessly across the Atlantic. Then he switched on the powerful LF transceiver and tuned it to the frequency of the Bandar Abbas naval base. Sipping the wine, he pulled the microphone close.

"Bandar Abbas base, this is Iranian warship *Yunes* calling. Bandar Abbas, this is *Yunes*, Captain Jamshid Bakhtiar Reza in command. I am reporting that our mission is completed, but due to—due to onboard casualties, we are unable to return to base or proceed to our scheduled overhaul. You may cancel the overhaul." Reza laughed in his growing delirium, filled the glass again, and tried to concentrate.

"I commend the magnificent crew of *Yunes*. They carried out their orders and their duties with unhesitating bravery. They are a credit to the Iranian Navy, and a shining example for submariners everywhere. Generous provision must be made for their families. That must be done without fail. As for Captain Reza, tell his wife that his last thoughts were of her and their daughters. Here ends the last transmission of *Yunes*." Reza switched off the radio, rose, and walked to the command station, swaying slightly.

Initiating the automatic dive sequence, Reza listened to alarm klaxons that shouted the conning tower and forward torpedo room hatches were open. Another alarm joined in, screaming that the main induction valve to the diesel engines was also open. He hit the alarm override switches and selected maximum down angle for the forward dive planes. Then he stepped to the periscope and watched air venting from the ballast tanks in tall misty columns as the voids below filled with inrushing seawater. *Yunes* was snorting like some great surfaced ocean beast, anxious to return to the safety of its home in the deeps. He walked back to the navigation table.

Perched on the edge of the table, Reza felt the deck of *Yunes* begin to gradually tilt forward. When the laboring diesel engines drove the bow of the boat under the waves, seawater reached the open torpedo room hatch and cascaded into the compartment below. The dive angle increased sharply.

Reza held on to the table and heard pots and pans fall in the galley. Books, charts, and navigation instruments slid off the table along with the wine bottle and crystal glass.

We had crystal glasses on our picnics. We filled them with pistachios and licked the salt from each other's fingers. Sweet Minou...

At last he heard the sea reach the open induction valve and waterfall directly into the howling diesel intake manifolds. Then the Atlantic stabbed her cold salty spear deep into *Yunes'* heart, and killed her. Lights flickered and died as the ocean flushed through bulkhead doors and flooded the engine and battery rooms. Filling with icy water, her interior churned wildly as the black submarine plunged toward the bottom, two miles below.

Four hundred miles away, electronic ears of the National Security Agency heard the last message from *Yunes*. Thirty minutes later there was a series of pings from the speakers in Adams' laptop. It was the Intelink with a CRITIC message.

Parked near the small operations building at the Pentagon helo pad, Adams saw the flashing bar on the laptop screen. When he slid the ID card into the slot and keyed his password, the screen cleared and he saw a satellite photo of a submarine. Latitude and longitude notation indicated it was in the central Atlantic. Below the picture was a transcript of Reza's last message to Tehran. Adams read it and cleared the screen.

Far to the east of the Pentagon, beneath the arch of a starry ocean sky, the Zodiac motored westward in a light breeze, her outboard set to its lowest speed. Three men were asleep in the bows, and Chief Ali dozed at the helm. Suddenly, a familiar rushing and hissing pulled him away from dreams of a strange submarine, and he saw a dark shadow pierce the surface thirty meters away. His eyes widened in recognition. The huge sail of a nuclear submarine was gushing water and rising into the night air.

When the intense beam of light blinded him, the chief knew his dream was real.

CHAPTER 51

Adams peered through the small window in slammer door. Nothing to see. Earlier, the closed circuit television monitor in Doctor Holloway's office had shown him Carly tossing deliriously, a pressure-suited figure taking her blood pressure. Holloway had been at Adams' side since he arrived and did everything he asked—except allow him into the isolation room. They returned to the doctor's office.

"For the last time, Adams, you can do absolutely no good in there. Besides, you would get in the way. You can see everything from out here, and if—when she improves, I'll put her on the phone to you. Meantime, take a couple of these." He held out vial of white tablets.

"What are they?"

"Quarter grain phenobarbs. They'll drop your blood pressure."

"Forget it, doc. I don't want my blood pressure dropped. I just want her out of there."

"Okay, then drink more coffee. When you pop a valve I'll sedate you before your open heart surgery."

"Listen doc—Adams was about to continue harassing Holloway when his cell phone made its distinctive chirp.

"Jay? This is Tarsis." Encryption circuits cleared. "You might like to know I just got hard copy of an interesting gram from what's left of SOSUS. Together with amplifying reports. Seems a submarine fell two miles into the Atlantic deep around 1630 and hit the bottom going eighty miles an hour. Collapsing bulkheads, the works. She's buried in the mud around 66 West, 40 North.

"I also got a detailed workup of *Maryland's* waterfall. It matches data that P-3 recorded from the boat that got away from them in the eastern Atlantic. Looks like Iran's navy is down to their last two KILOs." Adams heard Tarsis chuckle grimly.

"That figures, George. I guess you know NSA intercepted a radio message from a sub at coordinates that match your SOSUS fix. The sub's transmission was *en clair*, and indicated they were in serious trouble. Screw all those bastards anyway—my heart bleeds for them. We'll deliver a special thank you to Iran when this is over, and if the Nixon policy on payback for germ warfare still holds, maybe they'll even glow in the dark. Thanks for the call, Admiral. I'll be talking with you soon."

"Hold on, Jay, I'm not finished." Another grim chuckle. "The attack boat I sent out to find that diesel was too late to help her to the bottom. But she found a Zodiac with four Iranian sailors in it, merrily yachting their way back to North America. How about them apples!"

Adams was silent for a moment, then said, "Somehow I don't feel my quarrel's with those submariners. If they were yours, I think you might even be proud of them."

"Yeah. I might at that." Tarsis heaved a sigh. "Too bad that skipper went down with his boat. I would've grilled him a steak on my patio and guzzled beer with him all night before he went to trial. Well, I'll send you a transcript of the interrogations. So long, Jay."

Adams snapped the phone closed and focused on the doctor, who was looking at him oddly.

"What's the matter, doc?"

"I suppose I never really considered the sort of things you do." He raised a hand as Adams started to interrupt. "No need to tell me to forget that talk about glowing in the dark. Anyway, you might want to go back to your work, whatever it is. I will keep you advised. And you have that helicopter, if need be."

"There may be trouble at the Pentagon tonight, doc, and I should be there. But I'm only minutes away. You'll stay in close touch? Okay?"

Holloway nodded silently. Adams rose and looked around the office aimlessly. Then he squared his shoulders, nodded in return, and softly pulled the door closed behind him.

CHAPTER 52

The Representative Condominiums
Arlington, Virginia

The Professor looked into shadows in the dark garage, then leaned on the fender of the Suburban, breathing hard. Strenuous effort was now almost impossible, and his face glistened with perspiration around the respirator he wore.

Fifteen minutes ago he sent Kasim back to the apartment for water and the codeine syrup that provided enough euphoria to enable him to carry on. When he did not return he switched on his cell phone, called the apartment and warned Kasim that if he did not return immediately, he would drive off without him. If that happened, the Professor promised, he would notify police of Kasim's location. They would be on him like lions on fresh meat.

While he waited, he slit open the smooth plastic bags of anthrax spores and carefully let the tan powder flow into the hopper of the agricultural fogging machine. There was sixty pounds of the dust, and he knew that amount could kill Washington if it was delivered properly. He finished sealing the hopper, gasping, and pulled the respirator from his face. He had been careful, but a thin layer of dust covered his hands and the fogger machine.

Why do I worry? Plague kills me long before these dust devils awaken in my lungs. As for that Kasim pig...

His cell phone rang, and Kasim's voice babbled at him even before he could answer. "They are coming! I see a helicopter flying this way—and vehicles from the

Pentagon!" There was a pause, and the Professor heard traffic sounds on the phone. Kasim must be standing on the apartment balcony. "Look, a car in the street! I am coming now—don't leave me!"

The Professor broke the connection and tried to think clearly. How could they have found them? He had watched the men and machines around the Pentagon at sunset, and they seemed to be doing nothing, just waiting. But somehow they found him. He dropped the cell phone in his pocket as the garage door burst open and Kasim ran wildly toward the Suburban, shouting.

"Quickly, we must go! Out the back! They will not come to the garage door right away, and we can escape—quickly, quickly!" Kasim was in the driver's seat, starting the engine even before the Professor closed the Suburban's rear hatch.

"Very well, drive us away. If it is to be our fate, we will be gone from here before they find us. Drive." The Professor slammed his door as the Suburban's engine revved.

The black SUV roared down the hill on the east side of the condominium building, lights out, tires squealing. Kasim accelerated into a right turn at the bottom, and then turned right again into the next intersection. A second after they passed, two unmarked ONI cars skidded into the crossroad in the opposite lane and turned up the road that led to the rear of the building, the garage entrance.

Anticipating Kasim's fear, the Professor twisted in his seat, winced at the pain in his chest, and produced his pistol.

"Drive carefully. Go down to 23rd Street and turn north onto Route 1. Then go toward the 14th Street Bridge and turn off on the George Washington Parkway going north." The Professor slowly screwed a silencer onto the gun's barrel, his pale blue eyes fixed on the profile next to him.

Kasim smiled weakly when he saw the weapon. "Good! Very good!" he said. "We take a car from kids in a parkway overlook and then go north. I'll get money from a bank in Maryland or Pennsylvania. We will get away—you're right!"

The Professor coughed violently, then said, "You will drive where I tell you to drive." He was breathing hard, but his hand was steady on the gun resting on his lap.

The Suburban was already on the ramp to the parkway when Adams leaped out of Horst's Crown Victoria. He trotted up to the two men in dark suits blocking the entrance to the condominiums. The fix on the cell phones had taken a few minutes to reach him, and more time was lost before he and the other units could reach the building. The Nighthawk hovered above its roof, beating waves of whooshing air down into the street, gently ruffling Adams' hair.

"Building surrounded? Back entrance? Garage? Basement doors?"

"It's all covered now, sir. A roach won't get out without us stomping it." The young intelligence officer blinked anxiously under Adams' cold stare.

"Good. Now holster that gun before you scare the shit out of the citizens, and stay alert out here." Adams strode into the brightly-lit lobby, glancing at the expensive furnishings.

"Where is Mr. Tarik Kasim's apartment?"

The grandmotherly Middle Eastern woman behind the reception desk was cringing against the wall, as far away as she could move from the stern young man with a gun that stood behind her desk. So big and handsome, she thought, and he spoke such good Arabic.

"I told this man, we have no Mr. Kasim," she managed to stutter, "but Mr. Tarik is in number 1212."

Adams sprinted to the elevator bank without replying. Gorski had already called all the elevators to the ground floor and had immobilized them.

They found the door to 1212 unlocked, the apartment empty. Captain Alexander cautiously opened the doors to the balcony and then stepped out.

"Hell of a view of the Pentagon, Mr. Adams. Do you think they were going to use that sprayer machine off this balcony?"

"Wouldn't be very effective from here even if the wind was right, captain. Send your troops and the others through the building. Start at the top and go down. Make it fast and open every door. I think they saw us coming and flew the coop, but let's make sure." Adams holstered his handgun and pulled the radio from its belt clip.

"Cristani, Adams, over."

"Cristani, aye."

"Have Duggan start the helo into a slow spiral orbit away from the building. Find that damn black Suburban. They can't be more than a minute or two away from here. Out." He punched another channel button that was flashing.

"Adams, over."

"This is the Spookmobile, still out front. The vans hold a fix on two phones, and calculate both to be moving east over the 14th Street Bridge toward D.C." Horst paused, then added, "Correction, they are heading north now. Probably on the GW Parkway, over." Adams was bolting for the door as he answered.

"This could be it! Alert the Pentagon perimeter. I'm on my way down."

When Adams and Horst roared across the Pentagon's south parking lot, they were advised the cell phones had stopped moving, and were now located on the east side of the building. Distorted antenna patterns made it impossible for a good fix until the vans could get closer to the area. Adams was puzzled.

"East side? Why the *east* side? Are they on Route 110? They can't possibly be closer than that, Fred, or the perimeter watch would have seen them. They'll have to keep moving on that road or get nailed by the guards. I don't get it, but let's go to the east." Adams used the car's radio to order the Nighthawk back to the Pentagon, and to sweep the grounds from the River Entrance to the south parking lot.

The Crown Victoria flashed past two checkpoints and rounded the southeast corner of the building. Then, across the Potomac River lagoon, Adams could see the lights of Columbia Marina glinting through the trees.

"There! They've got to be in the marina or in the parking lot for Lady Bird Johnson Park. Or next to that frigging seagull monument on the parkway. Keep going, Fred. Get on the north access road and then make that turn south, down to the parkway. When we get near the marina, lights out." The blue cruiser's turbocharged engine wound up as they accelerated across the long Pentagon parking lot, dodging parked cars. Adams was on his walkie-talkie as Horst swerved the Crown Victoria into the exit lane and slowed.

"Cristani, this is Adams. Slide your chopper over the river, due east of the Pentagon. You'll see the Columbia Marina and a parking lot across the parkway near the river, just north of a low sculpture of seagulls. Stay dark, and stay high enough over the Potomac so your noise doesn't spook anyone in the marina or near that monument. Use night vision gear and ready the searchlight. Keep this channel open. Out" Adams adjusted the radio's earplug and his lip mike.

Finally out of the parking lot and on the parkway, they were slowing down, easing south, paralleling Lyndon Johnson Park. Horst switched off the headlights. There were no cars in the lot along the river, so they turned into the marina entrance.

CHAPTER 53

Adams and Horst coasted the car into the marina parking lot. They saw the Suburban, dark and still, backed up to a dock gate that sheltered under an ancient pin oak. They could not yet see the night watchman sprawled near the open entrance. Neither could they see the Park Police officer who routinely patrolled the marina lot at night, shooing away lovers. He was sitting behind the wheel of his parked car, a bullet hole in his forehead. The Professor's silenced gun had been as effective this night as it had been in training, long weeks ago.

With considerable difficulty, Kasim and the Professor had lowered the *Typhoon II* fogger to the deck of a large cabin cruiser at dock number 34. They had positioned the machine near the after deck railing, and its muffled Honda power plant was humming, ready to be engaged to the spray impellers. The Professor waved to Kasim above him on the raised bridge, and shouted for him to start the yacht's engines.

"Kasim, you are now our gallant captain. Engage your motors, sail up the river, and I will release a cloud of death that will cover the entire city. We will spray them until we are near the Chain Bridge, and then we turn south and spray them again. Tomorrow, Washington will wish we had given them the nuclear bomb instead."

Kasim waved back, shouting over the boat's rumbling diesels. "Then we can motor all the way to the bay. They will never find us!" Kasim's anxiety was turning into a strange elation. Below him, the Professor threw the mooring lines into the marina waters.

A few yards from the gate to the dock, Horst braked the darkened car to a stop and Adams keyed his throat mike.

"Cristani, do you hold them? They're on a boat alongside a pier in the lagoon. We're next to the Suburban at the gate." Adams squinted into the gloom. *A boat. Why a boat?*

"Roger, we see them. Orders?"

"Horst and I are going to rush them. When you see us move onto the dock, get over that boat and switch on your light. If they so much as twitch, shoot the fuckers."

Horst eased his door open and the cruiser's dome light went on, illuminating him and Adams. The Professor's head snapped toward the light.

"They've seen us! They're moving the boat away from the dock. Light 'em up, Cristani, light 'em up *now!*"

Side by side, guns drawn, Adams and Horst pounded down the dock as the yacht's engines began to move her deeper into the lagoon. Suddenly, the helicopter's searchlight, brighter than the noonday sun, outlined the white boat in a shimmering radiance. Adams reached the end of the dock and went into the classic hand gunner's stance: right arm crooked slightly to bring the sights up to his eye, left hand under the gun butt.

Steering the cabin cruiser toward the exit to the Potomac River, Kasim looked back at the marina and saw Adams and Horst on the dock, aiming pistols at him. He laughed and rammed the throttles forward. The sudden acceleration knocked the Professor off his feet and sprawled him near the buzzing fogger machine.

Fifteen yards away, Adams centered Kasim's smirk just above his gun sights and fired twice. The first bullet whipped by his ear and made a starry hole in the windscreen. The second bullet hit Kasim on the point of his chin, shattering the jaw bone into bloody shards. He fell and rolled off the bridge to the deck below, clutching his throat as the yacht picked up speed. Even over the methodical blasts from Horst's gun, Adams could hear Kasim's bubbling screams.

"This is Cristani." The SEAL's calm voice in his headset drew Adams' eyes up to the hovering Nighthawk. "One man's down. The other has a weapon and is crawling around a machine on the fantail. It must be that sprayer, and it looks like it's putting out smoke. Request guns free. Over."

"Take 'em, Cristani! Hit 'em with everything you've got!" Adams shouted into his mike, emptying his gun at the departing boat. He watched the yacht motor away.

The fogger's running. If they make it out to the Potomac—they'll get the whole city!

Automatic weapons cracked and sparkled from the Nighthawk's open door as its rotor blades slashed the night air. Then the hovering machine dropped and turned toward the yacht as it gathered speed and moved away.

Knocked off his feet by the sudden acceleration, the Professor lurched to his knees on the fantail and saw Kasim, shrieking and rolling on the forward deck. The boat was not under control now, but it was still headed for the river. Good, he thought, I started the machine, and we can still destroy many killers of children before this night is done. Then he looked up at the searchlight that turned night into day. A helicopter. Must all things begin and end with helicopters, he wondered. On his knees, he raised his pistol to the hovering shape and shouted.

"Allah, give me my vengeance now!"

Adams screamed at the helicopter, "The minigun! Use the minigun!"

As if Lieutenant Duggan heard Adams' command, there was a high-pitched roar, like the sound of celestial canvas tearing, and a gout of flame hosed down from the rotating six-barrels of the machinegun slung below the helicopter. The white boat began to disintegrate into a cloud of fragments.

On the dock, Adams and Horst fell prone as wood, upholstery, Plexiglas, chrome, aluminum and steel deck fittings flew madly into the air and skipped across the lagoon. Thousands of bullets danced through the boat's decks, ricocheting, tearing through her sides and singing around the engines.

Adams watched the shattered boat sink and heard the sprayer gagging, choked by the lagoon closing over it. Above, the helicopter ceased firing and hovered, its searchlight probing the debris-strewn surface. Wiping moisture from his face as the helicopter rotor blades wafted spray around him, Adams wondered how much anthrax he was breathing. His cell phone chirped, and he mechanically put it to his ear.

"Adams, this is Doctor Holloway." The voice from Fort Detrick was somber. "Miss Truitt died five minutes ago. We just couldn't get ahead of pneumonia or the plague, and her heart couldn't take it anymore. She was not in pain when she died. I am very sorry. She was a lovely woman. Adams? Adams, are you there?"

CHAPTER 54

Morteza Dehesh's face was cold iron, his features motionless. Only his eyes moved, two glittering furnaces of rage. He read the report from Bandar Abbas a third time. How? How could it have ended so quickly and so completely? He leaned back in his ornate chair, put his elbows on the Louis XV desk and stared into the distance. A full minute passed before he prodded an intercom switch. The usual voice answered.

"Yes, Excellency."

"Go to Major Doctor Suleiman. He is in our suite at the Esteghlal Grand Hotel. When you wake him, apologize for the late hour and bring him to me immediately." Dehesh released the button, took a deep breath, and called to the tea boy always on duty outside the library.

"Mustafa! Bring two glasses and the best Armagnac brandy."

It was midnight when there was a discreet knock at the study door. A street guard let the doctor in and retreated, closing the door behind him.

"Ah, doctor! How nice. Sit down. Sit down here at the desk. I must apologize for taking you from your evening's rest, but there are some matters we must discuss tonight." Dehesh's teeth gleamed at the edge of the lamplight.

Doctor Suleiman was cold, almost numb despite the small fire that burned in the carved marble fireplace. Standing in the doorway, shivering, he said, "I apologize for my robe and slippers, Excellency, but the guard who came said not to change into uniform."

Dehesh indicated the desk chair opposite him with a graceful wave. "Please do not trouble yourself, doctor. You and I do not stand on ceremony. You and I, we've done historic things together, have we not?" Suleiman could only stare at Dehesh, nodding as he walked to the chair and sat.

"So. I'll wager you cannot guess the amazing news I just received from our navy friends in Bandar Abbas. It seems that they have lost one of their submarines. What do you think of that?"

"I... I don't know what to think, Excellency."

"No? I suppose not. We are not sailors, are we? But there are still many matters we do understand, yes? Like the deaths of the two men you recently trained. Like the death of a very expensive agent in America. Like an attack on the Pentagon that failed." Dehesh's voice rose with each sentence until his final words became a high pitched scream. "Like the failure of our weapons to destroy *anything*!"

Doctor Suleiman was close to shock. His heart fluttered, and he had to purse his lips very firmly to keep his teeth from chattering. But he could not stop his hands from trembling. Dehesh smiled again.

"Forgive me for shouting, doctor. It was rude, and I did not mean to distress you. Here, let us have a brandy. It will calm us both." Dehesh poured a large measure into a snifter and offered it across the desk to Suleiman. The doctor's eyes widened, and he shrank into his seat.

"Think it is poisonous? Please don't be so silly, doctor." Dehesh poured an ounce into his own glass, and drank it. "See? 1938. An excellent year for Armagnac. Drink. Drink deeply." The doctor managed to sip from his shaking goblet. The amber liquid warmed his stomach and then seemed to reach his clammy hands. He sipped again.

"Now we drink together, like colleagues," said Dehesh calmly. "So, like your good colleague, I must advise you that we know of the message you sent to your doctor friend in America. We could not break the cipher, but in light of recent events, what else could it be but betrayal? Tell me doctor, my former friend, why did you do it? Why did you betray our country and dishonor yourself? Why did you betray *me*?" Dehesh seemed genuinely curious.

The courage that comes to some men when they face certain death now graced the doctor. His hands stopped trembling. He sat taller in his chair, drank more of his brandy, and looked into Dehesh's eyes.

"I did it to *save* our country, not to betray it. If you had succeeded, if you had used a biological weapon to kill Americans, they would have answered such an attack with their nuclear bombs. It has been their policy since Nixon renounced the American biological warfare program. Iran would be utterly destroyed. You and I and our families would be burned to ashes." The doctor looked serene, and sipped his brandy again.

Dehesh still looked curiously at Suleiman and said, "Surely you are not a fool? Don't you understand the men we sent were never sure who was their master? That all the weapons they carried were made in Russia? Nowhere was our hand to be seen, and the two men would have been silenced forever once their task was done. You know America would take great care to be absolutely sure of who attacked them before they would even consider launching their atomic missiles."

"I tell you, Excellency, they would have discovered everything," replied Suleiman. "Think of all our messages, of the Russians who sold us the weapons, of the submarine, of all the details—even our own people. Somewhere, somehow, they would find out that we sent the weapons. Then the blood of our families and millions of Iranians would be on our hands. No, I had to warn the Americans. Not to save them—to save us!" Nodding to himself, the doctor looked up. "May I have more brandy, please?"

Dehesh continued to regard Suleiman with bemused fascination, and poured another large measure into Suleiman's glass. "Impressive. You go effortlessly from medicine to strategy, doctor. However, I know a little about both myself, so drink, then listen carefully." Dehesh filled his own glass.

"I thought it a possibility the Hamas idiots would succeed in their attacks, doctor. Difficult, but worth a try. Think of it. If they had succeeded in killing only a hundred thousand Americans! The blood of our soldiers and sailors who died in the attack on Bandar Abbas would be avenged. Our honor would live again! But I did not imagine our avengers would fail because they were betrayed by you. That they would die uselessly, completely ineffectual.

"Even so, doctor, there is more, much more. Think. You know it already. For two years you explained to me your success with biological weapons. All the wonderful bugs you make that kill pigs, chickens, cows and wheat fields. Do you remember my people were always in your laboratories, always anxious to have samples of your germs? Do you remember I gave your research much thought? That I supported all your projects? I see by your face you do, and that you now understand why I needed your excellent work to launch my second attack—an overwhelming and absolutely untraceable attack on American farms and livestock.

"Please forgive me for not telling you, doctor, but I suspected you might be a traitor even before you sent that message to America." Dehesh sniffed delicately at the brandy, looking at the doctor over the rim of his glass.

"I have been in close contact with commodity brokers in Zurich and Hong Kong. They tell me that if one somehow knew American wheat and meat would become diseased, one could do very nicely with futures contracts on Australian and South American food products. I was also told the Americans would suffer as much as sixty billion dollars in losses in the first year alone. I will make a billion or two. At least I think those are the amounts they explained to me."

Dehesh, watching the doctor closely, reached into his desk drawer and produced a small pistol. Its engraving was inlaid with gold that glittered in the lamplight. Suleiman looked at the gun dispassionately, and raised his glass to his lips.

Dehesh leaned forward. "I will not ask VEVAK to torture you and your family until your bodies break and your minds dissolve. I will not do that because you truly think you are a patriot. Yes, I believe you do, doctor."

The little gun's blast was surprisingly loud. It filled the room and stirred the crystals on the chandelier above.

"Mustafa! Come take the glasses and trash away."

EPILOGUE

Sophie Giltspur and Jeremiah Adams were the last mourners to leave the gravesite in Salisbury. Adams was glad for the misty spring shower that cooled his face. Ranger lay near the mound of freshly turned earth, his brown coat glistening with rain.

"Time to go, Jeremiah," Sophie said softly. "You're soaked through."

"It's not over Sophie. It's not over by a long shot." Adams turned away from the grave, wiping droplets from his cheeks. "Damn rain."

"Let the limousine go, Jeremiah—I'll be your chauffeur today. I've towels in my car for Ranger. We'll all go to my flat. While your clothes are drying we can drink some of that Southern Comfort I bought. Come along now."

Adams sat, dripping small puddles on the floor mats of Sophie's silver BMW. He was vaguely aware of her hand resting on his knee after they moved off.

On the border with Canada, hundreds of miles northwest of the churchyard in Maryland, warm spring weather started the southbound tourist season early. On the Canadian side of the Pacific Highway border crossing, Mr. and Mrs. Fahad Matar and their infant daughter waited patiently in line. Their large white recreational vehicle had been washed and waxed before they left Vancouver, and it was well stocked with canned food, diapers, and cartons of baby food.

Matar had been watching "borderlineups.com" on his wireless laptop all morning. The site's real-time video feeds of the border crossing showed the backup at the Pacific Highway station was now perfect. Not too long, but still crowded. They had cleared the Canadian border post with ease, their Lebanese passports, US visas, Canadian residency stamps, and applications for Canadian citizenship in impeccable order. They would reach the American side just before lunchtime, as planned.

An American customs officer stepped out of a small booth and directed the RV to an inspection lane beside a long machine, higher than the RV's roof.

"Good morning. Passports, please." Tired and hungry, the customs and immigration officer standing in the open vehicle door was brusque. He looked through the documents carefully, and was scanning the faces above him when Matar spoke.

"Why do you stop us here? Because we are born in Lebanon?" *It is their famous X-ray machine, just as the training officer told us. Nothing to fear.*

"Just a routine random check, sir. It has nothing to do with your nationality or where you were born." The custom officer's voice sounded like a taped recording. "Is this trip for business or pleasure?"

"We are tourists."

Another uniformed officer approached the vehicle leading a small spaniel. The two officials conferred briefly, occasionally looking up into the RV door. *As the dark man in Tehran told us, they bring a filthy dog to smell us.*

Matar looked impassively at the customs officers, then relaxed his grip on the steering wheel and flexed his fingers.

"Where are you planning to visit on this trip?"

"We go down the Pacific coast." *And other places.*

"Planning to visit wine country, Mr. Matar?"

"If we have time." *We will make time.*

"Okay, please step out of your vehicle, sir, and take your wife and child with you. This officer is going to inspect the interior."

Matar sighed and drummed his fingers impatiently on the wheel. Then he rose, motioned to his wife holding the infant, and the three tourists descended to the tarmac.

"Look and inspect everywhere you like."

The small spaniel nosed around the RV's neat interior, and then headed straight for the diaper hamper. The handler opened the lid and then hastily closed it, dragging the dog away. He checked closets and cupboards, stacks of clothes, boxes of diapers, and the larger boxes of baby food, occasionally pushing a radiation detector into corners. He nodded at the other officer as he left, his dog unhappy to be pulled away from the interesting hamper.

"Will you be leaving anything in the United States, Mr. Matar?"

"Dirty diapers." *Do not fear these people, the Tehrani told me. Drink my wine, he said, and fear only me.*

"Uh huh. Well, we won't delay you much longer, now." The customs officer looked at the control booth next to the large vehicle X-ray system and thought about lunch waiting in the customs house. The operator gave him a thumbs-up.

"Welcome to the United States, Mr. Matar. Have a pleasant visit." The officer was rewarded with a shrug as he handed the passports back.

Matar started the RV and moved away slowly. Once he was clear of the customs buildings, a malevolent curtain fell over his swarthy face. He glanced at the woman seated next to him and grunted in Farsi.

"Yes, we leave them something in America. We leave them Karnal bunt and flag smut for wheat. Swine flu and hog cholera for their filthy pigs. Newcastle virus for the chickens. Special foot and mouth disease for cows. And something for their unclean wine leaves, too." His scowl deepened. "We are on our way now, Noor. Put the brat back in her bed."

"We are lucky they did not open those cans of SIMILAC baby food, Fahad. Or check the bottom of the diaper hamper." She rose from her comfortable chair, cradling the infant.

"Why lucky? They look for atomic bombs. Remember what the man in that Tehran *koucheh* told us. These people are fools—they do not know what to look for! We bring no bombs, no hashish. Only interesting powders we leave them. That is all." He laughed raucously.

On the other side of the Rockies, Route 15 crosses the Canadian border at Montana. It wanders southwest, almost all the way down the United States to the Mexican border. Another sparkling white RV was approaching the border, and in it was a happy family that owned a popular Lebanese restaurant in Calgary. They were on their way to visit a restaurant in Chicago owned by a partner.

But first, they were going to pass by the big cattle stockyards of South Dakota and Nebraska. Then, after some old-fashioned polo rice and *chelo kebab* in Chicago, they planned to double back through the wheat fields of Kansas. They would zigzag through the rice paddies and hog farms of Arkansas. And they also intended to pay a visit to the great fruit orchards and citrus groves of Florida.

They had lots of time.

THE END

ACKNOWLEDGEMENTS

It is not customary for an author to acknowledge help with the writing of his novel. But *The Woolsorters' Plague* is grounded in so much research that it could be called "faction" instead of fiction. Readers, especially those in government, the military, intelligence, security agencies, and law enforcement, are quick to find faults in portrayals of their jobs. I tried to encourage those experts to "suspend disbelief" by bothering friends and colleagues for advice and help. They include:

Ejner Fulsang, an indefatigable editor who focused me on the mysteries of how to handle the literary 'point of view,' and

J.P. Tristani, a Marine fighter pilot who explained the wherefores and how-to's of loft bombing, and

Jean-Loup Combemale and Gardner Brown, diesel submariners who gave me an understanding of snorkeling and the joys of living in a cramped, noisy and foul-smelling world for days and weeks—not to mention the meaning of, "green board, pressure in the boat!"

Chris Flaesch, Marine Captain, business partner, graphic designer, and high technology advisor, and not least,

My patient wife Dorothy and my children, an amazing family of proof readers, editors and critics.

There were several others who did not wish to be named, but they know I remember them, and that I am grateful for their help.

Of course, all errors and flights of fancy are entirely my own.

ALSO BY CHET NAGLE

"A page-turning tale of counter-terrorism, as explosive as today's headlines."
W.E.B. Griffin & W. Butterworth, authors of Men at War.

"Iran Covenant is an action-filled, technically accurate novel—or a scenario on which an intel forecast could be based"
George H. Wittman, columnist for The American Spectator.

"Nagle delivers cutting-edge, real-time action in Iran Covenant. A novel every bit as intriguing as its title."
David Hagberg, best-selling author of Allah's Scorpion.

"Chet Nagle knows what goes on behind the scenes in Middle East politics and the war on terror. Characters are vivid, drama intense, and depiction of a fanatical Iranian regime all too real."
Arthur Herman, author Gandhi & Churchill

CPSIA information can be obtained at www.ICGtesting.com
Printed in the USA
BVOW040308161211

278493BV00001B/7/P